Life in the Chastity Zone

First paperback edition April 2020

Book design by Madhat Books

ISBN: 9798633782684

For my mom, Randy Jean.

For being the most loving and supportive person I know.

You made me believe that anything is possible.

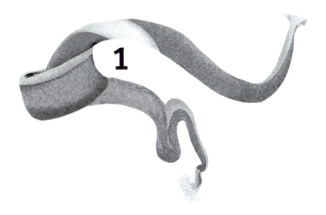

1

"What the–?" I jerk the steering wheel, making a turn off of Highway 75, heading up the little knoll. A condo complex lines one side of the road while a sledding hill dominates the other side. A snowplow passes me, splashing muck on the drivers-side window and windshield. I roll my window down and back up to give it a quick clean while gunning the accelerator a little harder, still keeping my eyes on my target. I can see a shadow of someone in the passenger seat. Where did he pick up this girl? I'm so angry now that I can't see straight. Slamming my foot even harder on the accelerator, my SUV growls through the snow—not the day to be speeding in near whiteout conditions. I can't get close enough to see if it's his cheesy license plate BU2TFUL, but then again, how many atomic red Jeep Wranglers are out there with "Architects Know All the Angles" tattooed on the spare tire cover? Right?

My heart's pounding as I grip the steering wheel.

"What is going on, Grant? Everything was falling into place—you, me, our future. Until now," I blurt out. I want to think that I'm reaching him. Telepathically. I'm trusting that the course I took on quantum mechanics a few years ago is finally coming in handy.

Hmm ... no answer. Maybe I'm not focusing hard enough.

The images I had as a kid are flashing rapidly through my mind, throwing off my concentration. Like being a top female structural engineer in LA, having a perfect architect husband and the sweetest steel beam-and-glass home perched in the Hollywood hills with a view looking out to the Santa Monica ocean. "Dammit, Chase, focus!" It takes me a bit, but I manage to clear my head as we both speed down the other side of the knoll. "You had better not ruin my plans, Grant Stevens, because I guarantee that I'll throw a shitload of—Aargh!"

I shriek and slam on the brakes as a group of bundled-up sledders dart in front of my car. On cue, they give me a deer-in-the-headlights look, waving their saucers in my direction; my car skids on the ice and comes to a shuddering halt on the two-way road, which now looks like a tunnel. Snow, piled high on either side, press against the wooden fences of the adjacent homes. I've lost sight of the jeep. I can barely see two feet in front of me. I muster up a wan smile, waving an apology to the pedestrians, clumping to safety, some mouthing out a string of merited expletives.

"Yeah, you're right! I'm such a jerk. I'd do the same thing if I were in your ... sleds." My moment of remorse. I doubt they can hear me.

Setting the four-wheel-drive button to high again before shifting into drive, and this time with a death grip on the steering wheel, I shoot through the narrow yet multicolored Idaho roadway, passing by the Sun Valley Lodge. My heart sinks for a moment as I notice the white Christmas lights that light up the iconic hotel and every inch of the property. From the trees to the lampposts to the fences and the brightly lit ice rink, everything is a blur of color in this dreadful weather. The holiday decor is something I look forward to seeing every year that our family visits Aunt Kate, who actually isn't related; she is my mom's best friend. Her holiday shindigs are nothing but the best. Ironically, Aunt Kate has her act together compared to the rest of my crazy family. She is like the calm amid a storm.

There are bright red taillights in front of me. "Ah-ha, I got him!" I let out gleefully, making a fast turn onto a familiar road just before Dollar Mountain; the snowcats the only beacon of light in this winter nightmare. It's a wide berth lane providing enough room to fishtail, even though my SUV clips a few snow-laden evergreen branches. A gust of wind throws a pile of snow on the windshield, obscuring my vision. I plow into something; the SUV skids. I jerk the steering wheel hard; ice and slush push their way into the wheel wells, creating a harsh grating sound.

"Ahh!" I yelp. The car starts spinning like the Disneyland Tea Cup ride before coming to an abrupt halt, smacking into a wide snow-covered area. Fortunately, I don't have to contend with other cars behind me. "Phew! Thank God!" I utter even though I have no idea what to expect of the exterior damage. My relief is momentary. In my peripheral vision, I spy something heading in my direction. Reflexively, my gloved hands shield my face as I brace for impact from an airborne snowman tray filled with two-dozen frosted cupcakes. There's a small thud and then silence. Taking a quick peek to my right, I assume the interior damage isn't too severe, considering the snowman tray has made a perfect landing on the passenger seat. Wrong!

The cupcakes I slaved over earlier today have taken on a different form—a surrealistic one, to be exact. Crumbs are EVERYWHERE. Random patterns of frosting and remaining batter have not only landed on the front of my shirt but also on the floor, the windows, and—just in time for the holidays— a dripping-off-the-rearview-mirror version.

"Hmmm ... I imagine Picasso would be proud," my lame attempt at humor. With everything happening so fast, I don't know whether I should laugh or cry. My logical mind tells me that the best I can do is to focus on the rent-a-car and not my dad's booming voice when he sees the damage.

"Okay, time to get this baby out of here." Trying to bolster my confidence, I put the car in reverse and rev the engine. The tires' spinning action only sinks the SUV deeper into the snow, mud splattering the back and sides to the top of the windows.

Letting out a huge sigh, I unbuckle the seatbelt and direct my attention toward the only thing left in my control: the windshield wipers. Not so. The swishing movement of the blades and the hypnotic snowfall catches my attention. I can feel myself getting sucked into a catatonic state. A persistent tapping on my window breaks my brief reverie. After everything that I've been through in the last hour, I half-expect a stodgy police officer to be on the other side, ready to hand me a hefty ticket. It's not. Recognition sets in after blinking a few times.

"Chase? Is that you? Unlock the door!" I hear Grant's voice; he's in a panic, pulling like crazy at the handle. I sink in my seat. My gloved hands come to the rescue, covering my face a second time.

"Are you okay? Say something," he's yelling.

He opens the door, eyes wide. He brushes a lock of his blond hair away from his tropical-ocean-surf eyes as I barely make out Aunt Kate's old, dark green Victorian-style mansion between the rhythmic wipers. The only house of its kind, with its three stories and ornate leaded-glass windows, it towers over the other well-kept homes on her street. It makes perfect sense, considering that the road used to be the entrance to the world's first single-chair lift on Proctor Mountain back in 1936. I shake the historical trivia once my eyes pan the gorgeous outdoor decorations. It's like a winter wonderland all over again; twinkling lights tastefully sprinkle the small pines flanking the front door and the long walkway that leads to her mini-parking lot, equipped with a three-car garage.

Well, whaddayaknow? I guess I made it to Aunt Kate's Christmas party after all.

"Chase!"

Sarcasm quickly sets in once I remember why the hell I was madly racing through a blizzard. "Who else do you expect, one of Santa's elves working overtime? Of course, it's me. Who's that girl in your car?" I say all in one breath, glaring at him as I crane my neck to meet his six-foot-six stature.

FREEZE...

* * *

You see, a month ago, Grant, my fiancé of the last six months, sent me a text:

> Grant: Sorry, Chase, I'm taking a pause.
> **Me: What does that even mean—a pause?**

No response.

> **Me: You're pausing to test the field?**

Again, no response. My patience grows thin.

> **Me: We're over?**

Grant, you are getting on my last nerve!

> **Me: Are you ghosting me?**

Why don't you answer me?

> **Me: You cannot ghost me!**

Undoubtedly, I was in a state of denial while he followed through with his new plan.

* * *

"There's no girl in my car, Chase." Grant gives me that look like I've just gone loco. No, HE'S the one who's gone loco. I can't bring myself to speak up. Another person walks out and pushes himself in front of Grant. He puts his perfect face up to mine, producing a dazzling smile. I'm instantaneously mesmerized.

Crumbs cover the front of my white sweater and leggings. I brush a piece of frosting off my nose before I turn my legs and attempt to exit the car gracefully.

"So, I *finally* get to meet the famous Chastity Morgan," says Perfect Face, grabbing my hand and helping me out of the car.

"You're the person I'll never be able to live up to. I don't know whether to bow, curtsy, or kill myself, but come here!" He leans his five-foot-eleven frame into me. "Give me a hug!"

I mutely let him hug me since I can't seem to find my voice.

"I'm Brody Masterson!" He says into my neck.

He's gorgeous, and I'm not exaggerating; a runway-model—perfect-ten beautiful—with penetrating gray-blue eyes, porcelain white skin, and dark black hair. Brody wraps his ravishing arms around me, and I can feel his ripped Adonis muscles through his puffy down jacket.

"You're gorgeous!" I can't help but stare at his pouty lips, so close to mine. "Did I say that out loud? Oops!"

Brody laughs. "Thanks!"

Grant is pouring over me as Brody continues. "Why don't we go inside, warm up, and enjoy the party while we wait for someone to pull your car out of the snow-covered flower bed. Whoops! From the looks of it, I think you plowed into Miss Bilby's vegetable garden." He points towards the smashed up wooden tomato posts sticking out from underneath the hood of my SUV before turning back towards Grant, "Could you please grab our tray of cookies from the back seat?"

Bilby? Our tray? My brain is in a jumble.

"Wait! Bilby? Aunt Kate? You mean Mrs. Carter. She got married a few months back," I say to Brody. "And who's 'we,' Grant? And what happened to the girl in your car?" I repeat, staring at his jeep wrangler, expecting someone to pop out of it magically. "There was a girl in your car, right? And who's this guy? Your cousin, maybe?" My mind is desperately trying to put two and two together as I look at the handsome duo.

"As he said, Chase, there was no girl in the car. Just me and Boo." Brody glances over at Grant for approval, only to notice that he's frozen in place. "Ah ... you didn't tell her, did you, Grant?"

"Me and Boo? W-Who are you?" I'm confused.

Grant looks miserable. His blue eyes wildly pan the immediate area, as if preparing to make a quick getaway. The snow's falling in big sticky snowflakes, blanketing the cars packed tightly into the driveway. He's not going anywhere anytime soon.

6

No one's responding, so I keep rambling, · hoping that someone will tell me what the hell is going on. "Where have you been for the last month? I've been calling you every day. We need to finalize the menu, pick our song—"

He takes a deep breath and lets out one solitary word: "Vegas."

My vivid imagination conjures up a scene where Grant and Brody are in a nightclub. Club lights illuminate the dance floor where a bunch of women surrounds the boys in a mosh pit of flesh. I'm standing in a far corner of a room. I spot Grant, looking back at me through a mountain of cleavage. He gives me the two-thumbs-up sign. A giant-sized bouncer comes up behind me and slaps my ass, snapping me out of the horrific image.

"Did your new friend Brody take you to a skanky nightclub and set you up with a bunch of women? Is that where you've been the last month? Is it?" I step in closer, snow crunching underfoot in my clunky wilderness boots.

Grant's eyes flicker to the ground as he kicks around the fresh powder, lost in thought.

"What? What is it?" I throw up my hands. "Is there more? Did you cheat on me, too? OH. MY. GOD. You did, didn't you? Did you pick up some weird untreatable disease?" I scream, tugging on my "security blanket," a pink-and-blue scarf wrapped around my neck.

"Brody's the most incredible person I've ever met," he continues, putting an arm around the gorgeous hunk. "We met on a wakeboarding trip to Lake Havasu. We went to the Bellagio Hotel in Las Vegas and..."

"WHAT?????? You're not making any sense, Grant." I'm in a tizzy. Fiddling around with my hands, I pull off my gloves and stick them in and out of my coat pockets. My movements capture the light from the car headlights, striking the Tiffany ring on my left hand at the exact angle to create a stunning spectrum against Grant's form-fitting leather jacket. I grab the ring and start twisting it furiously, cutting short the brilliant rainbow performance.

Grant offers no comment on my display. Instead, he keeps to his impromptu script. "Our ceremony—"

7

"Ceremony?" I cut in. "Wait! What did you say? Ceremony? What about our wedding?" I'm on the verge of tears, but I will myself not to cry.

My mind suddenly flashes to another imaginary scene with Grant and Brody standing hand-in-hand on the cliffs of Laguna Beach, the turquoise ocean shimmering below. I'm in my princess-cut Vera Wang dress, standing next to Grant with a bouquet of pale pink roses in one hand and the wedding rings in the other. Grant recites his vows, "I take you to be my lawfully wedded husband, to have and to hold—" I let out a scream: "STOP." But no matter how much I scream, my attempts to stop the ceremony are futile. My constant shrieking snaps me back to reality. I feel the heat rising on my face.

"Chase, where did you go?" Grant's hand is on my shoulder.

"DON'T TOUCH ME, YOU, YOU..." *Liar, marriage wrecker.* I can't even wrap my head around an appropriate word as I jump out of his grip.

Looking beyond Grant and Brody, I notice movement at Aunt Kate's bay window; guests are pulling back the curtains and gawking at the crazed outdoor scene.

In a moment of clarity, everything solidifies.

"You, slimy bastard! I. SAVED. MY. VIRGINITY. FOR. YOU!!!!" Screeching now at the top of my lungs, I feel as though I've morphed into the White Witch. "TRAITORS!" *Did I say that out loud?* Both Grant and Brody appear frozen in place. The terrorized look on their faces with hair standing on end are sure indications that I have successfully turned them into stone statues.

"Chase," Roxie giggles, "what are you guys all doing out here?" She's oblivious to the outside drama, standing there at the main entrance on Aunt Kate's wraparound porch with her hands on her hips in her sexy "Mrs. Claus" getup—red dress with white trim, red stockings, furry white boots, and a hat to match with a big jingling silver bell at the tip. "Come on inside so we can get this party started!"

* * *

Now some would call the two of us twins—tall—both 5' 11",
slender, and athletic with icy blue eyes. In the looks
department, our resemblance is uncanny, except for the fact
that Roxie is a brunette and voluptuous. I'm a blonde and
average in that department, which is fine by me because Roxie
can never find the perfect bra that will keep everything intact.

It makes sense we would look-alike since her father Mason
and my dad are identical twins. They were inseparable growing
up: attending the same college as roommates. When it was time
to marry, they bought houses across the street from each
other. The brotherly closeness trickled down to us girls; it was
inevitable—fate even—that Roxie and I would become … well
… bosom buddies.

Two years after Roxie was born, her mother, my Aunt Mary
Ann—messed up, depression perhaps—ran away. While I have
my anxieties, Roxie, who grew up without her biological
mother, has abandonment issues, choosing to play the part of
the "bad girl." It's more complex since she and Uncle Mason
have unresolved issues, such as never wanting to discuss the
big ones, like why her mom left. Fortunately, Roxie gained a
"mom" when my mother "adopted" her as a second daughter.

With that being, besides looking alike, Roxie is the total
opposite of me, especially when dealing with the flirtation
game. She can seriously enrapture any man she wants with
just the crook of her finger; I swear. Roxie may drive me nuts
at times, but the bottom line is that we're inseparable. She's
my wild "life of the party," partner-in-crime cousin.

* * *

"Chase, Roxie's right. Let's go inside so we can get this party
started. How about we try this again and be grown-ups about
this?" Grant reaches out to hug me again.

"DON'T TOUCH ME!" I scream a second time. Before he can
lay a finger on me, I push him away, but he recoils, throwing

me off balance. Before I know what's happening, I'm slipping, arms flailing like a first-time ice skater. "Ahhh!"

Roxie charges down the steps through the snow.

I can hear Charlie singing "American Girl" before I hit the ground.

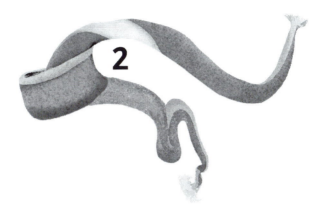

2

The scent of burning wood overwhelms my senses. I blink a few times before fully opening my eyes. There's something cold on my forehead. I reach over to touch the ice pack. "What the hell?" I mumble. My throat is dry; I can't speak anything above a whisper.

Roxie kneels by my side, brushing the knots of cupcakes from the ends of my hair with her fingers. "You took quite a tumble, kiddo. Good thing Grant and I broke your fall because you'd be in the hospital right now with a concussion. So, did you two have a wild cupcake make-out session, or did you want to go for the Christmas red-and-green look? Either way, it suits you."

I'm so out of it. I can't even think of a snarky comeback. I may feel a bit tired and have a slight headache, but I'm grateful for the cushiony softness beneath to help lessen the pain.

"I have a concussion?" I start feeling around for a bump but to no avail. "Did I pass out?" totally ignoring Roxie's question. It takes me a few minutes of looking around to realize that I'm lying on a plush leather sofa in Aunt Kate's impeccably clean, giant chef-like kitchen. *Who puts a couch in their kitchen, anyway?*

Aunt Kate, of course. She claims it's the best R & R after slaving over the stove. 'You can relax and take in the wonderful smells at the same time. That's my motto, and I'm sticking to it!'

"You're fine, you, silly head!"

I ignore Roxie's comment. I pan the room and marvel at the organized room, now decorated with a couple of small trees laden with gilded ornaments and twinkly white lights. At the center is a combination large-chopping-block-and-stove island with a circular hanging unit above that houses every pot and pan imaginable; it sits parallel and across from me. The couch sits perpendicular to the mini-bar, which is nearest my head. Beyond that is the pass-through window, decorated with ornate cherry wood shutters, that looks into the great room. The opposite wall includes an array of cabinets that hug snuggly around a second stove with an attached microwave, a bay window above the sink, dishwasher, and refrigerator. Off to one side is a back entrance with two sets of steps, one leading down the basement and the other upstairs. More cabinet space flank the remaining walls, all filled with enough canned and dry goods to keep her and Uncle Herb, her new husband, well supplied in case of an unseen disaster.

Aunt Kate, who is always one for convenience, enjoys adding practical modern ideas to the charm of this old place, including the great room—1500 square feet of combined dining-and-living space, which accommodates her humongous parties. I should know; I helped with the revised floor plans and knocking down walls. Well, in all honesty, my dad was the master engineer. I was just his summer intern. I like to think I added insight into her renovations, including a high-top bar that fits in the living room corner, directly opposite the gigantic, raised brick fireplace, which has a two-foot-deep ledge to seat five.

Marrying Uncle Herb has kept Aunt Kate grounded. He's ten years younger, and a couple of inches taller than her five-foot-four frame, and ruggedly handsome with slightly weathered tan skin, dark brown hair styled neatly into place, thick, brown eyebrows that enhance his doe eyes, and a somewhat scratchy yet deep voice. Uncle Herb sells real estate and likes to sneak out at night to drink beer at the cowboy bar while watching the latest sporting match. While Uncle Herb is a far cry from Aunt Kate in the social sector, I can't help but admire how comfortable he is in home decorating as he is in cooking a prime roast meal. I guess there is truth to the "opposites attract" thing.

And then there's Aunt Kate's peculiar fashion sense, which I find a bit bizarre at times, like the crimson mink jacket and snakeskin stilettos she usually sports around Christmas time. But that's Aunt Kate, and it certainly matches her youthful spirit—short bleached blonde haircut, polished white skin from all her laser treatments, and toned body from all her personal-trainer sessions. Underneath it all, she has a heart of gold, and I love that she's as cool as Uncle Herb.

"How did I get on the kitchen couch?" trying to regain my voice but to no avail. I begin groping around my neck, feeling for my security scarf, which is still intact, thankfully. "Wait. Did you say that Grant helped break my fall? Oh, God, he touched me? Where's Grant?" I try to sit up, my eyes swiveling around the kitchen a second time. "I need to give him a piece of my—"

"Chase," Roxie interrupts. "You need to calm down, okay? Here, take some Ibuprofen and drink this water." She shoves the pills into my mouth and puts a tall cup of water to my lips. I comply with the unwelcome deed. "Now's probably not the best time to get all upset with Grant. You make yourself sick when you get all emotionally wound up? So, no throwing up. Okay?"

I add a weak smile to my nod.

"But his friend?" Roxie continues. "Jesus, he's stunning. That one's all man, with sexy, hot-out-of-the-oven buns of steel. Can you introduce me to him, Chase, once you feel better, that is?" she says, all in one breath. I roll my eyes, watching her morph into the "infatuation zone." With a dreamy look plastered on her face, Roxie glances longingly in the direction of the pass-through window, hoping to make eye contact with Brody.

13

"I'm Dreaming of a White Christmas" streams through the sound system. From my vantage point, I have a pretty decent view of both rooms. Gazing through the pass-through window, I spot a familiar picture on the wall in the great room just beyond the kitchen's entrance. I'm on my knees in the sand; the colorful scarf that Charlie gave me earlier that day used as a headband. I am sitting between Charlie, Roxie, and Grant while holding a "Happy 28th birthday". It brings back warm memories.

I can't believe that everything changed the following day when—.

I have to look away to keep from tearing up. "The past is the past," I mutter under my breath. "And now I have to be strong and move forward."

"What did you say?" Roxie responds.

"I said that I couldn't let a little pain bother me; I have to be strong. Right, Roxie?" I lie, staring at the one photo, amongst the collage of others, that has had a life-changing effect on me.

"Absolutely! Strong!" Roxie mimics robotically, still gazing over at Brody.

"Chester, NO!" Aunt Kate's yelling, followed by dog saliva dripping into my eyes, breaks the momentary spell. Roxie quickly grabs tissues from the box on the end table and lands them on my face. In between wipes, I glance at my mom's friend who, like a Russian circus contortionist, snaps her fingers and then grabs the dog's collar with one hand while balancing a tray of sandwiches with the other. *Amazing!*

"At least someone loves me," I respond weakly, my voice crackly and still in a whisper. I involuntarily rub the Saint Bernard's ear, cupcake frosting, clinging to his little whiskers. He rests his head on my tummy, another round of saliva drips all over my white sweater.

"I'm so sorry, dear. Are you okay?" Aunt Kate sets a plate of tempting cucumber sandwiches over to one side and out of the dog's reach. I nod affirmatively. She gently pats my face; the compassion in her eyes immediately fills me with a sense of peace. "Now, you sit and behave, Chester." She gives the dog a quick pat before gathering up the tray of goodies and heads towards the pass-through window. I don't recognize the sea of ladies on the other side, all in their late fifties, early sixties, and dressed in either designer apres-ski attire, red and white festive attire, or god-awful ugly Christmas sweaters. But they all have one thing in common: they're all greedily swarming over the finger food like wasps at a picnic. Buzzing sounds would be a welcoming relief to their sickening camel-chewing ruminations as they add whispering—most likely about the new "Grant and Chastity" intrigue—to the mix while taking turns to eye what I'm doing on the couch. The husbands, oblivious to the rumor mill, huddle around the mini television, planted atop one of the high-top bar shelves, their eyes glued to a football game. A chorus of periodic cheers or boos provides the only sign of their presence. Shaking my head ever so lightly, I close my eyes. *God, is this what I have to look forward to when I'm their age?* "Spare me," I blurt out unexpectedly.

"Do you bowl?" Roxie spontaneously responds, giggling at the corny comment Uncle Mason used to make when we were teens and vocally opinionated about everything. I smirk briefly before reality hits. I can tell the meds are working; niggling thoughts overtake the numbness in my head. I tug on Roxie's dress to get her attention, ignoring the fact that she's still zoned out—this time swooning over Bing Crosby's silken voice.

"Rox, can you believe it? I was forty days away from giving myself up to who I thought was the perfect man. I waited so long for my 'happily ever after' moment. I was looking forward to starting a family and living my dream life. But now it's all gone. Gone! What am I going to say to all the guests? I've got to call the venue, the caterer. Mom will flip when she—" Roxie leans in to hear what I have to say. It helps that I don't have much of a voice. At least it won't activate rumormongering antennas amongst the older ladies in the kitchen.

"Don't worry about it now," Roxie says, placing two of her fingers on my lips. "You just need to regain your strength."

"At least now I know that my lack of experience isn't why he went searching for greener pastures," I ramble. "And you know what that means?" My stiff upper lip trembles. "It means that I'm still a thirty-freakin'-year-old vir—"

I stop dead, noticing new activity by the kitchen entrance. The loud, distinctive nasal cackling could only mean one thing;

the Prissy Posse has arrived. *Jesus! I haven't seen them in two years. Do they still come to Aunt Kate's holiday bash?*

"Holy shit! Did you see who just walked in?" I whisper to Roxie, pointing toward the kitchen entrance, panic written on my face. "That's the last thing I need is them ganging up on me, pretending to feel sorry for me."

Roxie looks up. Her eyes widen. "Crap!" she mouths. Surreptitiously grabbing the sofa quilt, she covers me up to my nose.

"What the—"

"Shush! I've got it under control. Shut your eyes," Roxie whispers. "Trust me."

* * *

Even though I feign sleep, my mind flashes back to high school, and the day they distributed the yearbooks. The Prissy Posse, I called them behind their backs, because they were always so flawless—flawless style, flawless grades, flawless boyfriends— was sitting around the giant oak tree in the center of the campus, swapping books and happily signing away. My copy, which mysteriously disappeared during my first-period class, magically reappearing at my usual lunch table. I remember the apprehension I felt, sitting on that scalding hot perforated metal with the sun beating down in the ninety-degree June weather and wondering what was hiding within the pages. Pimply faced me donned in my pastel-pink uniform and band-aids to cover up my zits braved opening it only to find that the book conveniently lands at its centerfold. There across the binding in bold black lettering was a message that at once made an indelible mark on my brain: "Chastity Ann Morgan, most likely to be a spinster with a hundred cats."

"This is all bullshit! Bullshit," I spouted under my breath. The anger I felt that day is still fresh in my memory. "Whoever wrote this doesn't even know how to insult me properly. I'm allergic to cats, the morons! First, Mrs. Callaway tells me I will never get into college with my SAT scores, and now this."

* * *

"Merry Christmas, Roxanne!" Lizzie Anderson (lead "Priss" with her immaculately polished nails, silky hair, and unblemished, peaches-and-cream complexion) says loud enough to get head turns from other guests in the kitchen; she's holding a box of tissues. "How's Chastity? I heard there was quite a commotion outside earlier. The guests seem to be all abuzz," she says, her brilliantly white teeth accompanying her condescending smile. She's wearing skinny jeans, a red-and-white angora sweater that hugs her figure, suede in-the-moment-boots, and too many diamonds to count. Jewelry covers her, making her look unnaturally frosted.

"She's resting," I hear Roxie reply flatly.

"Well, we came to help." Lizzie turns to wave over the remaining trio.

"Oh, look!" I squint enough to see Julie Harris point at my face. Her ginger red hair--as red as her matching lipstick and sweater she's adorning--is nothing to the pear-shaped diamond bracelet that she purposely flashes for everyone to see along with her very protruding belly. "Her makeup is a mess. Dear God! What horrible monsters would be so cruel to her, especially at Christmas time? Here," I see her pull out a pink bag from her oversized purse. "Let's fix her up, girls, and make her beautiful once again." She's looking at Joan for help, who's standing off to the side with her phone at the ready, probably to post a party Instagram pic. Donned understatedly in a red sweater dress with nude tights and no bling, Joan Rush is the "least prissy of the posse," at least that was Charlie's reasoning when he shocked Roxie and took her to the senior prom.

"She's sleeping," Roxie interjects civilly, blocking them from getting any closer to me. She leans into them. "What part of what I just said don't you understand? When she's awake, you can discuss helping her. But in the meantime, get your goddamn hands off her or else," I hear Roxie say through gritted teeth.

Lizzie throws her head back and lets out a loud laugh. Julie and Joan join in. "Or what? You're too funny, Roxanne. We were just trying to be helpful," Lizzie says as she turns and walks to the kitchen island toward the platters of food, the others trailing her like ducklings.

I squint again to see the threesome strategically plant themselves across from me on swivel bar stools so they can get a bird's-eye view of me. Lizzie (Elizabeth) with her pixie-styled blonde hair, now dyed white; Julie with blunt-cut red hair; and Joan with her black-haired bob and noticeable widow's peak are all magically the same height—a whopping 5' 5". I glance at Roxie, who eyes them warily, as they perch like hawks waiting for their next prey.

And why am I surprised to see them? Their moms and Aunt Kate are close childhood friends who all attended the same all-girls high school Roxie, and I attended. Three charming ladies, ending up with sappy, clone daughters. *What's the probability of that happening?* A lot, I guess.

I squint for a third time to see Lizzie, Julie, and Joan leaning in close and whispering while staring at Brody. As he gracefully glides into the kitchen to add a few more snacks onto his already-full plate, their eyes follow him as he moseys back into the great room. The trio resumes their bar activity once he stands by Grant. Joan grabs a glass of booze and immediately chugs it down in a couple of gulps. Lizzie, who usually fixates on her figure, throws her cares to the wind and grabs a brownie. Sucking in small portions, she produces loud salacious moans. It makes me sick to my stomach, listening to her.

Last, there's Julie, who looks uncomfortable with her noticeable baby bump. God, she looks like she's about ready to pop! Why anyone would want to make a baby with her is beyond me. I couldn't care less who the father is. I don't know, and I don't want to know. I take a peek and see her seductively lick the last bit of frosting from a cupcake. I can feel bile rising in my throat. I try to keep from throwing up, but it's too late. I'm too shocked to be embarrassed by my projectile vomiting.

"Whoa, Chase!" Roxie pops up like a jack-in-a-box and then sprints off to get supplies.

A chorus of blood-curdling screams gets my attention. I look up just in time to see the unanticipated reaction of the not-so-perfect-anymore Prissy Posse, grabbing cocktail napkins from the small kitchen bar to cover their noses. Even though I feel drained, my olfactory glands are entirely operational, and the stench is undoubtedly foul.

In my peripheral vision, I see Julie duck-walk out the kitchen entrance, probably looking for the nearest bathroom.

"I'm so sorry," I weakly say, pointing at Lizzie's feet. Lizzie screams a second time, realizing that my puke sprayed her designer boots.

"OH MY GOD ... OH MY GOD ... OH MY GOD" Lizzie's new mantra as she stares down at her muck-covered boots. Scurrying to get out of the kitchen, she is suddenly airborne. I see her reach for a nearby stool, which smacks the ground as her derriere glides in my direction. Lizzie grabs the couch's end table and manages to right herself. Relief washes over her face until she realizes that she is standing in the middle of my oozing vomitus substance.

"OOOOOH FUUUUCK..."

Dead silence follows.

That is so not a super slo-mo *A Christmas Story* moment. Joan dropping the F-bomb catches the attention of everyone in the kitchen, plus a few heads in the great room.

There appears to be activity brewing in the great room as well. I notice Mrs. Stevens, who seems to be clueless to the kitchen drama, moving straight for the far end of the great room. In an element of surprise, she corners her son Grant. Barely hearing them, I wish I were a fly on the wall so I can catch every word. I strain my neck to get a better view. His deer-in-the-headlights reaction lets me know that she is going for the jugular as she thrusts her hands up in the air in a fit of frustration and begins screaming in his face. So caught up in the moment, I don't make a connection when a blur of color passes in front of me. Witnessing that moment is bittersweet because, on the one hand, I'm so angry with Grant that I could spit. On the other hand, I'm off the hook having her as my mother-in-law, which was something I wasn't relishing since she has the personality—and looks to boot, no joke—of Cruella de Vil.

Another blur of color passes me until I realize that Aunt Kate and Uncle Herb have morphed into custodians, donning rubber gloves and carrying floor brooms, mops, a vacuum, disposable masks, *and* sawdust—of all things. *Where in the heck did they find the sawdust?* Uncle Herb starts on the floor while Aunt Kate attends to the bewildered Lizzie, moving her gingerly over to a chair so she can help in the removal of her tainted shoes.

Roxie, returning with her own set of supplies, sidles next to me on the couch and hands me a glass of water. She places a cool washcloth on my forehead.

"I'm so sorry," I mumble, trying to get Lizzie's attention.

You can hear Cruella's unintelligible rants from the great room. Just as Uncle Herb collects the remnants of newly dusted odious ejecta, I see Cruella's head bobbing in the direction of the kitchen, Grant trailing close behind and looking like a guilty puppy with its tail between its legs. I lean my head back and feign sleep again.

"Chastity, I need a word with you about—"

I never found out what Cruella had on her mind. The moment the mother and son enter the kitchen, they both begin gagging uncontrollably. At the same time, my parents and brother Henry enter through the back entrance, my mom looking like a dwarf against my six-foot-tall dad. Snatching a whiff, Mom throws an arm over her mouth. Henry grabs a kitchen rag to cover his nose and mouth, but once he puts two and two together—viewing both the floor scene and Lizzie, who is crying uncontrollably, he erupts in wild laughter.

Henry can be an annoying jokester, but he respects me as his big sister. His entrance into the world when I was twelve was a surprise to us all, especially when my mom thought she couldn't have any more kids— at least that's what her doctor said. So much for doctor's predictions! My brother may drive me crazy sometimes, but he means the world to me. Regardless of his age, he looks older than he is because he's matched perfectly in height and appearance with my dad—the same big-boned structure and blonde hair. Plus, the girls—and even guys, I'm told—flock around him, he's that cute.

The fact remains that he's got time to think about settling down because he's still in high school. But, me? I'm thirty-freakin'-years old.

"CHASTITY ANN MORGAN!" That would be my dad. His distinct baritone voice is a breath of fresh air to the surrounding chaos as he towers over a sickly-looking Cruella. He's wearing his usual wannabe cowboy getup, which makes him stick out like a sore thumb with jeans pulled up too high around his waist, plaid flannel shirt, cowboy boots, and a black cowboy hat that sits a little too tall on his head. It's hard to imagine he's a Structural Engineer and professor at our local university when he insists on wearing that ridiculous outfit for every special occasion.

Like a racehorse with his blinders up, he fixes his eyes on me.

"We leave you for an hour while you take your time getting ready for this wonderful party and now look at you. You look like a train wreck. What happened to the cupcakes you finished this morning? Why are peanut butter frosting and sprinkles in your hair? Did you throw up? Oh, for goodness sake, don't tell me you're pregnant." he rambles like he always does. Somehow, he still believes I'm a kid that he can order around.

"PREGNANT?" Cruella shouts between coughing fits. She turns to Grant and shoves a finger in his face. "How dare you! I raised you … better than that. You just couldn't … keep your pants zipped … until your wedding day, could you? You're just like your worthless father."

Grant, speechless, opens and closes his mouth like a fish out of water.

Julie, back from the bathroom, peeks through the pass-through window along with Joan.

Henry composes himself and agilely zigzags his lanky frame across the kitchen to where Grant is standing and slaps him on the back. "You dirty dog, congratulations! Christ, Chase finally let you pop her cherry! Took her long enough."

"What in God's name is going on here?" I can tell by the direction of her voice that Nana, my grandmother, is near the kitchen entrance. I sit up as I see her saunter in like a catwalk model on a runway. Her perfectly coiffed, stark-white hair matches her queen-bee family status. Whatever she says, goes.

"Chastity Ann, is it true? Are you pregnant?" Without waiting for an answer, she turns from me to my grandfather and starts to yell. "I need another martini. Somebody, please refill my glass! Mitchell!" She's undoubtedly had one too many, her olfactory glands unfazed by the kitchen reek, which has fortunately toned down a bit, thanks to Herb's ingenuity.

"Preston, your daughter is pregnant? Why didn't you reinforce what I taught you and your brother Mason? No goddamn milk for free!" Nana's voice is booming again, her voice ricocheting off the stained-glass windows.

"Honey, I think it's time to clear up the confusion." Nana and Cruella move aside as Brody grabs Grant's hand and leads him to the entrance of the kitchen like it was the next planned event of the evening. I have a clear view of them from the couch. "Can we all have your attention, please?" he says, looking at the gathered group in the kitchen before turning his attention to the guests in the great room.

Aside from occasional gagging and coughing, I'm shocked by the sudden reduction in noise from both rooms as they fix their eyes on Brody.

Grant, who suddenly gains composure of his reflexes and finds his voice again, realizes that he has a captivated audience. "Ah, well ... while we're talking about pregnancy..." a cheesy grin accompanies his awkward opening. "This is probably a good time to make an announcement."

Silence suddenly blankets the rooms.

"So, to clear things up right off the bat," Grant continues. "Chastity is not pregnant." A chorus of murmurs breaks forth. "Wait. There's more I have to say. Even though Chastity and I are not getting married," another round of murmurs erupts, "I have one thing to say to you." He walks over and bends down so that he's at eye level with me. "Chase, always remember that no matter what life offers, you will always be my best friend." A wave of "awes" fills the rooms.

Here's my chance to punch him, except I can't. I'm mesmerized. He's as sexy as all get out in his pale pink sweater—one of a select set of tight-fitting garments that makes him look hot.

Grant waits for the sound to die down again. He stands back up to continue walking back to Brody. "In fact, the other news is … I'm already married." Grant proudly puts his arm around Brody. "Ladies and gentlemen, meet my husband."

Dead silence hangs heavily in the air; you could hear a pin drop.

Roxie breaks the void with a loud gasp.

Cruella de Vil screams out, "YOU'RE MARRIED TO … *HIM*?" She looks like she's about to faint.

"You're WHAT?" my mom follows close behind.

Oh, boy! The shit just hit the ceiling fan!

The momentary shock on the faces of the bedraggled trio shifts to smugness, which I wouldn't be surprised is a sign of satisfaction that a portion of the yearbook prophecy may have *finally* come to fruition. I still have no proof it was them, but a gnawing feeling at the back of my neck grows as I watch them grin like Cheshire cats.

This evening has turned into a living, breathing nightmare. My dad's face turns pale. My mom seems beside herself, which is understandable. She hooks an arm tight around his nearest arm. *Not a good time to talk to her!* I make eye contact with Roxie, my sign to her that I need to get out of here. Fast. Eventually, the party chatter resumes, providing a perfect diversion. Roxie wraps a fresh blanket around my shoulders, anchors her arm around my waist, and boosts me up to a standing position. The two of us slowly shuffle our way across to the back of the kitchen. Before we turn to go upstairs, I notice Grant standing near the refrigerator, nursing a fresh bottle of beer. Alone. Somehow, as weak as I am, I manage to lock eyes with him.

"Get over it, Chase!" His grin sends shock waves through my body.

My jaw drops. *What the hell are you thinking, asshole.* Except I can't get the words out. Instead, I have another comeback. "You just told me that I'm your best friend, and now you want me to get over it?" I'm amazed that I have enough energy for sarcasm.

23

"I'm going to need my ring back," he says, looking down at my hand.

"But—" I begin furiously twisting the ring again as he holds out his open palm.

"By law, it's not yours to keep. It's a family heirloom."

"What? Are you a lawyer now?" Roxie gets right in his face. "You broke her heart, and now you want to do this? Well, fuck off! It's not the time nor the place to ask for the ring." She sticks her finger in his chest like it's a knife.

Grant unlocks eyes with us and, as if we didn't exist, turns and walks by us and into the great room. Roxie shoots daggers at him as he passes.

I'm confused. I'm also so dizzy I can't see straight. All I want is to get to the bathroom as quickly as possible.

* * *

I've often wondered why this room even exists in such a large home. Aunt Kate calls it the "guest" bathroom. *Seriously?* It's the size of a matchbox, which would be perfect for someone like Peter Dinklage. The room is covered in dark floral wallpaper, and the bathroom contains a teeny tiny sink and decorative oval mirror above it with a toilet—complete with a pull-down chain that makes a booming flush sound—smooshed to its right. And here we are—two five-foot-eleven women scrunched in this slightly oversized doll-house version, on the third floor, no less. I feel like Alice, except I don't remember anything in the story about her vomiting.

Whatever.

After all the things I've been through this evening, nothing seems to faze me. I promptly collapse onto the carpeted floor, head in the toilet. Roxie, who is on her knees, begins dispensing toilet paper and wiping my face when there's a light knock at the door.

"Sorry!" Roxie yells. "We're going to be in here a while. You'll have to use—what the hell?" The knob turns slowly. Roxie promptly stands, her hat bell hitting the wall and jingling like

24

crazy. Continuing to hand me tissues this time with one hand, she grabs the sink with the other while contorting her body into an arabesque; her foot outstretched just millimeters away from pinning the door shut.

It's too late. The door quickly opens, and a substantial rhinestone-studded flower emerges, followed by the head of a middle-aged woman. She smiles, batting her ultra-long fake eyelashes.

"Hey, can't you see my friend's sick?" Roxie points in my direction.

"Please, go away," I mumble, my head in my hands.

"I know this is not a good time—" The elderly Lady Gaga reflexively pinches her nose even though the burning sage that Roxie lit is doing a pretty decent job masking the repulsive odor. "I'm sorry to bother you," she continues, "but I couldn't help overhearing all that went on downstairs, Chastity, and ... and..." Trying to shield my eyes from the lights reflecting off her headpiece, I catch her staring at my head resting against the potty.

"Um ... I had to open up a lot of doors and climb a lot of stairs to find your hiding place. Call me when you're ready. I have the perfect guy for you. He just went through a breakup too." She slithers one of her glittering bedazzled arms into the tight space to deposit a gold-leafed business card at my feet before retracting it and closing the door.

"Mrs. Josephine Adelman, Matchmaker Extraordinaire. Hmm, the address says she's from New York City," I read aloud to no one in particular.

"Uh ... awkward," Roxie furrows her brows.

"Ee ... yeah. Let's get out of here."

I muster enough strength to get myself together.

* * *

Half an hour later, we're in Roxie's car and heading to only God knows where.

The sole customers of a nearby fast-food restaurant, Roxie and I make ourselves at home in the corner yellow-plastic booth, sitting in silence while slowly sipping away at the hot cocoas Roxie bought.

"I feel so numb," I announce impassively, breaking our unpremeditated vow of silence as the neon light flickers overhead.

"Well, I hated Grant for saying this, but he's right: you need to get over it, Chase. Don't you see it? He's not right for you. Plus, the writing is on the wall. Don't you get it? You need to be more like me; forget about marriage and your fairytale ending. You don't need to be attached to one man. You know what they say about marriage? Marriage is the last legal form of slavery."

Get over it. Grant's stark statement haunts every brain cell in my head.

"How the hell can he tell the world that I'm his best friend in one breath and then in another, he tells me to get over it— not to mention that he wants me to give him back the ring? We've been friends since college, a decade now. How the hell did he all of a sudden turn so two-faced? And what are you going to do about your dress? You're my maid of honor."

"The dress," Roxie says matter-of-factly, "is the least of my worries. I'm sure I'll find some use for it." Roxie gives me a knowing look. We sit in companionable silence as I slowly lick off the whipped cream. It's the perfect comfort food for my deflated ego as I stare out the window, hoping to watch the hypnotic falling snow. But with the cloud cover, regardless of the new moon, everything is pitch black.

"So..." my lame attempt to get back to our conversation. "Tell me that I've just woken up from a nightmare. Everything that happened back there didn't happen. Right? Please tell me it wasn't real."

"It WAS real, Chase."

"Great! What in the hell am I going to do now?" Grabbing my hair, I probably look like I'm about to pull every last follicle out of my head. Roxie—always one for dramatics—lunges across the table, cupping my face. Her eyes are as big as discs.

"Chase?" I have no choice but to stare back. "Listen to me!" She squeezes my cheeks together. I steal my reflection on the mirrored wall.

"I wook like a fookin' dook," I manage to squeak out.

"Okay. Sorry." Roxie releases me but keeps her eyes fixed on mine. "You are going to be okay. Do you hear me? Before you know it, we'll be packing our bags, getting on a plane, and heading home. And when we get there, you're going to start something new."

"Like what, Rox? Open a kissing booth to see if I can catch an eligible bachelor?" I humor her.

"Trust me, Chase, just trust me. I'll think of something."

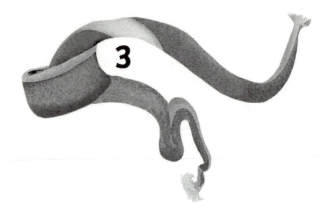

3

Two weeks later, I'm still in flannel plaid pajamas under my short pink parka with hair twisted in a ratty bun on top of my head. Now that Christmas vacation is over, it's time to leave this little Idaho ski town and head back to Southern California. I drag my feet along the snow-covered tarmac and walk toward an Embraer 175 jet, capacity seventy-five. It's a crystal-clear day with the sun glistening off the snow-covered mountains. The temperature, colder than usual, sends an unexpected chill down my spine as I breathe out a cloud of air. I'm usually paranoid about flying, but after researching the size of this plane, it doesn't bother me. Beyond that, I'm a hot mess, as I climb on board.

"It's nice to see you out of bed," my father says sweetly, patting my shoulder as we march down the narrow aisleway.

"How else do you suppose I'd get home if I didn't?" I roll my eyes as I drag my bag behind me towards my seat.

Dad ignores my question, tapping my shoulder again. "You know there is life beyond a man. There was a time when all you thought about was engineering, your degree, becoming Dr.

Morgan. I think it's time you go back and finish. You're practically done, with only two quarters left to finish before graduating. It'll give you something to focus on instead of your would-be wedding next month." He looks at me again and down at my hand. "Don't you think it's time to take that ring off?"

I look blankly at my father, who swiftly takes off his black cowboy hat, flipping it over, like he expects me to put the ring in it. I turn up the volume on my earbuds. *I'm not ready to be single and ringless.*

Doesn't he get that?

Although I'm hoping to have a relaxing ride home, I get the uncomfortable feeling that my wish will not come true.

Trailing my mother, brother, and Roxie down the aisle, I spot our seats ahead. I'm relieved that even though we've been told that the flight is at full capacity, at least my family will have most of the back section. That's a plus since it's right by the bathroom—just in case. *I sure hope I don't get stuck with someone who hogs the window and can't stop snoring.* Roxie's and Henry's assigned seats will be directly in front of mine. My parents, who have 21 C and D, will be on the other side of the aisle next to me. I notice a young couple who's already settled in, their earbuds attached. They appear to be in their own little world.

"Ugh," I huff. I don't realize until it's too late that my pajama top has exposed a little more than my midriff as I struggle to get my bag in the overhead bin. It doesn't help that my bottoms are ever so slightly riding on my hips. I feel eyes boring into my back. Glancing over my shoulder, I see him: a young, full-bearded, long-scraggly-haired man close to my height with a lustful smile and raised eyebrows. I notice lots of movement. His hands tucked away in his hoodie pockets.

"Must you? That's dis-GUST-ing!" I say loud enough that I can hear myself over the music. I'm also hoping someone from my family will take notice of the pervert before I settle down in my seat, except I can't sit down with him in proximity. Roxie's no help since I spotted her in her giant penguin sweater, taking off for the lavatory soon after depositing her carry-on. The rest of my family busily stow their luggage away, except for my mom, who glances briefly in my direction. Looking over the weird guy's shoulder, I can tell that she's staring at the guy's back. *Great! She had better not ignore me, that's all I have to say.*

"Chase, honey," my mom gets my attention. I wonder if there is hope after all. Maybe, she got over the initial shock of Grant's marital announcement. "Let me tell you about the horrible men I dated back in my day." She carries on where my father left off. "You dodged a bullet, and one day we will plan an even better wedding. Something outdoors in the spring when the flowers are in bloom."

Are you serious, mother? I've got a perv just about breathing down my neck, and you're going to tell me about your love life and weddings! Brilliant. Rolling my eyes again, I let out a frustrated sigh. I gently rub my temples; I can feel a migraine brewing.

The guy, still doing his "thing" in the aisle, looks at me longingly. I don't want to create a scene, so I remove my earbuds and politely excuse myself as I pass him and wiggle my way between the other passengers stowing away their carry-ons toward a male flight attendant near the cockpit.

"Excuse me, sir," firmly tapping his shoulder. He turns to look at me. I wasn't expecting to see a hunk with a full head of wavy dark hair and a dazzling smile in his spiffy uniform. He takes my breath away for a moment. His hazel-colored eyes look me over quickly. "Ah...," I briefly forget why I went to see him in the first place. "Ah ... there's a strange guy," I remember, "standing near my seat at the back of the plane. He's, ah, fondling himself under his hoodie."

"OH!" He puts his business face on again. "I'll take care of him right away, miss. Just stay put here for a mo—" he grabs my shoulders, moving me off to the side and out of the way next to the lavatory. Suddenly, I feel like I'm in a Marvel cartoon as I watch my hero come to my rescue. I've never seen a person move so fast in tight quarters. I watch in awe as he turns the guy around and seats him in the middle section of the plane before returning to me.

"What's your seat number," he smiles sexily.

"Ah ... 21B," I say quietly enough that he has to bend near me to hear my every word. Breathing in his cologne, I close my eyes.

"Mmm ... musk," I belt out.

"Excuse me?"

I open my eyes and see him give me a curious look.

"Um ... I mean ... I must get back to my seat."

"Well, you'll be happy to know that 21A is a no-show, so you've got that section all to yourself." He smiles widely. I promptly turn and head in the direction of 21B. He follows close behind. Settling in, I thank him profusely, especially when he gives me another one of his brilliant smiles and says he'll be back with some hot tea after the plane reaches its desired altitude.

I am about to replace my earbuds when I hear my mother's voice. "Granted, I never dated a gay man. Well ... at least I don't think I did. They certainly are well-groomed, well mannered, and devilishly handsome..."

"Mother!" I exclaim, trying to keep my voice down.

I have no idea how long she's been rambling, but one thing I DO know is that judging by the sea of nods coming from the middle-aged ladies in the mid and front sections, my mother has their full support. *Aaaarrrrgh!!!*

"Dear Lord, help me! This woman is in a bubble, I swear!" I mumble just as the engine roars, and the plane prepares to taxi down the runway. I close my eyes, hoping that everything I've witnessed is nothing more than a bizarre nightmare, and I can get back to a restful trip.

Once the plane is airborne, and the droning white noise from the engines reach a tolerable decibel range, I tell myself to concentrate on the only calming effect I've had this whole trip: Mr. Hunk, the flight attendant. Soft chuckling coming from across the aisle breaks my reverie. This time, it's my dad.

"I guess we're not getting you off the payroll anytime soon." He leans his torso across the aisle toward me to continue his monologue.

"What is that supposed to mean?" I say louder than expected, an unmistakable sign that I'm beginning to lose it with my parents' logorrhea.

31

"You know what you need since you seem uninterested in being a career woman?" Not waiting for an answer, he proceeds to ramble. "A strong man like John Wayne—tough, straightforward..."

"And with a bit of pluck," my mother adds, reaching across my father's lap so that she can get a better look at me.

"Oh, yes, that's perfect." My father grins from ear to ear, planting a kiss on her cheek.

I observe the strange interchange between my parents, my head bobbing side-to-side as if watching a tennis tournament. "Who's John Wayne?"

"WHO'S JOHN WAYNE?" My father screeches, giving me a look of disbelief as a few heads in the peanut gallery turn to see what all the commotion is about. He removes his cowboy hat, scratching his head. "What did they teach you in school? John Wayne was one of the most brilliant actors who was known for his cowboy roles!"

"That's it! I can't take it anymore. I'M NOT READY TO DATE! Henry, say something to make them stop!" I yell, my eyes pleading toward my brother, who's ensconced in his iPad. *Great help, he is!* "Roxie!" I kick at the seat in front of me. "Help me, please! This is not the day and age of arranged marriages! They have to be joking. Everyone knows I still want my career. This is all a trick, right? Reverse psychology to make me finish my degree and give up on my fantasy marriage, isn't it?"

My attention is quickly averted when I notice a guy jumping into the aisle, madly stripping off his tracksuit. *It's the pervert!* My thoughts start to run wild. He first throws his hoodie to the ground, then one shoe after the other flies towards our back section. He bends at the waist, stripping off his pants and twirling them overhead before throwing them toward the front part of the plane. *Great! Here we go! Why do quirky people always surround me? My whole family, and now this idiot in the aisle!*

First, he's giggling, then he's crying, and then he's laughing again. My hero, Mr. Hunk, returns and scrambles up to the miscreant, talking to him in hushed whispers. Perv, now down to his red-striped boxer briefs, produces a small container and opens it. I see a diamond ring flashing against the overhead lights. Sweat begins to trickle down the sides of Mr. Hunk. He seems to morph into high alert when he notices the weird guy shift into a tight fetal position and begins whimpering, rocking his body front to back. My brave defender scoots in a little closer to whisper in his ear. "Please put your clothes back on, sir."

"I killed my fiancée," the pervert yells. A litany of apologies follows. "I'm so sorry. I'm so sorry. I'm so sorry..."

My eyes widen at the thought of there being a murderer on the plane. My pounding heart feels like it's going to pop out of my chest at any moment, beads of sweat forming at my temples.

"Mom, I'm burning up. I can't breathe." Rubbing my neck, I unzip my jacket and angle the AC knob in my direction before pulling off my coat and rolling up my pants.

With no warning whatsoever, Perv leaps for the emergency exit door and pulls on the handle with all his might.

"NO!" I screech, leaping towards him, but the seatbelt jerks me back. Three flight attendants—two women about my age and one of them, my hero—rush to the scene. Successfully tackling him to the ground, they zip-tie his hands behind his back.

"What a moron! Everyone knows that the emergency exit doors bolt shut after ten-thousand feet," Roxie's laughs in front of me with her phone out, recording all of it.

"Chase, you're turning green, just try to breathe in and out, like this." A voice comes over the loudspeaker, cutting short my mother's deep-breathing demonstration.

"Hello, this is your Captain speaking." His voice makes me want to throw up. Trying to keep passengers calm is one thing, faking it miserably is another. "One of our passengers in need of medical attention will have to be escorted off the plane immediately once we land. Please remain in your seats until we give you clearance. At that time, you can retrieve your belongings and exit the plane. Thank you all for your cooperation and patience!"

I block out his message over watching the group help Perv to his feet and lead him to the flight attendant's station upfront.

"Excuse me," my mother flags a female attendant at the tail end of the troupe. "What's wrong with the young man?"

Separating herself from the others, she kneels to whisper. "Ma'am, that's confidential information. I'm sorry that I can't assist—"

"Confidential information, my foot," Roxie chimes in, she's practically standing on her seat, turning around so she can see us all. "I've got this whole thing on video, and believe me, I'll be posting on Facebook, Twitter, and Instagram. Let me tell you; you're going to have one hell of a time trying to keep this one a secret." She waves her phone high in the air, so the back half of the empty plane can see. "Look, miss," the flight attendant stands up, and fidgeting, she turns to address Roxie. "I don't mean to be rude, but I have to follow airline proto—"

My brother interrupts this time. "Protocol? That's a bunch of bullshit."

"Watch your language, son," scolds my father.

"The reason I ask," my mother dribbles, "is that I'm pretty certain I know that man. Well, at least I remember what he looked like when he was younger. That has got to be Stephan Dukas. The last time I saw him would have been, let's see, just before he started college, I believe. Yes, yes. That had to have been more than ten years ago. His mom always worried about him because he was so unstable. You see, I kept in contact with his mother all those years. I talked to her just yesterday, as a matter of fact; we went to coffee in the Sun Valley village. She commented that she's worried about him since she hadn't heard from him in over a week. You see, Sun Valley's a tight-knit community where everyone knows each other, especially during the holidays, kind of like Mayberry. You know, Andy Griffith? Certainly, his mother needs to know what's going on."

"Ma'am, I'm sor—"

"Yes, yes. I'm certain it's Stephan," my mother insists. "His mother must be worried sick."

I can't believe my mother is doing this. It's so unlike her to be so forthright. *Who the hell is Stephan Dukas? Never heard of the guy. This has GOT to be a bad dream!* I close my eyes, hoping that it all goes away, except it doesn't since I can hear everything they're saying.

34

The flight attendant pans the area before bending down again. She keeps her voice low. "Okay, listen. I know I'm breaking protocol. I start my master's program in a couple of days, so I'm out of here after today. Please keep this to yourself. I don't want this to come full circle. Is that understood?"

"Absolutely! You have my word." My mother places her hand on her heart like she is getting ready to recite the Pledge of Allegiance.

"You've got me on two accounts: I'm a mom, and if that were my son, I'd want to know what's going on, too. Secondly, you're right. The first attendant who got the lowdown on the guy identifies him as Stephan Dukas. He rambled on and on to him about killing someone—his wife, fiancée—I'm not sure. He's also carrying around a scary-looking passport; there are tickets tagged from Sun Valley to Los Angeles to New York and then to South America, Europe, and Africa—all on different airlines." She stops to look around again before continuing. "If you ask me, I think he's tripping out on drugs. He said something about swallowing a balloon packet that may have popped internally— Mollys, I think. It's all very Narcos."

I hear my mother say, "thank you" before the attendant stands up, smoothing down her skirt, and heads back to the station. I can't handle another incident. Feeling bile rise in my throat, I grab the vomit bag in the front seat compartment just in the nick of time.

"Guys, did you hear what she said?" So much for my mother's so-called "whispering" since it made its way to my brother too. "This is better than a reality show!" Henry laughs from across the aisle. "Shit, I could have gotten her whole spiel recorded if I didn't run out of storage."

"Son! What did I say before? Watch your language!" my father scolds a second time.

"This is so not happening," I mumble into the bag. I feel like I'm on the verge of bawling. "Why can't I just be around normal people?" Bending over to get tissues from my purse, I notice someone standing next to my seat. I look up to see a pair of smiling eyes; it's my brave hero, Mr. Hunk.

"Here's your cup of hot tea, miss. Sip it slowly; it's very hot." He sets up my tray and places the cup with a couple of creamers, sugar packets, and a handful of napkins. "I also brought you an extra pillow and blanket for a nap if you'd like to stretch out afterward."

Like a magician's hat, he pulls the items from somewhere in the beverage rack and plants them in the empty seat next to me, lightly grazing my chest in the process. Caught off guard again, I can't help but blush.

"We need you back up front," a female flight attendant says in passing.

"Um ... thanks!" I blurt out.

"You're welcome. By the way, could I have your phone number?" He hands me a napkin and a pen. "I'd love to call you sometime if you don't mind."

I gladly jot down my number and return the items to him. Halfway down the aisle, he turns to give me a wink. I manage a smile and a finger wave. Stunned by the calming change of events, I robotically grab the napkins to get my face back in order before wrapping my hands around the welcoming tea and reminiscing about Mr. Hunk. I never knew rest could feel so good after a shit storm. *Maybe there's hope after all.* That's my last thought before drifting off into a deep sexy slumber.

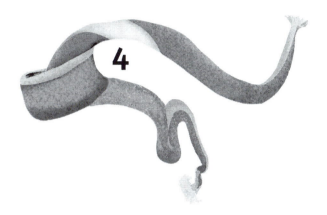

4

"Boston? You've got to be kidding!"

A "Vincent O'Connor" shows up on my cell. I don't usually answer unknown calls, but his name has a lovely ring to it. I was utterly clueless about the 617-area code.

"Call me Vince, Chastity, or do you prefer Chase?" He releases a light chuckle that is as sexy as all get-out.

We spent the first twenty-eight minutes rehashing the Stephan Dukas incident before I asked him where he lives. Even though I've muted the TV, I can't get my eyes off of Lucille Ball wrestling in a vat of grapes. I imagine myself in that scene with Grant, except that I knock him out cold.

"Hey, think of it this way: you could be in Alaska. Almost six hours of flying time isn't too bad from Los Angeles."

"I don't believe in long-distance relationships. They don't last, Vincent—I mean Vince. I mean, don't get me wrong—and by the way, call me Chase. I appreciate everything you did for me with that "weirdo," but—" If he could see me—a faded Pink Floyd T-shirt with Daffy-Duck PJ bottoms, lying on the navy paisley couch in the den with my greasy hair sloppily gathered in a bun—he wouldn't give me the time of day.

"I understand what you're saying, and if it's any consolation, I couldn't agree with you more." His soothing voice has a calming effect on my rising frustration. "All I'm saying is that when I met you, I could feel this magnetism. It's weird, I know, and I don't like to put a lot of stock on "feelings" because they're so fickle." He pauses to take a deep breath. "But you? There's something about you..."

"Vince, you sound like a nice guy and all, but—"

"OK..." he cuts me off again. I should be angry, but strangely I'm more aggravated with myself for being impatient. "This is going to sound weird, but here goes. Have you just come out of a bad relationship?" My jaw drops. The silence is so thick you can cut it with a knife.

"Hello?" Vince sheepishly asks.

"Yes. I'm here. I'm just— How did you know?" I grab the couch blanket; chills run up and down my spine.

"Please, don't take this the wrong way, but I can read you like a book. You're edgy and irritable. Everything about your sweet face says that you've been beaten down as low as you could go." He takes another one of his deep breaths before continuing. "You see, I just got out of a bad relationship too."

"OH! Am I that obvious?" I quickly head to the mirror in the foyer to give myself a close look over. "Well, yes. Listen, I don't want to make you uncomfortable. If you need someone to talk to, I'm but a call away, unless I'm 33,000 feet above the ground." That sexy chuckle, again!

"Fair deal," I giggle back, thanking him for his sensitivity, as I resume my spot on the couch.

"OK." More sexy snickering. "Now we're talking! How 'bout when you're ready, call me. Got it?"

"Got it!" I'm grinning from ear to ear after we say our brief goodbyes. My face defies my grungy appearance, which pales to when I dropped out of school two years ago during my fall quarter of grad school; I didn't eat, I barely drank, and I looked anorexic.

My mother takes a break from her baking. Wiping her floured hands on her apron, she pokes her head into the den.

"Who were you talking to for nearly an hour?"

The woman doesn't miss a beat, I swear. Maybe ultrasensitive hearing comes with motherhood.

"If you must know, it was the sweet flight attendant—the one who brought me the hot tea last week. He asked for my number before we deplaned." I'm flipping through the channels, not paying attention to her. "Oh, how romantic!" My mom walks over to touch my shoulder. "Are the two of you going to go out on a date? I think that's a splendid idea."

I'm surprised she never brings up Stephan after her long spiel with the female flight attendant. It's like she moved on to more important things like ... my love life, of course. In a way, she's like my grandma Nana with her perpetual marriage clock ticking, anxiously waiting to plan my big day. Not that I am any different than they are, I've been planning my fantasy wedding since the first time I watched Cinderella. If only life could be that easy...

Years ago, Roxie told me that she couldn't fathom that I'd want Prince Charming because "he's too freakin' lazy to leave his castle." *"If a Knight in Shining Armor is what you're looking for, then you're going to have to search for him. And when you do, I bet it'll be magical because he'll fight for you."*

Truth be told, as much as my parents drive me batty, I admire their relationship. My father adores my mom, and my mom thinks my dad is her knight in shining armor. I've never seen two people so devoted to one another, so in love. All I want—coupled with Cinderella—is to have a perfect marriage just like them.

"Ah, no. Vincent lives in Massachusetts, Mom. We're just friends." I retort.

"Oh..." The tone in her voice lets me know that since my love life is going nowhere, she's about to shift gears to the second most important thing in my life: my education. At least she's predictable. She stands as tall as her five-foot-five frame will allow her, and dropping my hands, she begins clearing her throat. *Great! It's soapbox time; I can almost see her self-proclaimed podium.*

"Chase, I thought that when we got home, you would start your life again and not just sit on the sofa binge-watching television." She grabs the remote, switching off Pastime, the station with old reruns. "It's a new year, for heaven's sake. I don't want to see this anymore. School is back in session in a few days, and I know you miss it. You think I don't have eyes, do you? I saw the course catalog in your room. You even had it opened to the Structural Engineering section. Opportunities like this just don't come around every day, Chase. Look how hard you had to fight to get into college."

"But, Mom, what about contacting the guests? And then there's the caterer and—"

"Don't worry about it. I've got it covered," my mom says matter-of-factly. "Right now, you take care of you, do you understand?"

I nod respectfully. *Wow! What's gotten into my mom? She sounds like... Dad.* Regardless, I can't help but admit that she's right. My college counselor reminded me every day of my junior year of high school that with my grades and my SAT scores, I most likely wouldn't get into any school. At the time, I wondered if she had a crystal ball and could somehow manage to foresee the future. She sure did look like a gypsy with her long skirts, gold bangle bracelets adorning her wrists, and giant beads wrapped around her neck a couple of times, not to mention the bizarre multicolored scarves she'd wrap around her head. Her words haunted me every day and pushed me even further to succeed.

"Plus, this is your dream school we're talking about," my mother continues where she left off.

As much as I hate her rants, I have to say that her timing is impeccable. In a seemingly orchestrated moment, a cacophony of noise erupts from the kitchen. The phone rings ad nauseam while the stove timer dutifully performs its part. Disregarding the eclectic chorus, my mother—with a look of satisfaction on her face and a lightness to her step—elegantly turns and sashays back into the kitchen to the hot pads. "Can you answer the phone, please? Oh, and your father booked you an appointment with the Head of the Department at 1:30 pm today. So, I say it's time for you to get in the shower," she manages all in one breath.

"Ugh," I let out loudly as I crawl off the sofa and walk around to the kitchen phone. "Hello," I pause. "Hey, you!" It's

Henry. He always gets me laughing when he spits out a chain of "let me guess"; it's like he planted a listening device so that he doesn't miss the latest intrigue while he's away. "Mom? Yes. Dad? Oh, yeah! Both are still on my case. Are you sure you don't want to drop out of boarding school and move home? Got it, I'll tell her. Love you to the moon and back!"

"Was that Henry?" my mom chimes in as soon as I hang up the phone, knowing that I reserve that tagline only for my brother.

"Yep. He said that he forgot his blue sweater, and please mail it to him as soon as you're able," I respond, fishing out a bag of popcorn from the pantry before resuming my spot on the couch.

"I'm surprised he didn't want to say hello." My mother grabs the bag of popcorn and promptly returns it to the pantry. The smell of freshly baked cookies wafts through the air.

I shrug, grabbing the remote off the coffee table, flicking the television back on. "Henry said he was off to tennis practice."

"Honey," my mom switches gears, "after your shower, make yourself useful." She scoops the cookies off the pan, places them onto a plate, and lightly covers them with a kitchen towel. "Take the cookies next door and introduce yourself to our new neighbors. Be sure to tell them I used fresh eggs from our little chickens in the back—. Uh, on second thought, don't tell them. They might be sticklers and turn us in."

"It just dawns on you now that we might not be allowed to have chickens? I'm sure they've already heard them, especially what's-her-name; she's louder than the rooster." I can't help but laugh, reaching for a cookie as I head back into the kitchen.

"You mean, Chickalette? Well, she can make Bruce look like a little chick at times, I admit."

It always cracks me up when she mentions the chickens' names like they were my childhood school buddies. One, in particular, I had as a kid—Happy—followed me around the yard. I used to dress her up in my doll's clothes and give her rides in the wheelbarrow.

Besides my mom nagging me about school and men, she's the perfect stay-at-home mom; she's sweet, loving, a bit quirky, especially with our mini-farm in the backyard. She beats to her own drum, which is always in motion—I think that's how she stays so fit, and best of all, she doesn't listen to a word my Nana says about anything—the old "plug your ears, my mother-in-law is arriving" trick. She might get on my last nerve with her doting ways, but when everything is said and done, she's still my mom, and I love her. "Just throw on something decent when you go over to the neighbors and keep it short." She bats my hand away from the cookie and shoves me in the direction of the staircase. "You need to get back to make yourself presentable for your meeting with Professor Wellington."

"But..." I protest.

"No buts. Your dad set this up, and you are going."

"Typical," I mutter under my breath as I head towards the shower.

* * *

Throwing my now-clean hair up into another bun, I grab the plate of cookies. Taking a shortcut, I head across our driveway to our neighbor's front lawn to their brick walkway that leads up to their pale blue colonial house with dark blue shutters, encasing the first- and second-floor windows. It's a replica of our house, except ours is white with black shutters.

The bell on the bright red door barely rings before a raven-haired girl with long braided pigtails, and smiling eyes opens the door.

"Hi! Oh my gosh peanut butter cookies with M&M's my favorite!" she says all in one breath, grabbing the covered plate. Wearing a giant toothy grin, she turns and shouts in the opposite direction. "Mom, our next-door neighbor is here!"

"How ... did ... you ... know—"

"That you brought peanut butter cookies with M&M's?" she finishes. "I bet you're wondering how I knew you were my neighbor too, right?"

42

My jaw drops. I must look like the town idiot, standing there with my mouth open and uttering, "uh, uh, uh." Calm and matter-of-fact, the little girl shrugs her shoulders fiddling with one of her long braids while giving me an I-know-something-that-you-don't-know smirk.

"Shh…" The little girl turns away to nothingness. "Not now."

Eerie. What? Does she have an imaginary friend?

A short-statured woman in pale-blue medical scrubs who looks as fit as a teenager without a line on her face and with the same long-raven hair jogs down the stairs. It's hard for me to determine her age. *Maybe she's my age. If she's forty, I hope I look like her when I grow up.* I watch as she pushes back the pile of boxes cluttering her front hallway before poking her head in the opening.

"Hi! Pardon our disheveled state. We are still unpacking boxes. I'm Maria Stanley," she extends her arm, giving me a warm handshake. "I see you've met my daughter Daphne." I look past her, waiting for someone else to pop out, perhaps the not-so-imaginary friend. "It's just the two of us."

I'm still numb from the initial introduction. I hear Maria rambling on about being an obstetrician and a single mother and needing a babysitter for her ten-year-old. That last part gets my attention. "Baby … sitter?" I gibber.

"Yes. Do you babysit?" Maria looks at me strangely, wondering why she had to repeat the question.

I produce a wan smile, doing my best to feign politeness while trying to figure out how to respond. Maria's phone, ringing in the background, comes to my rescue.

"Sorry, it's the hospital. I have to answer that." Maria sheepishly turns away and heads toward the kitchen.

My phone buzzes, too. I take a brief look down and notice a text:

Roxie: Hey, I think I've got someone lined up for you. When can you
come over?

"Uh, I better get back. Nice to meet you both," I blurt out all in one breath. Seizing my exit, I slowly back my way onto the brick walkway, except Daphne is on my heels. *Great! Now, what do I do?*

"So ... how are you settling into school?" my lame attempt at spontaneous conversation. "You know you can hear the dreaded school bell from your backyard. It rings every day. Even weekends at exactly 8:15 am and then at 3:15 pm." I fake a laugh, walking towards the sidewalk and then back up my driveway. "Brings back memories I'd rather forget every time I hear it." Now I'm rambling. *Why the hell did I say that, especially to a kid?*

"I know, bells and boys, right?" She puckers her lips, emitting a few smoochie-kisses.

I nearly trip over my feet as I pick up my pace, practically running up my driveway. *Kisses? How does she know this about my past? Nah, she couldn't know. Oh my God, I'm overthinking things again.* Another awkward silence follows. Daphne abruptly shifts gears, giving me a stern look while tugging on the suspenders of her overalls and nervously kicking around her red high-top Converses. "I'm worried about math and science. Maybe you could help me; those are your strong subjects, right?"

"Umm..." I will my feet in the direction of my front porch, my legs shaking involuntarily. "You're going to do great in school, by the way. Don't let that lady professor get you down. She's not what you expect. Oh, and did you know you are what my mom calls 'obstinate'?"

Daphne's comments throw me for a loop; I have trouble turning the front doorknob.

"That lady professor ... get you down..." I repeat, releasing a small but nervous chuckle. *Who is she talking about? And I'm not stubborn.*

Not waiting for me to respond, Daphne runs back down my driveway, shifting to the next thing running through her young mind: drawing a hopscotch course on the sidewalk. She pulls out color after color of chalk she had hidden in the front pocket of her overalls.

"Want to play with me later?" she nonchalantly asks as if we'd become fast friends.

"Wish I could." *Not!* "It was nice ... to meet you, Daphne, and I'll see you around," I holler before racing into the house.

Gently tapping the door closed, I let out a sigh of relief until I realize that she isn't quite finished.

"I'm sorry about your boyfriend with the cool leather jacket," Daphne says from outside my front steps. "Don't worry! Mr. Right will show up sooner than you think, he's been right in front of you the whole time. Just let it go!"

I peek out in enough time to see her give me an exaggerated wink. My mouth drops open. *Wait. What the heck?*

"Daphne, come back inside and finish unpacking your boxes," Maria yells from their front porch.

My eyes are fixed on her, watching her have a conversation like she was connected to Bluetooth as she runs across her front lawn, returning home.

If I think my family is weird, this kid—oh, lucky me, my new neighbor—has them beat!

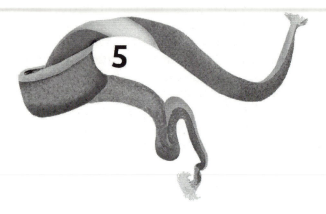

5

On the second floor of Boelter Hall, one of the engineering buildings at the University of California, Los Angeles, I walk to the far west-wing and fingernail-tap on a grey, scratched-up wooden door. The little bronze plaque reads, "Dr. Wellington, Head of the Department of Civil Engineering."

"Come in," a deep voice bellows. Tucking my ski cap in my backpack, I securely wrap my scarf around my neck before entering. "Chastity Morgan, I would like to say this is a surprise," the older man says, steadying himself against the desk as he slowly stands up. I feel like a giant to his five-foot-nothing stance. "It's nice to see you again."

I shake Dr. Wellington's wrinkled hand, staring at the tiny, older man a little more than I ought. I barely recognize him. He's aged a lot in the last two years, with large puffy circles under his eyes and deep lines zigzagging his face. The last time I saw him, he had wisps of white hair that lined his head like a basketball. Replacing his sport-themed hairdo is a thick and oddly shaped toupee. Regardless of the awkward appearance, Dr. Wellington has an uncanny resemblance to the cartoonish high school principal Mr. Rooney from *Ferris Buehler's Day Off*, albeit a cheerier version.

"You too, Dr. Wellington," I reply, shaking his hand weakly.

He wobbles a bit as he sits back down. "The joys of a hip replacement." He releases a little chuckle.

I begin to pan the familiar civil engineering books—Fortran Analysis, Engineering Mathematics, Structural Systems—to keep from staring at the spot of ink that's drenching the front pocket of his white button-down shirt. One of the pens in his pocket protector exploded. Next to the books is steel industrial shelving, made more for a warehouse full of supplies than a professor's office, and adorned with awards. He has one little window behind his desk with a few potted cactus plants on the sill that overlooks the section of parking lot presently under construction. Floor-to-ceiling bookshelves cover the remaining walls.

The plastic fluorescent ceiling lights beat down on me as I sink into the swivel seat situated in front of his oversized steel desk. It makes a loud gaseous sound as the plastic springs collapse. "That wasn't—sorry." All I can think of is the office scene from *It's a Wonderful Life* when a diminutive George Bailey asks for mean old Mr. Potter's help. I suddenly feel like a mouse in a cubby hole; my hands, reduced to paws, nervously twitch.

"What can I do for you?" he inquires while drawing attention to the only free spot on his desk where he has his laptop; he opens it, completely disregarding the remaining desk area, covered in messy stacks of loose papers piled two feet high.

I press the chair lever a few times, hoping to boost myself up to eye level but to no avail. "Well," folding my hands neatly in my lap, "to tell you the truth, I was sent here on pretense. My dad thinks I need to be back in school. It seems like everyone at home wants me to rebuild my life. Things are just happening way too fast for me. I guess I'm not thinking straight," I ramble, looking down at my hands, which are turning purple from clutching them together so tightly. *Breathe, Chase! Remember, ten seconds in, ten seconds out.* "Sorry. I just broke up with my fiancé. Wait. That's not right;

he broke up with me—more like straight-out got married under my nose, TO A GUY no less..."

I'm in a tizzy, and I need to cool down. Dr. Wellington's bug eyes are enough of an indication that I have successfully freaked him out. *Breathe, Chase! Dammit! Come on, ten seconds in, ten seconds out.* The nagging sound of a drill followed by a jackhammer jolts me back to reality.

"My life," I shout, compensating for the background noise, "is in a bit of jumble at the moment. As much as I hate to admit it, I think my parents might be on to something. It's time for me to go back and finish my degree and focus less on men and my fairytale fantasy." I take out my mini water bottle from my purse taking a couple of swigs to relieve my parched throat before resuming. "That said, I want to start over, pick up where I left off and finish my degree once and for all."

Silence looms as I catch him in suspended animation, staring at me, his hands frozen in place and hovering his keyboard. It feels like several seconds have passed before I think I'm in control again. I need to prove to the old doc that I have my act together, even though I don't.

"So ... as I was saying," I shout once again.

"Sorry, can you say that a little louder," he asks, cupping his ear. The drilling stops a moment later, but I don't notice a thing. Instead, my attention is diverted to a bunch of long, straggly grey hairs sticking out the top of his ears. I'm transfixed. *Wow! He almost looks elfin. I thought that only happened in folktales and—*

"Chastity," his nasal voice breaks my trance. "Chastity? Are you okay?"

"Ah, yes, sir. I was just thinking about my dissertation," I lie.

"Well, I hate to inform you," he talks slowly and sweetly as he closes his laptop and places his folded hands on top. "Professor Feldman rejected the first two chapters of your PhD dissertation, which means your degree is ... over. She said your research was not real life and that you didn't follow her suggestions on how to make your dissertation meet those standards."

48

I glance out the window, flashing back a few years ago, to the last day I was on campus. I was sitting at the head of a rectangular table in a small conference room lined with a chalkboard in the front and whiteboards on the other two sides. I can still smell the toxic fumes of the colorful markers that I used to scribble out my proposal. Five committee members focused on my every word, grilling me, asking me question after question about my proposed dissertation during the oral screening exam. Of the five, it was Professor Feldman who said that my research was not practical. She picked apart every page, finding supposed errors, wanting me to redo all my work. I was a deer in the headlights and couldn't hear anymore. I was beyond broken. Tears poured down my face as I picked up my paperwork, threw my blue backpack over my shoulder, and walked past the committee members without a single word, not even a goodbye, never looking back.

"Chastity, did you hear a word I said?" Professor Wellington asks, now standing, half leaning over the desk, concern written all over his face. "Are you sure you're okay?" His hand slides off when a few errant papers become airborne and hit me on their way to the floor.

I snap to and shake out the cobwebs. "Wait! Hold on a second." I ignore the gaseous sound the chair produces as I position myself on the edge of the seat, which miraculously catapults me to eye level. "She failed me? Why wasn't I given any notice? A letter? An email? I walked out. I never knew I was kicked out."

"You were given notice." He pulls off his glasses and rubs his tired eyes. "You never responded to the attempts we made to contact you."

I glance out the window again, "I wasn't in a good place."

"I know. Your father told us what happened, the accident. I'm so sorry about—"

I wave my hand, cutting him off. At the same time, I pinch the bridge of my nose, forcing back tears. "And I'm sorry to be the one to tell you that a failure like this jeopardized your degree." He pauses momentarily before continuing to make sure that I am listening instead of getting wound up emotionally. "The only thing I can suggest is for you to meet with Professor Feldman, plead your case, and apologize for walking out. After that, you need to figure out if you can reorganize your dissertation. I'm all on board for letting you continue. We always loved having you around, but this matter is out of my hands. She's one of your committee members; you need her to sign the paperwork for you to come back."

I slowly sink back into my seat, the gaseous noise a welcome sound to my jumbled mind.

"The only thing I have ever wanted besides a loving husband and a family of my own is to be a Structural Engineer. I wanted to follow in my father's and grandfather's footsteps since I was a little girl—designing and constructing buildings and teaching on the side. But now you're making that impossible because this is morally wrong. I did the work, and I did it well. My advisor, Dr. Wang, told me my project was fabulous and that I was on track to finish. Professor Feldman is a jerk who hates females! *The irony of it all!* Furthermore, I only stayed in school to finish my master's degree—almost got a PhD in the process—because of a promise I made to myself to stick to my plans no matter what. Why? Because I believed that engineering wouldn't let me down. It was the one stable part of my life that no one could take away from me, or so I thought. And now you're telling me my future depends on THAT woman? I would never have dropped out if I didn't lose—" I mumble, my face buried in my hands.

The floodgates open; tears begin to drench my face.

"To answer an earlier question of yours, no, I guess I'm not okay. I came here today to pick up where I left off to rebuild my life. Granted, my parents forced me into it, but you know what they say about your parents knowing what's best?"

"And you can do that if you go talk to Professor Feldman and redo the first couple chapters of your dissertation to her liking."

I'm fiddling with my hands, not sure how to ask him.

"Maybe you can go talk to Professor Feldman for me? Tell her I'm sorry."

He pauses for a minute, "Are you serious?"

"Yes," I say, matter-of-factly.

"No, I can't do that," he laughs. "I'll do anything else to help you out, but you have to face her yourself."

"Oh, God. I can't do that. It's morally wrong. My advisor should be the only one able to judge me and force me to redo my work. If he thinks it's fine, then it should be fine."

"Chastity, Dr. Wang doesn't think it's fine either. Talk to him. You'll see. My hands are tied. Your fate is in Professor Feldman's hands."

"This is nonsense. It's unfair. She hates me. She'll never let me back in. There's no way she'll change her mind." Holding back my tears, I let out a quiet "thank you for listening," as I stand.

I slowly turn to collect my purse, and as I'm putting on my ski cap Miss Harris, Dr. Wellington's much younger secretary with her skinny jeans and skin-tight turtleneck sweater, bounces in carrying a stack of papers, topped with multiple sticky notes. She chuckles when she sees me donned in sub-zero-temp attire. It may be in the mid-50s, but when my nerves are frayed, my body temp goes down, and I turn into a freeze baby.

Regardless of her ridicule, I tighten my scarf and "will" myself to stand tall before leaving the old doc's office. To do that, I have to muster up as much encouragement as possible. *I REFUSE to have her deprecate me! Time to leave, Chase. Put on your best face!*

As I extend my arm to shake his hand, I look up at the old doc and notice a couple of errant strands of his unkempt hairpiece pointing up, like they were stretching from a well-rested beauty nap. The movement continues; I can't help but not stare. *What the hell? That's not hair; they're legs belonging to a ... SPIDER.*

My eyes widen. My facial expression is enough for Miss Harris to take notice. Immediately looking in the same direction, she opens her mouth, but nothing comes out.

Oblivious to the unfolding events, Dr. Wellington sees Miss Harris's entrance as his perfect exit and stands to shake my hand. "Good luck to you, Chastity. I know you have what it takes to succeed, only if you want—"

"Dr. Wellington," Miss Harris interrupts, she's patting her blonde curls like a monkey rubbing his head. "Um, I hate to say this, but there's a spider nesting in your hair."

"A SPIDER? I hate spiders. Get it off me, Miss Harris. GET IT OFF. NOW!"

Miss Harris grabs the doc's back scratcher off his desk, papers swishing off left and right, and pawing at the designated spot on his shaggy mop she gets nowhere with Dr. Wellington, who has morphed into "berserk" mode, dancing wildly behind his desk. In one last attempt, Miss Harris rips off his toupee and flings it across the room like a Frisbee, knocking off an end table lamp before landing on a stack of books neatly piled on the floor next to one of his bookshelves.

"My hair, my hair!" The old doc drops to the floor and raises his arms to his head, his pudgy fingers barely making a dent to disguise his bald spot. It takes a moment for him to realize that he's made a fool out of himself. He slowly rises to a dignified stance.

"Miss Harris," Dr. Wellington utters a light cough before continuing. "Could you please hand me my toupee?" his voice barely above a whisper.

Grabbing the back scratcher again, the stodgy secretary walks over to the bookcase, and before pawing around, notices the spider's crumpled form on top of a textbook. She gingerly picks up the hairpiece and passes it along to the doc who, in turn, promptly plops it back in place.

Unbelievable! The strange office duo, so caught up in the surreal moment, don't even see me leave. I walk out of the building, passing all the construction, to the parking garage right next door with a victorious spring to my step. Even if crawling on my knees to Dr. Feldman to complete my degree daunts me, reminiscing on the office scene lightens my mood.

My phone buzzes just as I open my car door. It's a text from Grant. *God! You're the LAST person I want to talk to, you, asshole!* There's a bunch of heart emojis at the end of the message.

Grant: Can we please talk? You're still my best friend, and I love you! Remember? The five

musketeers forever! Please don't let my
decision to marry Brody destroy our friendship.
I have so much to tell you. Call me. 🖤 🖤 🖤

My happy moment snuffed, I'm about ready to puke. Madder than a bat out of hell, I fumble with my phone, trying to figure how to shut it down as I toss my backpack into the passenger seat.

"THAT has to be the straw that breaks the camel's back!" My voice starts at a mumble but grows steadily. "You tell me to get over it and give you back the ring, and now this text! Well, fuck it, fuck you, fuck Dr. Wellington, fu—" my tirade cut short when I look up to see a group of wide-eyed students staring at me from the car next to mine. I sheepishly finger wave as they speedily back up and exit the garage.

Once I get in the car, the dam breaks. I sink into my seat, mumbling through sobs.

"Grant, you were supposed to be my other half—the architect to fit my engineering designs. We would have made the perfect team. You're the perfect building. Don't you get it? You're, you're like a building, designed for the long-term lifespan. You have functionality, strength, rigidity, and durability. You even have the perfect base isolators that allow your sometimes-stiff self to move during an earthquake without breaking."

While I know that what I'm spouting sounds corny, I'm a freakin' engineer who's looking for precision. "But apparently, I wasn't *the* perfect fit for you, Grant!" I yell in the safety of my car, windows up, banging my fists on the steering wheel like a child having a tantrum. "Jesus, I'm a woman, for crying out loud! How could this be happening to me for the second time: I've lost another best friend. I'm done with marriage. It's time for me to explore another avenue."

Ripping the ring off my finger and placing it securely in the box kept in my purse, I rev the engine and screech out of the parking lot, ready for new adventures—Roxie style.

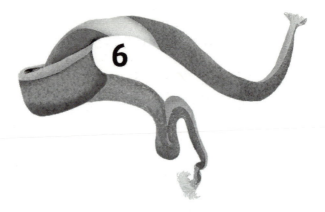

6

On the way home in bumper to bumper traffic on the 110 Freeway, I crawl through downtown and then past Dodger Stadium. While car horns blast at inconsiderate drivers every few minutes, I can't help thinking back to the times Roxie made out with guys she barely knew. It repulsed me. At the same time, I realized that I was jealous. Roxie has this ability to approach life with reckless abandon. This carefree attitude about life is something that I most definitely lack. I have yet to learn how to let go; I can't even share the freakin' pen in my purse for fear that I'll never get it back, that's how tight I am.

I turn onto our quiet little cookie-cutter street, where no one is allowed to park a car at night. Each house is some colonial version with dark shutters that frame the windows. Antique white street lights grace the corner of each driveway. The homes have wide sidewalks and rolling, green lawns that roll from house to house.

Roxie and another guy stand with their bikes in front of her house near the sidewalk. She leaves him there and heads across the street, bouncing in the direction of my house. She's wearing one of her getups—a rainbow-colored tutu, matching rainbow tights, a shirt with glittery writing on it, and her long brown hair pulled up into a high ponytail with a unicorn headband to top it off. I'm in no mood for company, so I hit the button to the automatic gate opener earlier than usual and pull into my driveway. Roxie beats me to the punch, jumping in front of my car, hands up in surrender. I lock the brake since I'm on a mini incline. Roxie knocks on the driver's side window and motions for me to roll it down.

"Hey, Chase! Guess what I figured out for you?" She doesn't wait for me to respond as I stare at her glittery t-shirt, *Here Comes Trouble*. I roll my eyes. "A set of post-breakup resolutions, to be enacted. Immediately. So, here goes..." And holding up a crinkled white-lined piece of paper, she reads:

1. Get out of bed.

2. Leave the house.

3. Travel the world and have adventures.

4. Meet a bunch of hot guys.

5. Have lots of sex.

6. If you're fortunate enough, fall in love.

7. Get married (which I wouldn't advise, but heck, it's your life!)

She hands over her prized work, all written in bright red marker like a teacher grading an exam. *The girl's a motormouth, I swear.*

"Granted," she continues, "number 5 and 7 could be interchanged, depending on if you still want to listen to Nana and hold onto your virginity until you walk down the aisle. If you're hell-bent on throwing caution to the wind, then stick with 4 and 5. In any event, it's time to stop living in the past and wallowing in what could have, would have, should have, and go out in search of your own—"

"Listen, I appreciate what you're doing, but I don't want to talk about this right now." I can't believe I manage to cut her off, rolling the window halfway up. "I've got way too much on my plate. Grant just texted me, and I can't take it anymore!" I snip. I'm angrier at myself for going back on my recent resolve than I am of her genuine concern for me. *I'm such a wuss! I have no backbone! Jesus, what's wrong with me?*

Roxie pulls back, yelling at me and almost falling in the process into the rose bushes nestled in front of my house under the dining room French windows. "Whoa, cuz! No need to be so snippy. I get it, all the more reason to hit the reboot button and dive right in, right? Plus, you're going to love this one. I stopped by the party center to pick up a few things, and lo and behold, I came across Amoremoji stickers!" She pulls little sheets from her back waistband, holding them up for me to see. "It's serendipity! So anyway, I've got it all figured out. You can use the stickers as a quick way to keep tabs on each resolution of the list..." She slips the sheets of stickers through the window, which lands on my lap. "What the hell?"

"You know, 'amore'? Love? Plus emojis!! Pretty cool if you ask me. There are heart designs too."

I open my mouth to protest, but Roxie plows right through my invisible shield.

"And don't tell me that you're not into emojis! Come on; you're the queen of histrionics. Like that word, eh? I just learned it today from my Word of the Day app. It means drama qu—"

"Roxie! Stop!" I cut her off a second time. "I know what it means. And I'm not a drama queen. I'm just having a hard ti—"

"Nope, not today," Roxie says, cutting me off. Her hands on her hips. "I'm not hearing it. No more wallowing for you. You need to get off this pity pot once and for all and get back to real life. It has been three weeks since the breakup—THREE WEEKS, and your mom says you've been spending more time on the couch than she cares to think about. So, no more. Since you're so anal about living life like an engineering project, let's stick to the plan."

"As if that's going to work, especially after hearing what Professor Wellington had to say to me. It's—"

"Jesus, stop being so goddamn obstinate!" Roxie's pulling on her ponytail, clearly frustrated.

"Obstinate? OH ... MY ... GOD ..." I pause, having an epiphany. If I missed seeing Grant for who he really is, maybe Professor Feldman was right. Did I do a lousy job on my dissertation? Oh. My. God, Daphne's words... Shit!

"Oh my God, what?" Roxie asks.

"Am I really obstinate?"

Roxie looks at me, eyebrows raised.

"The short answer is, yes, you are. But that doesn't matter now. You are still a true-blue engineer, so from here on out, you are going to go about dating like you would constructing a home—which, by the way, you are amazing at doing. If you can build a house, you can build the perfect life, piece by piece. You always told me to find a nice parcel of land, lay down the foundation, frame the house, put up the bearing walls, frame the roof, place the sheathing, and finally add the finishing touches. Grant proved to have a lousy foundation. Promise me you'll keep an open mind with the next guy, and USE THE AMOREMOJI STICKERS, for heaven's sake! Pinky swear," Roxie says, leaning into the car with her right pinkie extended.

Roxie's explanation gets my attention. "Wow, you've actually been listening to me all these years. Okay. Fine! After the day I've had, if it shuts you up, then I'll pinky swear." I let out a little laugh, rolling down the window a few inches more, sticking out my pinky.

She wraps her pinky around mine, tugging at it. "Good, that solves that. Now, each check you make on my list will bring you closer to the plan of plenty of sex, some love, and, and if you *really* must go there—something I don't condone, of course—marriage. Hopefully, you'll have a line of heart-shaped smiley faces after each one."

There's a slight pause in the conversation. It's quiet, except for the light rumble of the car motor, which, for some strange reason, has a calming effect on me. The brief pause allows me a chance to mull over her barrage of information. *Do I tell her that Vincent called me? Maybe not. She'll just ask me a million-and-one questions.*

Roxie's phone starts blaring. Flinching, I accidentally slam the horn. I look up to see a face appear in the living room window. I could swear it looks just like Nana—chuckles and a half-drained martini in her hand.

Okay. Weird. I'm seeing things. Nana's still in Idaho, right?

Roxie, who's engrossed in texting, is entirely oblivious to what I saw.

"Roxie! Did you see her?" I point surreptitiously at the window, but the figure has disappeared, and the curtains are back in place.

"See who? Seriously, Chase, you need to de-stress. You're so locked into old-fashioned ideas and your relentless goal to get married that you're beginning to hallucinate. There's no better time than the present, Chase. Come on, this is your time to go wild and—" she's reaching for the door handle.

The look of shock on Roxie's face is the last thing I see as I find myself lurching past the gate and into the garage. Not wanting to hear any more of her haranguing, I floor the accelerator, thinking I can make a speedy exit. In the rearview mirror, I catch Roxie's jerky jogging movements coming up the driveway, tutu bouncing the whole way. She's laughing hilariously.

"You had the emergency brake on, didn't you? God, I wish I had caught that on my phone," she yells between catching breaths. "Oh, geez! I almost forgot. I have someone for you to meet."

Seriously, Rox! You just don't give up, do you? Rolling my eyes as I step out of the car, I gear myself up for more of her bullshit, only to realize that she's rummaging through a collection of stuff in the garage. "Hold on a second!" I quickly grab my scarf to make sure it's knotted securely before running over to where Roxie has pulled my bright pink beach cruiser out of its slumber. "Oh. Dear. Lord," keeping my voice low, "you don't waste any time, do you? I suppose you're setting me up with the guy on the bike by your tree on your front lawn, right?" She playfully slaps my hands when I reach for my bike.

"You're going to love my stepbrother Brent," Roxie responds as she begins to wipe it down with a cleaning rag.

A few years after Aunt Mary Ann ran away, she sent a letter to Uncle Mason with no return address, saying that she remarried and had a stepson. Years pass with no further information about her mom and new family until Roxie received a surprise letter from a "Brent Kramer," who claimed they were related. They've kept in touch ever since. "Stepbrother? The one that lives in Vancouver that you've met face-to-face all of but what? Once?"

She stops suddenly, "Yes. So, what? We talk a lot over the phone. My dad's still in London on business for another few months, and I'm lonely. So, I invited him to crash with me until he figures out a place to stay. He's super fun and sweet and a super fabulous artist to boot. He's ideal for you, Chase." She's pushing the bike out of the garage and by the front gate.

A little head pops out of the next-door bushes, "That oddball? He's a far cry from ideal!" Daphne laughs. "I personally like the flight attendant, but he's a bit on the older side. You know, flawless people have a lot of flaws. I'd watch my back if I were you."

I jump like a jackrabbit. "Daphne!" I breathe out a startled sigh. "What are you doing hiding out in the bushes? What are you talking about, and how much of our conversation did you hear?"

"Everything, of course!" ignoring the first question. Daphne gives me a smug smile. She's wearing a unicorn sweatshirt with a hood that dubs as the horn, and bright pink pants to match with even pinker Converse sneakers.

"Right. Uh ... Roxie, meet our new, uh, neighbor, Daphne," I stammer, wanting to chuckle at her outfit choice, "Daphne, this is my cousin Roxie. She lives across the street with my Uncle Mason."

"Hi, Daphne. I'm Roxie." She extends her arm to shake hands. "I like your style."

The little girl eyes her, her mouth twisting into a grin. "I like yours too," and they weirdly high-five. "You create such pretty parties. Maybe you could decorate my house for my birthday party?"

Roxie grins from ear to ear. "Why, thank you! What a nice compliment. How did you know about my party decorations? Granted, my unicorn costume is a dead giveaway that I just came from a client's unicorn party, but still..."

The little girl shrugs before skipping around in circles. "My mom met your dad a few months ago when we were first looking at the house. By the way, cool bike, Chase and, oh— cool hat, too. Are those reindeer? They look like they're playing." She steps in a little to take a closer look.

"Ah ... oh, nothing," I laugh, giving a little pat on the top of her head, as I make a beeline up our front walkway for the front door. "I'm going to freshen up first, Rox. Nice seeing you again, Daphne." I put my key in the door, giving the lock a little shove.

"You don't want to go in there. Just saying..." Daphne shouts as she runs across her front lawn back to her house.

"What?" my lame attempt to patronize her. I turn the knob. I can tell that the door hits something.

"Ooph! Oh, heavens! My new top. It's ruined!"

Oh, Lord, it can't be! I'd know that voice from anywhere. It's Nana's. Peeking around the door in the main foyer to observe the damage, I see that she landed safely on the Victorian corner chair, empty martini glass in hand, her silk navy blouse, drenched in liquor.

"Nana, what are you doing here?" is all I can say, hand still on the door as I stand in the entryway.

"Don't you love me anymore?" she says louder than usual.

"Well, yes, of course, I lo—"

"Then why didn't you say it: 'Nana, I'm so happy to see you!'"

"Nana, I'm so happy to see you," I mimic. "But..."

"But. But what? What's wrong with your butt? You haven't been giving your milk away, have you? Lying down too much? You know, I've *always* taught you never to give your milk away for free."

"No, Nana, my butt's fine. I mean," my lame comeback. "What the heck do I mean?" I mutter under my breath.

"Ah! So, you HAVE given your milk away, haven't you?" Nana continues, putting the glass to her lips, not realizing until she tips it that it's empty.

"No. No, that's not it, Nana! It's just that—"

I notice movement in my peripheral vision. Our odd and slightly clamorous conversation draws a small but amused audience through the slightly opened door. A dark-haired guy with striking hazel-colored eyes parks his bike on our little walkway before joining Roxie, who has already made herself comfortable on my lawn nearest the front steps.

That must be Brent. Great, just what I need!!

"Well, then, spit it out. What is it?" Nana hammers, her red fingernails, tapping in irritation against her glass.

"Ah ... you surprised me ... that's all. I thought ... you were ... still in Idaho." I sputter, backing away, inching the door open.

"Oh, your mother filled me in with Grant and everything that happened on the plane. I couldn't bear staying away. We have so much to talk about, Chase, and—MY GOD!" Nana shrieks, standing up, reaching for my knit hat. "Please tell me you didn't wear that God-awful ski cap when you met with Dr. Wellington?" Nana says before catching her breath.

Holy shit! No wonder Doc Wellington and his stuffy secretary giggled. Great professional presence, Chase!!! The blood drains from my face as I recall the whole scene.

"Um..." I suddenly remember Daphne's warning: 'You don't want to go in there. Just saying.' *How the hell did that pipsqueak know Nana was home? Has she been spying on my house?*

"Oh yeah," changing the subject, "I just remembered that I promised to go with Roxie on a bike ride. We'll talk later." *Or not!*

And to think that I was deliriously happy when Nana decided to stay in Idaho longer, instead of joining us on the flight home, and that I wouldn't see her until the end of January. *So much for that!*

I turn to walk out, swinging open the front door, Nana following close behind me, still clinging onto her empty martini glass.

"Okay, if you must! Just remember, I'll be waiting. We need to have this discussion. It's for your own good, Chase, darling." Nana waves before twirling and shutting the door behind me.

I hear light chuckling growing into hysterical laughter coming from the front lawn as I approach.

"Bravo, bravo," the cute guy claps.

"Okay. Shows over," I quip, standing on the front porch.

"What the heck? Giving your milk away?" he guffaws, holding his stomach. "What is this? Victorian England? Who talks like this nowadays?"

"Keep it down. She can probably hear you," I say through gritted teeth.

"Our grandmother, that's who," Roxie answers quietly, her back to the house. "Is it ever too soon to talk about sex, Chase?" Roxie holds an imaginary glass, pretending to be tipsy. "Remember, don't give the milk away for free, don't *ever* give the milk away *for free!*" She says in an overly haughty way, slurring her words.

"That's enough! Quit it!" I'm close to tears, bent over, hands clutching my stomach. "I feel a headache brewing. Between Wellington and Nana, I need to lie down. And it doesn't help with Daphne around." I vigorously rub my forehead. "I take it that you're Brent? I'm Chastity," I say, giving his grungy clothing a quick once-over while extending my hand. "Listen, I'm going to have to take a raincheck. Sorry, for messing up your bike ri—"

"Brent Kramer, at your service. Hey, if you're not up to biking today, we can try—"

"She'll be fine," Roxie interrupts. "Why don't you take five, Brent, while I help her freshen up? Okay?"

"Sure, boss. Anything you say." Brent salutes Roxie as the three of us walk across the street. Brent enters the guest room while Roxie and I head to her room.

"So, what's your issue with her anyway? She's just a kid, Chase."

"You've got to be kidding, Roxie," raising my voice a bit. "The kid freaks me out. She knew Nana was at my house."

"Well, that's nothing. Daphne probably found out about her from your mom."

"And," I continue. "She knew about Grant."

"That's no secret. She could have gotten that from your mom, too. Don't you think you're stretching things—"

"She knew about the school bell," I interrupt. "No one knows about the school bell except you and me."

"Okay, that's freaky."

"That's what I'm trying to tell you, Rox. And then she says things about Nana, and it comes true. The kid scares me. Look at what she had on. It was almost like she knew what crazy getup you would be sporting today."

"Well," Rox reassures me, flinging open her front door, "we'll have to keep our eyes on her, that's all. There has to be some explanation. Maybe she just likes costumes like I do. In the meantime, let's get you fixed up."

* * *

"Here, take this," Roxie hands me a cup of water and two Ibuprofen. I obediently swallow the pills and place the drink on her nightstand as I snuggle under her plush down comforter. Her room hasn't changed a bit since we were in high-school. Her walls are painted lavender with long white curtains that tie on each with lavender bows. She has an eclectic mix of old movie posters like *Pretty in Pink* and boy bands like N'Sync. And then there's her ceiling, entirely covered in glow-in-the-dark stars. She was always one for making a wish on a shooting star, *"and what better way than on the ceiling with your imagination moving them"*—is still her motto.

"What are you doing?" I hear Roxie rummaging in her closet. "Oh, I know what you're up to." I let out an exaggerated sigh, pulling her purple quilt from the foot of her bed and up to my chin. "Please, don't dress me like a sleazeball. I remember the top you wanted me to wear to the football game last year; my boobs just about fell out of it."

"Oh, come on, Chase. You've got to live it up, especially if you want to go for 4 and 5."

"Rox, I think the thing I need to do is take one step at a time."

"Are you getting cold feet?"

"No!" I snap. "I'm just ... I'm just..." How can I tell her that I still want my fairytale life with Grant?

"Just what, Chase? Scared?" She pops her head out of the closet.

"No. It's just I'm still getting over Grant."

"Oh, hells, bells, Chase! Grant is history. HISTORY. He's goddamn married, Chase. He wasn't meant for you in the first place. Like Grant said, get over it! Now, lie down and rest. Let momma Roxie fix you up. I'm going to set the timer for fifteen minutes," she says in a motherly tone. "While you relax, I'll scrounge up some clothes for you to wear." Roxie heads into her closet before I can object any further.

Sleep hits me quickly once I settle into her soft bed.

* * *

A light binging sound from Roxie's phone wakes me up. I'm a bit disoriented, trying to figure out why I'm in my cousin's bed.

"Ah! You're up! Look what I picked out for the bike ride." Roxie holds up a pair of capris khakis and a light blue short-sleeved top with a plunging neckline. "I figured you'd be wearing your scarf. You could tuck in the ends so they won't get in your way when you're pedaling."

"Wow! That's really cute! Thanks, Rox!" I sit up, taking the clothes from her. I pull off my own and change into hers.

"Anytime, cuz!"

Looking out Roxie's bedroom window, I see Brent napping in the front yard on the glider under the oak tree. He reminds of an old timber-framed building, lightweight but sturdy and durable. I feel excitement stirring within me. I send an encouraging message to my frazzled brain: *This is it, Chase. You can do this!*

"Chase, you ready?"

I look down at my new outfit, securing my scarf in place first before slipping on my hat. "Yep!"

"Then let's get this show on the road." Roxie's energy level is contagious. Rejuvenated after a power nap, I clip down the stairs and out the door to meet hot guy number one.

"Hey, Brent, rise and shine!" Roxie yells before making a beeline for her bike.

Brent stretches, touching his toes a few times before walking over to his bike. My eyes feast on him for a few seconds before rolling my bike down Roxie's driveway towards the sidewalk. As I approach, I notice that he's no longer wearing his shabby-looking clothes.

"Oh kids, I just looked at the time, I need to run an errand before I get ready for my hot date," Roxie announces.

"What?" I spout. "You just met—what's his name?"

"His name's Trevor," Roxie finishes.

"Trevor. The guy you met yesterday in the grocery store?"

"Four and five, cuz. That's the name of my game!" Roxie turns around so that she's facing Brent and me. "All right! Let's get this baby started! Chase, this is my stepbrother Brent Kramer. Brent, this is my cousin Chase Morgan. Now you two go along and have fun. I have stuff to do before I meet up with Trevor."

"Uh ... where were you when we introduced each other?" I quip but could have readily been talking to a tree for all Roxie cares about as she quickly jumps on her bike and speeds down the road. "Your cousin is rather subtle, isn't she? Shall we?" Brent says, mounting his bike.

"Yeah, like a train wreck," I mumble, hopping onto my pink beach cruiser. "In a tutu."

"I heard that." Brent turns back so I can hear him. "That's funny! You've got a great sense of humor. I like that in a woman."

"Thanks!" I gaze at him, noticing his change of wardrobe; he's wearing a white fedora and dark-shaded aviator glasses, which makes him look sexy as all get out. *For being step-siblings, it's incredible how alike Roxie and he are about their get-ups.*

"Well," Brent taking the lead, "shall we?"

I give him an affirming smile. My mind takes off in another direction as I head down the street, imagining what he would look like shirtless and me rubbing his chest. Before I know it, I'm in a whirlwind of lustful thoughts. An anachronistic "clink-clink" sound of a kid's bike joins my salacious fantasies. *What the heck?* Locating the bell's origin, who do I see coming out of our new neighbor's garage but Daphne.

Oh, God! Not her again! I gear myself up for more weirdness.

"You forgot your helmet. Didn't your mother tell you that you should never ride your bike without it?" Daphne gives me another one of her silly smirks, clanking along on her purple bike complete with wispy pom-poms on the handlebars and a white teddy bear peeking out of her front basket.

"Yes, she did. But I'm an adult. I'll be fine. Thanks, anyway!" I smirk back at her.

"You'll be sorry!" She yells as she passes us on the sidewalk, turning the opposite way around the block. "Just saying!"

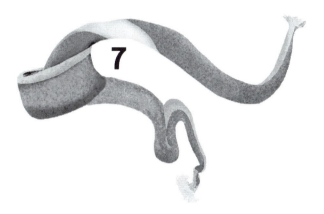

7

I race on ahead of Brent, trying to get away from Daphne before she says something else that makes the hairs on my arms stand up. Brent peddles fast to catch up; the huffing and puffing, a sure indication that exercise is not his forte.

"So..." he yells loud enough to get my attention, "I hear you were about to walk down that dreaded aisle."

I let out a sigh of relief, grateful that he didn't hit me with a barrage of questions about my new neighbor. "Yep, until my so-called Prince Charming decided to run off with another Prince Charming." I stand on the bike pedaling harder up an incline littered with an uneven asphalt, the loose pebbles rattling against the spokes.

I pan our little tree-lined California neighborhood, relishing the breath-taking view—a collection of small hills dotted with homes rests right near the Raymond fault line. The view never ceases to amaze me, regardless of the area's disturbing geographical history. I stare at a crack in the pavement, probably from plane slippage. I'm momentarily mesmerized at the fact that even if we don't feel an earthquake, the ground moves ever so slightly; that last part, a mixture of what was drilled into me from all my earthquake classes and my dad's logorrhea after significant earthquakes. Some kids learn about space or the weather. But in this region, it's all about tectonic plates and which regions are more likely to have a significant earthquake. "Another Prince Charming? Should have gone with the knight in shining armor instead." I shake my head slightly, trying to recall what I said that made him comment like that.

He rides up alongside me, chuckling, sweat dripping down his forehead. He's exerting a lot of energy up this mini hill. Watching him snaps me out of my earthquake trance. "Well ... nothing you could have done, kid. You just don't have the right plumbing, I'm afraid." He turns up an empty driveway making a sharp left onto the sidewalk.

"That was pithy! God, you sound just like Roxie." I burst out laughing, feeling a bit lighter. I slow down to enjoy the crisp winter air as we peddle along. "Funny, though, you make a valid point." While strolling at a steady pace with Brent in the lead, I ruminate on the newfound knowledge before continuing. "Oh well, doesn't matter ... Grant was just the wrong type of building. He looked and acted like..." I'm distracted again as I pan the surreal Christmas scene, keeping count of the number of deflated blowup Christmas lawn decorations that linger after the holidays.

"Llll ... like," Brent drawls, getting me back on track.

"Like the Empire State Building. You know, strong, statuesque, stately. The thing is, his beautiful façade hides what is really going on inside."

"Whoa! Hold up!" He slams on the hand brakes, his wheels screeching to a halt. I have to brake quickly so I don't ram into him; I skid onto a neighboring lawn. "So ... if I've got this straight, you equate men to buildings, correct?" He eyes me curiously like I'm bat-shit crazy.

"I'm a structural engineer. What can I say?" I feel the heat rising up my neck. I turn slightly, so he doesn't see me blushing. I know I'm an oddball, I just don't like when people point it out.

"O ... K..." Brent knocks his kickstand in place and walks over to the corner stop sign a few feet away to press the crossing-guard button before sidling up to it. He tips his fedora; mouth cocked to one side. "So... how would you rate me?" He waves his hands up and down his body like he's a new shiny toy.

"Hmm..." I play along, tapping my finger on my chin. "You're like the..." I pause, "Leaning Tower of Pisa."

He rolls his eyes and throws his arms in the air before grabbing his bike and walking it across the street. "I don't know if I should take that as a compliment. Okay, don't respond to that," he laughs, looking back at me, making sure I follow. "All I have to say is that you're a real find, Chase Morgan. So, if men are all buildings, what's your ideal one?" He mounts his bike once we get to the other side of the street, adjusting the seat before sitting down.

"Oh!" I let out another sigh, avoiding a pronounced bump near the curb as I catch up to him. "Good question. I ... I honestly don't know anymore. I used to think that the best type of man would be someone who could weather the rough times without having added reinforcements, like dampers or base isolators, to enhance performance; someone with a definite, long-lasting lifespan since marriage is one heck of a commitment."

"Marriage means monogamy? What a distressing word," Brent blurts out before hopping on his bike and peddling away. "Why can't we all be like dolphins and fuck the entire pod?" he yells out. A woman pushing her baby in a stroller stops with her mouth agape, giving him a hard stare.

"Oh! Sorry," I offer the shocked woman, hoping to soften the blow. "He's, you know, a little cray cray," my pointer finger loops circularly at one of my temples. She just rolls her eyes and continues on her way. "Fuck the entire pod?" I add.

I pull up alongside him, laughing. "You're nuts, you know. You scared the poor mom back there." I can't help but look him over; he's exceedingly handsome with his big pouty lips and long dark eyelashes that accentuate his doe eyes.

"No, I didn't. She's probably just a bored housewife. And what's wrong with having different partners without making it official? Who needs a wedding and a binding piece of paper? It's all a bunch of horseshit anyway."

We shift gears as we enter a narrow and semi-secluded street that backs into our local park. The street's entrance, riddled with bumps and dips, is the result of an enormous oak tree whose roots have relentlessly pushed its way through the concrete year after year. Public space surrounds the beloved tree for several feet before opening into a posh development.

My heart plummets. "I need all those things," I respond. "For me, they provide stability. It's about commitment, building a lifetime together—family and all."

Brent seems to ignore me, parking his bike under the giant oak. Fiddling with his phone in one hand, Frank Sinatra suddenly blares out with "Fly Me to the Moon."

"A little mood music." He throws his phone in the bike's side pouch. He whips out a joint, lighting it up. "You'll be fine. You don't need your fantasy wedding. We live in the modern world. You can have your family without a man. All you need is a little artificial insemination. Although, I think you'd have much more fun trying to have a baby than actually having one." He leans over, handing me the rolled-up piece of paper.

"No, thanks. I value my brain cells."

"Suit yourself." He takes a long drag, sitting down against the tree. I park my bike next to his and locate a spot near him but far enough away from the smoke's trajectory, the wind carrying it over his shoulder.

He takes another long drag. "I'm having such a problem cumming lately," he says while exhaling slowly.

My eyes widen at the random comment. "Coming?" I repeat, trying to figure his far-fetched statement. "Oh, yeah. Cumming. Cumming. You know, beating the old stick?" Brent states matter-of-factly, grabbing his groin.

"Oh ... I see." *Awkward.* I can feel the heat rising up my neck, again, realizing that I just made a fool out of myself. "So?"

"So, that means," he begins to laugh, "I'm not in my 20s anymore."

"So, my girlfriend," Brent air quotes, "who's not really my girlfriend but thinks she is, has been after me since I came to California. She shows up every night at Roxie's, wanting a piece of me. She gets frustrated when I can't deliver. Personally, I'm bored with her nightly routine. I really need to be in the right frame of mind, and she just doesn't do it for me."

"All right now! TMI!" I blurt.

If things couldn't get any weirder, I hear the distant sound of a contemptible chime.

"Shit!" I mutter under my breath. Impulsively, I jump on my bike and push the peddles as hard as I can, heading back home and swerving madly to avoid the chuckholes.

"Hey, wait up," Brent jumps to his feet and stomps out his joint. "What's the hurry? Is it something I said?"

"Ahhhhh..." A yelp of shock escapes as my bike catches on a tough divot and swerves off of the road. Before I know it, I'm off my bike and down a small incline off the road, somersaulting like a ragdoll in a dryer. I don't realize that I've stopped rolling until I open my eyes and see vegetation and smell something putrid. I'm too dizzy to identify what's in front of me. I close my eyes again and concentrate on breathing. I can hear someone talking in the background, but can't distinguish the message. It takes a few minutes for the dizziness to subside.

"Ouch," I wince, my head throbbing. My noodle-like limbs remain firmly planted in the dirt. I feel like a freight train hit me.

"Chase!" I make out the voice to be Brent's. "Chase!" He yells louder.

"I'm here!" I can taste dirt in my mouth as I speak. I wave my arms in SOS fashion, hoping the bobbling head coming towards me is truly Brent.

"Chase, are you alright?" He bends down, patting my body. "You took one hell of a tumble."

"Nice observation, Sherlock!" my voice squeaks. He's furiously brushing the leaves off of me. "Stupid kid, shoving me off the road like he owns it." I wipe the dirt off my mouth with the back of my hand.

"No one shoved you off the road, Chase. You took off like a bullet and hit a chuckhole." Brent peers at me curiously.

"But the bell; it was ringing and ringing..." I press my hand to my eyes, flashing back to a childhood nightmare.

* * *

Even though the closing clangs of the school bell were my signal to run home, there were times I just wasn't fast enough. On those days, another bell would ring, this time from the bike of Jeff Roberts, a 6th grader with a mad crush on me. He would always try to ambush me, hoping to steal a kiss. Jeff donned shiny saddle shoes and knee-high socks and fitted with silver braces decorated with dull green rubber bands, his rising hormones overpowering his post-WWII attire. His puckering lips (which resembled a giant fish) always at the ready to plant me a slobbery smacker.

* * *

"Sounded like a school bell to me. There was no kid on a bike. There's a couple in the park arguing at the end of the street but no kid around. Maybe that's what you heard. How about I call 9-1-1?"

I shake out the vivid memory. "What? And be totally humiliated when the paramedics strap me onto a gurney? I'll be fine in a minute. Or two. Just help me up … slowly. Let me see if my body will move." I sit up, wincing as my head spins again. I grab Brent's arm to steady myself, looking towards the park.

In the distance, I see two people who are clearly in a heated argument. There's nothing unusual, except for the guy's jacket. It looks just like the one Grant wore to Aunt Kate's holiday get together. Leather jackets in California aren't exactly a fashionable trend these days.

Stealing long peeks while massaging my legs, I observe the guy's body movements and can't get over how much he reminds me of Grant. The girl looks familiar, too, but I can't quite place her. Just when I've seen enough, I see the guy throw something down to the ground. He looks angry. The way he carries on, again, reminds me of—*Oh, my God!*

"Now, don't freak out." Brent interrupts my spying.

"Never start a sentence with don't freak out!" I look over at Brent. He's swatting at my hair, trying to get something out of it but not wanting to touch it. I try to move, but he holds me still.

"I said, don't freak out." He seems content to swat at my hair for a second. I manage to spy the couple in the park and watch as the guy walks away, leaving the girl sitting on the ground with her head on her knees. "Okay, got it, but I think we might want to move."

"Might want to move?"

"You know, because of the dog shit in your hair."

"WHAT?" I screech, pushing against the ground, trying to get my balance.

"Just a minute, how many fingers am I holding up?" he says, raising his hand, waving it in front of my face.

"None, you idiot! You're wearing mittens." I narrow my eyes. "When in the world did you put on mittens? You're so weird. Fifty degrees isn't that cold." I glance back again, but the two figures are now gone.

Brent laughs, "Says the girl wearing the ski hat, a weird one at that. I can only assume what the deer are doing." He takes his mittens off, brushing the dirt off my face.

"They're reindeer, to be more specific," I say, feeling only a bit perkier. I turn to pan the park, hoping to get a glimpse of the disgruntled couple, but they're gone. *Hmm...*

"Okay, humor me. It's not what I think it is, right? They're having sex, I'm guessing." He plops himself beside me, patting my knee. "I'm all ears."

"Rutting," I feign a laugh while tugging on my cap. "The appropriate term is 'rutting,' which boils down to them having sex. So, yes, you're right."

He elbows me back, pulling down my navy ski hat to get a better look.

"If you look closely, you'll notice that the bottom one is screaming with joy." I burst into laughter.

"Ah! I can almost hear her! Amazing! Well, aside from the imaginary, kid, I do believe your brain's working fine." He jumps up. "Wrap your arms tight around my neck. Are you sure nothing feels broken or dislocated?"

"No, just achy," I say, feeling a bump forming on my head. Daphne's words suddenly replay in my head, sending shivers up and down my spine: *"Don't forget to wear your helmet."* *That little girl is seriously odd.*

I dutifully obey, wrapping my arms around him, taking in his musky cologne in the process. Ever so gently, he scoops me up and carries me to a tree nearest his bike. I hold onto a thick limb as he slowly stands me upright. I watch his muscles flex when he lifts my slightly skewed bike and places it next to his. *I have to admit that he's sexy as all get out.*

"Maybe your problem is that you don't like having the dead deer brought to your doorstep," I spit out abruptly. He looks at me blankly. "You know, because of your 'cumming' problem?" I air quote.

"Hmm ... I can see where you're going with that. You're not as naïve as Roxie plays you up to be." He eyes me, cocking his mouth into a grin.

"Oh, really? Is that what she told you? That I'm naïve? I may be a virgin, buster, but that doesn't mean I don't know a thing or two about the birds and the bees and milk for that matter." I fold my arms across my chest. "For instance, I do know that men like to be hunters. Thus, the reference to 'dead deer,' as opposed to the excitement that comes with catching."

Still holding onto his sexy grin, Brent helps me onto my bike.

"You're actually a virgin?"

Silence. I glare at him.

"Well, I really put my foot in my mouth this time, didn't I?"

My imagination runs away with me as I envision a new contortionist act.

"Sorry, I'm not patronizing you." I can tell his apology is genuine. "I really like you—and I'm not just saying that. I *really* like you."

"Thanks! You're not as bad as I originally thought." I amaze myself just how swiftly I get back on my bike to backtrack home. After testing out the brakes, I pedal slowly, making sure to avoid pits along the way.

"Listen, Roxie won't be home for the rest of the night. Would you be—"

"NO," I interrupt. "Roxie has glorious ideas for me, and believe me when I say that I want to go there someday, but…"

"You're afraid," he finishes.

"No. Well, I guess, yes. No." I peddle faster to get home.

"Well, if that isn't indecisive?" he lets out another one of his sexy chuckles.

"I'm still processing everything that's happened," is my final answer, as I weave along the sidewalk making little S's.

"You mean Grant Stevens. Let me tell you something, Chase. He's a loser."

"Just because he dumped me for another guy? How can you say something about a person you've never met," I argue. "Being gay doesn't make him a loser. How do you even know him?"

"I've never personally met him. Grant's name has made its way through the grapevine, that's for sure. That's all I'm going to say. Let's leave it that you need to get over him and move on."

"What's with this 'get over him' deal? Grant said that. Roxie said that, and now you." Just talking about him, especially after witnessing the park scene, gets me so angry I want to spit!

"Consider it a sign. It's all good, kid."

"Don't call me 'kid'! I'm a grown woman, for heaven's sake," my voice raises a bit.

"My apologies, ki—" he catches himself. "It's endearing to call you that." Brent wears a sheepish grin. *Hmm … I definitely admire that in a man, humility, that is!*

We ride in silence for a while before I hear Sinatra's voice again.

"I hope you don't mind that I turned the music on again. 'Ol' Blue Eyes' always has a calming effect on me."

"Sure!" I have to admit that Frank's voice does something for my psyche. I feel my shoulders begin to relax.

We turn onto my street.

"So, I know you're not ready to do anything. Would you be interested in some pointers?"

"Like what?" my curiosity suddenly aroused.

"Like positions. Let me show you."

My eyes go wide, like a dummy doll.

"When you're on top, like this..." And with absolutely no reservations, he leans back on his bike. "Have the man maneuver your hips like this..." he demonstrates, his hands jerking the handlebars. "And you have to lean back just enough so that his junk hits your belly button just right."

Suddenly, my imagination kicks in, and I picture Brent sitting on a bronco—clothed only in a cowboy hat and a pair of slick boots—and lassoing a scantily-clad blonde.

The image disappears when I catch Mrs. Gormley, an older neighbor, popping her head up, like a groundhog, from her gardening to view his suggestive gyrations. There's a broad smile on her face. Okey dokey, *now!* I wonder when the last time she got hers was? I giggle quietly to myself.

Brent peddles alongside me as I decrease speed, turning into my driveway. "By the look on your face, I think you might like me as your sex coach. What do you think?"

"Ah," I release a light grunt, "let's not and work on being friends instead."

"Deal. Baby steps. It was a pleasure meeting you, Chase Morgan. Until next time." He tips his fedora, giving me a mini-salute. "And go ice yourself. I'm sure you'll have some bruises by morning."

"Shall do, doc!" I wave as he rides across the street to Roxie's place. "Okay, now. Done with date number one," I mumble under my breath.

* * *

I peddle up the long narrow driveway and deposit my bike in the garage. "Mom, I'm home," I yell, pulling open the backdoor.

"Hi, honey," my mom says, her back towards me, "you're in luck. Nana just left; she couldn't wait any longer." Hovering over the stove, stirring up some kind of sauce, she turns to look at me. She drops her spoon and runs towards me. "Oh, my heavens! What happened to you? Are you okay? What's that bruise on your face?" She grabs a couple of paper towels and runs them under cold water. She wrings them out before dabbing the affected area.

"Ouch!" I wince. "I just had a minor bike accident. No big deal, Mom." I finagle water from the refrigerator and down it in a few gulps.

"There you are," my father says, walking into the kitchen. "I ran into Dr. Wellington on my way out of school today. He tells me that you need to decide what you want to do about advancing your career. Winter quarter starts on Monday. Your mother tells me that you've been lounging around watching old reruns. Is this true?"

When my dad has an agenda, he gets so fixated that he can't see anything else. I'm used to it.

"Honey, look at your daughter. She's hurt."

I can tell by the look on my dad's face that my mother's words are unintelligible because he's not listening.

"I … um," he blurts.

My father looks like an old historic building, one with a stately outer façade with an interior that continues to weaken with age. It's also hard to take him seriously because he replaces his blazer and tie with a western shirt, a silly cowboy hat, and pointy boots when he gets home from work, and then pulls his jeans up so high around his waist he looks like a clueless nerd.

"I'm pretty sure it's your career," he continues. "Get over your pride and what you think is morally correct and go talk to Professor Feldman. She's a reasonable woman. You used to say that you wanted your engineering career no matter what, and you would never quit until you achieved your goal. You've been talking about being an engineer since you were five years old."

"Dad, I never quit, you know that. After everything … I just couldn't … continue… You know how difficult it has been," I stutter.

"He would have wanted you to keep going. You know that Chase," Mom interjects, placing her hand on my shoulder. I can see her eyes welling up. I turn away, willing myself to keep my tears at bay.

Buzzing from my phone interrupts the solemn mood and rescues me from entering into a full-fledged sob. I reach into my pocket, pulling it out to read the text:

Brent: Loved riding. Let's keep riding again and again and again until you scream for more!~Brent

Not the time to laugh, but I have no choice except to cover my mouth to hold back a fit of giggles. It takes all that I have to revert to a straight face.

"I want you to go back to school right now and apologize to Professor Feldman and beg her to take you back." Again, entirely oblivious to my comedic intermission, my father stares at me with one of his stern looks.

"Mm-hmm," I casually respond. I can't help but stare at his new boots. They have a giant carved eagle on the toe and some symbol I can't quite make out. My father is undoubtedly an oddball.

"Chastity, I mean it." His voice startles me.

"Got it. Tomorrow, I will." I grab some ice packs out of the freezer and walk past him, heading towards my bedroom.

Collapsing on my bed, I press the packs against my achy hip and knee before sending a quick text:

> Me: Roxie, interesting ride, learned about dolphins and other things. Thanks. It was way better than listening to Nana's lectures. By the way, I think I saw Grant at the park with a woman. It was really surreal. We need to talk.

I hit send. Tossing my phone in exchange for my computer, I take out Roxie's wadded up to-do list from my pocket and set to work, creating an Excel spreadsheet, making several changes in the process.

"I'm going to ax 2 and 3 because that's already happening. 'Travel the world' ... well, I'm going to focus on a guy first, so scratch that, too, for now. Sorry, Rox!" I mumble.

To-Do List (Week by Week)								
Completed by: Chastity Morgan								
Get Married: God only knows								
D = Date A = Amoremoji SR = Success Rating								
Meet a bunch of hot guys			Have lots of sex			Fall in love		
D	A	SR	D	A	SR	D	A	SR

I grab the finished product from my printer, the sheet of stickers and a pen, and head to the closet. Feeling like I'm performing a sacred ceremony, I part my clothing and prepare a clear path to the back wall, anointing the elements with slabs of Scotch tape. I close the ritual by entering the date, a number "7" for success rating because I like Brent, and place a smiley face from the sticker sheet under the "Meet a bunch of hot guys" category. With one swipe, my closet reverts to its usual form. *Voila! Done.*

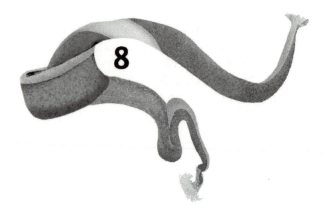

8

"Hello, CHAHS-dah-dee," Professor Feldman looks up from her computer, her heavy Russian accent lingering in the air like an overpowering perfume.

She may have aged quite a bit since the last time I saw her, but her image hasn't. Her dark hair now tinged with grey is still pulled back into a tight chignon, her glasses perched on her nose like a crotchety school teacher with a form-fitting, black turtleneck and matching blazer.

"Vot can I doo for you?" she says, radiating her authoritative, no-nonsense attitude.

"Hi." I walk towards her glass desk and take a seat on one of two miniature metal chairs with white-mesh seats set in front of her desk. Fiddling with my hands, I feel uneasy. Her office is the exact opposite of Dr. Wellington's messy booked-filled one. It's sparse but pristine. Everything about it exudes, "Look at me!" Condescension hangs heavily in the room as I pan it. A sleek, gilded lamp rests by her laptop on a large, glass-topped, modern desk with a near wall-to-wall snow white-colored sisal rug covering the concrete floor. Across from her desk and completely dominating the breath of the wall is an ornate glass display case replete with a plethora of awards. I'm sure she strategically planted it there, so that's the first thing she sees when she sits down every day. Structural blueprints encased within glass frames decorate the remaining walls. An oversized ficus tree, dressed in twinkle lights, hogs the corner next to the bay window. The window is at the left of her desk. I give a double-take, not sure how the tree fits in with the rest of her ostentatious display until I notice that the lights give off an uncanny resemblance to sparkling diamonds. I shake my head lightly in the hope of activating my gray matter so that I can give the professor an intelligent response.

"I want to finish my degree," I say, at last, as I breathe in slowly before I continue. "I made mistakes in my life, but I promise that I won't do it again." *God! What just happened? I sound like a six-year-old fessing up to my mom about stealing the proverbial cookies from the cookie jar.* My mouth is dry and feels like I'm about to have a coughing fit. I look down, and for the first time, I spy a water dispenser tucked neatly under her desk, hidden from plain sight.

"Do you mind if I get a cup of water? I'm feeling a little parched," I say with more boldness than I thought I had in me.

"Certainly, CHAHS-dah-dee. Can my secretary get you some coffee?"

"No, no," I say as I scurry over to fill a Dixie cup appropriately sized for, uh, a kid's tea-party set. I madly gulp and refill the minuscule container a few times while mentally gearing myself up for the rest of my confession. Coddling the last refill in both hands, I head back to my doll chair.

"Professor Wellington told me I failed my oral exam because you didn't like my work. I'm happy to redo it if that's the case." I spit it out as fast as I can before I lose my nerve.

She sets her glasses down on the glass top. Steepling her fingers, she places the tips against her nose and casts me a searing look.

"As a human being, I like you. You're an EENturesting VOOman who vohs dealt a bahd hahnd, and I'm really sorry for DAHT," rolling her Rs a little longer for emphasis. "To me, in-jah-NEER-ing iss about dee PEEyourest of dee PEEyour. EEt's for dose students who vant dahr degree more dehn anyting and are VILLing to take CREE-tah-see-zim vit-out valking out. I just don't beeLEEVE you are cut out for eet; I'm sorry to say. I, myself, STRAHggled. Bahk in my country, in-jah-NEER-ing for a VOOman was unHURED of. I came to ah-MAH- ree-CAH, and I POOSHT, I STRAHggled, and I fought for vaht I vanted. You don't haf daht kind of fight."

Her loftiness makes me so angry I want to bop her in the nose, but I don't dare reflect any weakness. Lost in my momentary reprieve, I tip the tiny cup to get the last gulp of water. I sit up straighter in my seat and muster up the strength to follow through with Plan A. I knew she would react this way, so I prepared myself for the worst.

"Actually, I do, Professor Feldman. I agree with you about getting dealt a bad hand. I've gone through some really hard times, including my fiancé … dumping me. I—"

Feeling my eyes well up with tears, I close my eyes and take in a couple of deep breaths. I hear the release of not one, but two tissues. I assume Professor Feldman picked them for me, so I ready myself. I begin to raise a hand in her direction when I hear someone stifling a sob.

I look up only to see a side of a woman I never dreamed possible. Professor Feldman sits there in tears, crying uncontrollably. I grab a handful of tissues and pass them her way. She utters a "tanks" as she quickly snatches them from me and covers her face with the whole wad.

The scenario catches me off guard; I'm not sure how to react, except to sit there patiently until she calms down.

The once-steely woman blows her nose a couple of times and takes another tissue to dry her eyes. "I'm … I'm … SO sorry you haf to see me like deece. I haven't cried like deece since … I don't remember dee last time. Vell, eet's BEEn too long." Professor Feldman gathers her hands again, this time cradling one within the other.

"I vunce had a love. He broke my hahrt so much so daht I promist myself I vood never get married. Two years later, I met Yosef. Vee fell in love and got married. I gave heem tree BEAUtiful children—two boys and a girl. He died five years ago.

82

Even though vee had a VONderful life together, I vill never forGEET my first love. I am SO sorry for your loss, CHAS- dah- dee."

I restrain myself from hugging her and, instead, give her a nod of acceptance.

"Um ... I'm not quite sure what to say—"

"Dehr's NUTting to say. Accept deece as a heart-to-heart female moment," Professor Feldman quips.

"Well, there's one thing that I'm learning from all this, and that is even though relationships can collapse and life can let you down sometimes, underneath it all, engineering is still in my DNA, Professor Feldman. It's what defines me. You may not believe me when I say this, but I have that fight in—"

"I understand more than you tink," she cuts me off as she begins ticking away on the keys of her laptop. "I'm going to do deece as a favor to your FAHtur since vee love HAFing heem as vun of our adjunct professors. Promise me daht I von't regret deece, CHAS-dah-dee Morgan?" a line of Rs following.

"I promise!" I blurt out, not even grasping what the hell it is I'm committing myself to. I hear the familiar humming sound of the printer. It takes a moment for me to realize that the sound is coming from under her desk. I hear rolling castors as she pulls out a sliding shelf to retrieve some paper.

"Iff I don't like your changes," she continues, "I *VILL* fail you. AGAIN. Understood?" She signs her name in perfect cursive and slips it into a manila envelope before handing it to me. "Take deece to your advisor and get his signature too."

I stand up, shaking her hand. "You're saying 'yes'?"

The old prof nods. "There's another ting you must promise me."

"Sure! Anything!" I blurt out again. What the heck's wrong with me? I don't even know what I'm getting myself into!

"Vut you VEETnesst today never leaves deece room. Do vee haf an agreement?"

"Yes. Absolutely. My lips are sealed. You won't regret any of this, Professor Feldman. I promise!"

I feel like I'm in a bizarre dream backing out of her office and into the deserted hallway. I lightly crinkle the envelope to make sure that the reacceptance papers are really in my hands and not a figment of my imagination. With a bounce in my step, I head a couple of doors down to my advisor's office to give him the good news.

I'm too excited to knock. I fling open the door and barge right in.

"Professor Wang, you won't believe this! Professor Feldman signed my paperwork to readmit me!"

I'm hovering over his cluttered desk, smiling like a schoolgirl who just got an A on her test. I can barely see his tiny weathered Asian frame behind all the giant stacks of papers. I can hear the older man giggling before I see him. His office, filled to the brim with documents, filing cabinets, and books topped with cans of cookies, makes it look more like a storage unit than an office.

"She can be rather scary, I admit, but don't let her bite throw you off. She's rather a softie under all that toughness," he chimes, pushing a pile of papers off to the side so he can see me.

I plop myself down in the little grey chair with its torn old upholstery. "Now, all I need is to get your permission to sign my paperwork and I'll be back in business."

"You don't need to ask," immediately putting his John Hancock on the dotted line. "You bring life to our boring department." He lets out a set of giggles as he reaches for a bowl of chocolate chip cookies before passing the paper back to me. "Don't tell them I said that. Truthfully, I never thought you'd come back after all this time. You worked harder than any student I advised. I never pegged you for someone who would throw everything away and walk out. You earned your bachelor's and master's degrees faster than any student I've mentored. Your father explained why you just dropped out suddenly. I'm so sorry for—"

"Please," I cut him off. "Not today. I can't relive it. Today is turning out to be a good day. Charlie would be so happy if he saw me now—" I take a couple of deep breaths to hold back my tears as the little old man eyes me curiously, munching away. "It's all good!" I continue, putting up my hand like a white flag in surrender.

"I know Professor Feldman will be watching me like a hawk."

"She's not the easiest lady to get along with," he winks. "We'll figure out a way to tweak your first two chapters to appease her without you having to redo everything."

I can't help but smile. My advisor's a rule breaker.

"Let's start you off right. I have a teaching assistant position that just became available. You only have two quarters left to finish before graduating, so let's get some teaching experience under that belt of yours. Keep in mind that you can take as long as you want to finish. No rush."

"Nope. I want to power through and complete my work in two quarters."

A young Asian woman lightly knocks on the door before walking in. She looks to be in her early twenties with long black hair, a tight pencil skirt, and a buttoned-up collared shirt that screams "uptight and proper."

"Ah, what perfect timing! Chase, I would like you to meet Alison Liu. I want the two of you to work together to TA my undergraduate class on Reinforced Concrete Design this quarter. She's on loan to me from Professor Feldman because I need some extra help."

My eyes go wide. "Huian Liu? From high school?" I spit out.

Alison glares at me with a catlike look that lets me know she'll claw my eyes out if I get in her way. "You must have me mixed up with someone else." I eye her again as she continues. "Of course, Professor Wang," donning her best Cheshire-Cat smile, "I'm sure the two of us will be best friends in no time at all."

"Yes," I give her a wan smile before turning to Professor Wang.

"Thank you again, Professor. I appreciate this so much," I extend my hand to shake his. He cups his hands around mine and gives me a hardy handshake.

I walk out the door, Alison follows close behind, her heels clicking loudly across the linoleum floor. Alison catches up and cuts me off in the middle of the hallway.

"Chastity Ann Morgan, we meet again."

"I knew it, Huian! You're the quiet foreign exchange student that stayed with Lizzie and barely spoke any English!" I inspect her again. "Lizzie sure did get a hold of you with the new look. And you're English is flawless."

"Obviously!" she snaps. "I stayed in the States." She glares at me again; her nose pointed as high as the Prissy Posse. Gone is her matted, never-washed hair and red, blotchy skin. In its place are shiny, silky hair and flawless makeup. "Let's get something straight. My name's Alison. I'm not the shy Huian you once knew, and I guarantee that I will win as top TA instead of you this quarter because you know why?" She pauses ever so briefly, so I don't have a chance to respond. "You don't belong here. You're only here because of your father, so you're in for the educational ride of your life. Enjoy it while it lasts."

"Right," I snap back, glaring back at her before she clickety-clacks down the remainder of the long hallway.

What the hell am I getting myself into now? The Prissy Posse seems to have a new and evil protégé, who, by the looks of it, has it out for me.

* * *

I pull into my driveway feeling a bunch of mixed emotions—happy to be back in school and on track, but at the same time terrified to be working with ... "ASSon!" I shout, excited over my revelation. "What a perfect name for the tight, ass-swaying bitch!

My moment of victory is short-lived when I see Roxie sitting on my front porch with a frown plastered on her face. She gives me a little wave as I stop my car in front of the gate.

"Hey, Rox, what's up?" I slam the car door and walk up to our little brick walkway towards her. I make eye contact with her immediately. Roxie's wearing fluorescent pink workout pants and matching running top, cradling her cell phone as if her life depended on it. "You okay? You don't normally go sitting on my front porch unless there's a rea— Oh, God! You

DO have a reason, don't you? You're giving me the willies, Rox. Now what?"

Roxie scrambles to her feet, sticking her phone behind her back. "I don't know, Chase. You don't look like you're in a good mood. I don't think you should see it." Just as I reach for it, she jumps out of the way, heading down the steps towards the front lawn. I promptly drop my belongings and fly forward, tackling her like we did when we were kids.

"GIVE it to me!" I lean over her, about to drop spit on her face. "Give me the phone Roxie!" I grab her hand, but her hold is secure. Instead, I pull her arm back.

"OOOOW! Let go!" Roxie screams.

"Say 'Uncle'!"

"UNCLE!!!" She promptly releases the phone into my hand.

"Now, that wasn't so hard, was it?"

"You're a royal bitch sometimes; you know that, Chase?"

"Bitch? Oh, you haven't *seen* 'bitch' until you meet ASSon."

"Ass who? What the hell—"

"Never mind. I'll tell you later. It's a long story involving Lizzie's foreign exchange student. So—"

"LIZZIE!" Roxie's eyes widen. "Exchange student? What?"

"Jesus. What's up with you, Rox? You look like you've seen a ghost. Okay, so what's on your phone that you're so upset about?" I take a seat on the porch steps, holding the little device in my hand.

"It's a video," Roxie confesses, sitting next to me.

"A video about what? Where?"

"Facebook. It's all over Facebook ... and Instagram."

"WHAT?" I yell. I navigate her Android to the Facebook icon and open it. "What's your password?"

"Here, give it to me." Roxie thumbs in her code and presses the play button to what I don't want to see, but I'm too nosey not to.

"OH. MY. GOD..."

My jaw drops as Aunt Kate's less-than-memorable Christmas party flashes in my mind. On the screen, I see myself covered in vomit. Grant is professing his love for Brody. The Prissy Posse, vomit-free, turn the video on themselves. "You weren't enough of a woman to keep Grant. You're such a loser, cat lady!" Lizzie, the queen of the Prissy Posse, mocks into her phone. The video shows Julie talking to Grant. He whispers in her ear while she subtly grabs his wrist. He yanks it out of her grip, walking away. The video goes black. I press stop.

Roxie and I make eye contact. She's been around me long enough to recognize that I'm stunned.

"They did write that yearbook prophecy!! I knew it. I knew that their sugary-sweet charm was nothing but a fake three-dollar bill! Those bitches! No one believed me, but I always knew!"

"I believed you, Chase," Roxie throws her arm around my shoulders, pulling me in.

"Since when did Grant become friends with Julie? Wait a minute!" not giving Roxie a chance to answer my question. "Remember when I told you that I could have sworn that I saw Grant in the park the day I was out biking with Brent? I couldn't place the girl he was with at the time. Oh, SHIT!"

"It was Julie," we say at the same time.

"What the hell is Grant doing talking to Julie?" I say, my voice growing louder with each passing second.

"Not sure," Roxie quickly quips.

"Well, I know one thing, from here on out I'm going to call Julie, Medusa; Lizzie, Ursula; and Joan, Maleficent! I think the witchy monikers suit them better."

"Agreed! But I hate to tell you that there's more," Roxie quips.

"Oh, God! Now what?"

"You've got to see what your mom got in the mail."

"What? Are you the mail police all of a sudden?" I yell in her face in shock.

"No. I stopped by earlier to borrow some sugar and saw the invite on the dining room table," Roxie replies matter-of-factly.

"What invite?" I jump up, grabbing my belongings off the porch.

"Take a look for yourself."

I am livid. I begin muttering a string of expletives as I unlock the door to the house.

"Hello! I'm home," I shout. The smell of cookies hits my nose the moment I walk in the foyer. I take in a deep breath, enjoying the aroma.

"They're not home," Roxie answers.

I give her a strange look as if she morphed into a mind reader.

"I happened to see them pull out of the driveway."

"You just *happened*..." I give Roxie a hard stare.

"I'm telling the truth! For real!!"

"Okay, okay! I believe you." I turn left and head toward the dining room table. I pan the room, noticing that everything is spotless. *Hmm* ... To the left of the table is the hutch, which gets my attention; the light is on. *Mom must have gone to that auction I saw posted on the fridge.* I notice a set of six sparkly water goblets, the newest in her pressed-glass collection. The mirror across the hutch on the other wall is free of streaks. Mom even changed the table runner: cream-colored with a Celtic "Tree of Life" symbol delicately stitched at each corner. My eyes catch glittery gold-leafed stationary that is lying on the table. It's an invitation.

"We invite you to attend the joining of two hearts ...' blah, blah, blah ... *'Harry Zinger III,'"* I read aloud. "Harry Zinger III? Wait! Is it who I think—"

"Medusa's marrying a gazillionaire," Roxie interrupts.

"Holy shit! How come all the bitches get the happily-ever-after, Rox?"

"Yeah, I'd like to see her walk down the aisle with a beach ball under her dress! Can't you just see that?"

"No. Not interested," I say, shaking my head. "Although, I wouldn't put it past her to go on a diet after the baby's born. Do you remember her high school mantra?"

"You mean, 'If you want to keep your man, keep your figure'?"

"Yep, that's the one!"

"Well, you've got her beat, Chase. Just look at you? You're perfect!"

I walk over to the dining room mirror, giving myself a once-over. *So much for my shapely body. What's the point if I can't keep a man interested?* My mind starts reeling back to the

Facebook video, and Ursula telling her that she wasn't "woman enough" to keep Grant.

"Wait a minute? Do you suppose Medusa met up with Grant to tell him that she's getting married?"

"Why would she do that? What's it to him?" Roxie comments, walking down the foyer and into the kitchen toward a plate of cookies on the counter.

"Don't know, but something just feels fishy," I reply.

"Well, who the hell cares anyway? You're free, Chase," she yells. "You can do whatever you want with whomever you want, and whenever you want, you know what I mean?" I hear the sound of saran wrap and then munching.

"You make it sound so simple, Rox. Life and relationships aren't like that."

"Look! Remember the list and the stickers?" she mumbles through a mouthful of cookies as she returns, handing me one.

"Right. I know. It's just that Grant makes me sick—" I wave my cookie around in a dramatic fashion.

"Oh, Grant, schmant. Just forget about him. He's a loser. Hey, let's just forget about all this crap. I've got an idea: I'm taking you to a super cool adrenaline-junkie movie with an after-party where you get to meet the stars. I think you'll find one of the guys, let's say, quite enticing." She tugs on my arm and points up in the direction of my bedroom.

Roxie rambles as we walk up the stairs. I don't hear a thing she says; my mind caught on the latest intrigue. I can feel my anger rising as I shove the entire cookie into my mouth all at once. "Rox," I mumble, cutting her off from her babbling. "I'm going to make tonight the time of my life."

"*Really?*" Roxie gives me her condescending look.

"Oh, please! You don't think I know how to handle myself?"

"Chase, when's the last time you had sex?" Roxie turns right to open the wide-sliding window above a large desk that includes a small goose-neck lamp, a mug filled with pens and pencils, and a potted succulent. Across the desk is my bed, adorned with a few throw pillows and dressed with a blue-and-white striped quilt to match my sky-blue walls, which I've had since I was a kid. A nightstand sits in the corner nearest the door. Parallel to my bed on the opposite wall is a white armoire.

A couple of shelves in the corner, off to the right, have what remains of my American Girl collection. Dotted on either side of my collection are shelves that include an assortment of family pictures. Roxie and I played with them regularly when we were little. To the right of my desk is my closet door lovingly draped with a poster of Johnny Depp, my fantasy man. Roxie sprints across the room and plops herself on my bed to stretch out her legs.

I look back at her, dumbfounded.

"That's what I thought. You haven't done anything with Brent. You're still a vir—"

"STOP!" I scream. "I know, Rox, I wasn't born yesterday." I grab a pillow off the bed, throwing it at her.

She grabs it mid-flight. "Yeah, right, like in Sex Ed class when Mrs. Bamstrong had to explain to you that you won't pee on your tampon if you put it up the right hole."

"That was the sixth grade, Rox. I know where to put a tampon. I'm going to catch one of these hot adrenaline junkies, and—"

"Holy smokes!" Roxie runs a hand through her hair. "It just dawned on me. You don't want to have a one-night stand; you think you can convince one of these movie star junkies to get married." She throws the pillow on top of her face to hide.

"And why not?" I walk into my closet to change.

"Oh, dear God—" she says, her voice muffled.

"And think of it this way, an adrenaline junkie will be the polar opposite of Grant. He'll be macho, honest, footloose, and fancy-free. He'll be the type that doesn't conform to society; he'll be the perfect guy."

"Oh, boy ... whatever, Chase. What are you wearing?" she changes the subject.

"Almost done!" I shout back.

The room is quiet, except for Roxie lightly humming to pass the time.

"Ta-da!" I jump out of my closet wearing black leather pants, black sky-high boots, and a bright red V-neck top. "I'll finish off my outfit with red lipstick. What do you think?"

Roxie stops, sits up, and looks at me seriously. "Are you sure you want to wear that? We have time for you to go back into your closet and change. Your scarf doesn't match your crazy ensemble."

I shrug. "Hey, you were the one that told me to take off my 'chastity belt' and have some fun. Plus, look at your outfit. You look like you stepped straight out of an 80s-workout video."

"But you don't get it, Chase. It's supposed to be 'fun.' I'm dressed in fun wear. You're turning it into a trap. What are you? Did an insect bite you during the night? God, don't tell me that you'll change at midnight into—" Roxie quickly jumps off the bed and lifts my top.

"What the hell are you doing?" I grab her arm and push it away.

"Just checking to see if you have an hourglass on your stomach."

"What?"

"You know, black widow? Spider web?"

"Oh, good God! If I'm Queen Clueless of Sexville, then what does that make you, Rox?"

"Uh, what about me?"

I give her dagger looks.

"Ok. Princess of Looneyville?"

"DEAL!"

We stare at each other for a few seconds before we break down laughing, tears running down our cheeks.

"Oh, God! I can't remember the last time I've laughed so hard." I grab a few tissues from my nightstand and hand them to Roxie.

"Seriously!"

After a long pause, Roxie continues where she left off as we head back downstairs.

"Chase, promise me—no traps. Just loosen up and have fun."

"But how do I find a keeper? Maybe I'll use reverse psychology, like if I give away my milk from here on out, one of these guys will eventually run with me to the altar, right?"

"I guess. Look, if you're that gung-ho about having sex, then use Sliquid, so your first time doesn't hurt."

"Slug-what?"

"Sliquid. S-L-I—"

"Q-U-I-D," Brent finishes. I hear him humming "Some Enchanted Evening" in-between spelling.

"What the he—." I open the door to see Brent sitting on the top slab wearing his signature Fedora, his bike leaning against the front porch. "How much did you hear?" I feign annoyance.

"Did you know that the acoustics around your house are perfect for sending clear sound waves? I could hear you gals all the way to the middle of the street. Helps to have your windows open a crack too."

"Oh..." I can feel the heat rising up the side of my face. "Um ... that's ... that's embarrassing."

"I found it quite amusing, to be frank," Brent calmly replies.

"How did you know about acoustics anyway?" I add.

"Oh, I took a class in Fundamental Acoustics back in college. It was thoroughly fascinating."

"I'm genuinely impressed with your knowledge of acoustics. I'm not impressed that you heard our conversation. Exactly, how much did you hear?"

"Well, let's just say I'm getting to know a whole new side to a queen and a princess."

"Awwwwwww, no!" I spit out.

"COOL!!! What did you hear?" Roxie butts in, appearing with another cookie in hand.

"Rox! Quiet it with—"

"Really, it's okay, Chase. Remember, I'm your sex coach. Right?" Brent throws his arm around my shoulder.

I let out a long sigh. "Right."

"Now, about the Sliquid—" he gives me a long, exaggerated wink.

"What about the Sliquid?" I rudely interrupt.

"Well, once you—hey, I bet you never saw a pe—"

"Yes, I have." I playfully shove him. "I did have a boyfriend, you know."

Rox and Brent look at each other, then look at me.

"That didn't sound good," Roxie offers.

"You know what I mean, you silly!"

"Okay, okay," Brent interrupts. "If the guy's the right one, you really won't need the Sliquid." He pauses. "Then again, you might need it for second base. On another note, I was hoping we could go on a night bike ride, and maybe if you're interested..."

"I'll take a rain check on the ride, Brent. I still haven't gotten over our first one." I look through my purse for my car keys. "Roxie, can you lock the front door."

"Actually," Roxie interjects as she checks the front door, "what she's trying to say is that she's hoping for a hot date with an adrenaline junkie at the Cialto."

"OOOOOOOOOOOOOOH, I see! Well, a quick pointer: he's a delicate fella. So, after you apply the Sliquid, you gotta handle him with care, like this." Brent demonstrates a slow, rhythmic massage in front of his pants just as Daphne comes around my car.

"Whatcha doing, mister?" she innocently queries, skipping up our walkway.

"Ahhhhhhhhhh..."

I've never seen a man turn five shades of red in a matter of a few seconds. It looks sexy as all get out.

"Are you here to see Chase?" Brent, subtle-as-a-train wreck, changes the subject.

Daphne pulls out the cookie plate from behind her back and hands it to me.

"They were absolutely scrumptious!!!"

"Why, thank you! I'll make sure to tell my mom."

"I hope you don't get too angry tonight," Daphne shifts gears suddenly. "He's silly; he doesn't mean it at all."

"Get too angry? Silly? What ... Who ... are you talking about?"

"You'll see!" Daphne gives another one of her cheesy smiles before turning away. "He's harmless and kind of funny and cute too." She pauses for a moment to look at us all.

"You're kind of strange, mister, but I like your hat. Bye!" She skips back across the lawn to her house, her pigtails bouncing the entire way.

"Why is it that she always shows up at the weirdest times? And does anyone know what the hell she was talking about, me being angry tonight?"

"No clue." Brent starts walking down the steps toward his bike. "But in case things go belly up, text me. I'll be right over," he winks, giving me his sexy grin as he hops on his bike and rides down the driveway.

I turn to Roxie and give her a hard stare.

"What are you looking at me for? I don't know anything. Remember, I'm the Princess of Looneyville?"

"Oh, Roxie, what did you eat for lunch?" I roll my eyes, getting in my car. "Come on, you ninny, let's get out of here before I get cold feet." I roll down my windows, revving the car engine.

"I hope you speak French!" Daphne giggles from her front lawn just as we're backing out of the driveway.

I slam on the brakes, "Huh? What am I missing with you?"

I hear Brent in the distance spilling out in a whole diatribe of French: *"Je t'aime ma petite ami." "Oui ma cheri,"* Daphne responds, giggling uncontrollably. She does a couple of cartwheels down her front lawn until she's standing close to Brent.

"What the fuck was that about?" Roxie looks at the two of them.

"Beats me, and I really don't want to know." I press the gas, backing out onto the street.

"Good luck with your exploration," Brent says, giving me a giant wink. "I'll be around, just in case."

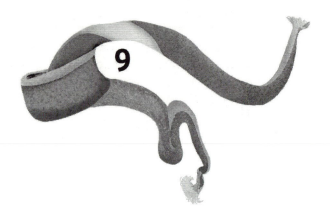

9

Roxie and I push through the doors of the old-fashioned movie theater known as the Cialto. Inside, wrought-iron chandeliers hang from vaulted ceilings laced with antique wood beams, the lights, perfectly dimmed to hide the gum-stuck floor and ripped mustard-colored corduroy upholstery on the ancient, creaky seats. There's a cold draft in the place since the doors don't meet plumb. Looking over the tight seating arrangement, we sink into the last two empty, rickety seats toward the back just as two guys walk onto the stage.

I nudge Roxie's shoulder hard.

"Ouch!" She rubs her arm; popcorn spills off her lap. "What was that for?"

My eyes widen in surprise. "Paul. Grant's college roommate, Paul."

He looks like he never left the Navy Seals with his buzzed haircut, full beard, and starched clothing. I remember the day when he signed up with them right after college, wanting to make a difference in the world. Staring at him, I no longer see a stocky guy, but a building—solid, mid- height, nondescript with an equally nondescript outer façade.

"Is that what you meant by I would know one of the stars?" I shake my head in disbelief, my thoughts drifting back to the first time Charlie brought Grant to meet me for what I thought was a set-up. He neglected to share that Paul, Grant's roommate, would show up unannounced, twenty minutes later. It sent me a message that I was just a person in their gang, instead of being a prospective date.

Roxie cocks her head to the side. "Told you tonight was going to be interesting," she winks, stuffing her mouth full of popcorn, looking like she just caught a canary.

I lean forward in my seat. "I wonder who the dreamboat is standing next to Paul? He reminds me of the Space Needle in Seattle—daring, tall, and definitely out of the mold. I'm beginning to understand how the whole shagging concept can numb a person's pain after a breakup."

"The Space Needle?" I can tell Roxie didn't hear anything I said after my Seattle reference. "Oh. My. God! Do you always have to sound like such a geek?"

"Hello, everyone, and welcome," our conversation interrupted with Paul's announcement, thank God! "Thank you for coming tonight to watch our movie, *Never Say Never*. I'm Paul Maxson, and I'll be the MC for the evening." He greets the crowd, pacing the stage. "And this guy beside me is my brother, Jaydon. In a few moments, you're going to watch us do things that may seem a bit crazy. Well, they are! So, don't try these the next time you hit the slopes."

That's Paul's little brother, Jaydon? What a hunk! I can't get my eyes off of this gorgeous-looking surfer guy.

"To start things off, Jaydon and I thought we'd give away a few prizes, courtesy of our skiing and snowboarding sponsors." Applause erupts from the audience.

"Catch the football, and you'll win this incredible ski jacket."

In one elegant swoop, Paul whips a blue parka around his back and slips his arms in the sleeves. Tucking his hands into the jacket's pockets, he struts around the stage, like a game show assistant. The audience roars with laughter.

"Catch the Frisbee, and you'll win these bright red ski goggles and matching hat. Sound good?" A chorus of hoots breaks out.

"Well then, let's get this show on the road, shall we?" Paul's voice suddenly blares through the microphone. "Jaydon, let it rip."

Jaydon scans the crowd. He raises his eyebrows when his eyes lock onto mine. He lets out a sly grin as he winds up and releases the ball. Seeing the flying object come straight at me, I reflexively slip out of my seat and drop to the floor, sending the football into the arms of a guy in the last row.

"Holy shit! What was that?" I blurt out from ground level to no one in particular.

"That would be a football," the guy answers loud enough for all to hear. The audience breaks out in uproarious laughter. I can feel the heat rising at the nape of my neck. "This obviously was intended for you, honey. Here, catch!"

He tosses it in my direction. Preparing for the worst, I shut my eyes and bury my head in my chest while lifting my hands aimlessly. To my surprise, I catch the errant ball. Wild cheers ring out from the crowd.

"Get up, Chase, for God's sake!" Roxie whispers. "They're cheering for you." Roxie proceeds to grab me from under my arms and attempts to pick me up.

"Jesus Christ, Roxie! I'm not a freaking four-year-old. I can get up by myself, thank you very much."

Except, I can't.

In my hurry to escape the prolate spheroid, I managed to wedge my hips snuggly between two rows of seats. Any amount of maneuvering does diddly squat. I begin to panic. At this point, Paul and Jaydon get restless and head over to see what's holding up their show.

"Hey, is everything okay over here?" Paul asks, looking down at me. I'm a hot mess. I've been humiliated to the nth degree. I'm trying to hold back my embarrassment, but it's no use; I can feel the blood rushing to my face and neck.

"Hey, honey, what's going on?" Jaydon adds.

"Don't ... patronize me! I'm stuck. I've ... had enough. I just ... want to go home," I say to Roxie.

"I'll handle this," Jaydon mentions to his brother. Paul runs back on stage, grabbing the attention away from my situation to the next prize giveaway.

"You know, you're not the first person to get stuck like this," Jaydon smiles sweetly. "The aisleways are a bit narrow."

"And that's supposed to make me feel all better?" I blurt out, accompanied by a coy grin.

For whatever reason, Jaydon finds my response hilarious and starts chuckling softly. His periodic hiccups—cute as all get out—attracts my attention; I can't help but laugh.

"Okay, I'm going to need your help … what's your name, cutie?" the question directed toward Roxie's boobs, which look gigantic in her push up sports top.

"Roxie, and this one here is Righty," she points to her right breast, "and the other one I like to call Lefty. You can call either of us anytime, lover boy." Roxie pulls out one of her party-decorating business cards from her purse and hands it to Jaydon.

"Thanks … Roxie, Righty, and Lefty!" Jaydon proffers smiling eyes as he tucks it in one of his back pockets. I let out a sigh, rolling my eyes, I've heard that line so many times over the years when men can't help but stare at Roxie's chest.

Jaydon grabs my hands. "I'll be ready to pull you up, Chase. Push at her lower back, Roxie, and gently rock her. Chase, place your boots on my feet."

We both do what he says. The rocking motion goes for about a minute before I hear a little pop as my hips dislodge from between the seats.

"Ah! That's the sound," Jaydon announces. "Now, on the count of three, let's get Chase standing on her feet. 1 … 2 … 3 …"

In Roxie's excitement, her gentle rocking suddenly morphs into a thrust, which catapults me up and beyond, throwing me against Jaydon and pinning him against the sidewall. My shock quickly dissipates when I get a whiff of his minty breath, followed by his intoxicating musky aftershave. He gently wraps his arms around me.

"Hi," Jaydon's smiling eyes meet mine.

"Hi ... Uh ... Thank you ... Uh ... This is awkward. I'm so sor—"

"Don't even give it a second thought. Maybe we can hang out sometime if that's okay with you?" he smoothly offers, tucking a loose strand of hair behind my ear.

He's tall but not too tall with broad shoulders and a golden tan, almost like he's fresh off a surfing trip to Hawaii. His blond hair is longer on top, falling in wispy layers, partially hiding his sky-blue eyes.

"Hey, let's get you cleaned up before you go on stage. You do know that you are the rightful owner of a snuggly brand-new blue parka?"

"Oh, God, no! I cannot go on that stage looking like this." I backstep towards the exit. Disregarding my rant, Roxie holds my arm and gets to work, straightening my top and fluffing my hair.

"Not to mention," I continue, "I can barely walk in these boots, let alone march down an aisle and climb onstage with everyone watching, especially with everything that hap—"

Jaydon grabs my hand and begins leading me down the aisle toward the stage. "You'll be fine. I'll be right by your side." The warmth of his hand numbs my irrational thoughts. All eyes in the crowd are on me as I do my best not to trip and fall.

"And congratulations to the winner of the Frisbee!" Cheers erupt after Paul's announcement. "Oh, just in time. Here's our winner of the football."

As I approach the stage, I notice in my peripheral vision the crowd standing to their feet. I'm overwhelmed by the ovation. Jaydon sees me stiffening up and immediately wraps an arm around my waist.

"Wow!" Paul yells. "What a nice show of support! Tell us your name?" feigning familiarity. "Chastity ... Chase Morgan."

"Well, Chase Morgan," Paul continues as he grabs a similar jacket designed for women from behind the curtain and hands it to Jaydon. "You are now the proud owner of this beautiful blue parka. Let's try it on for size."

Jaydon releases his grip, grabs the winning item, and begins dressing me, making sure to carefully tuck in my hair after placing the hood over my head. I'm surprised at how well it fits as if the jacket had a predetermined destination.

"Wow!" Paul utters, again. "A perfect fit! Congratulations, Chase!"

Another round of applause erupts, followed by another standing ovation as I shake Paul's and Jaydon's hands before reuniting with Roxie.

Taking off my prized coat, I slide back into my seat just as the lights go down.

* * *

"Paul!" I say, leaning against the lobby wall, behind a pillar, sipping on a beer and hiding from the crowd that's pouring through the exits. "Your movie was amazing!" I run over, jumping into his arms. "It was like a Warren Miller movie if Warren Miller drank thirty Red Bulls."

"Look what the cat dragged in after all of these years." He squeezes me into a tight hug, his lumberjack beard scratchy against my forehead.

"What's it been? Three, four years without even a word from you?" I can't help but pinch his side. "I don't even remember the last time I saw you."

"Ha ha! It hasn't been that long. I've been abroad and out of touch with everyone, not just you."

"I can't believe you haven't shaved this off yet; it's almost as long as my hair." I give his beard a little tug, and for a nanosecond, our eyes meet. "God, it seems like forever, and now you're a superstar actor instead of serving our country."

Back in college, Paul lit up a room in a matter of seconds with his jokes. A natural cut-up, Paul was always sweet, helpful, caring, and like most great friends, he brought the best out in Grant. At the time, I felt like I lived a charmed life surrounded by all these amazing men, and, of course, Roxie.

"Produced, directed, and did all the stunts ourselves," Paul says, exchanging his empty beer bottle for a couple of champagne glasses from the passing waiter. "Can you believe that someone offered us a contract for a series of our movies? I never dreamed that my playtime would become my work," Paul adds with a grin, handing me a glass; he clinks his against mine. "And what about you, smarty-pants engineer. Are you Doctor Morgan yet and taking the engineering world by storm?"

I sigh. "I dropped out two years ago, after ... everything. I just went back this morning to beg one of the professors to let me back into the program. She said something about my dissertation, not being real life. A bit ironic, wouldn't you say? I based my future on a false foundation, and then I was accused of *creating* a false one."

"You dropped out?" Paul's voice turns serious. "I listened to you talk nonstop about being an engineer for years, reshaping the skyline with your projects, running your grandpa's company, wearing a super short skirt you promised would bring in more customers."

"I never said anything about a super short skirt," I smirk.

"No, but at least it gave me a great visual," Paul laughs.

Confused thoughts begin muddling about in my head. Okay, that's a new one. He's never made flirtatious remarks to me. Ever.

A freckled boy, wearing an oversized *Never Say Never* T-shirt steps in front of him.

"Could you sign this? You're my hero. You're like Superman flying through the snow," the little boy bounces with excitement.

"And maybe while you're doing that, you could sign my top," a scantily clad woman with a dress made for a toy doll says seductively.

"Paul, Chastity's right, incredible movie," Roxie says, appearing by my side. She snatches the champagne out of my hands. "I wish I could do half the tricks you showcased." She downs the drink in one gulp.

Paul's smile goes wide as he releases a little chuckle, finishing with his signature. "Thanks for dragging her along. And thank goodness one of you does Facebook and stays in touch with all your long-lost friends. I've missed you girls, more than you know."

What a strange comment. I'm not sure how to interpret that one.

The three of us huddle closer together as we watch the lobby fill with people waiting to meet the stars. The drone of conversation builds with chatter about the movie.

"Hi!" interrupts an all-too-familiar voice. The wooden floorboard creaks as I pivot around and let out a noticeable gasp.

"Good God, not you." Grant's wearing a snug tan-colored T-shirt that accentuates his six-pack, tight jeans, and slick-looking black loafers.

I turn to Roxie. Guilt is written all over her face. "I need to head to the little girl's room," she spits out quickly. "I'll be right ba—"

"The hell you will, at least not alone." I grab Roxie by the shoulder and drag her over to the restrooms. "You knew, didn't you? What the hell is going on, Roxie? You need to fess up right here and right now."

"Chase, calm down. I'm sorry. He offered me this incredible band for my client's wedding next month, and I thought, what the heck, you can tell the dipshit off and put him in his place, and I can get the band. I saw it as a win-win situation!" Roxie rambles.

"What were you thinking, Rox? That's bullshit. BULLSHIT!" I scream, my voice reverberating off the ladies' room walls.

"There's more..."

"Oh, good GOD! Now what? Don't tell me you pulled Paul into this?"

"Paul knew," Roxie sheepishly admits. "He thought the movie and afterparty would ease all the tension between you two."

"Tension?! He ran off with a man!! A seriously hot, perfect, sweet man, but still!" I gasp. "Holy smokes! It's a conspiracy."

I head out of the ladies' room. Roxie doesn't follow. She knows I need space, so she goes about her business. I'm about to make a beeline for Paul when I see fans surrounding him.

"Fuck it all!" Pulling out my phone, I scroll through my contacts, find Paul's name, and begin madly texting, tears running down my face.

Me: How could you, Paul? This is so messed up!
You were a part of this whole goddamn set-up,
and why? So, you can get a good laugh: "Yeah,
there's that geeky girl who's got her head in
the clouds and doesn't know the first thing
about men." God, if you wanted to prove to me
that you're such a good friend, you could have
told me that your college roommate AND MY
FIANCÉ is gay! I thought friends were supposed
to be there to support one another, not knife
them in the back. Some friendship! Traitor!

Grant spots me at the ladies' room entrance and staggers in my direction.

"Dipshit," I mutter under my breath. Roxie got that one right. I have to hand that to her.

"Dipshit? I heard that." Grant grimaces in shock, looking at my makeup-streaked face. "I'm sorry, Chaysss," he drawls at a near-shouting level. "Don't be mad at them. It was all my idea. I called Roxie and Paul and bribed them. I needed to explain myself, and you weren't returning any of my texts and calls, and—"

"Grant," Brody interrupts, "this is not a good time, sweetie. You've had one too many." He snatches the drink from his hand.

I'm relieved that Mr. Perfect Face shows up, especially since I've expended my line of rants. Brody wraps one of his perfectly toned arms around Grant, steering him toward the exit when Grant yanks his arm away.

"Get your hands off me, Brody. I'm not finished." He pushes him away, but Brody doesn't budge. His substantial body is no match for his drunken husband.

I make an about-face, hoping to find shelter in the ladies' room and praying that he won't be bold enough to enter. I see a couple of women walk in, but then turn to leave when they hear Grant yelling in the room.

"Chayss, I'm sorry our engagement went up in flames so fast. You wanted a wedding and a family so bad, and then you were so sad, and I thought that if we started dating and got engaged and I gave you your perfect fairytale ideas, you could bury the past and move on and be happy again. He would have wanted that for you, you know?" he rambles. "I thought that's why he originally had us meet to fix us up. But then we didn't start dating until after he..." he pauses. "We were the five musketeers, you know: you, me, Roxie, Paul, and ... before we became the four musketeers, but then I started having these feelings toward men, and I didn't know what to do. I couldn't find it in my heart to tell you after Charlie's—"

"Don't you EVER mention his name!" I yell, shocked at how loud my voice is, forgetting that I'm slumped against the wall of the farthest stall. I can see Roxie's feet two doors over.

"Jesus, Chayss!" He bangs his fist against the stall. "How can you keep denying your pain? I'm not programmed to shut off like you. What's wrong with you? You never want to talk about him. About what happened that day. You need to grow—"

"I think you're upsetting her, honey." I hear Brody's voice again. "Come on, let's get you out of the ladies' room and head this way. It's time for us to head home."

"We were just finishing up. Chayss's a losssst cause..." he slurs a booming sound, a clear indication that he teetered right into the metal stall door.

I hear Grant's voice trailing away until it completely disappears.

I gather my purse and exit the stall.

"Come on, Rox, let's go home before he goes full Parseltongue."

Roxie quietly slithers out and washes her hands before leaving.

"I'm sorry, Ch—" Roxie begins.

"I'm exhausted. Can we talk about this later?" I interject.

"Sure," Roxie meekly chirps.

The moment we walk out of the ladies' room, my eyes pan for Paul. I can barely see him; the fan crowd nearly doubled in size. Over to one side, I see Jaydon standing alone, nursing a beer. Seizing my chance to escape, I quietly head for the exit, Roxie trailing close behind. Jaydon spots me.

"Hey!" he shouts. "Wait up, you two!"

"Oh, hey ... nice meeting you after all these years. Thanks for your help, you know, with the seats. We're on our way—" I rattle off.

"Can I get your phone number, at least?" Jaydon interrupts.

"Sure, she will," Roxie answers for me, pulling me closer to him.

"Uh ... I don't know, Jaydon. Your brother and I—"

"My brother means well; he wouldn't hurt a fly, even if it doesn't look that way right now. I got wind of this whole thing with Grant. I'm so sorry. That just wasn't right. I can't make up for my brother helping Grant, but I can tell you for certain that I am my own person, and I definitely beat to a different drum."

"Aren't you ... like on the young side? That would make me a cradle robber," suddenly blurting out my thoughts. "Oops! I didn't mean to say that." I can tell I'm blushing. *Shit!*

"Ha, ha," he produces a sexy grin along with his smiling eyes. I can feel myself melting inside, his musk aftershave wafting in front of me. "I often get that. I look younger than my age. I'm twenty-five. How does that sound to you?"

I gulp. "Actually, that works ... for her." Roxie answers for me.

Silence. After staring at each other for what seems like minutes, I began nervously panning the room.

"Hey, Roxie!" An adorable guy—tall with dark curly hair and brown eyes—breaks the awkwardness.

"Hey, Teddy, what's up?" Roxie smooths down her outfit and saunters over to where he's standing. It is apparent to me that she knows him from somewhere. *Only God knows where!* I watch as she hooks her arm around him, smiling widely. They give each other pecks on the cheeks.

"Hmm ... looks like she may be set up for the evening," Jaydon reading my uncomfortable thoughts.

"Ee ... yeah." I give Roxie this "what am I supposed to do now" look. She smiles sweetly and waves me in Jaydon's direction.

"Listen," Jaydon interrupts my jumbled thoughts, "I can take you home—not a problem. I've only had one beer, so I'm safe to drive."

"I … I don't know, Jaydon—"

"Look, you've had a rough night. I promise I'll be good to you. Plus," he bends over to pick up a plastic shopping bag, "this cherry pie from the dessert table was calling my name. The truth is, I can't eat this all by myself. Whattaya say?" Jaydon's gorgeous blue eyes give me the once-over as he wraps his arm around my waist.

"I can come over," he finishes, "and we can get to know each other, eat some pie, take it slowly. Watch another movie."

"Ee … yeah, okay," my heart starts beating faster than a percussion section.

Holy mackerel! Get your act together, Chase. You just met the guy!

"Well, what are we waiting for? Let's get this show on the road." Jaydon begins to usher me toward the exit.

I wave lightly to Roxie, who gives me a thumbs-up in return. I can feel an adventure brewing—an unprepared one, to say the very least.

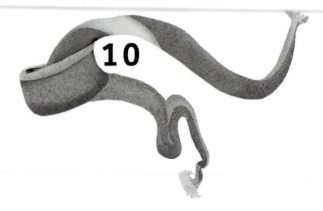

10

Red flags go off when we approach Jaydon's Dodge Ram. A thick layer of filth covers the truck's exterior. The passenger door makes an obnoxious knocking sound when Jaydon opens it for me. His chivalrous attempts turn sour when he tells me to hold off getting in so he can make the seat presentable. I watch as he scoops up a bunch of junk and dumps the contents in the back. The door, caught on who-knows-what, slams shut. Jaydon mouths "sorry" through the window. I quickly pan the interior before he gets behind the wheel. It looks like a bomb exploded in here; there are piles of dirty, wrinkled clothes, scratched Lotto tickets, and empty food wrappers from McDonald's scattered about, especially in the back seat.

"Sorry about that! It slipped my mind that I had come straight from work. It's a dump, isn't it? I practically live out of this baby." Jaydon's apology seems sincere.

"Well, since you put it that way, yes, it's a dump," I respond matter-of-factly.

Silence.

I don't know about him, but all I can think about is the condition of his truck.

"So ... tell me about yourself, Chase Morgan?" Jaydon's attempt at an icebreaker is working.

"Well, I'm in the process of finishing up my PhD, and—"

"A PhD? Wow! What a coincidence. In what? I'm halfway through a dual four-year master's/doctorate program in screenwriting," Jaydon enthusiastically volunteers as he pulls his car out of the parking lot, veering onto the street like an adrenaline junkie would—full speed ahead.

"Really?" Suddenly the truck isn't the center of my attention. I feel like I've just met someone who understands the higher-education process. I hold onto the door handle as he whips around the corner. "That's so cool! I've never met anyone working on a screenwriting degree. Is it challenging? I mean, I don't want to make it sound like you're studying a no-brainer career... I mean, writing is creative and all that ... I mean ... well, I don't know what I mean. I'm sorry. I don't know anything about writing. My father's an engineer, and, to be honest, he told me that if I ever wanted to be a writer, I needed to have a good day job." His eyes go wide. "That sounds pretty shitty. I think I just stuck my foot in it. Sorry!"

I sink down in the bucket seat a bit. *Chase! You idiot! Zip your mouth! "If you don't have anything nice to say, then don't say anything,"* I hear Nana's voice ringing through my head. Jaydon's brouhaha knocks me out of self-pity mode.

"God, I get that all the time!" His laughter tones down a little before he continues. "You know, it's not just my field of expertise; everyone in the Arts gets the same line, and I understand why. The scientific community has a history of providing job security while the Arts can be a catch-22. In my case, I'm already connected with "the best of the best" in Hollywood. Once I graduate, it's an easy slide into the field of entertainment."

"That's really awesome, Jaydon. I'm so happy for you!" I'm genuinely impressed, needless to say, with this hot six-foot-two dude.

"And you? What are you studying?" He slams on his horn as a driver cuts him off, forcing him to slow down to an acceptable speed.

"Structural Engineering." I smile widely at him, hoping he knows something about my beloved field of study. "You'll want to make a left at the next stop sign, and then my house is two blocks down, the white colonial."

"Structural Engineering," he mimics. "Hmm ... designing buildings, maybe?"

"Ding! Ding! Ding! You win!" I'm so excited at his response that I turn slightly and grab his shoulder.

"Really? What's the prize?" He gives me a s-l-o-w look-over.

Shit! I feel my heart pounding out of control again.

"Ah ... I'll have to ... think ... about that ... one," I stutter, the heat rising on my face. Knowing he's probably thinking sex, like all men do.

"How 'bout we start with some pie and see where it takes us?" Jaydon offers, showing off his sexy dimples that accompany his salacious grin.

"O ... K..." I feel myself falling right into the palm of his hand.

"What do you think you're doing, Chastity Morgan?"

I glance at my right shoulder and swear I see Jiminy Cricket. *Wait a minute! That's not him. It's a little female version ... of ME!* I keep turning my head, pretending that I'm looking out the window when I'm catching glimpses of ... whatever she is with long blonde hair, a pink dress, a pink top hat, a pale pink-and-blue scarf, and little glittery-pink wings. *Oh, dear God! Is this my alter ego, my conscience, or am I going loopy?*

"To answer your question, I'm your guardian angel. Now, listen; you barely know the guy, and now you're willing to shag your brains out to numb away that pain? You define that as 'love?' You want to give up your virginity for him?"

"Ahh," I say, dumbfounded.

Before I know what's happening, Jaydon slips a hand on my leg and gives it a tender squeeze before returning it to the steering wheel. I freeze, unable to turn my head to give him a response. Silence looms during the last couple of minutes before we get to my house. My thoughts run rampant as I listen to his deep breathing.

Am I in over my head, or what?

"This it?" he slows his car in front of my house, parking on the street.

There's a bright light bouncing between our driveway and the neighbor's bushes. "Chase…" I hear in a whisper. I look back at Jaydon, who is happily following me, pie in hand. "Chase, down here," the voice says again through clenched teeth.

"Daphne!" I can barely make out the little girl who's crawling on her stomach up the side of the bushes that separate our houses.

"Shhhhh…" She looks up at Jaydon, spotting him with the flashlight she has stuck to her forehead looking like a miner on a mission. She is decked out in black pants and a black sweater, clearly wanting to hide.

"Hey, who's th—"

"Wrong," Daphne interrupts Jaydon. She grabs my wrist and pulls me into the bushes.

"Wrong what?" I yell, trying to keep from falling.

"Wrong—" Daphne starts in again, but this time Jaydon cuts her off.

"Hey—" Jaydon pushes aside the branches, cutting her off.

"What are you two girls doing?"

"Nothing. Just telling Chase that her parents went out to dinner. Bye." Daphne's voice trails off as she runs across her front lawn to her porch.

"I didn't know you had a little sister." Jaydon looks at me for confirmation.

"No. Not a sister. I don't know how to explain her," trying to shake off the weird encounter as we head up the front walkway.

The house is dark, except for the front door light. A portion of me wishes my folks were home. Well, maybe not. I can imagine my mother greeting us at the door. *"Oh, Chase, you brought home a friend. How nice! Well, you've got the whole house to yourself; dad and I were just about to go to bed. I'm sure you two will be responsible while we're asleep. Good night!"* I suddenly feel like a guilty teenager, and I haven't done a damn thing!

"Let me turn on some lights so we can see where we're going," I ramble as I fumble to unlock the front door. I go off to the right of the foyer into the living room and then race across to the kitchen to release the sexual tension coursing through my body. "Make yourself at home," I nervously babble. "I'm just going upstairs to freshen up a bit."

"Take your time! Do you have any beer?"

"Yep! I'm sure my dad has some. Help yourself," I yell, running up the steps.

I hear Jaydon rummaging around in the fridge while I grab my makeup bag and make a beeline for the bathroom to fix my raccoon eyes. In a matter of minutes, I'm back downstairs and notice Jaydon fingering through my dad's CD collection.

"Wow! Elvis Presley, Fats Domino... You've got some great music here, Chase."

"Oh, it's not mine. My dad's a big collector of Rock n' Roll," I supply.

"Do you think he'd mind if I listen to some of them?"

"No, not at all. In fact," I subtly include, "my dad set up a multi-track player in the rec room downstairs so he can listen to his favorites while trying to beat the pants off me in ping-pong."

The words just finish coming out of my mouth when I realize what I just said. I swallow hard, hoping that Jaydon won't catch the maxim.

"Beat the pants off you?" He turns away from the CD stand to give me a wink.

Shit! Now I'm really in hot soup!

"It's just a saying, Jaydon, you know—"

"I know exactly what it means."

There's silence, except for the light slapping of CDs as Jaydon fingers through them.

Picking the sixth CD, Jaydon stands up and heads in my direction. "Then let the games begin!" he announces through his hand-cupped megaphone. I can't help but chuckle.

Near the bottom of the stairs, Jaydon spies a photo of Roxie, Grant, Paul, Charlie, and me skiing. He steps closer to the photo.

"When was that taken?"

"Winter break before we all graduated from college. About eight years ago." I brush it off, flipping on the stereo system.

"Who's the blonde with his arm wrapped around you?"

"Charlie."

"A boyfriend?" He scans the smallish but snug rec room, taking in the dartboard on one wall, a Haggard exercise bicycle at another, and the 1920's slot machine sitting on the counter across from the ping-pong table, which is the main room attraction. A quaint bar, complete with two stools, a sink, and a college-sized refrigerator is tucked neatly under the stairwell. "You have one hell of a rec room. Really sweet," Jaydon says, placing the CDs in the player. He pushes the play button; Fats Domino's "Ain't That a Shame" blares through the speakers. He takes another glance around the room before picking up a little wooden paddle—the one with red rubbery slick sides—off the ping-pong table.

"Not a boyfriend," I mumble a delayed response.

"Hmm... Mind if I grab another beer?" Jaydon appears to have ignored my comment; his voice muffled with his head in the fridge.

"Help yourself. I don't drink. How about a ginger ale for me?"

"One ginger ale, coming right up for the little lady!"

Jaydon throws the bottle up in the air and elegantly catches it behind his back. I proffer a smile, hoping to mask both my excitement and fear of the great unknown that accompanies this gorgeous hunk.

"So, are you any good—in ping-pong, that is?" he queries, popping off the lid of beer number two and quickly chugging it down.

"Am I good? Well, let's put it this way: I never lose," I tease.

"You're always the winner? Care to bet on that because there's more?" He puts his hands behind his back and begins to pout—another cute, sexy look. "I have a little confession to make."

"O ... kay," I jokingly drawl. "Then you had better spit it out, or forever hold your peace."

"I was the ping-pong champion in my college fraternity." He takes a big swig from his second beer.

Of course, he was; blonde surfer frat boy! My condescendence kicks in.

"So, what're we betting on exactly?" I crack a coy grin.

"Clothes," he says flirtatiously, stepping in closer.

"You want to play..." my eyes enlarge, "Strip Ping-Pong?"

He nods, breaking into another one of his sexy smiles.

"Oh..." I express my disbelief with a silly shriek of laughter. "Should I be worried about you?" "Maybe," he flirts back. "Pick out your weapon. The paddle with the training wheels might be just your speed."

"Fine. We'll play your little game of Strip Ping-Pong, but I get the red paddle. Hand it over. House rules." He hands me the red paddle with a full knight-in-shining-armor bow. "I'm partial to the blue paddle anyway. Matches my eyes."

"And no using your hocus-pocus hypnotizing gaze during the match," I add, laughing. I grab a ball and volley it in his direction, hard. He retrieves it effortlessly.

He releases a muffled snort of laughter. "Fine. Game on, Chase, let's do this. No mercy! Better chase that ball with those pretty eyes of yours."

"Bring it!" I reply, dancing like a pregame boxer.

We begin to rally like two Olympians. I can feel beads of sweat forming on my forehead. Elvis is singing "Don't Be Cruel" in the background. *How apropos!*

We rehash scenes from the movie; I include lots of positive criticism. Suddenly, I smack the ball harder than I should have. He catches the ball as it flies off the table.

"Hand over a piece of clothing." Jaydon goes to the fridge and gets two more bottles of beer and immediately pops one open. "Bottoms up!" he announces before chugging down.

"Don't you think you've had enough to drink?" I mention as I remove my new blue jacket, tossing it on the floor.

"Never!" He sets the empty container into the recycling bin. He grabs the wall as he totters slightly back in the direction of the table. He serves the ball back in play.

"So, tell me how you got into Structural Engineering?" Jaydon switches topics of conversation.

"Engineering's in my DNA. My father and grandfather are both engineers, and I always wanted to follow in their footsteps. I remember eating breakfast one morning when I was seven; I was making my way back upstairs when an earthquake struck. The floorboards were moving so violently I thought the house would crack open. I ran to my mother to shield me. All the while, my father stood watching the movement. I looked at him and wondered, what makes him not afraid and instead curious? After the tremors stopped, I asked my dad questions. He, in turn, took me to the library and helped me find books. I knew right then and there that that was what I wanted to do when I grew up: study earthquakes and how buildings respond on different surfaces."

Jaydon hits the ball back. "What do you mean, different surfaces?"

"Nineteen to sixteen. My serve, and clothing—you too. Off it goes!" I catch the ball and tap my foot, waiting as he pulls off his shoes and socks.

Jaydon takes a couple of swigs from his fourth bottle before we resume playing. I stand there, shaking my head.

"What I mean is wave propagation," responding to his question. "Earthquake waves travel at different speeds and intensities through different surfaces. A soft alluvial valley like Mexico City will move like Jell-O when an earthquake strikes. The waves resonate through the soil like a tuning fork." I slam the ball back, and Jaydon loses another piece of clothing.

"You're a hot, intense nerd. You know that?" He pulls off his T-shirt. Jaydon's down to his jeans, while I'm still wearing my pants and sweater.

"If I win the next point, you'll be down to just your undies. Hmm ... are you a boxers or briefs man?" I can't believe I just blurted out my thoughts as I bite my lower lip, trying to imagine what he's wearing. "Neither. I'm up to my last piece of clothing," Jaydon says, affecting a serious tone.

I squirm, bouncing from foot to foot.

"Ooooooooh..." I am entirely at a loss for words realizing that he's gone commando.

"You don't want to see my birthday suit?" Jaydon half-smiles, rubbing a hand across the top of his jeans. I'm so shocked I don't know what to think. I'm even more shocked when I find him suddenly standing in front of me. He reaches out and intertwines his fingers with mine. Leaning forward, he brushes a strand of hair from my forehead, and, in the gentlest manner, grazes my lips with a soft kiss. My heart's pounding again, and every nerve ending in my body is on edge.

"Uh..." I mutter unintelligibly, softly. I'm in a state of euphoria as I press my hand over his taut chest. He moves his kisses down one side of my neck.

"Uh..." I mutter again, "I thought you said we'd take things slowly."

"This *is* 'slowly.' Am I going too fa—"

"Yes, I mean no, I mean ... I'm not sure," I interrupt.

Jaydon moves to the other side of my neck, his hands sliding down my body, and in one fell swoop, turns me so, my back is against the ping-pong table.

"God, you turn me on. I want to fuck you right here," he whispers in my ear.

"FUCK ME? Right now? On this ping-pong table?" I chuckle nervously. "It ... it... won't hold us. Structurally it's not built for that kind of motion."

"Oh, really?" he smirks, pulling slightly away from me. "Sounds like you've tested your—what do they call it? Ah, hypothesis, I believe."

"No. It's ... it's just a mathematical certainty," I blurt in defense. "The plywood is not strong enough to resist the force of our bodies."

"I love it when you talk analytically to me," Jaydon whispers in my ear. Grazing his lips across my jawline, he lands on my mouth and kisses me hard before lifting me off the floor and gently setting me on the table.

"No! You'll—"

There's an odd scraping sound followed by a steep tilt downward.

"Whoa!" I yell.

Jaydon helplessly watches as I roll off the table. Grabbing the arm of my dad's La-Z-Boy recliner, I'm able to break my fall.

"Chase, are you alright?" Jaydon runs to my side and wraps his arms around me. "I'm so sorry; I should have listened—"

"Look—" I cut him off, aggravated that he didn't believe me. I let out a couple of cleansing breaths. "This is not exactly what I had in mind for this evening."

I allow myself to lean into his musky-smelling chest while he soothes my head with a light massage. I can feel myself slowly melting again.

"What ... did you have ... in mind?" Jaydon whispers, breaking the momentary stillness.

Like clockwork, my stomach lets out a loud rumbling sound.

"Ahhhhhh..." I chuckle lightly. "How about some of that cherry pie that you stole, if you don't mind."

"Are you planning on eating it or having me eat it off you," he says, kissing me on my head.

"Oh, ha, ha! Very ... uh ... funny! I never thought of that one. Let's start with sustenance," I sheepishly reply.

Jaydon stops kissing me and looks directly into my eyes. "Well, if the little lady says it's time to eat, who am I to argue?" He winks. We separate so he can gather his clothes before we head upstairs.

Once in the kitchen, Jaydon rummages in the freezer while I begin slicing the pie into eighths.

"Where do you keep your ice cream?"

"Bottom drawer, way in the back," I reply.

Jaydon pulls out a Breyer's container and opens it. "You've got to be kidding, right?" He points it in my direction where I can take a peek inside; there's barely a teaspoons-worth tucked to one side. "You know this is un-American? Pie and ice cream go together."

"I could have sworn there was a fresh container of French Vanilla," opening the freezer to see for myself, "right ... over ... well, I'll be doggone—"

Just as I shut the door and turn, Jaydon slams me gently against the fridge. I can feel his heart beating against my chest.

"Do you know why you don't remember seeing me much back when you and the ole' gang used to hang around the house?" He seductively whispers in my ear again.

"No." My feeble response is barely audible.

"Because every time I saw you, I got so flustered that I had to leave. You always made me so hot, Chase Morgan, and you still do. God, you have no idea what I'd like to do to you right now."

I'm melting fast. "What you'd like to do to me?" I mimic, my voice a bit louder.

Before I know what's happening, his mouth is on mine again, kissing me with such intensity.

"Ohhhh, fuck, Chase!" He shouts, his breath quickening. "You are *so* hot! Skip the ice cream."

"Oooooooh ... ahhhhh..." *God, it feels good!*

"Do you want me now? On the kitchen counter? Will it structurally hold us?" he chuckles into my ear.

It takes everything I have to keep focused. "Oh ... ah ... no," I manage.

He obediently pulls away. I'm still breathing hard, my heart racing.

"How 'bout we grab the pie and take a run over to the store to get some ice cream." He turns to me and begins rubbing my shoulders.

"Are you sure you should be driving? I mean, you had four bottles of beer."

"Six, if you count the two that I had at the Cialto," Jaydon adds.

"I'll only go," I say with a silky voice, "in one condition: I drive."

"Sounds like a plan to me!" Jaydon smiles widely before moving in to give me a long luxurious kiss.

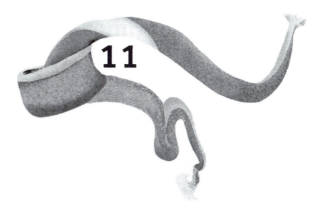

11

"Over there," Jaydon points to a secluded spot on the far left of Circle K's large parking lot near a line of trees.

"You must be joking! Why so far away from the store, let alone in the dark. I can barely make out your face," I say, my romantic feelings toward Jaydon rapidly diminishing, I try to put up a brave front, but my voice is noticeably shaky.

"You'll see." Jaydon squeezes my leg for the third time on the way to the store, winking before he exits.

He takes his time walking, staggering more like it. My thoughts run wild. I nervously wait until I think he's a reasonable distance from the truck before locking the doors. *What if he's some type of serial killer?* "OH, MY GOD!" I blurt out, frantically unbuckling so I can turn and check the crap in the back seat.

I grope around in the darkness. It takes a few minutes for my eyes to adjust to the light coming from one of the distant lamp posts before I identify items: a random mix of clothes, a couple of kitchen towels, nothing unusual. Something's poking out between one of the side doors and the bench seat. I pull on the loose end and discover it's a pair of lacy underpants. Looking closer, I notice that they're used panties.

"Eeeeeeewwww!" I fling the nasty underwear, watching them land on a backseat headrest. *Great! They can stay there. Yuck! I'm not touching them again!* I say aloud, establishing my new resolve.

I make an about-face and start opening compartments on the front dashboard, searching for anything that will confirm my worst fear. I reflexively cover my eyes when light glares from the glove compartment that pops open. A large, slightly crushed box flies out. The glow is bright enough that I can see details.

"What the hell?" I stare, mesmerized before grabbing a roll of condoms and pulling them open like an accordion. I dig in the box and realize that the packets come in different sizes and ... "SCENTS? I had no idea such things existed. *This* is just plain bizarre!" I speak aloud. Amusement over my new find quells my fears slightly. The list of choices engrosses me. "Peppermint Flavored condom? A breath freshener, maybe? Okay, I don't think I want to go there. What's this one? Glow in the Dark. Hah! Maybe Jaydon's afraid his one-eyed snake might get lost. Fruity Delight. Jesus, it's edible? Whoa! TMI."

Headlights aimed at Jaydon's car momentarily interrupt my probing. The car slows down as it passes and then drives off. I ignore it and return to my exploration.

"Apple Jacked? Really Romeo? Sir Richard's? What's this one? Mint Chocolate SHIT!" I scream. I jolt and drop the collection of packets on the floor. A flashlight suddenly glares into the driver's window, temporarily blinding me.

"Chase, what the hell are you doing here?"

I'd recognize that voice from across a football field. I turn the ignition key enough to let down the window.

"I could say the same, Roxie, and what are you doing spying on me, and why are you in ... What is that? Your Santa onesie from Christmas?" I can feel my annoyance suddenly rising.

"I'm not spying on you, you dimwit. Things went belly up with Teddy. I got your car back home, and then went to bed, except I couldn't sleep. So, I decided that I'd watch a movie instead, except I ran out of munchies. That's why I'm here."

She looks down at her pajamas as if a light suddenly goes off. "Ha, ha! Oh ... maybe I did run out a little fast."

"How did you know I was in the car?"

"When I pulled into the back entrance, I recognized Jaydon's car; I watched you guys leave the theater," Roxie admits unabashedly. "Anyway, it looked fishy, so I investigated— Hey..." she says, looking in the car. "Is that Double Ecstasy? Whoa, and Sir Richards? What the hell? Give me some of these."

"What?" I'm confused.

"Just give me some. Don't ask questions."

I dutifully grab a handful and pass them to her.

"2019 - 12. 2019 - 10. 2020 - 12. 2021 - 01," Roxie reads aloud to no one in particular. "This is not good, Chase. Not good at all!"

"What's not good? That Jaydon's a massive condom collector?"

"It's worse. He's a sex squirrel, which means that Jaydon's so addicted to sex he will get it in the worst way possible. What did he do to you?"

"Nothing, really. I—"

"What do you mean 'nothing, really'? He had to have done something to entice you this far."

"Well, he did do one little thing."

"Like what, exactly?"

"Well, the way he kissed me—"

"Really? You kissed a total stranger?" her mouth falls open. "Well, I'm proud that you were bold enough to let a guy you barely know, kiss you. That's a step up. Right?"

"I didn't let him."

"What?"

"It just happened so fast; I was shocked."

"Oh. So, Jaydon took advantage of you."

"I-I don't know. It felt good, that's all I know."

"Oh, dear ... I don't know what to do with you—" Roxie stops, her comment cut short when she hears feet shuffling across the asphalt.

"Someone's coming. Move over," Roxie whispers, pulling open the car door, banging it shut quickly.

I slide over to the passenger side while Roxie slips behind the wheel. A moment later, Jaydon peers through the window at me.

"Whatcha doing on this side?" Jaydon yells. "Aren't you driving," He teeters to the left; shopping bag sways in one hand while the other grabs hold of the car roof.

"Hey, isn't that the cute chick you were with at the Cialto? Ruby? Rhonda?"

"Roxanne," Roxie spits out. "Roxie for short."

"Yeah, Roxie, my brother's friend, with the big boobies, Righty and Lefty. So, you're all here to join the party?"

My eyes widen as I glance at Roxie, who is giving Jaydon dagger eyes. "Oh, boy, he's dead meat," I mutter under my breath.

"Actually, I came looking for Chase. Her dad needs her home."

"He does? What's wrong—"

Roxie cuts me off with another hard stare; her arms akimbo.

"Oh, poor little Chasie! Daddy says it's time to go home!" Jaydon mocks.

I might not understand what the hell is going on, but one thing I *do* know for sure is that I will not give in to derision. Just as I'm about to give him a piece of my mind, Roxie lays her arm across my lap, giving me another stern look.

"Sorry to burst your bubble, buster, but we need to leave, Jay—"

"But Chase promised to be my designated *D... R... I...* ver," Jaydon belches, cutting Roxie off. His alcohol breath is enough to make me want to gag. "We have a little business to take care of before she goes back home."

"It's time to get Mr. Maxson home, don't you think, Chase?" Roxie bursts out of the car and directs me to take her place behind the wheel. "Jaydon, the game's over; get in the car, I'll follow. Where are we dropping you off?"

"You're joking, right?" Jaydon's macho image promptly shrivels to the size of a mouse. "I didn't mean any harm. I just wanted some fun. Aw, come on, ladies, the night's young."

"Where to?" I blurt, surprised that the words come out of my mouth.

"You're serious?"

"Yes, Jaydon. I'm serious." I mimic.

"The Marblehead Hotel." Jaydon looks defeated as he flops into the car, depositing his grocery bag at his feet.

Roxie gives a thumbs up and jogs over to her car. We start up our engines, Roxie signals for me to go first. Jaydon is quiet during the ten-minute ride. It's comforting, listening to the road noise.

* * *

I pull in front of the valet; Roxie is right behind me. She decides to wait in the car. I stare up at the Avant guard building with a semi-circular design, admiring the bold look.

"You're not coming up, are you?" Jaydon says, sheepishly.

"No. I'm sorry, Jaydon."

"I'm sorry, too. I said some pretty stupid things. I didn't mean it. You're a really nice gal. Can you forgive me?" he says, placing praying hands against his chest.

He seems genuine enough.

"Sure. Let me walk you to the lobby," I give in. I grab the shopping bag with the cherry pie, sitting on the floor of the passenger's seat before I help him get out of the car. I hand him the bags, which he immediately grabs. Just as we reach the glass lobby doors, he sets the container on the handsomely-decorated flagstone walkway and wraps his arms around me, giving me a giant bear hug.

"I had a fun time."

"In a bizarre way, so did I. Thanks for rescuing me from Grant."

"Anytime." Jaydon still has a sexy smile, even when he's drunk. "Here," he hands me the bags. "Enjoy! I prefer apple, anyway."

"Thank you." There's no hesitation on my part to accept the gifts.

"See you around, Chase," he walks through the lobby doors as a man looking like he stepped off the cover of a GQ magazine, wearing tortoise-rimmed glasses and a brown suede jacket, holds open the door.

"Thank you," I smile. "I'm not going inside."

"*Bonne nuit, ma chérie*," he smiles back with his deep-set dimples. With my hands full, I can't catch my scarf fast enough; it drops to the ground. My mouth drops open as I stand frozen in place, staring at his dashing fellow who promptly rescues my beloved accessory.

"*Ton écharpe*," the man wraps my scarf snuggly around my neck, gently grazing my left earlobe and collarbone in the process. His sensual touch mixed with his cinnamon-and-cloves cologne sends a shiver of lust up my spine.

Suddenly, I find myself transported to the Eiffel Tower. It's nighttime, and the steel beams are aglow with thousands of twinkling lights. I'm standing underneath it, and this very man is wrapping my scarf around my neck, pulling me in for a passionate kiss. He drops down on one knee, pulling out a little red box.

"Chase," Roxie's yelling from the car.

I snap back, staring at this Frenchman. Somehow, I manage a "thank you" as he walks outside.

I shake my head, whisking the experience out of my thoughts, and head over to the car. Movement catches my right peripheral vision. I notice the Frenchman leaning his back against one of the hotel pillars, pulling out his phone. He spots me as I make my way to Roxie's car.

"*Au revoir, belle chérie.*" A little wave accompanies the lilt to his sexy voice. My French is limited to pet phrases. I have no idea what he's saying, but it all sounds so romantic. I'm oddly melting inside.

"Au revoir. Tu peux me prendre dans tout les sens." I smile in my best French.

"I can have you any way you want? Non. Tu es trés magnifique, ma cherie."

OH MY GOD! WHAT DID I JUST SAY???? I blush, walking towards Roxie's car.

"What was that all about?" Roxie spouts as soon as I get in the car. I plop the bags by my feet. I shrug, my eyes still lingering on the Frenchman.

"You do realize that you are not ready for 'no strings attached' sex? It's evident to me that you need to be married first," she continues without waiting for me to answer.

"Okay. Listen! I can think of some Amoremojis to stick onto your list, like a 'relieved face.' I'm not sure which one you could use for 'sex-crazed.' We'll find something to represent the boy toy and his variety packs," she laughs. I laugh along just to appease her.

"What's in the bag?" Roxie shifts over to the next thing. I've been around her for so long that I'm so used to her ADD mannerisms.

"Munchies! What are we watching?" My cheery response plants an immediate smile on Roxie's face.

"Oh, cool! A slumber party, like old times!! I was thinking of *Chocolat*. Can't go wrong with your teenage crush, Johnny Depp. But if you're up to it, I was thinking *Sabrina* with Harrison Ford and *Pretty Woman.*"

"Let's do it!" I raise my hands to give Roxie an enthusiastic high-five before she drives off.

I spot the Frenchman, again, as we slowly cruise past the hotel, "Remind me to kill Henry." *He's the one who's been teaching me naughty French phrases when he comes home from school.*

"Remind me to kill who?" Roxie gives me a strange look.

"Never mind," keeping my eyes fixed on my mysterious Frenchman. Silence looms as I gaze out the window. I imagine strolling hand and hand down the Champs-Élysées at Christmas-time with all the twinkling lights. We stop briefly to admire a window display, and he cups my cheeks in his hand, pressing his lips to mine.

"Hey," Roxie abruptly interrupts my fantasies. "Where are you? Earth to Chase, come in, Chase."

"In Paris," I answer catatonically.

"You're where?"

Popping out of my trance, I look directly into Roxie's eyes and respond with the first logical thought that comes to my head.

"It's time, Roxie. I'm spreading my wings. I'm going to Paris."

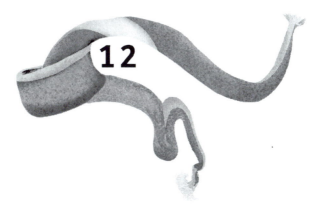

12

"*Essayons encore une fois.*" Madame Bohemond writes the equivalent on the chalkboard that takes up the length and width of the wall: let's try again.

She's about as American-French as they come—at least that's what her bio seems to indicate on the college website: "Sybil Bohemond emigrated from southern France to the U.S. with her parents when she was three. Her father used his professional chef skills to open several authentic French restaurants on both the east and west coasts..."

Her bubbly personality is infectious; her stereotypical plump "grandma" figure wiggles and jiggles when she laughs. To top things off, she has an enchanting, singsong voice. I'm mesmerized.

"Chase!" Roxie whispers while jabbing me in the ribs. Good thing we're in the back of the tiny classroom with a five-by-five seating formation. "Quit staring, and close your mouth. You look like some freakin' blonde."

"Well ... I am blo—"

"You know what I mean?" Roxie throws me her infamous dagger eyes.

"*Mademoiselle?*" Madame Bohemond gives me a warm smile. I swear her eyes twinkle when she does that.

"Uh … *Je m'appelle* Chase."

"*Je m'appelle* Roxie." Madame Bohemond points to her. She's wearing a beret and a little scarf tied around her neck to look more French than I expected. *Why am I surprised? Duh!*

"Je m'appelle Brent. Enchanté Madame Bohemond. Comment allez-vous? Vous êtes très belle."

Madame Bohemond blushes a deep red. "*Merci, Monsieur Brent.*" Without missing a beat, she moves onto the next student.

"See what I mean? I told you, I don't need to be here. I'm fluent in French and everything French- related," Brent whispers to Roxie and me. He gives me an exaggerated wink as the three of us sit back down in our seats. The slumber party set the right mood for me to pop the question about her auditing a week-long French immersion class with me. I was so excited when she agreed. That all changed when she showed up this morning with Brent. Madame Bohemond stands at the front of the small room, scrawling sentences in English and French on the chalkboard, which momentarily breaks my angry thoughts.

"As I told you, we are supporting Chase on her mission, right?" Roxie whispers to Brent through clenched teeth.

"Mission? You mean her ridiculous Paris fantasy all because a man spoke a little French to her and wrapped her scarf around her neck. I can do the same thing and save her the expense of going to Paris." Brent pauses. "Wait … I did do that."

"Shush, you two! I'm trying to catch her last comments before class is over," I say loud enough that the students in front of us turn their heads on cue. Ignoring their gawking glares, I'm determined to go about my business, scribbling out Madame Bohemond's examples in a stenographer's notepad. My mother keeps a stack full of them, which she uses faithfully—taking notes in shorthand every chance that she gets. The only problem is that she's the only one who knows how to decipher the Sanskrit markings.

"*À demain!*" Madame Bohemond announces suddenly. She points to a French-English chart.

"See you tomorrow," I read aloud.

"*À demain!*" Madame Bohemond repeats, this time looking straight at me.

"Ah! *À demain!*" I weakly smile as I gather my things and whisk out the door.

"Listen, Chase," Brent yells, trying to catch up to my speed walking as I head to the class Professor Wang assigned me to teach. "A few days ago, you were hell-bent on having a hookup, and now you want a Frenchman to "romance" you? No, I'll take that back—to woo you. You need to pick a lane and stick to it, or you are going to get nowhere in this dating game." Brent lifts his fedora, scratching his head. "I don't even think you're ready to date. Have fun? Yes. Date a man seriously? Not even close."

"Roxie, did you have to bring him?" I interject, feigning Brent's presence. "He's so annoying, plus I barely know him, and he thinks he's the Yoda of my dating life."

"I'm with Brent. Are you sure you're ready?" Roxie asks, totally ignoring my complaints.

I pull out my phone and see that I have five minutes to get across campus from Royce Hall. "Shit! I'll never make it," I mutter under my breath. I increase my stride a notch as I pass the courtyard and go down Bruin walkway. I can hear Roxie and Brent panting to keep up with me.

Out of nowhere, I hear Vincent's voice in my head: "Call me when you're truly ready to date. I'll be waiting." *Where did that come from?*

"Chase, did you hear what I said? Are you sure you're ready for this?"

Seeing the Math Science building, which is adjacent to Boelter Hall, in the near distance, I slow down a bit, so I don't have to yell. Brent and Roxie shuffle on either side of me.

"All right, I admit that I'm not sure!" I keep my voice low. "But, let's be real. Am I ready? Well, that's the $64,000 question, isn't it? Let me put it a different way: I'll never know if I don't go."

"And how do you suppose that will happen?"

I can tell Roxie's question is laced with sarcasm. She doesn't wait for my answer before she looks over to Brent and adds, "Do you know that she hasn't even gotten permission to go to this supposed conference? That's the excuse she's telling everyone—that she's going to Paris on an educational visit."

"Really? Now, that's my kind of trip." Brent shoots back, laughing. "La Ville-Lumière, the City of Lights. You know, a week-long class is not going to magically make you fluent in French or romance for that matter, Chase. I think you need to bring me along as your translator and sexual advisor." He gives me another one of his wicked smiles.

"I'm just fine. I've been listening to tapes on the treadmill."

"They make auditory sex tapes for the treadmill?" Roxie's eyes bug out. "Are they any good?"

"You're unbelievable, Roxie!" I roll my eyes. "French tapes, French tapes! God! I don't have time for this right now. I'll talk to you later." I rush past them both, heading to Boelter hall as fast as my legs will take me and hope for the best.

* * *

I swallow hard. My mouth feels parched. I grab my water bottle and take a swig before entering the brightly-lit room and set my things down behind the instructor's desk, which, positioned front and center, provides instructors with a clear view of students. Panning the large, tiered, and shell-shaped classroom, I feel the warm glow off the fluorescent lights against my back; beads of sweat begin to form and trickle down my spine. I feel more exposed than I've ever felt in my adult life.

Slowing panning the room for a second time, I count forty heads. They sit behind long tables, entirely indifferent to my presence: their laptops out, phones in hand, heads ducked down. Nineteen of the unfamiliar faces are women, which makes me smile inwardly at the thought of progress in my field since that's twice as many as when I started college. I rub my sweaty palms down the sides of my jeans before picking up a piece of chalk.

"Hello, and welcome to the first day of class," I say while writing my name on the chalkboard. "My name is Chastity Morgan, and I'm your teaching assistant and fill-in professor for this quarter's class of Advanced Reinforced Concrete Design while Dr. Wang is away this week."

I head back towards the right-wing chalkboard and scrawl a question:

Where do you place the reinforcing steel in a cantilever beam?

"This problem appears to be one that is simple, yet it's often the most problematic. I want to refresh your memory after the long winter break, so today we're going to go over some engineering basics, tension and compression, and where to place the reinforcements in a beam."

My chest tightens as I nervously glance around the room of expressionless faces before grabbing the chalk and setting to work on the problem. It's eerie how silent this huge auditorium is, and I concentrate even more to block this silence out.

"Excuse me," a male voice calls out from the back of the room. "How do we know that what you just calculated is correct? My calculations aren't anywhere near your solution, and I think you should've solved the cantilever problem like this."

My mouth is agape as the young man with thick dark hair wearing a black tracksuit approaches the front of the room. He grabs a piece of chalk and eraser and sets to work on the left-wing chalkboard. When he concludes, he high-fives his friends back to his seat.

I'm stone-faced as I assess his work. Did I do the problem wrong? Anxiety swirls around me. Is this the real reason I was nearly kicked out because I can't even calculate a simple problem correctly? Relief washes over me as I spot his mistake.

"Mister..."

"Miguel Alkstan," he finishes.

"Okay, let's see a show of hands. How many of you agree with Mr. Alkstan's calculations?" My eyes dart around the room as two-thirds of the class raise their hands.

Uh, oh, this isn't good. "Thank you." I let out a long sigh. I'm happy to see most of the women and a few men don't have their hands up. "I know I'm still a PhD student, and I'm human; I make mistakes. For everyone who did raise your hands, I'd like you to go up and scrawl your name next to Mr. Alkstan's answer. The rest of you, please scrawl your names next to my response."

"This is a pop quiz. Please take out a sheet of paper, a pencil, or a pen. Everyone on my side of the chalkboard, you will need to prove me right. Everyone on Mr. Alkstan's side, you will need to prove him right. If, at any point during the next thirty minutes, you change your mind about who you think calculated the problem correctly, feel free to erase your name and put it on the appropriate chalkboard. Now begin." After the end of thirty minutes, all but five students have their names on my side of the board.

"Here's the question on all of our minds: who's right?" I grab a piece of chalk, erasing my name on the middle board, and begin drawing out the problem.

"Your beginning level Reinforced Concrete Design class taught you that all concrete beams are reinforced with steel in the bottom of the beam. This is because a typical beam has positive bending. The steel is used to reinforce the tension stresses at the bottom of the beam since the concrete isn't strong enough in tension.

"Let me pinpoint where your classmates are wrong. In the case of a cantilever beam, it has negative bending. Thus, creating tension at the top of the beam instead of at the bottom. Therefore, the steel has to be placed into the top of the beam at the point of tension to reinforce the tensile stresses. That's the trick! Your classmates did not account for this negative bending." I put down the chalk.

"Would any of you five," I say, pointing to the group, "like to change your name to my board?" Four of them get up and come to my side. The guy with the ego, being a cocky ass, refuses to admit he's wrong. I look straight at him. "Mr. Alkstan, it's nice to see that you are firm in your beliefs, even if it won't do you justice during exam times. This concludes our class for today," I say all in one breath.

I take a seat on the stool. My body feels leaden, pain pulsating through my lower abdomen. My eyes close as I breathe through the pain. *Maybe my monthly crimson tide is coming early?*

"I hate to interrupt, but I'd like to introduce myself to all of you." I look up. It's my new worst nightmare: ASSon.

13

"I'm Alison, the other teaching assistant. I'm going to be in charge of Tuesday's and Thursday's question-and-answer sessions." She's wearing a tight black skirt and a bright yellow blouse with yellow kitten heels. With one hand on her hip, she looks like a bee in attack mode.

"Just so you know," Alison continues, her nose pointed towards the ceiling, "I am not on academic probation, nor is my father an adjunct professor in the department. Feel free to come and see me anytime you have questions."

My mouth drops open with a light pop. I notice ASSon turn her head in my direction.

"Oh, I didn't realize you were in the room. Nice to see you again, Chastity." Alison feigns a look of surprise. "By the way, you do know that the students rate our performance at the end of the quarter, right? That means if you ever want a job as a professor, you need to earn the top spot. Good luck to you." She turns, clicking her heels as she walks out of the room.

As soon as students clear the room and the door closes, I sink back onto the stool and start fiddling with my scarf. I reach for my cell and call Roxie.

"Hey, Chase!" She picks up on the first ring. "How was your first day of being an almost professor?"

"I was sweating when some smart-aleck student tried to humiliate me, but that was nothing compared to when ASSon walked in."

"Ass who?"

Why does it suddenly feel like déjà vu all over again?

"THE royal bitch," I shout, my voice echoing off the walls like an amphitheater.

"The royal bitch? That has got to be good." Roxie giggles like a schoolgirl. "Oh, I do love a good intrigue!"

"Alright, *Marguerite!*" I chuckle at Roxie's *Ever After* imitation. She's such a movie buff.

"Remember the day I talked to my advisor, and he gave me this teaching assistant opportunity?"

"Yeah?" Roxie's all ears, I swear. I can tell by the anticipation in her voice.

"Well, I'm not working alone; I have to share space with another TA, Feldman's minion. To be exact, she just so happens to be Lizzie's high school foreign exchange student, Huian Liu."

"Ooooooooooooh, so THAT'S ASSon! The shy nerdy girl with the greasy ponytails? She's harmless."

"Not anymore; she goes by Alison now, and the shy nerdy girl? Whoop!" I swing my arm to the side. "Out the window. Gone. Bye-bye! And I'm telling you, the new Lizzie version is a real piece of work. She makes me so angry I could spit farther than a camel, I swear."

"What the hell did she do that got you riled up?"

I hear the click of the side door as it opens, and a few students trickle in for the next class.

I continue to whisper while collecting my papers off the desk and stuffing them into my backpack. "So, the class was just finishing up when she struts in and not only introduces herself to the class but flat out tells them that she's not on academic probation and doesn't have a father who's a professor in the department. Then in front of them, she reminds me that I'll never earn a high rating from the students because I'm not professor material."

"Oh. That is so wrong. You're right, what a royal bitch!"

"That's what I'm trying to tell you, Rox. That is what I have to put up with just to get my PhD."

"That sucks! What is it with you, Chase? It's like the dregs of society gravitate to you. You've got the mean Prissy Posse, Grant—"

"Oh, that's real warm-and-fuzzy, Rox, and don't start up with Grant! He's another piece of work."

"More like a piece of SHIT!" she screams. I have to pull the phone away. A few students in front of the class look, wide-eyed, staring at my phone. A male professor walks in and storms past me, throwing his briefcase next to the podium.

"I'll say 'Amen' to that," I whisper, heading out the second side entrance.

I remind her that I'll be coming over at eight to study French and not to drag Brent along. She's convinced that he's not so bad. *I'll be the judge of that, Rox!* I give my scarf a light yank for good luck as I hang up and collect my things before heading towards the parking garage.

I must have missed the traffic rush, yakking with Rox because all I can hear is the rhythmic clicking of my boots. I grab the fob and unlock the car. I throw my junk on the passenger seat and start to get in when I hear a familiar voice in the distance.

"I'm so fucked up, Chase! I was a rotten son of a bitch at the theater. I don't blame you if you don't want to talk to me, but I could use some help—"

"Grant? Are you stalking me? You want your ring back that badly that you have to resort to this?" I manage to say as he slips out from behind a poll and heads my way. I shuffle in the driver's seat, slamming my door before he reaches my window. My poor attempt to shove the key in the ignition is enough for me to realize that I'm shaking like a leaf.

"Please, Chase..."

I flinch when Grant wraps onto the driver-side window, my heart pounding and my mind racing. It takes all that I have to close my eyes and take deep breaths.

"Please, Chase. You can give me back the ring later. Right now, I need someone to talk to, and you're the only one I can trust."

I wish I could say the same about you, buster. I take one last cleansing breath before turning the ignition a notch so I can let down the window a bit.

"Things have gone south, and I don't even remember doing it."

"Doing WHAT?" I shout.

"Chase..." Grant's face is plastered against the window, the aftereffects of booze wafting through the crack. His eyes are so bloodshot they look possessed.

"What the hell, Grant? You're drunk, and you stink of BO. What is going on with you?"

"Oh, God, you don't know half of it. The thing is I really don't remember having—" he wipes a stray tear with the back of his hand before continuing, "Brody keeps pressing me to adopt her and take on full custody, and—"

"Adopt? You mean like to adopt a baby?"

"You're quick, Chase. Yes, a baby."

"Don't mock me, you asshole!" Starting the car, I hit the gas and lurch backward. Grant pulls away from the vehicle and starts waving me down.

"No, no, Chase! I'm sorry. I didn't mean that. Please, forgive me!" He plops to the pavement and immediately starts bawling.

It's pretty embarrassing for me to see a grown man cry, especially when the acoustics amplify his sobs tenfold. I can feel my heart softening, but at the same time, red flags go up; In my heart, I don't trust him. Relying on the latter, I repark the car and roll down my window.

"Adopting isn't a bad thing, Grant. Couples do it all the time. I don't see what you're all upset—"

I hear footsteps coming through the garage. In the rearview mirror, it looks like Professor Feldman, but I'm not sure. Regardless, the person heads my way.

"I gotta go."

"But Chase—" Grant pleads loudly.

"CHAHS-dah-dee, iz daht you? Vaht are you still here vor?"

I was right: it *is* Professor Feldman. Her footsteps grow louder as she approaches.

"Grant, get out of here NOW," I whisper. He moves surprisingly fast for someone quite inebriated. I watch him go through the door to the stairwell.

"CHAHS-dah-dee, I'm so glahd to see you. I vonted to talk to you about your lab vork. I got your note." Professor Feldman bends a little to poke her head through the opened window.

"I'm sorry for the delay, Professor Feldman. I had a hiccup in my experiment and—"

"That's vhy I'm glahd I caught you. You have until the end of the week to get your rezults into me, or you vill be severely behind on your PhD timetable."

"Oh dear, and then there's the conference in Paris coming up, just before Valentine's Day—"

"I vouldn't vurry about dee conference," she interrupts. "You are not quite ready for dee caliber material dhey vill offer."

"In all due respect, Professor Feldman, I'm more than ready to tackle the informa—"

"Right now, it iz important for you to finish your experimentation. Conferences vill come and go, and vhen you're ready, I'll let you know. Good day, CHAHS-dah-dee."

And with that, the old professor turns and quickly shuffles to her car.

"Oh shit!" I mumble out loud as I start the car and close my window. "Now, what am I going to do? I've got to get to Paris, come hell or high water!"

* * *

"What do you mean you're not coming over to study, Chase? You're the one that got me sucked into taking this damn French—" I can barely hear her. I quickly turn the sound down to "Supermassive Black Hole." Playing Muse in the background helps liven up the room.

I'm stuck in the school's basement, which reminds me of the original *Frankenstein* movie with Boris Karloff. Gray and windowless, the cement bricks look mottled against the dim lighting. It doesn't help when the couple of goose-necked lamps I flicked on create the eeriest shadows. Every few minutes, I'll hear dripping coming from one of the old water tanks. There's even a cold draft that filters in through one of the vents.

"I know, I'm sorry. I stopped at home to shove some food down before I turned around and came back to school; I have to finish my project or Feldman's going to cook my goose."

I give a hard stare at the reinforced concrete column sitting in the middle of the room with its steel reinforcing rebar peeking out where the concrete has chipped away. Mindlessly setting my phone on a little table stand by the lab entrance, I carefully eye the column with its many wires connected like a heart monitor and evaluate the stresses before gearing myself up for work. I walk in perfect robotic fashion over to plug my computer into the circuit board and pull my ugly plastic goggles out from my backpack. "CHASE! CHASE! I'M RIGHT HERE! WHERE DID YOU GO?"

My mind shifts to *Honey, I Shrunk the Kids* when I hear Roxie's squeak.

"Oh, my God! Roxie," running over to the phone, I punch the speaker icon. "I'm soooooooooo sorry! I got caught up in my work."

"What's gotten into you, Chase, and who the hell cares about Feldman? You've got to stand up for your rights and—"

"She won't let me go to the conference, Rox."

"What?"

"You heard me."

"That's fucked up! Who the hell does she think she is?"

After explaining to her that Professor Feldman has a tenured position and can pretty much do whatever she wants, I walk over and recheck the wire connections. I can see the rebar changing from a straight piece of metal into a slightly curved one as it slowly works its way to its failure point.

"Oh, that's so wrong!" Roxie yells over the phone.

"I know, but if I want to get my PhD *plus* go to Paris, I have to prove to her that I'm engineering material—plain and simple. Oh, God," suddenly changing the subject, "I have to tell you what happened in the parking garage!"

"Don't tell me; Grant texted you again."

"Worse; he was stalking me." I proceed to give Roxie the blow-by-blow while sitting back in front of my computer. I push my safety goggles up to rub my tired eyes.

"*What??* He was drunk in the middle of the afternoon?"

"And he babbled on about adopting a kid, and then he bawled—"

"Adopting who?" Roxie interrupts.

"I never heard the rest of it—and frankly, I don't care—because Feldman stopped to talk to me." I type in a few changes, amping up the compression pressure at the top of the column. A piece of concrete flies, and I duck.

"OH. MY. GOD!" I have to strain my ear to understand what Roxie says over the cracking.

I crawl back up to my seat, readjusting my goggles so I can check the computer displacement results. At this rate, I can see the column rebar should fail by morning.

"It's Medusa's kid."

"Julie's kid? Why would you say something like that? Her rich fiancé probably got her knocked up."

"That's not what I heard..." Roxie demurs.

"From whom?" I retaliate, knowing that Roxie often catches gossip from unreliable sources.

"Facebook."

"Oh, great! Here we go," I mumble, leaning back in the chair and adjusting my legs on the desk, waiting for her logorrhea to start.

I don't want to hear more, but Roxie's on a roll, telling me that Medusa says that it's not her fiancés, so she's giving the baby up. Even though I've told her a thousand times that Medusa's nothing more than a pathological liar, she's convinced that the information is for real.

"What makes you so sure?" I blurt at last.

"Because Grant was a part of the conversation. Remember the park incident?"

140

"Yes, but did he say something about adopting?"

"No, nothing like that. It's just a feeling."

"Feelings are fickle; stick to facts."

"Fickle? Listen to your logic, Chase. You're the one that's been in denial about Grant, and don't forget about Charlie; you aren't processing the stages of grief for either of them."

"That's enough, Roxie! Okay? So, I've got my issues, but that doesn't prove anything about Medusa."

"Look. We'll just see how this whole thing plays out. Just promise that you don't start crumbling on me when the truth comes out."

"Fine. If it makes you happy, I promise not to lose it."

"And, do something about your love life, please. I want to see your chart plastered with Amoremojis before the year's up."

"Right." I can't even look at my chart now; it's so pathetic.

"And, you're going to Paris," Roxie adds.

"How do you know?"

"I've got a feeling."

"I've got to go, Rox. I need to get back to work. And seeing that I'm working with flying pieces, I need to monitor it and be more careful. See you tomorrow."

"Nighty night, cuz. Sweet dreams!"

And try as I might to want to believe that Roxie's full of hot air, I can't dismiss the nasty niggling feeling that she may be right.

"Sweet dreams, Chase," I mutter to myself. Now *THAT would be a miracle!*

14

Paul: Hey, boo, where are you? Don't go dark on me. I heard about the date with my brother. LOL. I'm going to Mammoth to shoot some footage. Call you when I get back.

"Seriously, Paul? No, I'm sorry, Chase?" I say a little too loudly. I glance up briefly from my phone to see a couple of students staring at me as they pass me in the hallway on their way to an 8 am class. I'm sure my hair looks a bit ratty, and my eyes must be utterly bloodshot after all the late nights I've pulled trying to move my work along faster. "He doesn't even have the decency to apologize for his slimy shift at the Cialto," muttering now on my way to Feldman's office. "Why do things like this happen at the most inopportune time? Chase, breathe!!!" I say, running my fingers through my hair right before flinging open the professor's door.

"Right on time!" I've been around Feldman's stogy secretary long enough to know that her cheerful smiles are as fake as her false teeth. "The professor is waiting for you. Oh..." She points to my cheeks. "Thanks, Mrs. Langmeyer." I feign a return smile, running my hand across my face to wipe the dust off, leftovers from my tests before I head into Professor Feldman's office.

"CHAHS-dah-dee!" She stands to shake my hand, pulling back when she sees my disheveled appearance. She hands me tissues off her desk instead.

"Professor Feldman. Sorry, the lab got incredibly dusty when the concrete started cracking."

"Shall vee head down to the basement? Yes?" She waves me forward to follow.

More like a "lah-BORRRR-ah-tory." I can hear Bela Lugosi's heavy Hungarian accent running through my head.

"I'll be glad to answer any of your questions once the demonstration is complete." I feign a smile as I try to keep pace with her down the hall in near silence. Her back is as stiff as a pole and her eyes as cold as ice, heightening my already nervous state. My fate is in her hands, and by the looks of it, she's not in a good mood.

"I'm sure you vill, my dear." She presses the button against the wall, and we immediately step into the elevator.

I can feel my heart begin to race.

"Breathe, Chase, breathe! How bad can it be? If she likes it, you'll be going to Paris and on your way to graduating, and if she hates it, you can resume your spot on the couch, watching old reunions!" I want to flick the little Chase Angel, who's not helping calm my nerves one bit, off my shoulder.

* * *

"Vell, I haf to say you've done a superb job, CHAHS-dah-dee. A superb job." She has her nose pressed up against the reinforcing bars, examining the jutting out spot in which they failed.

Thanking her profusely, I point out the response of the column and the point the column rebar ruptured and reached ultimate failure. I touch the surface midway down the column, explaining its length, width, thickness, and boundary constraints.

"I'd like to add that this project fits perfectly with the topics that will be discussed at the conference in Paris. If you would permit me to go, I—" I push my laptop in front of her, my results tallied on an extensive Excel spreadsheet. I'm a bit OCD about dotting my I's and crossing my t's.

She takes the computer from my hands and scrolls down the screen, handing it back to me. "No doubt, deece project vould fit in vell vit the conference, but I don't think you've got vut it takes to stand up to the presenters. They can be, how do I say ... ruthless?" she says, waving her hand as she walks towards the basement door. My spirits immediately plummet. *"This is the moment that can change your life forever. It's now or never, Chastity,"* the little Chase Angel screams into my ear.

"Professor, hear me out." I jump in front of her, blocking her way. "Please." Her eyes bug out as I release her arm. "I think that climate change is an important factor in the lifespan and resistance of a building. They say that swings in weather are precursor events to earthquakes. Significant temperature changes can cause expansion and contraction in the concrete that results in cracks and the breakdown of materials. That said, I firmly believe that I will benefit from this conference, which will help my research."

Silence.

Professor Feldman reminds me of "The Thinker," except fully clothed. I stand quietly, giving her time to mull things over.

"I see you've done your homework," I flinch lightly, surprised at Professor Feldman's swift response. "I'm sorry to say, CHAHS-dah-dee, dee spot has already been filled, and I don't have any more grant money to send another stu—"

I cut her off mid-sentence, letting her know that I called the conference office and found out that the university can send two additional students as long as it pays for hotel and flight expenses.

"I have—well, actually my dad has—accrued plenty of miles, which I can use; he won't mind. And my grandmother has offered to pay for my hotel. She's just happy to see me out of bed and not moping around."

"Hmm ... Vhy is it that you vant to go there so badly? It's only a two-day conference? Dat's a long way to go for two days." She stares at me hard.

I plaster on my best poker face, hoping that I don't give away my *real* reason for chasing love and a fantasy man, wrapping his scarf around my neck under the Eiffel Tower.

"Honestly, I didn't know that climate change would even be an issue until I started in the lab and saw the different factors involved in testing for the failure of materials. I thought that failure was only a result of site conditions and earthquake waves. Now, I see it is an imperative conference that I must attend."

Professor Feldman's eyebrows shoot up. "You haf a fierce determination, Miss Morgan. My friend, Doctor Milton, iz chairing the conference. Find him vhen you arrive. I'll let him know to expect you."

I fling my arms around her but pull back as soon as she stiffens.

"Thank you! Thank you! It's the moments that count, not how long they last. I promise you won't regret this."

"I certainly hope I von't." Her last words, as she turns, heading back to her office.

* * *

Thrilled to no end, I pull out my phone once I settle in my car at the parking lot just across the street. Without paying attention to the first contact on my list, I begin texting.

> **Me: I'm going to Paris.**
> Paul: You're going where? When?
> **Me: What? You know I'm going and when. Wait.
> Who is this?**

I stare down at my phone, waiting for a reply when it abruptly vibrates. I'm so shocked that I drop it and it lands under my left foot.

"Dammit!" I yell. At least my windows are up, so I don't have to worry about students ogling me. I slide the buzzing phone nearer to me with my feet, but the steering wheel is in the way. "Dear God in heaven! Why me?" I let out just before getting out of the car. I have to get on my hands and knees to reach the annoying gadget. Paul's name shows up as the caller. I swipe the phone icon.

"Paul?"

"What in the world took you so long to answer?"

"Why are you calling me?" I sink in my seat, gunning the ignition, turning the heater on high.

"You texted me."

"I did not," I respond emphatically.

"Yes, you did, you silly. You told me that you were going to Paris."

"Who told you that I'm going to Paris?"

"You did."

"No, I didn't."

"Take a look at your texts, Chase."

"Hold on a sec." I navigate to my messages app. Sure as shootin', there it is in plain sight. "What the hell..."

"Sorry, Paul. I thought you were Roxie. I gotta go—"

"Hey, hey, hey, don't hang up! I want to talk to you unless you're busy 'entertaining someone,' perchance my little brother? Say 'hi' to Jaydon while you're at it."

"He's not here. Besides ... wait! Why should I bother talking to you, Paul? That was a lousy trick you pulled at the theater. I thought we were friends. How could you do something so rotten like that?" I force myself not to cry as I adjust the heater, cranking it up a notch. "Do you know what it did to me to find out my fiancé married someone else right under my nose?"

Silence.

"I'm sorry, Chase. I didn't know about Brody. Heck, I didn't even know he was gay. I would never do anything to hurt you; I care about you way too much. And you're right; it was rotten of me to help Grant. He was so desperate to talk to you that he convinced me you needed to hear him out to help you both have closure. What I didn't expect was for him to pull a fast one on me; he got so stinking drunk and then treated you like shit."

I can feel tears welling up.

"Do you know what it felt like to have him not want me? To dump me and profess his love for someone else in front of a room full of people? I'm trying my best to put one foot in front of the other and move forward, and it doesn't help that I have to keep seeing him."

"I can only imagine. I'm sorry, Chase. Can you forgive me?"

More silence. I pull the phone away so he can't hear my sniffling.

"Actually," Paul continues, "there's more to the story that may interest you. I let him have it the next day—I stopped at his place and told him he had to make things right with you, or I was going to cut off our friendship."

"You said that?"

"Yes. For real."

I put the phone down and blow my nose hard.

"Chase!" This time, all I can think of is Matt Damon in *Downsizing* when I hear Paul's distance voice.

"Sorry." I take a deep breath before continuing. "So ... how did he respond?"

"Nothing. He walked away like a dog with its tail between its legs. I haven't talked to him since."

"Oh..." I'm at a loss for words.

"Let's talk about something else ... I suppose Jaydon planned this trip to Paris?" He suddenly shifts gears.

"No. This is in connection with my PhD. It's a prestigious environmental conference that will be held next week."

"Wow! I'm proud of you, Chase. You're really doing it! Good for you!"

"Well, it took some finagling on my part—"

"Finagling? You mean you didn't get chosen to go?"

"No, not exactly."

"Then ... Oh, wait! Don't tell me you're hooking up with someone once you get there, and you need an excuse to go. Right? It's a love jaunt."

"No. It's not a love jaunt, but I can see why you'd think that since Paris is known as the City of Love."

"Oh, you're hiding something, Chase. I can feel it. You forget that I know you way too well."

His light coaxing brings a smile to my face. It feels like old times.

"No, I'm not," I play along. I'm not about to tell him my dirty little secret. He'll think I've gone crazy.

"Yes, you are, Chase! I've known you long enough to know that you are a planner, and you wouldn't be traveling across the ocean just for a conference. Is there a driving factor because you hate long-distance traveling? I mean, come on, Chase, you have just enough tolerance to take a jet back and forth to visit your Aunt Kate during the Christmas holidays, and that's about it."

Silence.

"Chase? Are you still there?"

"Yes."

"Did you hear what I said?"

"Yes. I didn't think about all of that."

"Go see Dr. Brennan."

"My therapist? But I stopped seeing him a while ago. How do you know about him, anyway? We haven't talked since everything happened at Newport that day."

"Roxie. Roxie shared with me when you pushed everyone away. You need his help. Now."

Another pause. Why would Roxie share that with him?

"Fine. You win because, strangely enough, you're right. I'll call Dr. Brennan tomorrow."

"And try to get some sleep in the process."

"Right." If THAT'S possible.

"Coffee just the two of us when you get back from PAH-REE?"

"You mean without all your crazy fans swarming you?" I release a little chuckle. "Could happen."

148

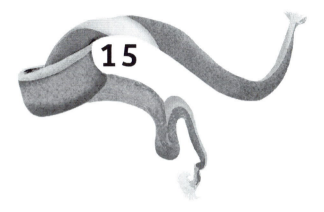

15

"Sleep. I need sleep... It's not rocket science... I don't have to climb Mount Everest... I just need sleep," I rattle off in one breath.

"On a difficulty scale from one to ten, this should be a one, but after staring at the ceiling night after night, listening to my heart pound in continuous insomniac rhythm, it's still a stubborn ten. Don't they say lack of sleep, day after day, can cause sane people to go psychotic? Is that really true, Doctor Brennan?"

My heart pounds so hard thinking about my upcoming flight; it feels like it's going to burst from my chest like the alien in that bloody fright flick, *Aliens*.

"It depends," Dr. Brennan calmly replies. The debonair-looking doc sits in a cushioned armchair. He's doodling on a pad of paper resting on his lap. I pan the room while I do my deep breathing exercise. Aside from his large mahogany desk and a tall bookshelf nestled in one corner, his office is nothing but welcoming. Light floral-patterned curtains complement the cream-colored walls, scantily clad with pictures of woodsy scenes.

Turning my attention back to Dr. Brennan, I can't help but wonder if he was even a former model with his silver sideburns and a full head of wavy, well-groomed hair.

He patiently waits until I complete a round of four deep breaths.

"Please, continue, Ms. Morgan."

"Yes. So, I've had severe anxiety over the idea of being trapped on an airplane for ten hours. I'm leaving for Paris in a few days."

Another ridiculously long pause passes. Silence seems to be the new trend that follows me.

"My mother circled the globe as a young woman. The impulse for adventure and transcontinental travel is deeply embedded in the Morgan family DNA, except for me. I'm afraid my last airline adventure maxed out my chromosomes to the point of having aviophobia at the highest level." Hands under my head and feet propped up on the lazy boy recliner, I revel at the accomplishments that led me to examine my mental state. For a brief moment, I stare at a multi-colored rug that dominates the floor. I'm lost in thought as the varied shapes play tricks on me; I swear that I'm looking at a graduation scene. I can even hear cheering in the background.

"Is that what brings you into my office today? Your fear of flying?" he asks flatly while taking his eyes away from his pad to look directly in mine. He appears unfazed by my astute self-evaluation.

POP! I flinch, Dr. Brennan bursting my imaginary congratulatory bubble. My intellectual attempt to escape the harsh reality that I don't have my shit together goes belly up. I have no choice but to resign myself to the fact that I need help.

"Yes." I breathe out a long, exaggerated sigh. "My cousin Roxie came up with this radical post-breakup resolution list in the hopes of getting me to conquer my fears and find love, especially since Grant dumped me, and last Saturday would have been my wedding." I grab a couple of tissues to blow my nose. Hard. "So, I say what better way to find love than in Paris, the city of love, right? Besides, Charlie and I dreamed of going to Paris since the first time we saw a picture of IM Pei's glass pyramid at the Louvre in our middle-school drawing class—the steel skeleton, the glass curtain walls, we um ... had these plans that we would go there on our 30th birthday, but then things happened as you know..." I nervously pick at my nail polish as a tear trickles down my cheek.

"Hmm..." He goes back to scribbling. "I'm sorry about your botched wedding plans," Dr. Brennan says sincerely. He pauses for several seconds, waiting for me to compose myself. "Let's deal with the issue of flying. How do you think you can overcome your fears?"

"Huh?" I ask, sitting up abruptly, one of my eyebrows cocked. "Is that a rhetorical question? That's why my friend Paul told me to come back to you. You are the wizard in the psychiatric department." My phone suddenly dings. He makes eye contact with me before his stare urges me to follow his gaze to the big sign on the backside of his door: PLEASE turn off all cell phones before the commencement of sessions! My sheepish grin says it all; I softly utter "sorry" while leaning over the side of the chair to reach my purse. "Let me give you three options," he says, his voice deepening like Barry White. He taps his pen against the yellow pad on his desk with annoying persistence. "Option number one: Flooding. Flooding means that you would have to face your fears head-on. In the case of flying, it means getting on airplanes—many of them, I might add—and taking multiple flights." I find myself mesmerized by his perfect, blazingly white game-show teeth. "Eventually, your body will learn through repetition to shut off the fight-or-flight adrenaline response and to accept flying calmly."

"It's a little late for that, don't you think?"

"When's your trip?" He looks up at me, tapping his pen against his pad of paper.

"In less than a week," I say, staring at the ceiling.

He scribbles again.

"When did you know you were going on your trip?"

I look at my hands, "almost a month ago," I whisper.

"Procrastinator. Okay, option number two: hypnotherapy. I can put you in a trance and make you believe you're not afraid to fly."

"Seriously?" I bolt upright, which slaps the recliner back into its flat bed-like position. My excitement overshadows the cringing look on the doc's face. "Like a circus show act? It sounds like a quick fix to me. But don't make me quack or chuckle out like a monkey."

"Must you do that, Ms. Morgan?" his eyes firmly set on the recliner. "That's an expensive piece of furniture."

"Oh. Oops. Sorry!" I put on my sheepish grin again.

"Never mind. Let's get started. I want you to make yourself comfortable on the recliner." I settle in; the doctor waits patiently. "Now, close your eyes." He reaches behind to turn on the stereo system; it immediately emits soothing ambient wave music.

"I want you to visualize the airplane," he says in a low, grumbly but sexy voice.

I erupt in a fit of giggles.

Dr. Brennan clears his throat, signaling his irritation. "Let's try this again, Ms. Morgan. Visualize yourself buckling your seatbelt, enjoying a refreshment."

"I can't do this," I erupt in another fit of giggles. "You have a 'phone sex operator with a Darth Vader' voice, and I can't get the imagery out of my head."

"I see." He places both his pen and pad gently down on the small end table next to his chair. "I'm going to break away from formalities and be frank with you. Chastity, you've been coming to me for quite some time now."

"Ever since Cha—"

"Charlie's demise."

"That's so harsh, Dr. Brennan. Must you?"

"What do you want me to call it?"

"Nothing. Absolutely nothing." I begin to raise my voice.

"Chastity, let me be clear with you that there's more to this fear of yours than just flying. You have a much greater fear that you've been suppressing for way too long. At some point, you have to talk about Charlie. If not, you will have a difficult time moving forward in life without some form of closure. Do you understand what I'm saying?"

Dr. Brennan intensely watches as I fiddle with my scarf while staring up at the ceiling. The spackling reminds me of the sand; I flash back to our fifth birthday. Charlie and I were down at the beach. Our towheads are nearly touching as we whispered kid things while collecting seashells. Once the heat got to us, we'd splash around in the ocean.

"Chastity, where did you go?" Dr. Brennan asks.

I sit up, looking at him, "I've come to terms with that." I pick at my nail polish.

"Okay, let's talk about why you believe you're winning even though you're failing at your relationships." I furrow my eyebrows. "I'm not winning. What makes you think I'm winning? I'm failing. I told you. I got dumped by my fiancé, who ran off with a man and is now contemplating adoption. Roxie thinks the baby is his with Medusa. In my book, that's not exactly winning. He broke my heart into a thousand pieces." A nervous laugh escapes my lips as pain pulses through my abdomen. I clutch my stomach.

"Are you okay?" he leans over his desk, and I wave him off.

"Just cramps." At least I think it is. It's the same pain I felt at school.

"Well then, as I was trying to explain, you are winning because you want your relationships to fail, because no man will ever fill that spot in your life, thus causing you to fail and win."

"That's a bunch of psychobabble. That makes no logical sense. I want to get married; thus, I want my relationships to succeed. DUH! Never mind all that, I just need to get over my fear of flying and check world travel off my list. You said you had three options for me. What's my third?"

He releases a frustrated sigh. He takes a quick peek at his hidden-from-view timer to see how much time is left. "Medication. I could give you a pill to ease your anxiety. Granted, it won't cure your fear, but it will shut off your fight-or-flight response. Chastity, life isn't about a checklist that you get through. You're running away from the underlying problem. Eventually, life will catch up to you. We need to talk about him."

I stare down at my ugly nails, hoping the unsightly image will help explain his medical mumbo-jumbo. Dr. Brennan opens a cabinet behind his desk and pulls out what looks like a pack of large posters. I watch as he sets up an easel in front of me. He places an enlarged picture of a bubble on the stand.

"Chastity, let me break down the "psychobabble," as you call it. Hopefully, this will begin to make sense."

"A little girl standing in a bubble?"

"Yes. Hear me out. What do you see her looking at?"

"The open field filled with daisies."

"What other views do you see?"

"Her reflection."

"That's correct. Does the open field scene look correct?"

"No. It's a bit distorted, but in a magical way."

"Why magical?"

"There's a shimmery quality to it that makes it look so appealing."

"Good. Would you say what the girl is seeing is true to life or skewed?"

"Oh, I think I know where you're going with this. You think I'm looking at life through a bubble, don't you?"

"So, to speak. Yes."

I can feel the heat rising at the back of my neck. *How dare he tell me what I can and cannot see!* I take a deep breath to force myself to calm down, remembering why I came here in the first place. I've been going to Dr. Brennan long enough to know that he's here to help me.

"You have an idea of what marriage looks like, but it's skewed."

"No, it's not," I ardently refute.

"Then tell me the number of people you know who are living in castles and are living happy-ever-after lives."

"Well, there's my parents..."

"They live in a castle?"

"No, but—"

"And they've never experienced problems?"

"Well, yes, but—"

"Then why are you so insistent in attaining an unrealistic goal?"

"It's not un—. I know I can achie—"

I stare down at my nails again, speechless.

"Chastity, what I'm trying to say is that your idea of winning—your goal in life—is skewed. You're caught in a bubble that, I'm afraid to say, you manufactured yourself. All you can see is your reflection and a distorted view of life."

"How can you be so pompous to conclude that I put myself in a bubble, doctor?"

"An imaginary bubble," he continues, ignoring my derogatory remark, "is a survival technique that a person creates when she or he is unable to face pain. The sad part is that people don't realize that their so- called comfort zone is also a self-made prison."

"Okay. You've roused my curiosity. How is an imaginary bubble like a self-made prison?"

Dr. Brennan pulls out another poster and places it over the bubble scene. It's a circular diagram labeled "co-dependency." I'm confused.

"Let me give you some scenarios to see if this begins to click. Amy has grown up with abuse all her young life. She doesn't know how else to overcome her troubles until Billy catches her unaware one day and offers her a 'feel-good' opportunity."

"Cocaine. Right?"

"Correct."

"How does that relate to me? I don't do drugs."

"Let me finish. Amy gets involved and finds that the cocaine allows her to escape in a euphoric state for a while, but then she dips into depression. The only way to get out is to take more cocaine. Now she's hooked: she lives for the rush but hates the sudden drop, and even though Amy doesn't like what it's doing to her, she doesn't know how to break the cycle because it's all that she knows and sees in her insular environment—her bubble. The same happens when people use alcohol to drown their sorrows. Both of these examples describe what's called 'codependency'—when a person relies on others for emotional and psychological support. The term also applies to relationships."

I'm in a contemplative mode, cupping one hand over the other and setting them in front of my mouth. "Using Amy again, let's say Billy starts showing her attention. She's not one for giving in to a guy's sexual desires, but since he seems to give her attention, she gives in. Soon it becomes almost a daily ritual, and while she's tired of the routine, she doesn't know how to say 'no' because he's the only person that makes her forget her troubles. It becomes a vicious cycle," he says as he points to the diagram. "Is this beginning to make sense?"

"So, you're saying that since I have trouble dealing with Charlie, I'm looking for something—in this case, a perfect relationship—that will ease my pain?"

"You know, you'd make an excellent therapist. You nailed it!"

"Mmm..."

The timer dings.

"Ruminate on this a while. In the meantime, I'd highly reconsider your trip to Paris."

"I can't, Dr. Brennan. For some strange reason, I feel destiny calling me. I've got to go."

"Well, then concentrate on what I've told you. Hopefully, that will deflect your fear of flying. If that doesn't work, get this prescription filled." He hands me a paper. I see "Anti-anxiety Medication" with "# mg" written on one of the lines. "Don't take more than two; three if absolutely necessary."

"Why? What are the side effects?"

I flinch when I hear a sharp knock on the door.

"Come in." Dr. Brennan raises his voice.

Ms. Finney, his receptionist, pokes in her head. "Mrs. Clark is here for her appointment."

"Thank you, Sarah." He promptly turns to me. "Our time has come to a close, Chastity. Make sure to read the paperwork thoroughly from your pharmacist; it should answer any questions that you may have about the product. If you have any questions, call my office."

"Thanks, Dr. Brennan." I shake his hand.

"See you next month?"

"I may. I need to 'ruminate,' as you say, on what you said first."

"Then do that. Don't hesitate to contact my receptionist when you're ready to set up another appointment. In the meantime, I wish you the best."

I thank him for a second time before grabbing my belongings and heading out the office door.

Great! Now my mind is more clogged than before. Dear Lord, get me out of this mess!

* * *

Daphne's waiting for me on the front porch when I arrive home.

"Oh, wonderful," I blurt out as I pull into the driveway. "What is it about people landing on my front porch?" I ramble loudly. Good thing, my windows are closed.

Daphne jumps up, soccer ball in hand, and gives me a little wave as I head into the garage. I'm barely out of the car when she greets me at the driver's side door.

"Wanna play soccer before you pack?" She spins the ball on her index finger while she awaits my reply. "You're good!" I'm genuinely impressed with her skill level.

"Thanks!" Daphne grins from ear to ear.

"So," I grab the ball mid-spin. "What's the story with you? Mind explaining to me how you know things about me—things I've never mentioned to you? You seem to have all the information. Are you some kind of psychic?"

"You were right, the peanut butter cookies with M&M's are divine," Brent mumbles, mouth full of food as he walks out the front door, Roxie at his heels. Daphne runs towards him and snatches the half-eaten cookie from his hand.

"What are you doing here, Brent? When did *you* start to get chummy with my mom?" I'm shocked by the bizarre scenario.

"Oh, I can answer that," Daphne shouts.

"I'm sure you can. Isn't that what you've been doing since you moved here?"

"Brent came over to Roxie's a few weeks ago asking about you. Roxie was in the middle of making cookies when she realized she ran out of vanilla. So, she and Brent went to your house to ask your mom for vanilla, which she had, by the way. Your mom laughed when she opened the door and saw Roxie. She was about to go to her house and ask for some sugar. The funny part is that they thought it would be fun to make cookies together. So, Roxie and Brent went back to get her cookie stuff and brought it over to your place. They loved it so much that they've been making cookies together ever since on Thursday mornings."

After hearing that, I feel like I'm the new kid on the block; I'm utterly clueless.

"Where was I when all this was happening?"

"Playing 'mad scientist' in your *laboratory*," Brent volunteers, doing a lousy job of mimicking a Bela Lugosi accent.

Lovely.

"I was NOT playing, Brent! I was working on a criti—" I quip, rolling my eyes.

"I know, I know. I was just pulling your leg. Don't take it so personally, Chase. Now that your project is over..."

"That was only the first stage," I interrupt. I must have been turning red in the face because the motley little trio begins staring at me.

"Okay. No need to get huffy, Chase," Brent replies calmly. "Let me restate that: Now that you've gotten part one of your project completed, maybe you can join us during our baking parties."

"I'll take a rain check. In the meantime, I have a trip to get ready—"

"Oh, speaking of your trip, Daphne thought it would be nice if I got you an umbrella."

Roxie gives me the one-moment signal while she runs in my house and returns, grinning from ear to ear. "I hope you like it," she hands me her prized gift. "It was the last one left at the art museum store."

I let out a slight gasp when I open the canopied device and recognize the full-blown scene of Monet's "The Picnic"—one of my favorite art pieces.

"It's absolutely stunning, Rox, but why bother with an artsy-fartsy umbrella, let alone an oversized one?" I give Roxie a confused look.

"Because rain is in the forecast. And you're going to get drenched. And the whole wet look doesn't suit you."

I shouldn't be surprised by Daphne's comments, but I am. I turn, and crouching to her level, I give her my full attention.

"That's really sweet, Daphne." I try not to let it slip that my remark is as condescending as all get out. "I hate to break it to you, but The Weather Channel shows sunny skies all next weekend."

"I'm not talking about here. I'm talking about Paris."

My impish grin slowly disappears when I pull out my phone and check the forecast for Paris. *100% chance of rain all weekend,* I deduce. *OMG! What is it about this kid? She's driving me crazy!*

"Okay, Daphne, time to fess up. How do you know all this stuff?" I'm visibly frustrated. "Did your mom buy you a cell phone? Do you tap our phones?"

"Um, they told me," Daphne points to Roxie and Brent.

"You know what I mean, you little squirt," I yell as she heads for the front lawn, juggling the soccer ball on her knees. Roxie cracks up when Brent steals the ball and begins dribbling it away before he turns and kicks it back to Daphne. She retrieves it and sends it back to Brent, who throws in some tricks before maneuvering it back to her.

"He's outstanding," I comment.

"Mesmerizing even," Roxie adds.

"So..."

"So, what?"

"I assume you bought a special umbrella for yourself, too. I can't imagine you going with one of your crappier ver—"

"Chase, I'm not going with you," Roxie interrupts.

"What do you mean that you're not going with me?" my face flushing abruptly. "You told me if I got the thumbs up, you would go. You know that I can't fly alone."

"Sure, you can, Chase. You're going to have to because ... well, for one, my dad won't lend me money for the trip, and secondly, Brent's going to help me set up my wedding-coordinator website. This is a big weekend for me—it's Valentine's weekend, and since lots of couples get engaged during this time, my phone will be ringing off the hook. Daphne said that I've practiced enough party planning and decorating to spread my wings and go out on my own."

"When did a ten-year-old become your financial advisor?"

"She's amazing, isn't she?" Roxie looks admiringly at Daphne. I look like I'm about ready to barf.

"The boys you're going to meet are really cute, and one's very familiar, but be careful. My mom says French boys are all oo-la-la this and oo-la-la that," Daphne yells as she runs past me. "He's not what you think."

"Spill it out, kid; you're a psychic, aren't you? Tell me, will I find my husband on this trip?" I'm about to run after her when Maria hollers that dinner is ready.

"So, here's the deal," Daphne responds, pulling me down to her level as she heads toward her house.

I didn't know I was supposed to be making a deal ... WITH A FUCKING TEN-YEAR-OLD!

"If you want to be my friend," she continues, "don't ask me any questions. Anyway, it's not the answers that will set you free."

My mouth drops open with her last statement.

"Don't worry, Chase," Brent chuckles as he pats my shoulder. "Remember, you're going to Paris. Men, especially handsome ones, are everywhere. It doesn't take a psychic to tell you that you'll meet one of them."

"And don't forget to add hearts and a smiling face with smiling eyes Amoremojis next to world travel!" Roxie adds. "You're making progress."

I wriggle away from the two and make a beeline for the front steps.

"You guys are driving me crazy. I've had enough for one day. I'm going to finish packing." Without looking back at them, I wave them off with an *"au revoir mes amis"* before heading through the front door.

"Boys? Familiar? Not what I think?" I mumble under my breath. "Right."

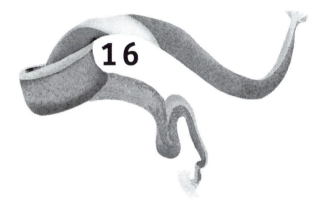

16

I can't believe my mother is coming with me. She stepped in soon after finding out Roxie's plans fell through. I half expected her to sit me down last night and lecture me on the "dos and don'ts" of romance along with a package of feminine products to keep me safe—just in case. Instead, she wished me a good night's sleep and reminded me to take a pill first thing in the morning before she turned in. *"It will take the edge off when we take off."* True to form, the anti-anxiety pills I've taken the past five nights seem to be doing the trick.

"Good morning, ladies," our Uber driver chimes as he promptly loads our suitcases in the trunk before opening the doors for us. "My name is Bill—Ole Bill, actually—and I'll take good care of you!"

He could have said, *"I'll treat you well if you do the same while dancing like a monkey,"* and I wouldn't have cared less. I am as docile as a lamb and feel as calm as a kitten all snuggled up in the back seat. You can almost hear me purr.

"Thank you, Bill." My mother ups her feminine charms as she places a crumpled bill in his hand.

I dreamily pan the view from my window en route to the airport. Unfortunately, the quiet ride is short-lived and dramatically shifts when we get caught in bumper-to-bumper traffic. I can feel my "fur" begin to bristle. *So much for my calm demeanor!* Before I know it, I have chipped at every single one of my freshly-painted nails. *Ugh!!* Bill notices a flareup with my nerves.

"Miss," my intrepid chauffeur yells over the outside noise. He looks directly at me through the rearview mirror. "Trust me; I know all the secret routes. I'll get you to your plane on time. Just don't you worry your pretty self. You're in good hands with Ole Bill."

Regardless, he appears unflappable, his world an imaginary oasis amid a sea of freeway chaos. Bill is, no doubt, a stalwart driver. The fiftyish-looking father figure handles the vehicle like he is tackling an obstacle course, aggressively darting in and out of traffic. Adding to the challenge, he munches on a huge brownie, the chocolate wafting in the backseat. I can't help but breathe in the delectable smell. A chorus of horns, coupled with his unrepeatable commentary laced with colorful metaphors, follow his every maneuver. Turning the radio to his favorite station, Ole Bill nods his head in time to a barnstorming country tune. Seriously, Heavy Metal would have been more suitable to the action-packed scene unfolding before my very eyes. Regardless, he appears unflappable, totally caught up in an imaginary oasis amid a sea of freeway chaos. *I wonder if Dr. Brennan would consider this a codependent bubble?*

A surreptitious glance at my mother lets me know that she's comfortably ensconced in the plush cab seats. She leans over and pats my knee approvingly.

"Just think, Chase, we'll be at the City of Lights before we know it. I can picture it now—the Eiffel Tower and brooding Frenchmen with their smoldering, cinematic stares. Doesn't that sound romantic? Think of those things instead of traveling over the unforgiving expansive ocean," she chuckles. *Unforgiving ocean ...* I purse my lips together, eyes wide.

"Seriously, this is a piece of cake, Chase. Think of the trips Nana and I took. We were trekking through the African safaris and rappelling down diamond mines. We even hiked to the top of the Mayan ruins well before it became a global Instagram bucket-list trip. Most who do reach the top don't come back down carrying a five-pound, green-and-white-marble chess set as I did. Sometimes I wonder if she was being motherly or trying to kill me."

Although mom inflates the stories each time she brings up their international experiences, I can't dismiss the fact that she may be right. It's a possibility that I may find my one true love in the most passionate city in the world. The last thing I'd want is to get tagged as a "spinster." *Does anyone use that word anymore, or am I stuck in the 1950s?*

"Ladies," Bill announces before he unloads our luggage in front of the Air France entrance, "I think you better put it in high gear. It looks like a madhouse with lines flooding out the terminal door. Good luck and bon voyage!"

Mom hands him more cash. A trail of thank-yous can be heard through the terminal as we battle our way through the crowds to check-in. Several layers of line dividers packed with an undaunting number of passengers, along with their luggage, make it look like everyone—including mothers, uncles, and cousins—decided this would be a good day to go to Paris. *Oh, lucky us!*

The sexy French attendant gives me a devious smirk when she opens my passport and doesn't see any previous destination stamps.

"Your first time flying internationally, *Mademoiselle*?"

"*Oui*," I squeak, embarrassed that I have not accrued globetrotter status like my mother and Nana.

"Not to be ashamed. You'd be surprised at the number of first-timers. They all say they're afraid of flying overseas," the French attendant lightly chuckles like it was jumping over a puddle on the sidewalk. I produce a fake smile.

"Oh, but she's going to love it," my mother interjects, "aren't you, Chase?"

If looks could kill, my glare would have immediately turned my maiden voyage into a solo experience. "Chastity, once you experience Paris, you'll change your name for sure."

163

Growing more annoyed by the second, my widened eyes and plastic smile are enough to make Jack Nicholson's iconic grin for *The Shining* look like child's play. I am beginning to dread my impulsive decision to find true love.

The attendant notices my discomfort. "Just joking! You'll be fine. Enjoy yourself and bon voyage."

I snatch my ticket and head toward the double doors of the lounge for a bit of respite. I can hear my mother's footsteps trailing behind me.

Looking at the wall-to-wall black frames that showcase yellowed, historical photos of the downtown LA skyline, my anger dissipates. I'm fascinated with the architectural designs that were produced during a time of limited resources. My train of thought is interrupted when I hear laughter coming from another corner of the room. I pan the vast space filled with an eclectic mix of multicolored square sofa seats and side tables that are strategically placed by the floor-to-ceiling windows, which overlook the runway and the taxiing jets until I see a cornucopia of hipsters hugging their iPhones.

To the left of the stilyagi (a not-so-nice term I would never say out loud yet my dad has used so frequently that it sticks in my mind), three men recline on their sofas in a grouping close to the bar where a harried yet cheerful bartender fills a line of Bloody Mary glasses. He pours spiked tomato juice and garnishes each one with a stick of celery and a green olive skewered by a toothpick. I stop dead in my tracks as I spot Mr. Handsome, the Frenchman from the hotel; he's helping an older woman open her suitcase. He's wearing a gray sweater with a white button-down shirt peeking out and thick tortoiseshell glasses. His façade looks stately with a beautiful old-world architectural design; if he were a building, he would be Versailles. His giant dimples are making my heart flutter. I briefly smile at him but avert my stare. Flustered, I reach for my phone and send a quick text to my last contact, confident that it's Roxie.

Me: Remember the guy from the hotel? HE'S HERE! It's a sign.

Dr. Brennan: Excuse me, I don't recognize this number. Please, identify yourself so that I can offer you help.

"What?" I say a little louder than expected. On cue, the three guys on the sofas look up from their drinks and give me the "deer in the headlights" look. I turn away embarrassed and swipe my phone to see who texted me. "SHIT!" I can't help but look over my shoulder and see if the guys are still gaping at me; they are.

"How the hell did I get Dr. Brennan?" I'm careful to mutter under my breath. "Something's got to be wrong with this phone. I need to upgrade it when I get home." I text an apology.

Me: I'm soooooooooooo sorry, Dr. Brennan. I thought you were someone else. This is Chastity Morgan.
Dr. Brennan: No problems! How are you doing, Ms. Morgan? Is the anti-anxiety medication helping?
Me: Yes. Yes, it is. I've been taking one tablet every night, sleeping like a baby. Thanks for asking.
Dr. Brennan: That's good to hear! I hope you've re-thought the idea of going to Paris; it's not good timing.
Me: Well, actually, I'm at the airport waiting to board the plane.
Dr. Brennan: Hmm ... it looks like you made up your mind. I hope you're not going alone.
Me: Oh, my mom is with me.
Dr. Brennan: That's good! At least you're not alone. Remember, if your anxiety spikes, you can safely take up to three pills; just avoid alcohol.
Me: Right. I recall reading that in the pharmaceutical paperwork. Thanks for the reminder. Wish me luck!
Dr. Brennan: Yes, indeed. Have a good trip, and don't hesitate to contact me.
Me: Thank you, Dr. Brennan.

"Flight 1415 will be ready to board in a few minutes, starting with passengers needing wheelchair assistance," the intercom blurts. I can tell it's the same sexy French attendant making the announcement. Her message sends shivers down my spine. I can feel perspiration beading up around my hairline. *I'M. NOT. READY.* My mind begins to race in a thousand different directions. I look at my phone to check the time and start counting. *It's been six hours since my morning pill. Maybe it's time to up the dosage.* I fumble around in my purse to find my prescription.

"Chastity." I flinch when I hear my mother's voice. "We should think about getting in line."

"I know," I impatiently spout. "Give me a moment, Mom. I need to take my pills." I begin opening my water bottle.

"Okay. I'll go ahead and save a spot for you."

"Great," I wave her away, tossing all three tablets in my mouth. I'm about to take a slug of water when I remember something the pharmacist told me: *"If you chew the pills, they'll go through your bloodstream faster."* I start chewing instead. They're not the best-tasting medicine, but I've had worse. I take a couple of gulps to wash down the gritty feeling in my mouth, cap my bottle, grab my luggage, and make a beeline to where my mom is standing.

* * *

"Wow, your father really splurged with his miles. This is incredible," my mom loudly announces as we enter the first-class cabin. The segregated quarters are tight but cozy with two seats to each side and extra head padding. Standing behind Mom, I can't see much beyond her, except for the passengers' pillows and blankets getting tossed about as they settle in their seats before positioning the cuddly sleep accessories. Finally, I spot Mom looking down at her ticket then over to her assigned spot. I notice the back of a man's head in 2D. *Oh, shit! Don't tell me somebody took over her seat!* Mom

166

nods to no one in particular and starts heading in a different direction.

"Mom, where the hell are you going? You're supposed to be next to me."

"I think fate might be knocking at your door, honey," she spouts as she spots an opening at 2A.

Now that my mom is out of the way, I see that the mystery person is none other than Mr. Handsome. As much as my heart melts when I look at him, I'm irritated that he's snuggled up in my mom's designated spot. He doesn't notice me glaring at him; he seems to be locked in his world, offering a sweet smile to a child coming down the aisle. I let out an exasperated sigh.

"Excuse me, *Mademoiselle*," the female flight attendant says, tapping me lightly on my shoulder while carrying a tray of drinks.

I reflexively slip into the nearest seats, 2C, to be exact. Feigning Mr. Handsome's presence, I can tell in my peripheral vision that he's looking me over, his sexy dimples amplifying his radiant smile. As soon as the flight attendant plants herself in the next section, I leap out of my seat and dart in the direction of my mom, except the upright transition leaves me disorientated. Before I know what's happening, I'm leaning forward with no idea how to break my fall.

"AAAHHH!" I yell, flailing my arms madly. I'm surprised when a set of arms grabs me by my waist. "Chastity," my mother scolds. I can hear her, but can't quite make out where she's at since the first-class section is spinning. "I hope you're not drunk. You know what Dr. Brennan said—"

"I know—" I shriek, not intending for my response to come out so forcefully, but it did.

"*Mademoiselle*," the female flight attendant says again, this time grabbing my shoulders, "are you drunk? Your eyes do look rather glassy."

"I've got it," my handsome prince interjects. Suddenly, I hear Tchaikovsky's love theme from Romeo and Juliet.

"Did you hear that?" I ask Mr. Handsome.

"Hear what?"

"Oh, never mind." I'm losing it. What the hell is going on?

"Here, let me get you organized. You can have the window seat. You deserve it after all you've been through."

After WHAT I've been through? I don't get it. All I know is that my hero has the dreamiest voice. Fortunately, first class stops spinning as I settle in by the window.

"So, you've had one too many? The trip hasn't even begun."

"Listen, I'm not drunk. I think it's my anti-anxiety medicine, and—"

I feel a slight wave of panic as I recall the massive gas attack that generally accompanies moments like this.

"Oh, God! I forgot to mention my fear of flying produces a rather malodorous side effect," I blurt loud enough that I see my mom turn her head. I can't believe my candidness—so unlike me.

"Would you pass this to my daughter in 2C," Mom says to the man next to her. He reaches out to Mr. Handsome, who graciously accepts my anti-gas medicine, which I didn't think to bring. My mom has a way of jumping in at the right moment.

Embarrassed, I grab the bottle from Mr. Handsome, pop a capsule in my mouth, and bend over to reach my water bottle.

"You know, I haven't stopped thinking about you since we first met at the hotel." He gives me one of his gorgeous smiles— dimples and all. I feel myself melting again. My mom's words come back to me, *"I think fate might be knocking at your door, honey."* And then there are Daphne's words about "someone familiar."

"We haven't properly introduced each other. *Bonjour, je m'appelle Jacques-Pierre,*" he says and then gently kisses my hand nearest him. I swallow hard.

"I'm Chase," I croak, sounding more like a frog than the woman of his dreams. "Chase Morgan."

"Pleased to make your acquaintance, Chase Morgan," as he kisses my hand a second time. My mind flashes to me in my Cinderella white dress, riding along in a royal carriage on my way to Versailles. I step out of the carriage, running up the stairs, late to my wedding.

I snap back into reality at the sound of the flight attendant in our area, shutting the main cabin door. *Oh no, I'm trapped!* A feeling of imminent distress rumbles in my stomach. I clench my muscles and try to hold it—*I'm not going to smell up this airplane.* My chest is a tight knot of fear. My neck muscles contract as if I'm wearing a boa constrictor. I can't breathe. I start to perspire; my heart beats out a staccato rhythm. *Shit!* Another pill has to help. I unlock my seat belt so I can pull open the drawer under my footrest and grab my purse. Madly scrambling the belly of the front section, I locate the bottle and have to apply extra pressure on the safety cap because of my clammy hand. I open the bottle faster than expected and pop the first pill that lands in my palm. *I know Dr. Brennan said a maximum of three, but this is a dire circumstance.* I hurriedly retrace my steps so I can buckle up and wait for the end to come over the unforgiving ocean.

* * *

"Bonjour! This is your captain. At this time, I ask that all passengers fasten your seat belts and turn off all electronic devices. Once airborne, we will be in the air, barring turbulent weather, for approximately eleven hours and forty-nine minutes..."

I catch the "barring turbulent weather" and anticipate more profuse sweating. Instead, I feel my body relaxing, cool as a cucumber and as giddy as a little girl. *These pills work fast.*

"Please," he continues, "give your full attention to Michelle, your flight attendant who will guide you through Air France's safety directions on emergency equipment and exits."

Michelle presses a button, which starts the instructional guidelines; she mimes each point in perfect synchronicity with the recording. In the background, I can hear the plane engines roar and feel the jolt as it backs up and begins to taxi. I should be frantic, but I'm not. For whatever reason, I lose interest in her important demonstration and start jabbering away with Jacques-Pierre.

"So, what do people call you? Jacques-Pierre? Jacques? Pierre? JP? Maybe you have a nickname—"

"You can—" Jacques-Pierre begins, but I immediately cut him off.

"By the way, my full name is Chastity Ann Morgan, but you can call me Chase. And what part of France are you from?"

"I'm not—"

"You know, I'm surprised that I'm going to be flying over the ocean. I'm happy as a clam. It must be the three pills, I mean four, that I took. I might die of an overdose, but that's okay. Is there something wrong with me?" I can't keep my mouth shut. *What the hell?*

"I think you're just—"

The plane jolts on takeoff, and I grab his arm.

"I'm still a virgin did you know that I'm a thirty-year-old virgin the plane could crash right now and I would be a virgin I've never had sex because my Nana always tells me to not give my milk away until I find Mr. Right I thought Grant was my Mr. Right but then he married another guy can you believe that he dumped me for a guy I bought pink furry handcuffs and edible body paint and a gorgeous see-through nightie sheer white with little pink bows I made him dinner with champagne and oysters the two of us ate he did compliment and wonder about my extravagance in creating such an elaborate multi-course feast I excused myself and slipped on the nightie put on the handcuffs and rubbed a bit of the body paint on my chest for dessert I walked into the living room and he stood up from the dining table as if he'd just been shot from a cannon silverware tinkling the oyster plate skidding away and onto the floor would that have worked on you would you have wanted to buy this un-milked cow you know you could be him you could be my Mr. Right you know what I think I think you're Mr. Right you know you're adorable I love your cute dimples when you smile you know what else I think I'm falling for you in fact I think I'm in love with you god I could fuck you right now mind if I kiss you…"

Suddenly feeling like a puppet, with someone manipulating my strings, the unbelievable happens: I unbuckle my seatbelt and wrap my arms around Jacques-Pierre, giving him a full-fledged kiss.

After that, everything goes dark.

* * *

The rumbling sound of breakfast trays jolts me awake from my drug-induced slumber. I open my eyes and notice the down blanket that's covering me, a pillow under my head, the seat reclined. *When did I fall asleep? I don't remember going to bed. How out of it was I?* I blink a few times to adjust to the light. I feel dried drool on my chin. I look up to see Michelle, my trusted flight attendant, passing out hot hand cloths. She hands me one, and I immediately wipe my face. I feel like a zombie with a bad brainy hangover. I glance over at Jacques-Pierre.

"Good morning," he says in the same cheery state. He takes a sip of his coffee while looking through Air France's catalog. *What did I tell him a few hours ago?* I wrack my brain. My memory is fuzzy. I remember getting dizzy, Mom passing me my Gas-X, and Michelle doing her safety demonstration. I remember starting a conversation with Jacques-Pierre, but for the life of me, I have no idea the topic of discussion.

"Here's some coffee and an omelet." Michelle materializes magically beside me.

"Thank you." My tummy begins to rumble. I'm famished. I glance over to Jacques-Pierre, who looks quite content eating fresh fruit and a croissant, a sure sign he intends to avoid further conversation. *Did I say something off-color? Oh, God! What if I blabbered about my sex life, or lack thereof? He's got to be too embarrassed to talk to me.* My mind frantically tries to access what I said before I fell asleep, or more like passed out.

"So..." I begin, "I think I may have passed out while we were talking last night."

"*Oui,*" he responds with a quizzical expression and a smirk on his face. "*Oui,* you did pass out, but not before sharing how much you would love sex and something about a lost engagement? And that *J'ai envie de toi.*"

I TOLD HIM I WANTED TO SLEEP WITH HIM? I can feel the heat all over my face; I must be red as a beet with embarrassment. I see him flip his bangs off his face, nodding.

"Oh, my God! I am sooooooooooo sorry. It was the anti-anxiety pills. I didn't know what I was saying."

"You made *Ulysses* look like a kid's book," Jacques-Pierre replies.

"Excuse me?" I am clearly lost.

"Stream of consciousness. You know, James Joyce?" he counters.

"Oh, the book! I get it! I struggled through that during a college literature course—couldn't understand— Wait! Are you saying I was, like, babbling?"

"Extensively." He gives me another one of his sexy grins. "You even said I had cute dimples." "OOOOOOHHHHHH..." I begin to slink down in my seat. I'm totally wordless.

"It's okay. Really. My cousin did the same thing—"

"Tell you about her sex life?" I genuinely show interest.

"His. He's gay and afraid of flying. On his one-and-only time that he came to the U.S. with me, he wouldn't stop talking for ten minutes straight about all the romances that went awry—including spicy details. He was so loud and obnoxious, I didn't know what to do to shut it up, so I did the most logical thing I could think of: I kissed him."

"NO..." I'm shocked.

"*Oui!* And you know what?"

"He passed out after that," I finish.

"Exactly."

"Jesus!"

"By the way, I'm not French; I'm Swiss," Jacques-Pierre brings up, out of the blue. "I take it from your experience that this is your first trip to Paris?"

"It's my first for everything. First time to Europe; first time to Paris; first time on a double-decker airplane." "You'll be enchanted with the City of Love." Jacque-Pierre's dimples reappear. "What are you planning to see?" He leans nearer. "I noticed your Monet. You must love art."

"My Monet?"

"Your umbrella."

"Oh, yes! *The Picnic*; it's one of my favorites."

"Mine is Monet's *Water Lilies*." His voice is sing-songy as he stares into my eyes.

I'm mesmerized. I feel a new rush, the thrill of being the center of his attention. His imposing aura, in concentrate form, could run engines for years. *Maybe Mom and Daphne were right: fate sat us next to each other for a reason.*

I finish my last bite and retrieve a creased piece of paper from my jacket pocket.

"I have my list right here," I wave it in front of him before reading. "Number one, the Louvre; number two, Notre Dame; number three, the Eiffel Tower; number four, Arc de Triomphe; and number five, Sacre Coeur, but that's after I finish sitting through the conference lectures." I take a long sip of my coffee.

"No shopping? Not even for handcuffs?" he says.

I choke, spitting coffee everywhere.

"I uh, um…" my mouth goes wide. "Please don't tell me that I said something about that?"

"Pink furry handcuffs, to be exact. Correct?" He winks. "To seduce your ex-fiancé?"

We look at each other and burst out laughing.

"Seriously, no shopping? Isn't that what all American women love to do?"

"Well, I guess I'm not your typical American woman. My version of shopping is discovering the architectural marvels first hand since I'm working on my PhD in structural and earthquake engineering."

"An engineer? *Vraiment?*" He leans in closer, mouth agape. "It is very odd for a woman to be an engineer? Is it not?"

Odd? I wouldn't call myself strange. He's munching away on a piece of his croissant, slathered with French jam. Sunlight peeks through the side windows.

"Well, maybe you're looking at it according to percentages. Even though there has been a slow uptick of women engineers over the years, about eighty percent are males. For me, engineering is my passion. Did you know that high-rise buildings are designed to sway in the wind, sometimes even as much as two feet?"

Jacques-Pierre looks genuinely surprised, "Ah, I'm in the same field, so to speak. I do roofing." he enthusiastically mentions.

Did he just say roofing? Like Gunnar, the German guy who camped out at my house for two months, working in slow motion, stripping off his shirt fifteen seconds after he arrived? I suppress a chuckle at the vivid image of Gunnar's washboard abs. Roxie found every excuse in the book to sit around our house that summer. We couldn't take our eyes off him, and he knew it. He teased us, calling us jailbait. Roxie threatened to hose Gunnar simply to watch water drip down his stomach.

I glance surreptitiously at Jacques-Pierre's hands. *Smooth, manicured nails, minimal cuticles ... in much more excellent shape than mine.*

"You know, even though I run an international roofing company," Jacques-Pierre volunteers, "I went to business school. My grandfather started the company in 1908. Today, the family business has grown into one of the biggest and most profitable in the world, with over thirty facilities. We employ over 3,000 people in North and South America, Canada, and Europe. I even have a plant in Egypt."

I listen as he talks on and on about his business and projects. His energy is infectious, and I want to curl up in his arms and listen to him for hours. I wonder if he has abs like Gunnar?

"I live on a plane more often than not. It gets a bit lonely, but ... I love what I do," he says, shrugging. "I spent my childhood in the mountains of Lausanne—summers by the lake, hiking in the mountains, and winters skiing. I was even a ski instructor. A special one." He takes off his glasses, rubbing around his deep-set eyes.

"What makes a ski instructor a special one? Your good looks and charm?" I can't help but laugh.

"I was kind of..." He pauses. I see him trying to order his words. "How do you say in English, I offered special services." He accompanies his air quotes with a wink. "An ... escort."

I screw up my face, sure that I've heard him correctly, but not willing to acknowledge it.

"You look like I just spoke to you in Mandarin," he chuckles. "I'm not particularly proud of what I did back then, but it did satisfy my raging hormones."

He must have noticed me turning bright red. He winks again and pats my hand gently.

Over the intercom, the captain makes an announcement, "*Nous allons atterier bientôt.* Please, tighten your seat belts."

"Do you need to squeeze my hand again?" Jacques-Pierre says, "I really don't mind." He smiles sweetly and leans forward, resting his elbow on the armrest, tightly against mine. I close my eyes, wishing I'd never taken those little pills. *Which is worse? My panic attack or total humiliation?*

Before I can answer my private thoughts, the jet touches down. *Thank God!*

"*Bienvenue à Paris,*" the captain announces.

Paris! I want to jump up and down and scream, but instead, I sit quietly in my seat, pretending to be the quintessential calm, urbane traveler. At least the drugs helped me weather the long flight. I stifle a yawn. Even though the effects of the drugs are waning, I'm a bit concerned about walking straight. Jacques-Pierre brushes his hair out of his eyes, fidgeting. "I'll be at the Hotel Comtesse for lunch today at 12:30 p.m. You and your mother should book a table—I'd love to continue our conversation."

"That sounds lovely."

He smiles, "I leave on the red-eye tonight for Lausanne, but there's an art exhibit I sponsored if you and your mother would like to join me for an evening cocktail at the Musée—"

"Honey, we made it," my mother says, cutting off Jacques-Pierre. "You forgot your scarf." She ties it loosely around my neck. "See? An uneventful flight." She peers past me to Jacques-Pierre. "And I must say that your seat companion is quite handsome. Wouldn't you agree?"

An uneventful flight? I want to ask her if she was on the same plane, but I back down. I stand, wobbling, feeling jumbled within a huge washing machine.

"How are we going to tour with you in this state?" My mother gives me a worried look.

"Mom, give me an hour nap, and I'll be good to go." I turn to say goodbye to Jacques-Pierre before disembarking, but he is gone.

"Oh." I'm visibly shocked.

"Oh, what, honey?"

"Never mind," I say, my shoulders suddenly slumping. I pull my suitcase out of the cabin door.

He didn't wait for me to say goodbye. My heart feels like it's going to break.

17

"Hello, Paris!" I whisper into the taxi window, selfishly basking in my breathtaking commentary and leaving out my well-traveled mother, lost in another world. It's Sunday, and the streets are vacant since it's too early in the morning for anyone to be up, except church-goers. The cab driver maneuvers the vehicle through the ancient byways like a pro. He's the silent type, a blessing to my haze-filled brain. The glow of golden lights suddenly enraptures me as he drives right up the Champs-Elysees and through the center of the Arc de Triomphe.

"Oh honey, wasn't I right? Isn't Paris magical?" My mother interrupts my reverie.

"Yep, magical," I robotically reply. Reality hits me when I hear my voice and acknowledge that I'm still half asleep, my body in a full-on slumber from the drugs. Our driver pulls up in front of our brightly-lit hotel, the outdoor lighting attractively captures the 19th-century Beaux-Arts architecture. I look up at it in awe.

A bellman arriving to gather our bags catches me off guard. He speaks to us in perfect English. I give him a look of surprise as he transports them through the hotel entrance. The hotel is known for its elegant interior design replete with elaborate floral arrangements. Tall glass vases, which are dwarfed by even taller ones, are each filled with brilliant gem-like pebbles, long stalks, and the most exquisite flowers. We dodge a group of photo-snapping German tourists, armed with not one but two cameras on each shoulder, gleefully babble away in their native tongue.

"*Bonjour, Madames. Bienvenue Marie Antoinette's Quatre Hotel,*" says a greeter in the lobby who is helping to point visitors to the front desk. The air inside the entryway is near balmy; I have to suppress the urge to peel off layers of clothing like an instant replay of Jaydon and our ping pong match. I can't help but wonder the purpose behind this blast of heat. *Why would a hotel want their guests to endure a sauna? It makes no sense. Maybe the floral arrangements need a greenhouse setting.*

"This hotel is incredible! I still can't believe Nana is paying for all of this. Whatever you said to her, maybe you should say it more often; I could travel like this all the time," my mother says, wide-eyed and scanning the lobby.

"Mom, why don't you check-in. I'll meet you in our room in a few. I'm going to register for the conference." My mother dutifully nods, busying herself at the front desk. I follow the signs for the conference check-in.

I slow my pace as I spot the desk. Standing there a Frenchman in his early 40s, dressed to the nines in a navy pinstripe suit with dark brown hair combed and set in place, his cheekbones defining his chiseled features. My thoughts immediately shift in a naughty direction. *Ooooh, I'd love to get my hands on him, undressing him piece by piece, kissing his luscious, pouty lips. If he were a structure, he would be like the one we just saw, the Arc de Triomphe, stiff but stately and exquisite, just like his hard p—*

"*Bonjour, Mademoiselle,*" his voice snaps me back to the present.

"*Bonjour, Monsieur.*" I reach for the counter to steady myself, feeling light-headed either from my wild fantasy or the balmy heat. *God, maybe this is what menopausal women have to put up with!*

"*Mademoiselle,* are you okay?"

I fumble with the translation in my head: *Je suis chaude;* I am hot, or *j'ai chaude;* I have hot. I pause for a second. "*Non, je suis chaude.*"

"Oh," he abruptly stands up straighter, rifling through papers.

"Is the air conditioner broken?" I fan myself with a conference brochure.

"Whatever do you mean?" His eyebrows, shooting toward the ceiling.

"Je suis très, très, chaude."

"Ugh... Can't you at least pretend to be an American who speaks French properly?"

I hear the familiar voice and slowly turn to see ASSon shaking her head, tilting it back a little as she releases a little laugh.

Pretending to mouth a whisper, ASSon leans next to the mysterious gentlemen, "She meant to say *j'ai chaude*, I am hot, not, I am horny."

I slap my hand across my mouth. "I didn't say that," I muffle behind my tightly cupped hand. Heat abruptly rises in my cheeks.

"*Oui,* you most certainly did," cackling, followed by a sardonic laugh. "Hi, I'm Alison Liu," she states to the man, "I'm here to check-in for the conference, and this is Chastity Morgan, who's also here for the conference."

"Ah, yes, Darlene Feldman's students. I am Dr. Milton." He stares into my eyes, reaching for my hand, gently squeezing it in his soft palm. I look over at ASSon, who looks shocked and mortified.

"Oh. My. God," ASSon sucks up to Dr. Milton. "I am so sorry, professor. I had no idea ... I didn't mean to embarrass..."

He glares at ASSon before letting go of my hand and reaching down to retrieve two hefty packets. "You girls have a little time to set your bags in your room before our first lecture begins. Everything is outlined," he says as he hands one to each of us, "and everything is mandatory. Dinner tonight is optional. It's at the Musée Rodin, and I highly recommend going."

ASSon morphs from mortification to downright stupid as she opens and closes her mouth rapidly like a fish out of the water while watching Professor Milton disappear into an elevator. I'm too caught up in my thoughts to throw her an offensive line or two. *How can this guy be Professor Feldman's supposed friend? The guy is drop-dead gorgeous, like supermodel gorgeous, and he certainly is not the "boring engineering, slide ruler, pocket protector" type of guy I was expecting. All I have to say is that this will be one helluva conference!*

* * *

I wait until everyone empties from the lobby. I welcome the momentary silence and begin flipping through the program while contemplating events before the first lecture. *Lunch is at 1:30 pm. Check. Okay, I can squeeze in seeing Jacques-Pierre for lunch at 12:30 pm and still make it back in time for the mandatory meal. Double-check.*

My phone buzzes, I see my mom sent me a text:

Mom: We are in room 214.

I locate the tiny lift that's already crammed with people clad with conference badges. ASSon unabashedly waves me down, annoying impatience visibly written all over her face.

"I don't know why she let you come," she spouts loud enough that everyone can hear. Under the circumstances, it's near impossible to ignore her, but I do my best and hope she gets lost in her phone. She appears to be madly texting away.

"Nonetheless, you're here," she says, not missing a beat, "and I guarantee you'll find a way to mess things up, and when you do, I'll be there to document everything." She looks up from her phone and gives me a sinister smile—the lift pings. I squeeze myself off to the side, allowing the glorified box to vomit its contents into a long corridor lined with pale blue carpet, landscaped photos of Paris hanging on the walls, and wingback chairs placed between every other door.

"See ya," ASSon announces to no one in particular as she takes out her key and heads toward her room. Unlocking it, she quickly enters and shuts it with a pronounced slam. I can't help but flinch. I catch the lift doors from closing and make my exit, heading slightly in the other direction of the hallway. Unfortunately, my room is diagonal from ASSon's.

I give a little knock, and my mom lets me in. "Hi, mom. I need a nap. As luck would have it the queen of mean—ASSon— is here," I say in one breath as I kick off my shoes, drag the comforter—duvet and all—from the bed designated for me, and plop myself on the puffy sofa in the little living room. I begin fluffing one of the pillows.

"I was just about to text you that I was going down... What did you say? Ass who?" my mom shouts as she's about to close the bedroom door.

"Later. I'll tell you later," I say, wiggling my feet under the puffy duvet. I quickly scan our room before I close my eyes. The exquisite chic Art Deco design, complete with a subtle floral wallpaper pattern, and set to a sky-blue backdrop, tastefully accents the heavy floor-to-ceiling blue drapes.

Bzzzzz...

I feel the cushions vibrating. Opening an eye, I see Roxie's picture light up my semi-silenced phone. "Hey, you! You made it to Paris!" Roxie shouts soon after entering my password. Her giant grin fills the FaceTime screen. She has multiple ponytails sticking out of her head with lots of pink ribbons.

"What's with the hairdo?" I laugh.

"You don't like it? I'm the stylist. Wait until you see Brent." Daphne giggles, her face off to one side. The screen wiggles before Brent shows up with a curly-haired blonde wig sitting atop his head.

"Don't you even think about commenting," Brent shouts, trying to cover his new makeover with his hands.

I can't help but burst into a fit of giggles.

"I don't think you will have much luck with the ladies sporting that look. Hey, wait a minute! What time is it over there?"

"It's one-thirty in the morning," Daphne happily announces. "We're playing beauty salon."

"What in heaven's name are you..."

"We're babysitting," Brent interjects.

"Maria got called into work," Roxie adds.

"She had an emergency C-section," Daphne finishes.

Momentary silence.

"Brent came over to help me," Roxie starts in, "with my first bridal shower coming up next month when Maria called asking if I could spend the night after I got Daphne to bed. She wasn't sure what time she'd be coming back."

"Wait! And Brent..."

"He's got a hot date." Daphne smiles into the phone. "So, he can't sleep over."

"A hot date," I repeat, a smirk on my face. "Looking like that?" I burst into a fit of giggles again. "What kind of date starts at one-thirty in the morning? Boo—Tee—"

"That's enough out of you. And besides, no matter what, I will always be the Master Swordsman! So," Brent conveniently changes the subject before I'm given a chance to say another word. "Did you find a hot Frenchman yet?"

"Possibly."

"Possibly?" Roxie juts in, jamming her nose into the screen. "Oooh, it's the guy on the plane, isn't it? Or the deskman? Did you get their numbers? They're both so cute. Super dreamy. You're opening yourself up, Chase. Look, I'm so happy that I put one of your kissy Amoremoji stickers on each hand." Daphne shows the tops of her hands. *The guy on the plane? Deskman? This kid knows way too much.*

"ROXIE!!! You're supposed to hide the stickers!"

"I had some extras with me. We're using them as payment to the beautician."

"I gotta go. I need a nap before the conference takes off. So good to see you guys. Even you, Daphne."

Daphne gives me the biggest grin. "Happy hunting. I do love a good scavenger hunt."

"Hunting? Huh? What are you talking about now?"

"Have fun, ki— Oops," he catches himself. "We'll hold down the fort while you're gone," Brent offers without commenting on his faux pas.

"And remember to take lots of pictures, especially of your new romantic interest," Roxie adds.

"You guys are too much. Love you! Hunting? You're a funny kid, Daphne."

I click off, place the phone onto the coffee table, and rollover again. Sleep embraces me within seconds.

* * *

"Ooooooooooooooh... God! Yesss... Kiss me, baby! Kiss me now!"

Jacques-Pierre and I are going at it. He has me at the edge of the bed. I'm sitting on his lap, his hands cupping my derrière, lifting me as he kisses me deeply this time.

"More, more," I yell.

Boom, boom...

"What the hell?"

Boom, boom...

"That's how the French do it, my love," Jacques-Pierre replies sweetly, whispering in my ear, before kissing me again.

Boom, boom ...

I bolt upright, startled.

Boom, boom...

"Knock it off, would you? What is it, an emergency?" I grumble, dragging myself to the door. I look through the peephole: it's ASSon. "Why am I not surprised?" I mumble under my breath. I open the door a crack.

"You have ten minutes—What the hell happened to you?" ASSon rattles off, looking at my disheveled state.

"I was napping before the first session," I reply flatly.

"Well, don't make us both look stupid by being late," she yells back as she heads for the lift.

"Right. Thanks, as always!" I add once the lift doors close. "She's already driving me crazy, and the conference hasn't even begun," I say to the empty corridor. "What a dream killer, too."

I bustle around the living room and the bathroom, getting ready. I poke my head into the other bedroom. My mom's mouth is wide open, snoring loudly. I decide to write her a quick note that I'm heading out and will see her for lunch. Grabbing my purse, I dash for the lift and press the button for the lobby.

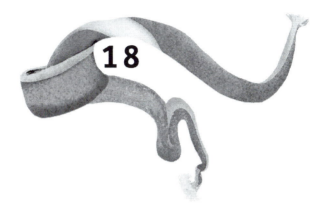

18

The lift pings, letting me out near the conference welcome area.

"Bonjour, Mademoiselle."

I jump, startled. *"Bonjour, Mon—"* I stop myself mid-sentence, swallowing hard. It's the sexy Frenchman, Dr. Milton. "You again." *Why does my ability to speak vanish around this guy? He's magnetic. That's why.*

"*Oui*, yes! It's me again. How delightful! *Mademoiselle* Chastity, are you enjoying your visit to Paris so far?" He flashes me the biggest smile.

"Oui, j'ai bien joui," I say, trying to be polite.

He checks me out with little subtlety. "Me, too. I had one last night." I look back at him, confused. He breaks out in laughter.

Laugher continues to my right. It's ASSon. *"Oui, j'ai bien joui?"*

My eyes widen with horror.

"Um," I whisper to the gorgeous French professor, "didn't I just say, 'yes, I'm enjoying this trip?' Why is she mocking me?"

He looks at me, "No, *Mademoiselle*. You said that you had an orgasm."

My phone drops from my hand, banging on the marble floor. I'm mortified. I scramble to pick it up. I'm nearly vertical when ASSon grabs my arm and begins dragging me toward the corridor that leads to the conference doors.

"Funny that Darlene never mentioned her students had such a keen sense of humor," Dr. Milton chuckles.

"Ha, ha..." ASSon utters a fake laugh in return. "Bye, professor. See you at lunch."

I wait until we're out of earshot before I express my genuine gratitude. "Thanks for getting me out of a pickle."

"Maybe you could just stop talking before you get us kicked out with all of your sexual innuendos."

"You're absolutely right," I humbly concur. "I'm really sorry. The week-long French immersion class didn't go into verb conjugation or direct translation. I guess I didn't realize—"

"Just think next time, okay?" She plops me in a seat near the back before catching a spot in the conference's front room. I feel so low that I'm delighted to be lost in the backdrop. I muster whatever remaining dignity I have and get my pad and pen ready for note-taking.

* * *

Twenty minutes pass before I start to shake my head, trying to fathom why the speaker is in rambling mode. *Good heavens! His PowerPoint presentation says it all. He could have finished ten minutes ago.* Checking the time, I see that I've got fifteen minutes. I drown out the speaker's droning; my thoughts suddenly fixated on meeting up with Jacques-Pierre for lunch. With the lights dimmed, and all eyes focused on the stage, I figure this is my chance to escape. Bending down, I duck out the back door.

"Sneaking out, are we?" Dr. Milton winks as the doors let in a blast of hallway lighting.

"No, um ... I was just getting some fresh air."

"Uh-huh. You look like a lady on a mission. I won't tell. I'm very good at keeping a secret." He smiles, gently resting his hand on my forearm.

"Ha, ha! Good one, Dr. Milton." I'm gratefully relieved when a conference member approaches him, monopolizing the professor's attention.

I send my mom a quick text that I'm going to hail a cab, so she needs to get downstairs ASAP. It's not until I enter the main lobby that I notice the rain. *Great! And I left my umbrella in the room, not taking Daphne's advice!* I see a taxi parked just outside the entrance and head for it. *"Excusez-moi"*

"Bonjour, Mademoiselle." The driver rolls down the passenger side so I can talk to him. *"Bonjour. Pouvez-vous me prendre à l'hôtel Contesse?"* I ask sweetly, crossing my fingers behind my back in hopes that I didn't say something obscene.

"No, Mademoiselle. Les rues sont bloquées là-bas à cause des émeutes."

I give him a confused look. "Did I hear him correctly? Did he just tell me that the streets are blocked because of riots?" I speak louder than expected. "What the hell would they be rioting about anyway, especially in the rain?"

"Oui. You heard me correctly, *Mademoiselle.* I believe it is about the recent tax hike, and weather doesn't stop the French, especially when we're passionate about something.*"*

I suddenly feel like an idiot. Here I am, battling with French translation when all the while, I could have carried this conversation in my native tongue. And why? What's worse is that my emotions seem out of control, rolling over from embarrassment to worry in a matter of ... seconds. "But you don't understand. I'm supposed to meet someone at 12:30 for lunch. Isn't there any other roads you can take to get me there?" What the hell has come over me?

"I'm sorry, *Mademoiselle.* I can get you there, but you need to expect heavy delays."

"Oh, no! Now, what am I going to do?"

The little Chase Angel on my shoulder adds: "What do you mean 'what am I going to do?'. Go inside, of course."

Sirens wail in the distance. It's an eerie tone. The hairs on my neck stand up.

"I am sorry, *Mademoiselle,*" the driver continues like sirens blaring are an everyday occurrence in Paris. "Can I take you somewhere else?"

"No, no. Thank you."

"Then I suggest you go inside, *Mademoiselle,* before you get soaked."

I slowly turn back to the hotel. In a daze, I make my way through the front doors and will myself to take the lift to my room.

What the hell is wrong with me?

The lift doors open, and Mom is standing there, looking spry and ready for adventure.

"Chase, darling," My mom for a moment sounds just like Eva Gabor as I step out of the lift. "I thought you'd be outside waiting for me in the cab, and why are you all wet?"

"We're not going."

"We're not going? Why?"

"The driver said they blocked the streets near Hotel Contesse because of rioting."

"Rioting?"

"You heard me correctly. Taxes." I grab her arm and wheel her around.

"Taxes? The people are rioting about taxes, and in the rain, no less?"

"Yes."

"Well, then let them protest. We can find something else—"

"No, there's nothing else to do. We were supposed to meet up with Jacques-Pierre, and now that's not going to happen. How am I going to connect with him again, Mom?"

"Oh, darling, don't—"

I can't wait for her answer. I promptly march down the long corridor back to our room. Robotically, I unlock the door, slam it shut, drop my things on the cushiony carpet, and just about ripe my wet jacket off before plopping myself on the bed. I immediately begin bawling.

"What is wrong with me," I mumble into the fluffy duvet. "Why am I so emotional over a lunch date with a man I barely know? Oh, God, not now..." I lift my head and let out a full-forced yell realizing that I'd been so focused on the trip that I lost track of my cycle.

"Oh, Chase—" My mom looks like she's about to cry, too, when she unlocks the room door and sees mascara running down my face.

"Why me? This is NOT the time to get my period!"

Grabbing my phone, I swipe over to the calendar app and start counting.

"I can't believe it! I just can't believe it!" I sob again.

"Chase! Honey, these things happen." She dutifully wraps an arm around my shoulder as my phone buzzes:

```
Alison: Where are you?
```

"Not now, ASSon!" I yell into my phone. It buzzes a second time:

```
Alison: Seriously, where are you?
Me: If you really must know, I'm not feeling
well; it's that time of the month. I'm in my
room again.
Alison: I'll believe it when I see it. I'll
come up and see for myself as soon as lunch is
over.
```

"Well, just peachy!" I yell at the top of my lungs.

"Chase," my mom calmly pats my leg, "honey, let me get you something to calm you down."

"I'll be fine, Mom. It's just my usual emotional crisis!" I mumble into my phone again. "She will be up here in five minutes. CRAP! CRAP! DOUBLE CRAP!!"

I scurry into the bathroom and wipe off the excess makeup, strip down to my undies, throw on a robe, whip a towel around my drenched hair, and hop into bed just as I hear a light knock. "Coming." I use my garbled voice for cover.

"Holy cow! You weren't lying. You look terrible!" ASSon's always timely with her unsolicited opinion. "Oh, hi, you must

189

be Mrs. Morgan," she plasters on a fake smile as she shakes my mother's hand. "We met briefly in high school at a bake sale. You make the most delicious peanut butter M&M cookies." My mother smiles, waving her inside our room.

"Thanks for the encouraging words, Alison."

"Hey," she says, overlooking my sarcasm, "I have an extra supply of Midol if you need some."

My jaw drops momentarily. I'm genuinely taken aback by her shift to thoughtfulness.

"Well ... actually ... I could use a few-day supply. I was so busy getting ready for the trip that I overlooked this little tidbit."

"That's very sweet of you, Alison. I'm going to pop down to the gift shop and see if they have any new novels and see if they have any feminine products. Be back soon, honey," my mom says.

"Hey, what are friends for..." Alison pipes up before my mother disappears out the door.

Did she just call me a friend?

"I have the worst periods. My cramps are so bad that I'm usually in bed for two days straight each month. No joke! But we are at the conference that could define our careers. You've got to pull it together and get the HELL OUT OF BED!"

"What?" I snap, she's done another one-eighty.

We're staring at each other, like two opponents ready for a boxing match.

"Say, listen," she breaks up the awkwardness, "Fine. Lie down before the 1:30 talk. I'll buzz you ten minutes before to give you time to dress? Dr. Feldman's judging both of us," she says, letting out a long, exasperated sigh, "And you're not helping me one bit."

"Okay, then. I'll set my phone timer. Thanks."

"Okay," she hands me a full bottle of water. "See you later. Please pull it together; this conference reflects on both our futures."

"I will." *So that's why she's being semi-nice. She's worried about her future.* I quietly close the door before dashing into the bathroom to pop two tablets. Setting my timer for half an hour,

190

I plop back down on the luxurious bed. Slumber hits me quicker than I think.

* * *

"How does this feel?" Jacques-Pierre gently nibbles on my neck.

"Oh. My. GOD! I didn't know your little kisses could excite me so much. Keep ... going... Yes ... don't ... stop..." I give out a scream.

"That's it, *ma cherie.* I want to get you so hot you can't stand—" A light chime of a lullaby interrupts the moment.

"Don't stop," I persist.

"Oh, but we have to. Times up. I hope you enjoyed your session. Please don't forget to make an appointment with my receptionist before you leave."

My session? I look over at the hot guy who is no longer Jacques- Pierre, but Dr. Brennan. "Chastity, these sexual distractions will only repress the pain for so long. We need to talk about what happened that day."

"YIKES!" I yell out ... again and abruptly sit up. "Ooh, my head." It takes a few seconds before the room stops spinning, the lullaby still chiming in the background. I grab my phone and turn off the alarm. There's a pack of tampons sitting next to the lamp.

"Wow! What a dream! Where did *that* come from?" I mumble while hastily putting myself back together for the next session and grabbing the needed supplies.

"Mom, thank you," I knock lightly on her door before sticking my head inside. She's flat on her back, again, mouth open and gently snoring. I scribble another note to let her know that I'm feeling better and that I'm heading to the conference room.

* * *

I peek through the conference window. The room lights are dimmed. The only light emitting is from the PowerPoint projection. I carefully slide in and begin tiptoeing toward a back seat when Dr. Milton taps my shoulder.

"So sorry I'm late," I whisper, looking sheepishly at the professor, "the French food is a bit rich for me. My tummy wouldn't cooperate."

"You're right on time. I just sent Darlene an email telling her how lovely you two are." He smiles. I notice movement behind Dr. Milton and spot ASSon sidling up to him.

"Oh, there you are, Chase. You're looking better. I hope the meds helped."

"The meds?" Dr. Milton looks confused.

"Girl stuff, professor," ASSon adds.

"Ah, yes. So..." he eyes us both, "Are you excited for the next lecturer?"

"I am," ASSon volunteers, speaking in her usual haughty voice. "His roofs are unreal. His latest birdcage design and use of steel is a masterpiece. He uses materials that won't deteriorate with climate change. Jacques-Pierre's roofing company dominates the market—"

"Jacques-Pierre?" I blurt.

"Jacques-Pierre Beaumont, to be exact," Dr. Milton interjects.

"Our next speaker..." the emcee's voice drowns out the audience's chatter. "...needs no introduction. A man with international fame, please put your hands together for Jacques-Pierre Beaumont."

The crowd immediately goes in an uproar and provides him with a standing ovation as he walks over to the podium. I can't even clap; I'm too stunned. *He never told me his last name, but who has two first names and owns a roofing company?* I grab a glass of water from the waiter's tray as he walks through the seating sections and promptly gulp it down. My mind is a ball of confusion. *What is HE doing here, anyway? And how the heck did he get back here in time with all the rioting going on?*

Dr. Milton pulls up two chairs for ASSon and me as the cheers die down, and everyone returns to their seats.

There at the front of the stage stands my seatmate. *I am SOOOOO HAPPY that my alarm went off on time.* "Thank you, Jesus!" I suddenly blurt.

A couple of "amens" come from the other side of the room. My embarrassment quickly turns into a broad smile when I realize the apparent appropriateness of my acclamation, especially when Jacques-Pierre winks at me, communicating his lustful thoughts from across the room. I see some in the audience turning around in their attempt to spot his alluring connection but to no avail. Donning a pale grey suit with a crisp white shirt, Jacques-Pierre paces around the stage as he talks, nervously brushing his hair out of his eyes every few sentences. He commands the room, all eyes on him, drinking in every word. At the end of his thirty-minute lecture, he says thank you, makes eye contact with me again, and slips out the side entrance.

I bolt from my seat towards the lobby. My eyes scan the crowd, and I don't see Jacques-Pierre anywhere.

"Is there something you want to tell me?" Dr. Milton comes up behind me, laying his hand on my shoulder, startling me.

"No, why do you ask?" I have my phone out, texting my mom that the session ended, and that she needs to get down to the lobby now.

"I wasn't born yesterday. Are you looking for Mr. Beaumont?"

"Fine. Yes," I say, frustrated because I am. "Long story short, he was my seatmate on the flight here. I stood him up for lunch, and I'd like to make it up to him, but now he's not around."

"May I offer a piece of advice?"

"Sure."

"I think you'd like to go to the *Musée d'Orsay*. And when you're there, make sure and ask for the *Exhibit of L'homme nu dans l'art de 1800 a nos jours*. I'm sure you'll find it ... intriguing."

"*Exhibit of L'homme...* So that's where Mr. Beaumont is heading?"

"Just ask for *L'homme*. Someone at the museum will point you in the right direction."

That doesn't sound correct. "Are you sure it's *Musée d'Orsay*?" I say. "Isn't *L'homme*: the man? He specifically said he loved the water lilies and that he was going to an art exhibit there. That means Monet and Monet's paintings are housed in L'Orangerie. I googled it."

I notice ASSon sidling up to the professor, again. *Dear God! Must she do that?*

"What are you two talking about?"

"I was just telling Chastity that I want to share a cab with you two for dinner tonight. Plus, I have some extra paperwork that I think Professor Feldman would love to see. Have fun, Chastity." With no warning, he scoops Alison's arm and leads her away, glancing over his shoulder to give me a little wink.

* * *

Twenty minutes later, Mom and I collapse our hotel umbrellas and walk through the doors of the Musée d'Orsay and follow the signs to *L'Homme*. There's a short queue of ladies waiting to enter the first of the exhibit's four rooms.

"Now remember, if you spot Jacques-Pierre, tell me, and I'll go say hello. We have to find him, Mom. I think he's the one."

"The ONE?" my mother laughs. "That's a bit extreme. First, you hate men and won't get off the couch, and now you think some random Frenchman is the ONE? You are a hopeless romantic that watches way too many Hallmark movies."

"He's Swiss, Mom, and no, I'm not."

We step inside the first room, and I grab hold of Mom's arm.

"OH. MY. GOD!" I say, bursting out laughing. My eyes feel like they are going to explode. All around us, every image on the wall is ... a penis. Penis after penis and more penises promised in the next three rooms, a colorful penis-fest—skinny, bent, curved, soft, minuscule, gigantic, erect; It's a Penis-O-Rama, a universe of penises.

My FaceTime rings loudly. I see Roxie's face. "Shit!" I say much louder than necessary. I look away from my phone a moment to observe that I am the center of attention. "Sorry!" I weakly spit out. I madly rummage in my purse to locate my earbuds.

"Hey, you." Roxie's eyes suddenly widen, and her jaw drops, her focus not on me, but what's directly behind me in gargantuan proportion. "OH. MY. GOD! Are you in a sex museum?"

"No, I am not in a sex—" I stop dead, noticing all eyes are on me, again. "No," I quip, "but I have to say that I feel like Dorothy in Oz on her first fateful adventure—if the Scarecrow, Tin Man, and Lion had shown her their appendages."

"Ha, ha, good one." Roxie bursting into a fit of giggles is so contagious that I cup my hand hard over my mouth.

"Rox, I'm literally surrounded by serious art connoisseurs," I whisper into the phone. "I can't believe they're able to walk through this exhibit without cracking a smile. You know the adage 'when in Rome'? I can't tell you how many times I've had to take deep breaths going from one form of media to the next. There are penises all over the place—some rendered in oil, some sketched in pencil. They're even sculpted in bronze, and the list goes on and on. It's incredible."

"Cover your eyes!" Roxie laughs, shielding Daphne's eyes.

I hear giggles in the background.

"Is that Daphne? Rox, she shouldn't be seeing—"

"I need a face with an open mouth Amoremoji sticker, Aunt Roxie!" Daphne interjects.

Aunt Roxie? When did that happen?

"The whole Amoremoji thing is for Chase, not you silly," Roxie's response to Daphne.

My mother tugs my arm, gamely pulling me to the next canvas, I turn my phone towards the large oil painting in Renaissance style of a curly bewigged reclining man. He is nude and he has a hooded penis that is larger than him, and his member is held by a hammock that is hooked to the ceiling. I glance at mom. She's in an open-eyed coma.

"Mom," I hiss, trying to get her attention, snapping her out of her instant shock. "Mom." She blinks.

"Kid, whoa, where the hell are you?" Brent says, his face pressed against the phone. "I think that's a wee bit advanced for you."

"Hey, KID," I sarcastically respond, "I thought you were going on a date!" I laugh.

"Look at this one." I pull my mom and point my phone toward the photograph of three famous French soccer players wearing nothing but shoes. "Can you believe this? It reminds me of when Roxie took me to a sex shop," I whisper, stepping closer to the photograph.

"*Excusez-moi, Mademoiselle,*" says the guard, motioning for me to take a step back.

I shrug. "But I can't examine the photograph from this distance." He crosses his arms, moving between me and the picture. I retract and move on to the next piece.

"You went to a sex shop?" My mother says a little too loudly. "Roxie, you took Chase to a sex shop?" My mother grabs the phone from my hands, laughing, saying hi to the three back at home. Their mouths are moving, but she can't hear them, which is fine with her as she waves "goodbye" and hands the phone back to me.

"Roxie dragged me in to buy pink furry handcuffs, Mom," leaning close to her ear so I can whisper. "What could I do? Her persistence wore me down. The first thing we saw was the section of rabbits, the new ultra-perfect-posh dildo—that's what the bedazzled sign said. It also said, 'Turn me on!' So, of course, I couldn't help but turn it on. Vibrating like crazy with a mind of its own, it knocked over the entire display. I fumbled with the off switch, but the not-so-little bugger wouldn't cooperate. I had a runaway penis on my hands."

"*Shush,*" I hear the woman behind me, a set of curious and startled eyes focusing on me. I'm exasperated at this point.

"Well, it did," I boldly say to my audience.

"I never," the vexed woman says before huffing and stomping away to the exit.

"The penises sure didn't help lighten her mood one bit," I say to the remaining crowd as I pop a piece of gum in my mouth before returning to my phone. "Some people don't have a sense of humor." A few chuckles erupt, both from the onlookers and the phone.

"Did you finally get his number?" Daphne randomly asks.

"How did you know about Jacques-Pierre, Daphne? And why in the world are you all still up? The sun should be rising soon."

She casts her eyes down, passing the phone to Roxie. "I keep trying to tell you—knowing who or how or when won't help you. It's about the journey that gets you there." The little girl says in the background.

"And the bad news isn't always bad news. My mama says it's about how we recover that defines us." Daphne has her face pressed up against the phone again. "Love you. See you when you get back."

"Bad news? Are you telling me I won't find him after all?" A burly guard is staring at me, stepping in closer. "If I don't hang up now, my phone will get confiscated. We'll continue this conversation later. Bye." I pop the earbuds and stash the whole phone getup in my purse as we silently follow the crowd out of the last gallery.

"Do you think Jacques-Pierre's name is on one of the paintings? Maybe he loaned one to the museum, and that's what he meant by sponsoring the exhibit. Let me run back in and check the plaques. Maybe he put down his contact information."

"No." She grabs my arm. "You can't go back in there. The guard might have you arrested."

"Okay then, let's stop to regroup. You lived in Paris, Mom. What museum should we try next?" I follow her towards the exit.

"Honey, do you realize how many museums there are in Paris and how little time we have before nightfall? That's like trying to find a needle in a haystack."

My stomach growls.

"Honey, was that your stomach?" My mother asks, glancing at her watch. "Let's go back to the hotel and get something to eat."

"But what about Jacques-Pierre? I can't lose him before I even find him! I have a gut feeling that he really is the ONE."

"You haven't lost him. We just don't know how to find him. I'm all out of suggestions, plus I'm jet-lagged. Please, can we go back?"

"Fine."

* * *

When we return to the hotel, I spot Dr. Milton by the concierge desk. "Mom, I'll meet you back in the room, I just need to figure something out," I say, heading towards the professor.

"So, was it a success?" Dr. Milton asks. He's standing with ASSon, who is inquiring about using the house car.

Disapproving eyes accentuate my shaking head.

"I don't understand," he shrugs. "You didn't like the exhibit? I was hoping you'd enjoy ... the sights."

He glances down toward the floor. I follow his gaze to see what he's looking at, and there's nothing there. Then it hits me. *Wait! He's not looking at the floor. He's looking at himself in a "private" display.* I give a cursory glance and notice a sizable bulge on his pants.

I flush red with embarrassment and with anger.

"The nerve of you! How unprofessional, inappropriate, how ... Goddammit ... somewhat arousing?" *Oh god, did I just say that out loud?*

"CHASTITY!" ASSon screeches out. "Please, disregard everything she said, Dr. Milton. She's high on drugs," she rambles a mile a minute.

I meet his stare, trying to maintain my seriousness and hoping he'll overlook my faux pas. I clear my throat. "What I meant to say..."

"Chase," he interrupts, "I was just having a little fun with you. All kidding aside, did you find what you were looking for?"

"No, I didn't."

"Come to dinner, ride with us. The concierge was just pulling around the house car."

I shake my head, reaching into my pocket for my key. I head toward the lift. "I better not."

"Ah!" he laughs, jogging over. "I almost forgot. Your friend," he winks, pulling out a white piece of paper from his shirt pocket, "left this for you. He said that he saw you in the audience." He smiles, raising his eyebrows, waving goodbye.

I'm stunned. I flip over the card: Jacques-Pierre Beaumont.

I'm giddy! He found me! Love found me! The ONE found me!!!

"Merci beau cul, Dr. Milton."

"Oh. Thank you. I work very hard on my sculpted ass, as you so eloquently said." He stifles his laughter, "I think you meant to say *merci beaucoup*. Unless you really think I have a nice ass," he winks.

I did it again. Why am I mangling my French into so much flirtation? I blame my frigid sexuality. "Oh. My. God! Please don't tell Professor Feldman that all I say is pervy things to you." I join in on his laughter.

Heading back to my room, I feel a new high—and so much better than the anti-anxiety meds. I can actually put Amoremoji stickers next to "met a bunch of hot guys" on my Excel Spreadsheet when I get home.

"YEAY!!" I whisper, giving myself a thumbs-up.

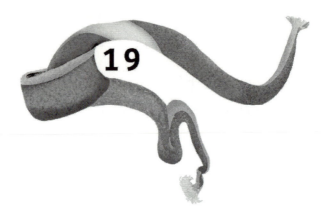

19

"And why is it exactly that we're flying to New York instead of Los Angeles?" my umpteenth attempt to get my mother to fess up. We're close to landing after a near ten-hour flight. All I know is that mom is in cahoots with Roxie and she tight-lipped about it. "Roxie said she had to stay home this weekend."

"How many times do you need to ask, Chase? She needs our help in scouting a location for her new Bridezilla client that she picked up yesterday, and while we have a little time to spare, we can check out the sights and sounds of the Big Apple. That's all!" She nurses a coffee as she stares out the window, purposefully not making eye contact with me.

I twist my body, leaning my torso into her lap. "Why is it that I get this strange feeling there is more to what you're telling me? I know you two; you're up to something. All I have to say is that it had better be worth it. I just want to get home; I'm so tired of flying." *And popping anti-anxiety meds. I can tell I'm a bit loopy; my eyelids feel heavy, and my body feels so numb I can't will myself to move my extremities, but this time I made sure I didn't OD. The last thing I need to do is blurt out my sex dreams to my Mom and more random strangers.*

"Relax, Chase. Everything will be fine. Roxie has it all figured out." She tries to reassure me, giving me one of her "I know what's good for you" looks as she shoves my shoulder, pushing me back into my seat.

Resigned, I recline my chair to its extent and close my eyes. All I want is to hear from Jacques-Pierre, the ONE, not extended flight time to another one of Roxie's adventures.

* * *

I spot Roxie immediately as we leave the customs section at JFK; she's yelling our names and waving her arms wildly with delirium. She's wearing an oversized T-shirt that has "take a bite out of the big apple" scrolled across her breast line and a blue foam Statue of Liberty crown on her head. I notice people standing on either side of her, creating a wide berth. *Good grief, Roxie! You do not understand how ridiculous you look right now and how many men are staring at your knockers like hungry animals.*

"Oh, my GOD, HAPPY VALENTINE'S DAY! I'm so excited to see you two! Chase, you will love, love, love what I have in store." She immediately wraps her arms around me, bouncing up and down like a jackrabbit.

"I can hardly wait," I respond, deadpan, my body not moving. Roxie, so caught up in her happy moment, doesn't catch my sarcasm. *Plus, I am not a fan of Valentine's Day, watching all the happy couples, considering that I'm still single.*

"Come on, Mistress Zombie, with your bloodshot eyes." Roxie nudges me toward Baggage Claim. "Let's get your suitcases. I have a taxi waiting for us. We will drop your bags off and then head on our way."

* * *

The three of us now crammed into the backseat of a beat-up yellow taxi that reeks of cigarettes are en route to what Roxie describes as the best way to see New York City.

"Trust me, Chase, you will love this!" She rolls down the window, leaning her head out; the fresh air a welcoming relief to the little smoke chamber.

Whenever Roxie's this hyper and adds the words "trust me," big red flags pop up in the back of my head.

Traffic is bumper-to-bumper, and horns are blaring every few seconds. Somehow, we manage to ride alongside a double-decker tour bus full of preteens. Taylor Swift blares from a boom box on the top level, and a gaggle of girls is singing and swaying to "Shake It Off."

"Okay, what do I say to Jacques-Pierre?" I direct toward Roxie, my phone in hand, and email open. "I stood him up," I continue, ignoring the teen display, "What do you say after you do something like that?"

"EE-YEAH! Turn it up," Roxie gives one of the girls a thumbs-up. "Like the music?" a cute chaperone yells down to Roxie.

"Can't you tell?" Roxie's head hangs out the partially-opened window. "You should check out Velo," Cute Guy spouts.

"What's Velo?" Roxie plays along.

"The best of the best nightclubs. They play a bunch of pop music."

"Velo. Hey, thanks," Roxie yells, cupping her hands together like a megaphone. "Maybe we can hook up there."

"Maybe," he winks.

"Hook up?" my mother interjects, leaning forward, eyeing the two of us.

"Oh, Auntie, you know what I mean? Coffee," Roxie laughs, snatching my phone, her fingers moving a mile a minute.

"Meet for coffee in a nightclub? Kids these days! They make little sense," my mom mumbles to no one in particular. "When I was your age..." she pauses for a moment, her jaw hanging open. "I was changing diapers." She lets out a long sigh, "those days were so much simpler." Her phone blares out, and she takes the call. "Oh, yes, Preston. We made it ... She's a little drugged."

"I can hear you, Mom," I say loud enough to get my mom's attention. "Tell dad that by a little, you mean a lot!" Mom rolls her eyes and continues talking away to my father.

I turn back to Roxie, straining my neck to see what she's typing, which she's hiding from my view. "Roxie, what are you doing?"

"Chase, if you're finally ready to date, why not call that sweet pilot Vincent from our Idaho flight last Christmas?" my mother asks, clicking off her call. "At least he lives in the states."

"Vincent? Why am I just now hearing about Vincent? He contacted you after all that plane craziness, and you're not jumping at the chance to see him?" Roxie adds.

I ignore both of them, eager to see what Roxie wrote as she tosses my phone back at me.

"Sent."

"Sent? I didn't have a chance to read it, Rox. What did you just do?" I madly scroll over and open the email to Jacques-Pierre:

From: ChaseMorg@mylife.com
To: jacquesp@mera.fr
Subject: Paris

Dear Jacques-Pierre,
I enjoyed meeting you on my flight. I'm sorry I wasn't able to join you for lunch. There was a riot that blocked traffic that day. If, by chance, you ever make it to Los Angeles, please let me know. Having lunch with you would be fantastic.
Warmest regards,
Chase

My demeanor quickly lightens up. "You never cease to amaze me, Rox!" You were paying attention the whole time. This is great—no, more than great. It's perfect. Thanks!"

"Don't mention it." Roxie gives my arm a little squeeze.

The tour bus moves forward, and the cabbie slams on his brakes, tossing us forward before changing lanes.

"AHHHH!" I screech, my gleefulness instantly squashed. "Oh, great! What type of driver deliberately pulls up behind a bus?" I say louder than expected.

"Lady," the cabbie answers in his hoarse voice, "if you want to get to your ride on time, then this is where I have to go."

"Ride? What do you mean by 'your ride'?"

"What he's trying to say," Roxie flashes a dirty look in the cabbie's rear-view mirror, "is that we're going to switch rides to get to the first thing on my agenda."

"Agenda? What the hell are you talk—"

My question dangles as the bus pulls into a parking lot, and the teens begin oohing and aahing, pulling out their phones to take pictures.

"Here, we are, ladies! Enjoy your flight."

"WHAT?" I scream as I exit the taxi after my mother. "What flight? I just got off a ten-hour flight." I grab hold of my security blanket scarf, making sure it's securely in place.

And then I see it.

"NOT. A. CHANCE. IN. HELL—" I gasp, my stomach making a merry-go-round loop as I stare at the helicopters lining the large helipad. "Roxie, you've gone completely cuckoo. You're an absolute lunatic!" I turn back towards the cab, my hand lingering mid-air to open the door, but it's gone.

"Isn't it great?" Roxie happily skips over to talk to the three guys standing by the first whirlybird. One guy who looks vaguely familiar, but I can't place him waves to the teens on the bus before entering the bird. The other two who have uniforms—I assume are pilots—wave us over.

"Isn't this the best?" My mother grins from ear to ear as we head toward Roxie.

"Not you too? Are you mad?" I raise my voice, shaking my head. "I'm not about to get into a tin- can bird. I had to be doped up to get to Paris from California and from Paris to here. I'm not about to get on a helicopter; they crash all the time, Mom. What are you thinking? Or maybe you're NOT thinking." I'm so flustered my eyes ache from the stress of my impending doom. "I don't have your genetic makeup for adventure!" I plant my feet, not moving.

"Good morning, ladies!" a handsome man with strawberry-blond hair interrupts, approaching us, "this is First Officer Carter, and I'm Captain Dan. Before we begin, we will brief you on safety rules, so, if you will follow me to the hangar, we'll get started."

I raise my hand like a diligent student, "I can't go, I'm high on dru—"

"Don't even think about it," Roxie yanks me forward, eyes on the pilots. "You do a lot of squats, don't you?" She looks at First Officer Carter, who rolls his eyes like it will be one heck of a long day. "Delicious, wouldn't you say?" she whispers in my ear through gritted teeth, tugging me along. "Chase, knock it off. You can't go around telling people you're drugged. What are you thinking?"

"What am I thinking? WHAT AM I THINKING?" I scream. "What are You ... UGH! THIS is a trip ... to hell!" I scream, but the rotor blades drown me out. I feel like a lamb being led to slaughter.

* * *

Ten minutes later and huddled in a small corner room of the grey, industrial-sized building with other tourists, Roxie, Mom, and I dutifully watch a safety video on the wall screen. On an intellectual level, I'm impressed. The rest of me is a ball of anger at my cousin and sheer terror at the many ways the video relates how something can go wrong and why we need to wear life vests in case of a water landing, which translates in my mind to a crash landing. Sure enough, after the short instructional film, First Officer Carter shows how to use a life vest. My stomach flips a couple of times.

"Roxie, I'm not joking, I can't do this." Tears are welling up, and there's desperation in my voice. "Sure, you can, cuz! Believe it or not, you need this!" Roxie's confident voice reverberates off the walls.

"No, I don't..." My phone goes through a series of buzzes. Not wanting to appear like I'm distracted, I give my phone a cursory glance and notice Grant's name. *Oh, Lord, not now. What the hell does he want?*

"HOLY SH—" I say in one breath, holding back an expletive.

```
Grant: I was going to wait until I saw you
again, but since you won't
talk to me ... I have to tell you something.
Grant: Okay, here it goes...
Grant: Brody and I adopted a baby girl named
Maddy. We want you to be
her godmother.
```

Oh. My. God. This makes no sense...

* * *

My mind flashes back to seven years ago when we were just out of college, and the five of us— Roxie, Paul, Charlie, Grant, and I—were all at the cross-town rivalry football game, USC vs. UCLA. Roxie leaned over the seat in front of us, oohing and ahhing over the little towhead in front of us, sitting on her mother's lap. The toddler wiggled her pom-poms, wearing a silly expression and giggling wildly. Within a matter of seconds, the toddler's laughter turned to loud wailing when her mother set the pom-poms down as she took a sip from her Coke.

"This is the exact reason why I never want kids," Grant said bluntly, nursing his frothy beer. "Never?" Paul chuckled. "You're exaggerating. One day you'll want to be a dad."

"No, I'm serious, man; I mean never."

* * *

"BABY?" I say, my voice reverberating throughout the room. "They have a BABY? A BABY GIRL? And they want me to be her godmother? WHAT THE FUCK version of Cinderella's bloody fairytale is this?" All eyes turn to me. It's suddenly eerily quiet; you can hear a pin drop.

"Chastity!"

"Sorry, Mom!"

Captain Dan clears his throat, immediately squashing the low murmuring that starts up among the tourists. "This ends your safety training," He makes eye contact with me, giving me a warm smile and a wink, which does nothing to calm me down. I'm a nervous wreck, sweating profusely and now freaking out over this new information. "This will be a twenty-five-minute flight," he continues, "so make use of the restrooms before we board the choppers in ten minutes. The number on your vest indicates which one you'll be boarding."

"Where did the two of them magically find a baby, and how were they able to adopt so quickly? None of this makes sense." I whisper to Roxie robotically as the three of us hold back from the crowd. "Plus, he never wanted kids." And then it hits me. "Oh, fuck! You don't think the baby could be Medusa's, do you? I mean, how could she give up her baby when she's marrying the mini-mogul father? He must be having a fit. I wonder if he'll break everything off," I ramble. "I guess Grant's drunken mumbling about adopting wasn't nonsense after all."

"Chase, I'm not deaf. What are you talking about? And watch your language," my mother speaks up.

"Sorry, Mom."

"He married a man, which means he likes men and sleeps with men! He never slept with you. Maybe we shouldn't jump to the conclusion that he knocked up the Prissy Posse bitch."

"Roxie!" my mom blurts out, "and who are you calling a 'Prissy Posse bitch'?"

"Mother! Auntie Olivia!" we say in unison.

"Well … I'm just repeating what you said," my mom glares back at the two of us. "I hate to be left in the dark, you know?"

"It's Julie," Roxie volunteers.

"Julie? Had a baby? She's not even married yet." My mom genuinely looks shocked.

"It's a rumor, Mom."

"Something I found on Facebook," Roxie adds. I make eye contact with her and mouth "TMI" as we head toward the pilots on the helipad.

"Facebook. Everybody keeps talking about Facebook. Sounds like the perfect gossip session, if you ask me," my mother concludes. My mom's eyes shift from Roxie's to mine when she notices tears welling up again.

"Chase? What's going on?"

"I ... can't..." I fan my face with the ends of my scarf, hoping to keep myself from bursting. "What she's trying to say," Roxie butts in, "is that she's still hurt about Grant messing up her wedding plans."

"But, what about Jul—"

"Let's not jump to conclusions. It's just the rumor mill running amuck. Right, Auntie? In the meantime," Roxie places her arm around my shoulders, "you need to get out of the safe little bubble you created and try new things. You wasted two years of your life dating Grant, every day planning your fairytale life together. You weren't meant to be married to him," placing her hands on my shoulders. "Confucius had it right when he said, 'our greatest glory is not in never falling, but in rising every time we fall.' The way I see it, you have two options right now: obsess about this baby news, or face your fears and get on a helicopter. Plus, remember that you said you wanted to have an adventure, and there's no better way to see New York City than from the sky. C'mon, go with the flow, Chase. A helicopter ride around the Big Apple will be amazing! Plus, think of your ... spreadsheet."

"Spreadsheet?" My mom is forever the inquisitive one.

"Oh, Auntie, it's just a code word for experiences."

"Kids these days..." my mom shakes her head. "We need to hurry along; our pilots are looking rather annoyed."

"I ... I ... can't do this," I stutter.

"Yes, you can," my mom and Roxie say in unison, walking on either side of me.

* * *

"Just in time," Captain Dan shouts as we approach our designated bird. "And Happy Valentine's Day, ladies!"

We return the greeting as a group while finding our seats. The tin-can bird is cozy but unquestionably roomier than I expected. With windows on both sides, my stomach does another lurch at the openness of everything around me. I feel like I'm standing near a cliff. On the flip side, the view is nothing less than breathtaking as I hold on to the ends of my scarf with both hands and hope that my nerves don't get the best of me.

Captain Dan and First Officer Carter announce that it's time to suit up and to put on the headsets. Before I know it, I feel engulfed by my new getup, especially when the giant harness secures me in my seat.

"We have a special passenger with us today," the Captain announces through the headsets. "May I introduce to you, Doug Holzman."

"Oh, my God! You look just like ... like..." Roxie grabs my arm with excitement.

"Like Tom Cruise?" Doug offers. She releases a little chuckle when she sees him staring at her chest and silently mouthing the words on her T-shirt.

"Like Tom Cruise," she mimics, her eyes wide with lust.

"Who's Tom Cruise?" my mother raises.

"Better than John Wayne, Mom," I insert.

Doug lets out a hardy chuckle. "Well, I know very little about John Wayne, but I can tell you, it helps to look a lot like Tom since I'm one of his stuntmen," he adds.

"And ... and ... oh ... oh... Don't tell me," Roxie is in game-show mode, "you're going to jump out of the helicopter, right?"

"WHAT?" My turn to shriek. "You've got to be joking? Listen, I'm having a hard-enough time with flying, let alone some guy who's going to commit suicide."

"Heavens, no, ma'am; I'm a stuntman. I'm a part of an action-packed movie. A camera crew will film me as I parachute out."

"Roxie?" I furiously shake her arm, "We. Are. Not. Doing. This."

"Chase, you'll be fine. Trust me."

"That's what I'm afraid of."

"Just think about it," Roxie ignores my jarring comeback, "how many times in your life do you get a gorgeous stuntman on your flight? We're all going to be in a movie."

"Most likely, you won't—" Doug's efforts to dispel confusion go flat.

"Just think we'll be famous. Maybe we'll get to meet the *real* Tom Cruise when this is all done ..."

"Actually—" Doug gets cut off again.

"You'll arrange that for us, Doug, won't you?" Roxie proposes.

"I ... I ... can't promise—"

"Well, try, at least for my cousin," pointing to me. "She's a big fan of his. Please?"

"I am not—" Roxie quickly shushes me and places a finger on my lips.

"I can't guarantee anything, ma'am..."

"Pretty please?" Roxie gives him one of her sweetest smiles. He lets out a long sigh.

"I'll see what I can do."

"Thank you! Thank you! Thank you!" Roxie claps her hands like a giddy school girl.

* * *

"Yes," Doug whispers, "Velo tonight after the shoot. One of the guys bought a table." Roxie's eyes grow wide with excitement. She swipes her phone and sends me a text

> Roxie: Did you hear that?
> **Me: Hear what?**
> Roxie: Doug's going to Velo tonight too.
> **Me: Velo? What's Velo?**
> Roxie: Don't you remember that guy from the bus? He said Velo is "the best of the best nightclubs. We need to go."

210

My eyes grow big as saucers. I turn toward her and subtly shake my head.

> Roxie: Amoremojis, Chase!

Rolling my eyes, I half expect a reaction from my mom with our back-and-forth texting. She seems lost in another realm, staring at the views from the window and sitting next to the stuntman, clueless that the guy will commit suicide any moment now.

I give a cursory glance at Doug and can't help noticing that his Tom Cruise features remind me of Vincent. My mind goes back to our phone conversation, which I begin to twist. Before I know it, Vincent is in the rec room, his hands immediately cupping my face. I'm ripping off his shirt and pulling his rock-hard body towards me, kissing him furiously. He slips his hand up the small of my back, pulling me in closer, lifting me onto the ping pong table.

"*Ready for me, Chase?*" Vincent asks. One of the wooden legs of the table makes a loud cracking noise.

"Yes! NO! OH GOD, NOT AGAIN!" I yell out loud.

"Yes, no, what, Chase?" Roxie looks confused. The remaining passengers have their eyes glued on me. My mom looks like she's just seen a ghost.

"Ma'am, are you okay?" First Officer Carter interrupts.

"Oh ... I'm ... reacting to a Facebook post..." I fabricate, keeping my eyes on my phone while madly swiping.

"Facebook..." my mom mutters. "Couldn't you find something better to do on your phone? I hear there are apps for Solitaire. You should try that."

Light chuckles flow through the headsets. I turn beet red as I give my mom a wan smile and mouth, "thanks."

I feel the heavy rumble as the rotor blades increase speed. The helicopter vibrates like a washing machine during the spin cycle. My teeth begin to chatter as I snap out of my love trance. The pilot pulls back on the throttle, and we are airborne.

"I watched the safety video," I yell into the headset again, totally forgetting my last shrieking episode. "and everything there was about what to do when the helicopter crashes. Sorry,

I'm not a good swimmer. I don't want to imagine myself flailing around in the Hudson River."

"We can hear you loud and clear, ma'am. Please tone it down," Captain Dan responds. I can hear another light chorus of laughter from everyone in the tin-can bird, including Doug, who seems distracted by something outside his window. "You're in good hands," First Officer Carter offers. "We've given this tour thousands of times, ma'am. Just sit back, relax, and enjoy the view."

"That's easy for you to say," I counter quietly.

Soon, we're up so high my stomach feels strangely weightless. I close my eyes, and I imagine falling out, the long expanse of seconds, becoming a wicked comet approaching landfall—the only thing separating me from death is a thin pane of glass.

"Earth to Chastity. Come in, Chastity," Roxie says through her headset, kicking my leg. "For God's sake, open up your eyes and enjoy the view."

"Here we are, folks," Captain Dan interjects. "We're about to fly over Coney Island and the Statue of Liberty before heading towards Central Park, Yankee Stadium, and circling the Empire State Building. You might want to get your cameras ready."

I open my eyes. The sky radiates a pink-and-orange glow from the sunset. "Wow," I say under my breath. The views are spectacular. *Roxie was right. Maybe that's the key ... I need to relax and enjoy each moment and try not to overthink things before it—* "SHIT!" I scream, knocking off my headset. "PULL UP, PULL UP! You're heading straight for that BLIMP!"

"What blimp?" Roxie looks around.

"Blimp? I don't see a blimp." My mother swivels around in her seat, looking amused.

"WHAT BLIMP?" I yell louder. "How can I be the only one seeing this? We're heading straight towards the giant white balloon right over there," I point.

A rush of strong wind blows through the helicopter. My hair and scarf whip around my face like a tornado.

"WHAT THE—" I frantically part my hair only to find the door opened and Doug crouching down with First Officer Carter standing at his side.

"Girls, calm down. The blimp is hovering above Yankee Stadium. It's much farther away than you think. We will not hit it," the first officer says, "The camera crew is there waiting for Doug. Please, put your headset back on, ma'am."

I gape. "FUCK THE BLIMP! Is he going to JUMP? I thought he was joking." I find myself screaming uncontrollably. I can't help it; I'm about to watch a guy plunge to his death, or fake death, or whatever the fuck this stunt is. "HEY, STOP!" I'm leaning forward, the seat harness pinching against my chest. "I don't care who the hell you are. You can't do this in front of us. This isn't part of our tour." I weakly yank his shirt.

"Oh, my..." my mother mumbles words that don't make any sense.

I hear a consecutive set of clicks as I replace my headset. I look over at Roxie; she appears to be snapping photo after photo. "This is so COOL," she whoops. "We're in a movie."

Doug looks back at the three of us. "Really, it's not as far as it looks," he says in the headset before he removes it and then promptly jumps.

"OH. MY. GOD!" I release a long breath, eyes glued to the window. "Not as far it looks?" I'm breathing hard. "Is he insane?"

"Catastrophe averted. See, it was all part of the filming. Now can you please tell me thank you. The view is spectacular. And watching a man jump from this far up was incredible," Roxie laughs as she texts:

Roxie: And I bet you momentarily forgot all about those baby texts too!

"Did you see a parachute? Did you see a splash?" Ignoring the vibration on my phone, I madly pan the windows.

"LOOK!" Roxie shouts, pointing.

My mom and I swivel to the right and see something white billowing in the sky.

"It's Doug," my mom yells.

"And he's heading for the Hudson River," I add.

"Ladies, ladies..." First Officer Carter butts in, "look who's waiting for him to land." He passes a pair of binoculars to me. It takes me a moment to focus before I see a whole slew of people scurrying about—some with cameras, some in a boat waiting for him to land.

"See," Captain Dan adds, "he has a crew helping him; he's just fine."

"BUT?" I say, aghast. "Hello, a man just jumped out of a moving helicopter. He could drown. No crew will be able to work that fast to save him."

"He'll be fine," Roxie says, matter-of-factly.

"How can you be so nonchalant about a man jumping to his death?" I feel the heat rising on my face.

"I guess I watch too much reality television. I highly doubt the crew plans to kill him, although that would make for an interesting scene—"

I snap off the headphones again. "STOP IT, Roxie! That's morbid!"

"I'm just saying..." Roxie mouths, giving me a lopsided grin. "Hey, I have another idea. Let's find Doug at Velo tonight. That'll prove he's still alive."

"What did you say? Roxie, take your headphones off," I gesture.

"Why?"

I give her a hard stare and nod my head in the directions of my mom and the pilots. "Text me," I mouth and gesture with my phone.

"Oh..." Roxie begins thumbing me her message.

Me: Ha, ha about the baby texts. I don't want to talk about that now.

Let's talk about that and Velo later. In the meantime, I'm going to enjoy the view.

I place the headset securely on my head a second time while giving her a wink and grinning widely. Roxie gives me both thumbs-ups before I start snapping pictures.

* * *

The helicopter descends slowly and lands lightly on the helipad. Captain Dan turns off the engines and removes his headset. The rest of us follow suit. I listen as the rotor blades wind to a stop.

"So, ladies, did you enjoy the ride?" he asks, the helicopter "unfasten seat belt" binging.

"Did we enjoy it? It was fucking amazing," Roxie says, grinning from ear to ear. "Ah, sorry, Auntie Olivia!" My mother purses her lips, which Roxie fluffs off, extending her hand to the captain. "Thanks for letting us be part of the movie and for all the excitement. What a treat!" "Happy to hear it," Captain Dan chuckles.

The three of us hand our headsets to First Officer Carter and unbuckle the monster harnesses. Still reeling with the experience, we exit the metal bird, returning our life jackets before carefully climbing down to the stable ground. For some strange reason, I can't help but feel giddy. Roxie sees my smile as I loosen my scarf around my neck.

"See, I told you we'd survive. We're going clubbing tonight, cuz, and you're going to LOVE it." She bounces around, wiggling like a schoolgirl, grabbing the end of my scarf and giving it a little flip. I roll my eyes.

"You girls can count me out of your next excursion. I've had enough excitement for one day," my mom chuckles. "I do think it would be a good idea to check out Jardine's Lookout while you're out. It's supposed to have amazing views of the city," she announces. I look over at Roxie, and I catch her wink.

Dare I tell Roxie that I'm feeling light as a feather for a different reason? As ludicrous as it sounds, she might have completely cured me of my fear of flying. Now THAT'S one significant weight off my shoulders.

But what to do about Grant and the baby? Well, that's a whole other story—one I have no idea how to tackle.

20

I feel like a dead "single woman" walking. The quiet excitement over conquering quells my fear of flying in preparation for a night on the town. I'm a nervous wreck, and Roxie, who instigated this whole affair and ought to know me the best, ignores my incessant grumbling, seeing that my attempts to sway her are futile.

"Listen, Rox," I lean close to her in the back seat of this taxi, "I must be half-crazy, going along with your idea of clubbing. What's gotten into you? How could you be so willing to go to a nightclub? You hate them."

"Well, you're right. I admit that it's not my usual protocol; I boycott them on principle alone because I don't want to stand in line to be looked over like a piece of prized meat."

"And you're changing your tune because why?" I spit out, flipping up my hands in frustration. The cabbie driver eyes me in the rearview mirror. I lower my voice, "You want to go stalk a crazy guy that likes to jump from helicopters? You already know that a nightclub is not a place to fall madly in love."

"I know that. The goal of this mission is twofold: for you to hook-up with a hot man," she says with great enthusiasm, "and for me to find Doug. He's the next best thing to Tom Cruise, and you know how I am obsessed with Top Gun."

"Hook-up?" I say blankly. "I am not about to have a one-night stand. I thought I could with the boy toy, Jaydon, and look how that turned out. I'm not genetically programmed to have a fling." I sit back in my seat, folding my arms across my chest.

"I'm not talking about sex. Hook-up, you know—flirt, dance, kiss, enjoy the company of a man." She presses her finger against the corner of my mouth, forcing a smile. "Are you sure you don't want to stash your scarf in your purse? Doesn't scream 'clubbing attire' if you know what I mean."

I give her a hard stare. It's useless trying to knock sense into my cousin, especially since we're right around the corner to our destination. I succumb to the dreaded task at hand and go with the flow. I look at my phone; it's 11 o'clock. We exit the taxi and approach the velvet rope, the cordoned entrance to Velo. Roxie addresses the bouncer, a tank of a man in a suit.

"We're on the VIP list! Here's our invitation," waving the magic wand, so to speak, in the air. The card she hands the bouncer is courtesy of the concierge at our hotel. He felt sorry for me after I vented to him about my whole Paris debacle. He took such pity on me; I'm surprised he didn't escort us here himself.

"The club doesn't open until midnight." the guttural voice of the bouncer matches his Brobdingnagian proportions. I suddenly feel like Gulliver. It doesn't help that his menacing glare gives me the willies. Ironically, he shifts over to a smile, probably to remind guests that he's kind underneath his monstrous appearance. What's even more bewildering is the fact that while I'm a club rookie, Roxie, who avoids night clubs like the plague, acts as if she's been doing this for years.

Roxie responds to the bouncer's warm smile with uproarious laughter. "We're born and raised LA girls; the nightlife starts much earlier than it does in Manhattan or any other Gotham or Metropolis for that matter." Roxie grasps for possible nightclub locations. She grabs the card from his stubby, sausage-sized digits and stows it safely away in one of her back-leather pants pockets that seem to shimmer in the light. "We'll be back," she finger-waves.

"Shouldn't we go back to the hotel for a little while?" I keep my voice low, hoping Goliath doesn't overhear our conversation as we head back on the street. A bus suddenly approaches, coughing up its diesel fumes. I hold my breath and cover my face as the bus floats pass.

Roxie pulls my arm like I'm some blind person and walks briskly along the wet city streets.

"Or we could go to Jardine's Lookout as your mom suggested," she counters. "Nana also told me it has amazing views of the city lights, and it's just a few blocks from here." She looks both ways before crossing the street.

"Since when does Nana or my mom know about the New York hotspots?" my heels clickety clacking across the pavement, trying to keep pace.

"Beats me, but they both insisted we go, and you know Nana. I'm afraid to come back and face her if we don't."

"We're walking ... the whole way?" I query, and Roxie nods. I give her a double-take. She may have her crazy antics and outfits, but it never ceases to amaze me how she adapts to Manhattan life over a course of a few days. *I guess when there's a will, there's a way. I just wish I knew what really motivates her.*

The night air chills. In LA, no one in cocktail attire would walk more than a few yards. A few blocks are a long way to walk in a short dress and spike heels. I fear blisters will greet me soon enough. I dodge a puddle. The reflection of the moonlit sky shining brightly in the water catches my eye. It's beautiful against the dark backdrop.

A car stereo bass booms, and I grasp my purse tightly against my body. "I can't believe you're having us walk the streets of New York at night," I say, eyes darting in every direction, wishing I had room in my tiny purse to pack pepper spray. "It's not safe."

"This is Midtown, not East Harlem." Undaunted, Roxie forges ahead. "We're fine. Stop being such a worrywart." She pulls my hand as if we were still young toddlers heading to the swimming pool.

A few minutes later, we're hurrying up a set of steps to a marble lobby; it's virtually empty.

"Where's the sign for Jardine's Lookout?" I ask, noticing a scarlet glow coming from a distant corner.

"Ah, a scavenger hunt, my specialty." Roxie takes out her phone.

"That glow feels vaguely reminiscent of an opium den, don't you think?" I drop my voice to a whisper.

"Nah. But I definitely think we should follow the lantern-lined corridor. That's what these reviews say." We walk down the hallway and locate the elevator up to the Far East. We board with another couple, and I push the button marked 53.

"Here we go," I say, turning to Roxie as the elevator doors close silently.

After ten seconds, her brow furrows, and she frowns with alarm, "Why aren't we moving?"

"We're not moving? Is the elevator stuck?" I sound more than alarmed—Roxie should know better than to prank me. The couple snickers and look at me like I'm crazy. A moment later, the elevator doors open, and I rush out, crashing into a stout, middle-aged man with a greasy comb-over. I immediately begin eyeing tourists with their jerky walking and drug-induced motion.

"Hey, watch your step, lady," he says, wiping beer off his arm. He turns to look at me for the first time. "Well, hello, sugar lips."

I cringe. "Sorry. Excuse me," I say, collecting myself as a gaggle of women with teased hair and acrylic nails pass through the corridor, the bachelorette party sashes, indicating that they are celebrating a colleague about to enter the institution of marriage. I just hope Roxie and I depart before the obligatory male stripper makes an appearance.

"Oops, sorry about that," Roxie says, appearing next to me and pulling me away from the stranger.

"That wasn't funny. You caused me to freak out and run smack into that lecherous pervert."

"Sorry, I wasn't joking. It felt like the elevator had stopped." She whips her head around. "Wow! This feels like we're in a different historical period, like the Orient of the 1930s." She points to the espresso- colored gallery tinged with twinkling amber lights that bounce off the mirrors as if we've now become trapped in an Asian-themed disco ball. The bar, veiled behind screens with intricate designs of dragons, tigers, roosters, snakes, boars, and the Chinese horoscope, adds an air of mystery and enticement to the decor.

"Mrs. Adelman?" I sputter, composing myself. "What ... what are you doing here?" I stutter, staring at the lady wearing her signature bedazzled jean jacket, skinny jeans, and a silver, shimmery top.

"Chastity, it's so lovely to see you." She looks past me to Roxie. "And you are?"

"Roxanne. I'm Chase's cousin. We met at Kate's Christmas party when you invaded our bathroom moment."

"Vivien said one granddaughter; she didn't tell me you would need matchmaking services too." Mrs. Adelman smiles widely, like she just won the lottery.

"What do you mean 'services'?" Roxie questions. "My grandmother told me to make sure to see the views of the city from this specific bar. She didn't tell me anything about a matchmaker."

The woman is waving her hands for us to follow, taking a seat at a corner table by the window. "Let's all have a seat. I brought along a brochure since you didn't look me up. I did give you my card after all."

Roxie is looking past me at the mist, obscuring everything. "Oh God, wouldn't you know, we walk all this way and then this. The view is as bad as the prospects at the bar," she says with haste, flipping through the fluorescent pink pamphlet. "This is not a way to start the evening out. Oh. My. God..." Roxie leans over, whispering in my ear. "Her fees start at five thousand dollars. Is she crazy? No wonder you never looked her up!"

"I vet all of my bachelors. They are the best of the best. Only the finest single men are available. I will scour the world to find you a husband if that's what it takes." Mrs. Adelman is pushing contracts in my direction. "But that's not what it will take for you, Chastity. I've already found your future husband. He is the perfect trifecta of love—brains, beauty, and body. His name is—"

"This all sounds really lovely," Roxie interrupts. "May we think it over? We need to be at Velo in ten minutes to meet up with our friends." Roxie is practically shoving me out of my seat, pushing me towards the elevator. "Bye, we'll be in touch," Roxie waves.

"Why do we have to leave? She said she found me a husband." I slam the button that takes us down. "Don't you get it, Rox? I WANT TO GET MARRIED. What part of that do you not understand? Plus, I wouldn't mind looking like Cinderella at the ball wearing a big white poofy wedding dress. Rox, we can't leave now. We need to go back and talk to her and be polite. This is fate, don't you get it? I left her card in the bathroom that night, and now look, she found me and found me a husband!"

"OH. MY. GOD. You sound cray, cray. First off, I thought Jacques-Pierre was the ONE, and second, how are you going to pay her astronomical fees?" She looks at me and then back at Mrs. Adelman. "OH, I see. You think Nana's forking it up as she did for your Paris trip, and that's why she ambushed us?" Roxie says as we board the elevator. A pregnant woman and her husband who can't keep their hands and mouths off one another join us along with a peculiar interloper who pushes close to me. He smells like sauerkraut and stinky feet.

"Hello, you're beautiful," says the drunk as he closes the elevator door. He has to be in his late sixties. I'm guessing Eastern Europe, but I can't discern the origin of his accent. Perhaps, he time-traveled from the upstairs room, taking advantage of the norms of that era—openly staring at women and breathing on them, which is not part of his charm. Either way, I quickly forget Mrs. Adelman because he's making my skin crawl.

"In the 'wild,' are all men Lotharios?" I whisper to Roxie.

She bites her lip, trying not to laugh. "You always encourage the serial killer types."

"No, I don't." Once the elevator deposits us in the lobby, Roxie pulls me toward the exit. The interloper keeps pace and buzzes around us like a mosquito.

"What's your name, gorgeous?" The interloper asks.

"Ex ... excuse me," I stutter, pushing open the giant glass doors to the street.

"Her name is Annabelle, and it's her birthday, so we must be going," Roxie blurts out.

The interloper pushes in closer. "I'll join you. Happy birthday, Annabelle! Where's your party?" He reaches for the end of my scarf, pulling me towards him.

"Don't you dare," I yell, karate-chopping his hand. He winces, letting out a lame "ouch." The freed scarf sends me bumping shoulders with Roxie as I fly toward a parked car. I catch myself from nearly toppling over it when I hear the sound of a vehicle approaching; it's a taxi.

"Sorry, our cab is here; we have to go," Roxie yells as she grabs my hand, and we pile into it, slamming the door. "Sir, gun it, and lock the doors, please."

"Okay, lady," the driver obliges.

"That was CREEPY! That drunk was old enough to be a sleazy grandpa—someone my mother never warned me about," I say, leaning against the back of the bench seat. "My poor scarf needs a thorough cleaning," I wipe the dirty end against Roxie's pants just as my phone buzzes.

"Hey, I'm not a washing machine," she laughs, pushing my hand away. "Since it's still early by New York club-going standards, should I tell the driver to take us back to the hotel where we can rest for thirty minutes to recover from our visit to the Far East? Then we'll have a repeat try at Velo," Roxie asks as I type away on my iPhone.

No reply.

"Hey, is everything okay?" she asks. "You look weird, Chase. Did Grant text pics of the baby? Chase, you have to let it go," she rambles. "It's too bizarre to think about, and it's going to ruin our whole night if we do."

"Uh huh," I mumble, reading Jacques-Pierre's unexpected email:

From: jacquesp@mera.fr
To: ChaseMorg@mylife.com
Subject: Re: Paris

Ma cherie, Chase, I am so pleased and happy to have this message from you. For sure, I will be in Los Angeles to have lunch with you—whenever my travels allow. This is not easy to organize because I have to work a bit ... and Los Angeles is not a suburb of Lausanne. I wish you a lovely day.

My heart feels like it's blooming; *there's hope.* Maybe this handsome older gentleman is what I've been looking for, especially after escaping from Jacques-Pierre's exact opposite.

"What are you smiling about?" Roxie says, pulling my phone towards her. She reads his email. "He sounds so sweet but kind of vague and noncommittal." She hands my phone back.

A sudden pang of disappointment hits me. "Way to be a killjoy, Roxie. Well, I have to say that you're right. I was hoping for something ... a bit more..."

"A bit more what, Chase? A bit more ... romantic?" she teases. "You do realize that you know absolutely nothing about this guy, except for the fact he's Swiss, sounds French, speaks French, and owns a roofing company."

I rub my chin, "Yes, I'm well aware."

"He sounds like a genuinely nice guy, though. Maybe you could add in a questionnaire to your next email: Marital status? Girlfriend? Age? Sexual orientation? Sexual fetishes?"

"Now who's being ridiculous?" I laugh.

"Oh, for God's sake, it's just an email, not a marriage proposal. If you're going to make any headway in your love life and the Amoremoji list, you'd better start by being more open. And you said you thought he was the ONE. You need not have all the answers right now. We're young and in our prime; have a little fun."

"Believe me; I want to." My fingers start punching letters. I need to reply with a message that is perky and fun, yet matches his noncommittal tone. "Done."

From: ChaseMorg@mylife.com
To: jacquesp@mera.fr
Subject: Re: Re: Paris

Yes, Lausanne is far from here. Maybe one day, your travels will bring you back to America. Paris was a marvelous way to spend a weekend.
Chase

"Look, I just pressed *send* and off it went, no turning back now. That was easier than I thought."

"For once, sit back, relax, and be patient," Roxie says, patting my shoulder as we fly through the streets of Manhattan.

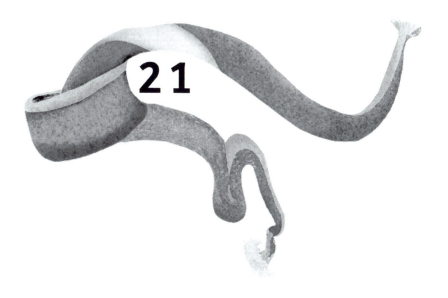

21

"We're in! Now what?" I say to Roxie as I pan the grumbling queue. For a fledgling club rookie, I can't get over how Roxie maneuvered the immediate attention of the hulky bouncer when she flashed our VIP invitations. I catch his seductive smile as we enter.

"Remember, don't give too much information away. Time to find the hot stuntman." Roxie steers me down the dimly lit circular staircase.

"I can barely see in front of me." The stark black walls doing nothing to help my spatial senses as I move along slowly, careful not to misstep.

"Quit your grumbling, Chase. What do you expect? Velo is an underground club, and they mean that literally because the entire multi-level dance space is beneath the street."

"Multi-level? How do you know all this?" I grab the railing, slowly making my way down the darkened steps in my treacherous heels. I'll be the first to admit that I'm clumsy and shouldn't be wearing these death-trap shoes, but Roxie was insistent: *"men love women in heels plus they make your bum look smaller."*

"Facebook," Roxie quips, bouncing down the steps with no problems at all in her spike heels. She stops, looking back at me, holding out her hand for me to take, like a mother to a child.

"Figures."

"And the bar is on the first basement floor," Roxie rambles on like a game show host, leading me forward, "and there is a huge area for tables, and a balcony that looks down on another level that makes up a massive dance floor, and—"

I never hear the rest of what she has to say. Pulsating Dubstep and raucous laughter drown her out as soon as she opens the soundproof door. Oscillating red and white strobe lights for Valentine's Day blind me. I break the hold of Roxie's hand to shield my eyes. A sultry voice cuts through the confusion.

"Welcome! My name is Lynx, and I am your host. Can I reserve you lovely ladies a table or do you already have a reservation?" My mouth drops open. A Chris Hemsworth look-alike only with black slicked-back hair, Lynx's bodybuilder physique takes my breath away. I can't help but stare at his tight black pants and how the V-neck T-shirt hugs his body.

"Uh..." I croak, staring at his protruding chest hair. "Rox, I didn't know we were supposed to make re —"

"I'll handle this," Roxie butts in. "Lynx, like the cute pointy-eared cat?" she replies, placing a hand on his burly bronze arm.

"Yes, like the cute pointy-eared cat," he repeats with a million-dollar smile. "Table reservations begin at one thousand dollars, plus one round minimum of bottle service."

"One thou—" I spit out.

"Chase, let me handle this, please!" Roxie's face is beet red.

"Fine. Fine. Have it your way!" I back off when Roxie gets this charged up. It's not worth trying to reason with her.

"Over there."

Roxie points Lynx toward a quiet corner. I watch as Roxie lightly flirts with him en route, touching his arm, whispering in his ear. *Good God, Rox!* I roll my eyes. The dance floor lighting changes into a blaring disco ball and blinds me again. By the time my eyes readjust, Roxie, and Lynx return. "We've got it all figured out," Roxie announces, "and ... Oh. My. God! There he is!" She excitedly points to her target as he rushes by, a gaggle of women surrounding him.

"Hi, Doug!" Roxie madly jumps and waves her arms wildly. "Remember me? From the helicopter ride?" She opens her arms, waiting for an immediate embrace.

Doug looks over and gives a wan smile before he and his harem disappear through a club door marked "PRIVATE."

Roxie looks at me and walks towards the door after him.

Lynx gently touches Roxie's arm. "I'm sorry, ma'am, but Mr. Holzman informed me that his Valentine's party is a closed event."

"Closed? What do you mean, closed?" Roxie's high-pitched voice cuts through the immediate area. Heads turn. "He all but invited us to join him." Roxie is furious; she can't find the words to vent. Her mouth opens and closes like a fish out of water. *Time for me to step in!*

"We can't afford a thousand dollars. Sorry to bother you, uh..."

"Lynx," flashing his toothy smile. His shimmering teeth hypnotize me.

"Lynx." My turn to mimic. "We ... we ... we..." Sounding more like I'm announcing an exit to the ladies' room, I force myself to finish my impromptu speech. I pull on Roxie's top. "...need to leave, right, Roxie?" Reflexively, I grip the railing above the dance floor as a wave of people enter the area and start bouncing, gyrating, and moving like electrons to a Pitbull tune that booms louder and louder.

"Hola, ya tenemos una mesa. Las damas pueden unirse a nosotros."

We turn in time to catch sight of two men in similar attire and hair color, strutting down the dance room stairs, chests puffed out like fighting roosters. I eye the taller one who didn't speak. He looks like he's straight out of a Martha's Vineyard catalog, the preppy type with khaki pants and a grosgrain belt. The look works for him with his freshly showered brown curly hair, lean build, and the confidence of someone who knows what he wants and takes it. If he were a structure, he would be the Chrysler Building; his façade screams sexy, sleek, yet established. He catches my eye, smiling, and then walks over to Lynx and hands him what looks like a wad of money.

"Did that guy just say that they had a table and that he was inviting us?" Roxie whispers in my ear to confirm that she heard correctly.

"Why are you asking me? High school Spanish was a long time ago. I barely understand it let alone speak it, except for some choice phrases Henry taught me. Did you see that?" I say all at once, my eyes widening. I freeze, staring.

"See what?"

I spy Roxie staring at the other guy.

"Chase," she changes the subject, "did you get a look at the way his pants hug his scrumptious ass? He's so sexy. Not just his looks, but his words and gestures are enticing. I wonder if he knows Doug. He looks like an actor. Maybe he can get us into his party."

"The stash Mr. Slick gave to Lynx," I whisper, ignoring her comment.

"Huh? What stash?" Roxie says a little louder than I expected, eyes panning the room.

My eyes widen even more; I give her the hand signal to tone it down. "The secret stash," I whisper. "He had a packet in his hand—"

"What? Are you nuts? Have you been watching cop shows again?" Roxie leans into my ear. "I think you're hallucinating."

"No, I'm not. I'm telling you that I saw—"

"Ladies," Lynx interrupts, "it looks like Lady Luck is in your favor. These kind gentlemen have invited you to their table. Shall we?" He escorts us to the other side of the dance floor to a semi-secluded and muted section. I'm greatly relieved about the change since I was growing concerned about my hearing with the ever-rising ambient noise.

"Now, girls, don't get into any trouble." Lynx teasingly chides, winking at Roxie, squeezing her shoulder. I turn to find Roxie gazing longingly into his eyes. *Dear Lord! He's so not her type. She's always dated the handsome geeky guys that looked more like skinny beanstalks. He's most definitely handsome, but not guys like this who looked jacked up on steroids. Tonight is getting weirder by the minute.*

"Trouble?" Roxie purses her lips, gently grazing his arm. "Didn't you know, that's my middle name?"

He's shaking his head, laughing. "Save me the worry by staying at your assigned table where I can keep an eye on you two."

Roxie winks, pinching his side as he departs.

Ignoring Lynx and Roxie's coquettish mannerisms, Mr. Slick and his sidekick pull out chairs for us to sit. "Well, isn't this cozy? Boy, girl, boy, girl." Mr. Slick starts right in.

"White Christmas!" Roxie shouts.

I nearly fall out of my seat.

"Very good! You like that movie, too, I take it?" he continues.

"It's one of my favorite Christmas movies; I watch it religiously every year. Say, you don't mind me asking? You look like an actor. Do you know Doug Holzman?" Roxie's enthusiasm is over the top, making me uncomfortable.

"Yes, Mr. Holzman. I know him well, and, no, I'm not an actor."

"Oh, you do?" Roxie jumps out of her seat. "Do you think you could talk him into inviting us to his party?"

"Well, there's no guarantee, but I'll see what I can do," he chuckles lightly before subtly shifting gears, pulling out the seat again for Roxie.

"And, how about you, Miss..." Mr. Slick turns toward me, sliding one of his hands across the table and gently placing it on my hand nearest him. I shiver slightly. "Oh, you're cold. How rude of me! Lynx!" he claps his hands together twice. The brawny host suddenly appears, looking annoyed.

"Yes, sir!" He plasters on a fake smile.

"Could you turn down the air? Miss..."

"Chastity. Call me Chastity."

"Miss Chastity," he continues, "is cold."

"Certainly," Lynx eyes Roxie for a moment and gives her a subtle wink before he skitters off to a far corner of the room and begins working the keypad like it was his cell phone.

"Oh, forgive me, again—so rude of me. My name is Carlos. And yours?" he takes hold of both of Roxie's hands, looking deeply into her eyes. "You know, you have the most beautiful blue eyes."

Roxie takes to Carlos's charm like Daphne does to my mom's peanut M & M cookies.

"You look so yummy; I could eat you up!" She smiles, but something in her tone of voice makes me realize this is all a show. She couldn't care less about him. Her whole mission is Doug.

"Roxie!" I yell, giving her a hard stare and gentle kick under the table.

"No apologies necessary. That was a very nice compliment, Miss..."

"Roxanne," she blurts.

"Roxanne. What a beautiful name!" Carlos swoons. The two of them gaze into each other's eyes way too long for my liking.

"SO," Carlos abruptly slaps a hand on the table. I flinch. "What brings you lovely ladies to Velo?" "We're visiting New York for the weekend. I took Chase—"

"Chastity," I clarify.

"Chastity on a sightseeing helicopter ride. Her fiancé dumped her a few months ago, and I'm helping her—OW!"

I kick her hard this time, giving her another bitter stare.

"I'm so sorry to hear that, Chastity. How could a man leave a woman as beautiful and sensual as you?" he leans forward across the little table.

"Uh..." feeling myself succumbing to his seduction. "I'm sorry." Attempting to change the subject, I look at Carlos' near doppelgänger. "You are?"

"*Manuel. Mi nombre es Manuel.*" He reaches across and holds my hands. His hands are warm and soft to the touch, chills of lust run up and down my spine.

"Oh, I am such a poor host. My apologies once again," Carlos bows his head. "This," pointing to Manuel, "is Manuel. He doesn't speak English. He lives in Costa Rica and imports bananas to the States. Basically, he grows bananas, and we eat them. Thus, we lovingly call him Banana Man."

"Banana Man. That's funny! We eat his bananas," I fictitiously chortle. The men's eyes widen and my cheeks flush red.

"You know what I mean. Not that we eat his..." I look down at his pants and back up, the men catching my eye, "that wasn't meant to be sexual ... Oh, dear God ... Hey, I can speak ... a little Spanish." I'm surprised at my unexpected candidness. *Who am I kidding? I just need to change the subject.* *"Hola, mi nombre es Chastity. Tu eres caliente."* I speak slowly and close with a smile.

Manuel's eyes widened. He breaks into a salacious grin, drawing my hands closer to him.

"Oh, no! What did I say?" I can feel the heat rising at the nape of my neck.

"You just told him that he's hot," Carlos giggles.

"Oh... Did I? I didn't mean—" I pause, processing what I just said. "Isn't that like saying *enchanté* in French? Nice to meet you?"

"¡Sin disculpas! Eres una mujer hermosa." Manuel kisses the tops of my hands.

"What did—"

"He said that he forgives you and that you're hot, too," he paraphrases.

"I ... I ... am?"

"Quiero joderte," Manuel moves his chair next to mine, our thighs touching. He places his hand on my knee.

"How romantic! What did he say?"

Roxie looks like she's just seen a ghost.

Carlos lightly clears his throat. "He says that he wants to make passionate love to you."

"Oh! Oh! Well ... I ... I..." I stutter, envisioning Manuel and I lying on a patchwork blanket. We just finished our picnic in the middle of his banana plantation. He leans down, cupping my face in his hands, pressing his sumptuous lips against mine. My heart pounds like a drum, reaching its high-intensity last note.

"Chastity, *quiero joderte,*" he unbuttons the top of my shirt, kissing my neck. I lean my head back, savoring the feel of his lips.

"BULLSHIT! That's not exactly—" Roxie starts in, ripping me out of my fantasy.

"Ladies," Carlos breaks in, "how about we get you both a drink, and I'll check on Mr. Holzman while I'm up?" He doesn't wait for a reply. In perfect choreography, the men stand and lightly bow before heading over to the bar.

"Did you hear that?" Roxie whoops once, the men out of earshot. "He's going to talk to Doug!"

"What did Manuel *really* say, Roxie?" I reply.

"Oh ... That." Roxie bends over and whispers in my ear.

"HE SAID WHAT?" I shout over the music, but my voice is completely drowned out by the blaring noise. "Yep. He wants to fuc—"

"Don't say it!" I put my hand over her mouth. "I feel like a piece of meat. These guys..." I shake my head. "Okay, listen. I know you don't like Carlos."

"I know, but I like the table. Do you want to stand all night while we try and get into Doug's party?" Suddenly, my phone pings. I hit the icon and see the beginning of an email from Jacques-Pierre. I quickly enter my password to reveal the rest of the message:

```
------------------------------------
From: jacquesp@mera.fr
To: ChaseMorg@mylife.com
Subject: LA lounge

Bonjour. The first time I saw you was at the lounge
before the flight and I fell totally under your charm. Tu
est tres belle. I wish you a lovely night.

------------------------------------
```

I sigh as love endorphins release into my bloodstream. *Under his charm, like he was under my love spell?* I shake my head with disbelief.

"Oh, my God, Roxie, listen to this...," I read the email before pausing for a second. "Do men really talk like this? I know he sounds scripted, like something out of a romance movie, but I can't help but imagine a future life with him."

She releases a muffled snort of laughter, "Breathe, Chase. It sounds like you finally found a guy who wants to sweep you off your feet. Now, if I can only keep you from sabotaging yourself," Roxie says, unable to hide a bit of exasperation. "By the way, what in the world were you doing that he found so charming?" she questions.

"I don't know. I passed him once in the lounge and then boarded the plane, took my meds, slumped down in my seat in a very unladylike way, and confessed to everything but murder while the flight took off."

"Did you wear a skirt like Sharon Stone in *Basic Instinct,* acting all saucy, because that would explain why he found you so charming?"

"Oh, God, no! I wasn't going commando on the flight."

Roxie erupts in laughter. "See, I think that's the key. You were casual and being yourself, totally oblivious to his charm. Fate intervened and allowed the two of you to sit next to one another. Imagine how thrilled he was. Just be cool! He clearly likes you."

She covertly turns to see if she can see Carlos and Manuel; they're still waiting at the packed bar; bar flies swarming their every move.

"Now that that's settled, here's my plan." Roxie looks left and right before continuing. "Notice how they were seducing us with their eyes? Well, we're going to do the same thing, but this time sway a little. They won't be able to resist it. They'll take the hint that we want to dance. Maybe even get us into Doug's party when they see our dance moves. Trust m—"

"Wait. What the heck?" I quickly turn my head like I didn't see anything.

"What the heck what?" Roxie turns just as a bottle service girl passes us by, a giant champagne bottle in hand, sparkler lit, singing happy birthday as she marches towards the adjacent table.

"Don't look!" I say through gritted teeth. "There's a pencil-thin brunette that went up to Manuel and sidled next to him. I saw him put something in her cleavage before she walked away."

"He what?" she's leaning so far over in her chair it's about to topple over.

"Keep it down. You heard me," I whisper, grabbing the chair, righting it.

"That's weird."

"Yeah, I wonder what that was all about?"

"They're coming," I whisper, sitting up straighter.

"Act calm," Roxie quips.

"Ladies, white wine. Complements of Mr. Doug," Carlos announces upon their return. "He'll have to take a raincheck. He's sorry he can't see you tonight."

"That's a bummer!" Roxie blurts as Carlos hands her a glass. She sets it down with a thump.

"Aren't you thirsty?" Carlos queries.

"Sorry. I'm not much of a wine drinker."

"Oh, pity! You're missing out!" Carlos feigns a pouty face.

"Mmm ... Burgundy? What vintage?" I feel like an expert, having grown up with a dad who is a connoisseur of great wine.

"Ah! I see you know your grapes. 2014?"

Roxie and I practice our eye thing. I wonder if it's working, but I can't get the strange scenario I just witnessed out of my mind.

"It's superb!" I exclaim. I gulp it down a little faster than expected. Truthfully, I never drink alcohol. I just smell my dad's wine, take a sip, swish it around and spit it out.

"*¿Te importaria bailar?*" Manuel stands and bows toward me.

"*Bailar?* Dance. Right?" *I guess it's working.* I give Roxie a cursory glance.

I stand but promptly sit down. The room starts spinning like the beginning of the teacup ride.

"Whoa! I think I drank that a little too fast. I'm light-headed, but I'll be okay." I take Manuel's hand, who promptly helps me up again, and let him guide me to the dance floor. I hold on tight to his arm. The psychedelic lights are blaring, blinding me. "When in Rome..." I hear Roxie yell as she joins the crowd and wildly moves around the dance floor with Carlos shielding her from knocking into other people. I look over and see a man doing the splits; his pants so tight I expect them to do their own dance. *Hope he hasn't gone commando!*

The room starts to spin. Manuel holds onto me securely as the mood shifts. I move in tune with Lou Bega's "Mambo No 5." Manuel moves flawlessly and sensually with the music. I relax into his touch. It feels good to touch a man again.

His hands wander up and down my arms. We weave in and out of the crowd, and he shelters me when anyone gets too close. My arms wrap around his waist, and his fingers run through my hair. His chest has a sun-kissed tan, glistening with sweat. I gaze into his eyes, and my lips part as he strokes my cheek with the back of his index finger, tilting my chin to meet his lips as his lips touch mine.

"OUCH!" I wail, grabbing Manuel's arm to steady myself. A sharp pain radiates from my lower abdomen.

"OUCH!" I wail again as the pelvic pain continues to pulsate in another horrific wave.

"I have to go," I say, doubling over, clutching my stomach and getting dizzier by the minute.

As I grasp his biceps, he brushes a thumb against my lower lip, sending another chill of desire up my spine. He smiles, hooking his arm around my waist for support, walking me off the dance floor. I pass Roxie, tapping her on the shoulder, indicating that it's time for an abrupt departure. I barely make it up the winding staircase, closing my eyes and letting my hand be my guide as I cling onto the railing. Carlos and Manuel follow us close behind.

"Ladies." Lynx is at the door. He looks between Carlos and Manuel, grabbing Roxie's arm. "Don't go..." the men look at him, and he lets go of her arm, not before giving her a small peck on her cheek, whispering something in her ear.

"Are you alright? You're turning green," Roxie says with concern, locking arms with mine once we exit.

"Yep." I press my lips together in a tight line to stifle another sharp twitch. *What's going on? Is this what being drunk feels like?*

235

Manuel rapidly says something in Spanish to Carlos, but I can't translate.

Lynx appears, hailing a cab. I hear the name of our hotel and no stops between here and there before Manuel helps me into the waiting car. I'm so tired I can barely keep my eyes open. I feel nauseous too. Moments later, Manuel helps me out of the cab, guiding me through the revolving doors that lead to the empty lobby. I look out and see Roxie in a full embrace with Carlos. I look into Manuel's eyes. For some strange reason, he reminds me of Gaston from *Beauty in the Beast*. Empty, narcissistic. The room starts spinning again; I feel my legs get weak.

"Roxie!" I yell out. Manuel's strong arms catch me before I collapse.

He puts two and two together, and carrying me over to the chaise sofa in the lobby, plants me securely in place before running out to retrieve Roxie.

From my vantage point, I see a few dozen men in black suits standing around a fancy town car with a line of black Suburbans behind it. "What the hell is that all about?" I mumble to no one.

"Jesus Christ, Chastity, you're scaring me. Are you okay?" Roxie rushes to my side. I hear her breathing fast, her hand is first on my forehead, before checking my cheeks.

"Why are Carlos and Manuel going with those guys?" My words are barely intelligible. Roxie has to bend down low to hear me.

"What does that have to do with how you feel? Are you going paranoid on me? Let's get you back to your room. Do you think you can stand up?"

"But ... but ... I saw all those men in suits usher them into a town car." I push my palms against the sofa to hoist myself up. I immediately clutch my stomach, bending at the waist.

"Forget the room. We need to call your mom and get you to the nearest E.R., Chase."

"No. No. I just need to lie down and turn on my hot pad. It's the same pains I've been having lately, just much more intense, and my head, I think I'm drunk. It's not a big deal. I probably drank the wine too fast. If I don't feel better in the morning, we'll call a doctor."

And then everything goes dark.

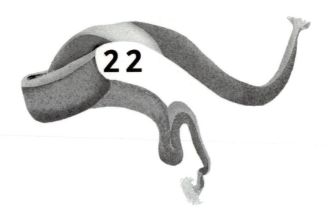

22

I slowly open my eyes, but can't make out a blessed thing; everything's blurry. I blink several times before I notice that the window shades are down. *White window shades? I thought mine were blue.* I rub my eyes lightly and look at it a second time. *It's definitely white. I don't remember changing them! And the size? Geez, did someone redecorate overnight? Why wasn't I told about—*

"Nurse, she's awake."

"Who said that? Who's in my room?" I croak. I cough uncontrollably.

"Whoa, whoa, whoa! Chase. Here's some water. Sip on it slowly."

With my eyes closed again, I reflexively put out a hand to receive the welcoming drink and quickly obey. "Is that you, Roxie?" sounding more like myself after a few swallows.

"Yes. You were out for about twelve hours." I feel the mattress bounce a bit as she must have taken a seat. "Twelve hours. Holy sh—"

"Nana's here too," Roxie adds.

"Nana? In my room? What's going—"

This time, with eyes wide open, I pan the room and realize that I'm not in my room. At all. Or the New York hotel room.

"What's happening? Don't tell me I'm in a hospital? OUCH!" I attempt to sit up, but my head is pounding.

"Okay, I won't tell you that you're at Gracie Square Hospital." She pats my leg, plastering on a fake smile.

"Your humor stinks; you know that?" I close my eyes again, letting this news sink in.

"Yes, but that's another story. Here, let me help you up." Roxie wraps her arm around my shoulders and slowly lifts me to a sitting position. Nana repositions my pillows.

"Hi, my little love," Nana grabs hold of my hand, giving it a little squeeze.

"Nana, what are you doing here? What's going on?" She's wearing sweatpants and a sweatshirt that mildly looks like pajamas. I close my eyes and open them again to make sure I'm seeing correctly. My uptight prim and proper Nana never wears anything that's not starched or pressed to a crisp.

"Your mom called. I got here as soon as I could so I could relieve her; took a red-eye flight. She's at the hotel resting. She's been a nervous wreck, pacing your room for hours."

"Chase, you blacked out at the hotel lobby. Do you remember?" Roxie interjects. "After the hotties left us."

I look between the two of them as Nana's mouthing the word *Hottie* like it's fresh in her vocabulary. "No. But I remember having stomach pain. Well, more like pelvic pain, and then my head felt so dizzy. Is that why I'm here? Did I get dumped again—this time on Valentine's Day, slip and fall, and knock myself out AGAIN?" I press my eyes closed as visions of Idaho, Grant, and flailing on ice skates swim past me.

"Nice to see you have your sense of humor back," Roxie offers, "we'll know more when the doctor comes in."

"Ms. Morgan?" A dark-skinned Indian woman pokes her head in the door. "Hi," not waiting for a response, "I'm Dr. Patel. You've had quite a long nap. How are you feeling this afternoon?" She's petite, half the size of Nana, and doesn't look a day older than twenty.

"Afternoon? What time is it?"

"It's 2:12. How are you feeling?" Dr. Patel repeats, grabbing my wrist, taking a quick check of my pulse. "Well, my head hurts, and my stomach doesn't feel quite right; I think I'm hungry," I tell her. "And I feel like I'm having horrible cramps but more towards my tailbone if that doesn't sound crazy."

"Hungry is good. I'll order you soft food for starters."

"Soft food? Why? Did you remove one of my organs?" I can feel the heat rising at the back of my neck. "Which one?" I begin to grope my body for signs of stitches.

"I assume you ladies are family. Yes?" looking at Roxie and Nana.

"I'm the grandmother, and these are my granddaughters. My daughter-in-law, Chase's mom, is staying at a nearby hotel," Nana jumps in, standing up, properly introducing herself.

"I'm Roxanne Morgan," Roxie stands, vigorously shaking her hand.

Dr. Patel nods. "Thank you! I have Mrs. Morgan's number listed. I'll update her as soon as I'm done here," she scribbles on her clipboard. "Ms. Morgan, do you consent to me going over your prognoses in front of these family members? This is just protocol."

"Uh ... yes... Why wouldn't—"

"Then, I need your signature right here." Dr. Patel hands me a clipboard and pen. I scan the document and scribble my name, hoping that I haven't signed something I'll regret later.

"What's going on, now I'm worried?" I ask, handing back the signed document. "Did you take out my appendix? Tonsils? What?"

"No. We didn't remove anything. I ordered a battery of tests, and the results showed several things. For one, and you have a very rare condition called levator-ani-syndrome."

"Levator ... what? Syndrome? Is that BAD?" I say a little too loudly.

"No. We'll talk about it in a second. The second thing is that tests found MDMA, methylenedioxy-methamphetamine, in your bloodstream," Dr. Patel announces.

"MDMA?" I'm confused.

"Better known as ecstasy. Are you a drug user, Ms. Morgan?"

"WHAT? No. Absolutely not. I've never touched the stuff. EVER!" My eyes have to be bugging out. I'm clearly shocked. "I'm not a druggie—" I look at their faces. "I'm not! Okay. Fine. I like my anti-anxiety meds for flying, but those don't count. Roxie, tell her—I don't even drink."

"ECSTASY? The drug that makes you want to fuck your brains out?" Roxie's mouth drops open, forgetting that Nana's in the room.

The doctor glares at Roxie. She mutters, "Sorry, Nana," before quietly moving next to me.

"No one is accusing you, Ms. Morgan," Dr. Patel continues. "I'm just collecting facts. Where were you last night?" She's looking at her clipboard, taking notes.

"We were at the Velo," Roxie volunteers. "There were two sex—" she catches herself, glancing at Nana, "Spanish guys, who paid for our table, and—"

"Roxie! TMI," I whisper through gritted teeth.

"Did they provide you with any drinks?" Dr. Patel adds, ignoring my sudden rant.

"Yes. Red wine. Why do—"

"But I didn't drink mine. I don't like wine," Roxie volunteers again, interrupting me.

"Yes, and thank your lucky stars because it saved your lives," Dr. Patel points out to Roxie. "It did?" Roxie answers weakly.

Dr. Patel turns back to me and continues where she left off. "When did you notice pain in your abdomen, Ms. Morgan?"

"Soon after ... Oh, my God! Are you telling us that they slipped *that* in our drinks? I never drink. I just got so nervous, and for some reason, I gulped it down. But I never, ever drink. You have to believe me."

"More than likely, Ms. Morgan, yes, they slipped the MDMA into your wine. As I said, both of you are very fortunate women. You could have been raped and found dead in an alley instead," Dr. Patel states matter-of-factly.

Silence, except for the hard "flump" from Roxie when she plops into the chair by my bed. Nana's mouth drops open, looking horrified.

The last statement throws me for a loop. I feel bile rising.

"Quick! Grab that—" Dr. Patel points to the plastic bag under the hospital tray, which Nana retrieves. Dr. Patel opens a plastic bag under my chin and hands me a couple of wipes when I'm through.

"I'm sorry, Dr. Patel," I say feebly.

"No need."

"So, are you telling me that we were a date-rape set-up?" Roxie mumbles, eyes now wide with shock. "They didn't look like the type. They were so preppy and handsome and charming ..." She's rambling like she does when she's uncomfortable.

"Date-rape?" Nana says feebly, her eyes wide as saucers. "In my day and age, women of your age would be married and not going to nightclubs." She sits down on the little seat, fanning herself with her purse. "That's why I specifically instructed your mom to get you to Jardin's lookout to meet Mrs. Adelman. You both need husbands. You don't need to be going to nightclubs, where you meet men looking to date-rape you. Are you sure, Doctor? That these vile men were up to no good."

"I'm afraid so, Miss..."

"Mrs. Morgan. My last name is the same as Chase's."

Dr. Patel nods to Nana. "We've had several incidents recently and are working with the police to nail down the perpetrators. If you're okay, I can have an officer interview the two of you."

"Oh, God!" I start shaking. Roxie wraps the bed blanket around my shoulders.

"Yes. We'll be glad to talk to an officer." Roxie's voice is a near whisper. This is a side of my cousin I rarely see. I can tell she's affected by what Dr. Patel has to say.

"I'll need you to sign this," Dr. Patel gives each of us clipboards and pens. "Someone will be in to see you soon. Now, about the levator-ani-syndrome, Ms. Morgan. When did you first start noticing the severe pain in your tailbone and lower abdomen?"

"About two years ago," I provide. "But then it went away and came back after my fiancé dumped me."

"And have you had trouble getting pregnant, that's assuming that you're sexually active?"

"I always told my granddaughters never to give away their milk until they're married," Nana jumps in. Dr. Patel smiles sweetly.

"Nana!" I shout.

"Well, it's true!" Nana unashamedly admits. "First, a date rape drug, and now you want me to hear about the sexual activity of my granddaughter? I need to call your mother. I can't take much more today. You're going to give this old lady a heart attack."

"She's still a virgin, Nana. I, on the other hand—" Roxie confesses.

"Roxie!!!" I'm visibly livid.

"Okay. No worries! You answered my question. You do know that as a future reference, you shouldn't conceive. It would severely damage your body and you would no longer have a normal life."

"You mean, I won't be a great-grandmother?" Nana blurts. "That can't be true. We need a second opinion. A husband needs a wife to bear children."

"OH, FOR HEAVEN'S sake! Nana, get off it. We don't live in the Victorian age. Chase isn't getting married to be a broodmare. She's marrying to have great sex!" Roxie's practically shouting.

"ROXANNE!" Nana snips. She visibly flinches as she takes a seat in the empty chair, looking exhausted.

"What are you saying? That I can never have—" I burst into tears, crying uncontrollably. Roxie hands me a box of Kleenex.

"You can see a specialist who can run more tests," Dr. Patel continues. "Studies show that it's a very rare condition and that 1% of women ever get it. Can I be candid with you, Ms. Morgan?"

"OK," I say between sobs.

"My personal experience working with women who have this condition is this. Levator-ani-syndrome typically affects A-type personalities—those who are overachievers or have suffered some kind of tragedy."

"Oh, my God! She lost her—" Roxie begins.

Silence as Roxie, Nana, and I look at each other.

"Ms. Morgan, I can refer you to a specialist in the area."

"We're not from here," Nana provides. "The girls were just visiting. We're all from Southern California. The Los Angeles area, to be exact."

"Oh, really?" Dr. Patel perks up. "I'm a native of that area. I could probably connect you with someone there. I have a colleague that I refer to a lot of patients: Dr. Brennan. He's rather well known in your neck of the woods."

"I know, he's my doctor," I admit. "Do we have to talk about this now?"

"No, we don't. I do encourage you to see Dr. Brennan. He can help."

"He's my shrink. I don't think he can help with that area." Tears start pouring down my cheeks.

"Yes, and no. Relaxation and meditation are a big part of controlling the pain. When you heal your inner self, you heal a lot of things." She looks at me sweetly, "I'll also leave you with a pamphlet on stretches that will help and also a list of foods to avoid and a suggested relaxation app. All these things together should minimize the pain."

"Oh, so I may still have great-grandchildren?" Nana claps. I turn away.

"There are no guarantees. For now, Ms. Morgan, I'll write up a prescription that will get you back on your feet. In the meantime,"

I hear something vibrating on the chair by the window.

"Is that my phone?" I interrupt Dr. Patel.

Roxie rummages around in my purse. "Here," she hands it to me, along with my scarf. "I thought you might like to have it with you." I wipe my nose before I wrap the scarf around my neck and give my phone a swipe. I see that someone sent me a text.

"I'll sign the release papers once you talk with the officer," she tells me. She watches as I set down my phone to blow my nose. "You know, I've seen some miracles in my day. There's always hope. First, follow the protocol and reduce your pain episodes. From what your grandmother was telling me earlier, you're a very smart young lady. Maybe it's time you try to balance life, work, and play." She looks at me, producing a smile. "It was nice meeting you all. I need to call your mom, Ms. Morgan, before I get to my next patient." Dr. Patel smiles before exiting.

"Yes, yes! There's always hope," Nana mimics, taking a seat next to me on the other side of the bed, squeezing my hand in hers.

"Hope has been reserved for everyone, except me," I say, pressing my eyes together, fighting back another round of tears.

"Don't let me ever hear you talk like that again, Chastity Ann Morgan! Do you understand?" Nana wiggles her finger toward me. "There's always hope. You've just got to believe."

"Yes, Nana. I'm sorry," I whisper. My simple act of contrition isn't enough because Nana's diatribe on premarital sex continues, I swear, for another five minutes. The best I can do is avoid eye contact. Emotionally drained, I have enough energy to grab my phone off the bed and look at the new text. I read:

Paul: Where are you? I stopped by your house to surprise you. I was hoping to take you out for breakfast, but your dad said you were in Europe. You really did it? I can't believe it! You hate flying. Anyway, I tried to ask more questions, but he was rushing off in some crazy getup to go horseback riding. BTW, I saw Grant.

We need to talk. Listen. No more running away from me again, do you understand? I want to help you get through this, so don't push me away. Later.

I barely digest Paul's text when my phone buzzes again. This time, it's my mom. "Hi, Mom," I say groggily.

"Chase. The doctor just called me." I hear sniffles in the background.

"Mom?"

"I'm just glad you're safe." Her voice trails off as she puts the phone down. I hear her sobbing and patiently wait until she composes herself.

"Honey, don't worry, you can get through this. You always fight through everything," she says between sobs. "You can always adopt."

"Not now, Mom."

"You know," my mom ignores my comment, "life gives you curveballs, and you find a way to smack them out of the park. You're going to get through this, I promise. I'm on my way to the hospital now to pick you all up."

I press my eyes together to drown out the pain, as I did over two years ago.

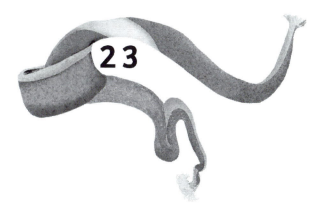

23

Three days have passed since our return from New York. Nana suggested I stay with her, and Gramps in their roomy guest bedroom while I recover. Pale-yellow walls, sprinkled with white forget-me-nots fit in perfectly with the lavender-accented curtains, bedspread, pillow shams, and wall-to-wall shag carpeting.

The warmth of the alcove room only gets better when I pan the array of vintage pictures and candle holders that cover two of the walls. There's an antique desk adjacent to the bed; a squat bookshelf rests against one of its long rectangular sides. Off to the left of the dormer window are a couple of hanging shelves filled with bric-à-brac.

The funny part about being at Nana and Gramps place is that their brick Tudor home, nestled among some big oak trees and barely visible from the street, is a few doors down from our house at the end of the block. They wanted to downsize and be close to their family after they retired. Nonetheless, it was a good call on my grandmother's part since the stress of the Velo incident was too much on my mom and my dad, even though he acts like nothing ever happened—I guess his way of coping.

"We've nabbed a couple of guys that fit their descriptions." Detective Lucas says through my speakerphone, as Roxie lounges on the bed and I lay on the floor on my back, bum pressed up against the wall, with my legs pointed towards the ceiling—one of the many stretches in the pamphlet Dr. Patel gave me. "And verifications are looking good, but you never know. They may still be out there. At any rate, don't be surprised if you see something in the news soon. Have a good day, ladies!"

"Geez! I wish I could find these sleazebag con artists," Roxie exclaims as soon as I hang up. "I'd give them a piece of my mind."

"Yep, and probably a couple of other limbs, too," I sarcastically add, placing my new emoji pillow against my headboard and new emoji bean bag lap desk on my legs. Both items are recent gifts from Roxie, her way of apologizing for what she put me through at Velo and the hospital. "Why would Detective Lucas bother to contact us if these guys weren't dangerous? Plus, they're pros, Rox. God only knows how many different names they go by," I say, as I type in the current aliases of the two men. "OH ... MY ... GOD..." I spit out slowly.

We give each other a knowing look.

"You found them?" She immediately grabs her laptop and madly ticks away at the keyboard, armed with the necessary information: banana exporter, land of origin, name, and the photo Roxie took of him exiting the club.

Three hours later (and a bag of tortilla chips, a jar of salsa, two bananas, and bottled spring water), all that our bloodshot eyes can find are strange websites forums that include comments about Banana Man from weird entry names like Dizzle Frat, MamaMucha, PootyToots, and Gotchabytheballs.

"Gothabytheballs? What the heck?" Roxie bellows out loud.

"That's a good one!" I can't help but laugh, except it still hurts when I do. I wrap my arms around my stomach. "OUCH!"

"Oh, sorry, Chase! Can I get you a hot water bottle or something? I'm sure Nana has a bunch stored up around here."

"I have Nana's hot pad right here!" I set my laptop on the bedside table and reach behind my pillow to pull out the little blue mat. Placing it on top of my tummy, I close my eyes, enjoying the warmth; it feels so good.

There's a knock on the door just when I'm about to doze off.

"Who is it?" Roxie asks.

"It's me. Daphne."

"I hope you don't mind, love," Gramps inserts as they walk in. "She said it was important."

At eighty-seven, he's always the epitome of elegance in his grey slacks, collared shirts for golfing (even though he can no longer golf because of a bad back), and sports coat. Nonetheless, he's still goofy Gramps, the card who wears old, gray sneakers with every outfit. Even right now in his bathrobe, his hair a bit out of sorts, and looking half asleep, he still has on his old, gray sneakers.

"What are you doing up? It's nearly eleven p.m. Does your mom know you're here?"

"I'll leave you ladies alone," Gramps interrupts.

"She's the one who encouraged me," Daphne responds, waving to Gramps as he leaves. "She walked me over. She just got back from the hospital," Daphne smiles widely. "I'm not exactly a baby, you know. Eleven isn't that late. Plus, I told her you had pieces of my science project that I needed for school tomorrow."

"Clever, kid—" I stop myself. "God, I sound like Brent. Where is the Master Swordsman, anyway? I'm surprised he's not joining us." I look at Roxie, who just shrugs.

"Beats me. Out of town on business, that's what he said."

"So, what's up, Daphne?" I ask, slightly groggy. She's wearing Minnie Mouse pajamas with her hair in two pigtails.

"I've got some news for you." She wriggles between the two of us on the bed.

"News? About what?" I inquire as I maneuver my body into a better sitting position.

"Can I use your laptop?"

"Uh ... sure. Why?" I'm curious now, reaching over to the table to hand her my pink device.

Daphne begins ticking away and opens to a CNN report with the heading "Drug Lord and Brother Arrested after a Ten-Month Search."

"Holy Sh-nike!" Roxie restrains herself.

"Who told you—" I begin.

"Nobody. I thought you might want to know." Daphne smiles sweetly, again.

Both Roxie and I must look like idiots, our mouths opening and closing like a beached fish. We scroll through the article that was published ten minutes ago. Two men are mentioned, including mugshots: José and Ymmer Ramirez; José (aka Manuel) identified as the drug lord and Ymmer, (aka Carlos) his chemist brother.

"Listen to this," Roxie says "A ten-month search for José Ramirez and his chemist brother, Ymmer Ramirez, is over. They have issued warrants in connection with the production and sale of a highly-toxic form of MDMA (better known as ecstasy) in Manhattan..."

"OH. MY. GOD!" I'm thunderstruck, slowly shaking my head. There's also something later in the article about a Ponzi scheme involving their father. *Jesus! I guess the apple doesn't fall far from the tree. How do people get mixed up in shit like this, anyway?*

"I have to go now. Could one of you walk me back home?" Daphne says matter-of-factly, bouncing off the bed.

"I'll take you," Roxie offers. "I'll be right back, Chase."

"And Chase," Daphne pops her head back into the bedroom, "when we let go of the past and start living in the present, life changes. Just saying..." She gives a little wave as she leaves.

My eyes stay glued to the doorway minutes after they leave. "How the heck did that little squirt know about New York and the men?" I mumble, still shaking my head. "And how does she sound like my shrink and Dr. Patel?"

"Jared, stop the car, man!" An ear-piercing scream startles me and revs up my already pounding heart. I'm startled a second time by the mad scratching at the door; it's Lacy, Nana's little King Charles Cocker Spaniel. I open the door; she runs into the room in full attack mode, barking at the window, like she's ready to bite a home invader. I shut the bedroom lights before pulling the curtains aside to see what all the commotion is about. The streetlights faintly illuminate the pavement below.

I slide down to my knees and peer over the sill. My eyes grow wide.

"OH ... MY ... GOD! This is absurd," I blurt aloud.

If the night couldn't get any weirder, there in the street in front of Nana's property is a stark-naked guy, sprawled out spread-eagle on the windshield of an SUV. I remain frozen, staring; I'm practically gawking as he slides his body down the side of the car. I gently push open the bedroom window, sticking my head out to get a better view. He's leaning into the passenger window as his friend hands him a pair of shoes. I've never laid eyes on such a tight, lean, and muscular body. I exhale. I didn't even realize that I was holding my breath. Even from this distance, I can see his ripped, golden Adonis muscles.

I race over to the little antique desk in the corner of the room, grabbing my phone.

"No one will believe me, Lacy, if I don't capture this on film." The sweet spaniel gives me an encouraging nudge to get my phone. I fiddle with it, turning off the flash, so I remain undetected. I enlarge the screen as much as it will go without distorting the image. The guy, wearing only shoes, stands in front of the car in the glow of the headlights.

"OH, MY GOD, Lacy, don't tell anyone that I've turned into a randy voyeur." The spaniel utters a light growl. "You promise?" I give her a light pat. She begins licking my arm. "Good, Lacy!"

I brush away my Peeping-Tom thoughts as I continue to stare, mesmerized. I'm flushed, breathing hard while trying to snap a photo of his tight derrière. I can't look away.

The car horn beeps, snapping me out of my trance. I dive to the floor and creep back up to peer out the window.

"Have I been caught?" I whisper. "Nope, no one's looking my way."

The guy is bent over in a pre-race position. For some weird reason, I feel like I've seen this before but can't place it. I set my camera to video and hit the play button. A loud blast of the horn pierces the darkness, and he is in a full sprint down the street. I follow as far as my view will take me until all I see is an ancient eucalyptus, and just like that, my streaker is nowhere to be found. I feel a twinge of disappointment since the show is over.

"Did you see that?" Roxie says, rushing into the bedroom.

"You saw him?" My eyes widen.

"Hell, yeah!" Roxie exclaims. "I had to cover Daphne's eyes on the way to her house. She fought me tooth-and-nail, wanting to see what was going on. I kept saying, 'Not for young eyes! Not for young eyes!' GOD, what a HUNK!! The whole scene was straight out of the movie *Old School.*"

"That's it! *Old School!*" I shout, happy to have figured out the scenario's familiarity. "What are the chances of seeing something like that, especially at this hour on our super boring suburban street?" I raise. "Where nothing remotely interesting ever happens."

"Seriously! How are you feeling?" Roxie says, changing the subject.

"Better, but I'm exhausted after all the excitement tonight. I need to get to bed."

"Sounds good, cuz. I'll see you in the morning, especially since I left on all the lights at my house. You know—makes it look livable to keep the snoops away. I better get going." Roxie gives me a hug and kiss before leaving.

Somehow, I manage to brush my teeth and get my PJs on quickly. Slipping under the covers, I'm out like a light as soon as my head hits the pillow.

* * *

The naked Adonis runner is dashing towards me on the sandy beach, his hair blowing in the wind, his ripped muscles flexing with each stride. I'm holding a bouquet of red roses as I stand underneath a canopy of flowers in my princess cut, giant poofy wedding dress, waiting for him—my groom. The wind starts raging, the flowers are blowing everywhere, and the sand is obscuring my vision. Everything abruptly changes to slow motion as his direction shifts, and he runs backward.

"WAIT!! Don't leave me!" I yell at the top of my lungs, trying to run forward, but my feet won't move; they're in cement.

BANG!

I wake startled.

BANG!

The tree branch slams against the windowpane again, as the Santa Ana winds are in full gale force, pounding branch after branch against the window panes. I wake up with a kink in my neck and the sun shining in my eyes.

Do I know where I am? Yes, Nana's guest bedroom. Do I know my name? Yes, Chastity "Chase" Morgan. Do I remember anything about last night? Hell, yes! Colorful images of the exhibitionist fill my thoughts along with the latest news of José and Ymmer via none other than a ten-year-old girl.

"I've got to have a talk with that kid," I mumble as I sit up.

"Chase, love, who are you talking to?" Gramps must have turned his hearing aids up; he pokes his head in the door.

"Oh! Morning, Gramps! Just talking to myself. What's up?"

"You missed breakfast. Your grandmother says it's time to get dressed and come downstairs before you miss lunch too." Lacy runs over to him, scratching at his legs.

"Oh, little love, that's where you've been all night. Protecting Chase, have you? You come downstairs too. We have something for you as well." He picks her up, cradling her in his arms as he heads back out the door.

"I'll be right down. Let me jump in the shower."

I climb out of bed and head toward the guest bathroom before venturing down into the kitchen.

"Good morning, Chase, darling! You were up rather late last night. Here, I mixed raspberries and Farmer's Market granola with some plain Greek yogurt to tide you over until lunch," Nana says, handing me a bowl. She's back to her old self, dressed in starched navy pants and a navy-and-white cardigan that has a bit of shimmer in the threads, as she sits back down in her favorite, padded ladder-back chair. The kitchen is a throwback to the 50s with its painted cabinets and yellow-marbled countertop, but I wouldn't expect anything less coming from Nana's fetish for vintage decor.

"Thanks!" I lean over and kiss her on the cheek. Taking a seat on another ladderback chair at the oblong breakfast table, I happily begin munching away, staring out at their glistening pool–something that Gramps insisted since he swims laps twice a day. Lacy paws my leg, begging for anything I'm willing to share my breakfast food. I place my bowl on the floor and listen to her lick the scraps while looking at my phone. "Nana, did you hear anything weird last night?" I'm scrolling through the last obscured photo. It should be a crime to look this good.

"No phones at the table, love," Gramps interjects behind the newspaper.

"Perhaps," Nana says, winking and letting out a little laugh. "Did you get a good night's sleep?"

"I definitely had very vivid dreams," I say with a huge grin, sticking my phone back in my jeans pocket.

"Mrs. Adelman called me the other day. She mentioned that you had not contacted her about her matchmaking services."

"Did she tell you her prices? They're obscene. Where would I come up with that kind of money?" I say in between sips of hot tea.

"That's not for you to worry about. I'm taking care of it. The important thing is for you to find a husband and not go around to any more nightclubs. That's why I went to all that trouble to set up the New York meeting."

"So, essentially, you want to buy me a crazy, eccentric husband because she's kind of looney with all her bedazzled outfits? I can't imagine a normal guy wanting to hire her, Nana." I say, throwing my hands up in the air.

"Oh, little love, I just don't want anything like New York ever to happen again." Her expression says it all; she's anxious. "But, never mind all that. I'll find you a husband," she says, giving me another wink.

"I know you mean well, but just for today, can we take a mini-break from the whole marriage hunt and instead have a late lunch? I feel like *Pollo Negro*—you know, the new Caribbean restaurant that just opened up? What do you say? Savory plantains sound good right now."

"Well, I have something special planned for lunch today," Nana smiles like a Cheshire cat as she briefly glances at Gramps.

She's up to something, I've seen that look a hundred times before.

"Oh, love," Gramps interjects again, "shouldn't you be teaching and going to your classes? Your father called this morning and said it's time for you to get back to school. 'No more hiding out.' Those were his exact words."

"I haven't been hiding out. You know that Gramps, and you know what's been going on recently. I've been avoiding dad because I can't talk to him right now. He doesn't handle trauma too well. Maybe you can talk to him. Tell him that the doctor said my body needs rest. I know he doesn't understand that concept, but then it goes back to him being in the dark about what happened in New York. His way of coping is, well, not coping. He is busying himself with other things so that he doesn't have to face what's in front of him."

"That sounds oddly familiar, little love," he gives me a long look. "Okay. For you, I can try to talk to your dad, love, but he's one hard nut to crack if you know what I mean."

"I do." I let out a huge sigh. "Alison's been covering my sessions. I was thinking possibly of going this afternoon and giving Professor Feldman an update. No need to worry." I give them both a kiss on the cheek as I deposit the bowl in the sink. "This has been a delightful sleepover. When mom suggested it, I thought you would be force-feeding men down my throat, but this has been like old times—playing cards, watching Wheel of Fortune, overeating jamoca almond fudge ice cream. Thank you both."

"Don't forget your binoculars next time," Nana winks.

"I knew you saw him!" I run back over, embracing her in a tight hug.

The doorbell rings. "Little Love, could you get that?" Gramps asks.

I scurry across the black-and-white checkerboard hall and pull open the extra-thick wooden door.

"I was just getting ready to leave, Roxie—"

"That wouldn't be a good idea right now. You'd miss out on all the fun."

My eyes are wide with surprise as Daphne runs out from behind Roxie. She throws her arms around my waist.

"Her mom got called into the hospital," Roxie explains. "A patient went into labor. Daphne has the day off from school, so Maria asked if I could babysit."

Roxie's phone suddenly lets out with a powerful choo-choo.

"That's a new one! Who is it this time?" I roll my eyes, knowing that she always sets up a different ringtone for each guy she meets. I watch her turn as she picks up; her voice goes all sappy and soft.

"I can't talk now—"

"Tell him that I approve," Daphne interrupts.

Roxie waves her hand, blowing her off.

"Tell who that you approve?" I question.

"I'll call you back soon." Roxie throws a kiss before closing her phone. She looks up from her phone and finds me staring at her.

"You mind telling me who the mystery man is?"

"Not yet," Roxie quips.

"Not yet? What do you mean, not yet? You always tell me about the latest and greatest in your—"

"It's not time," Daphne jumps in.

"Not time? Would someone please tell me what's going on?" I throw up my hands.

"I'm testing the waters with this one. He's ... special," Roxie admits.

"Hmm... It sounds serious. I thought you weren't one for settling down?" I counter.

"I'm not, but I may rethink it." Roxie grins.

My eyes get big.

"Okay. You're freaking me out right now, so how about I drop this, and if you want to tell me more some other time, I'll be all ears."

"Agreed." I extend my hand to shake on it. "Oh, by the way," the mistress of abrupt changes does it again, "We had a little run-in with the occupants of a silver convertible Porsche 911 Carrera on our way back from our morning donut run. The

Carrera was idling right next to me on Colorado Boulevard. I looked over and saw the most familiar guy with a buzz cut and full beard." Roxie wiggles her eyebrows—her signal for providing a hint.

I furrow my brows, missing her point. "And? So, did he give you the birdie or something?"

"No, you don't get it. The man behind the wheel was caressing the thigh of a long-legged blonde." This time Roxie gives me a playful shove.

"All right. I give up! I have no idea who you're talking about," putting my hands on my hips.

"Paul." Daphne sputters. "She's talking about Paul."

"Paul? Is he back in town? And he was with a girl? That makes no sense. When we were in New York City, he said he came by my house to take me to breakfast. He never mentioned anything about a girl. OH. MY. GOD! Maybe he met someone at the Cialto, and he started a long-distance relationship, or maybe he's turning into his brother. Either case," I ramble, "it makes sense with the Porsche." I roll my eyes again. "But, then again, I can't imagine him as a player. Something's not right."

"Ding, ding, ding! You got the player part right. But what about the girl?" Roxie looks confused. I watch as she shifts to "thinking mode" by screwing up her face and tapping her index finger on her puckered lips.

"Maybe he's in town to do some film and brought his cousin?" Roxie theorizes, "but then again, I don't think he'd touch his cousin like that."

"I can't believe Paul has a girlfriend, and he didn't tell us," my voice sounds brittle, as my thoughts head in a different direction, visualizing him making out with the leggy blonde and feeling a sudden pang of... *"A pang of what, Chase? Jealousy, maybe?"* The little Chase Angel sits on my shoulder yelling in my ear.

"Why do you care, anyway? You've never liked him romantically. It's Paul, Chase! He's been your brother from another mother like ... forever. Plus, why are you getting your knickers in a ticker? We're all just friends. Right? Friends."

A moment of silence as Roxie and I stare at each other.

"But then again, Daphne has been telling me something else. Go on, tell her, Daph."

Daph?

"Well, I like him a lot. Do you like him, Chase?" The little girl winks at me.

"Um ... yeah ... What have you been telling Roxie?" I kneel, grabbing the little girl's shoulders.

"Just girl talk." Daphne smiles, patting my arm.

I give her a sideways glance.

"What?" Daphne shrugs. "I just think it's weird that in this large city, we had a random encounter with Paul. Don't you think fate might be knocking at your door, trying to tell you something?"

My mouth drops open. My thoughts gravitate to the text Paul sent me while I was in the hospital. I never responded to him; I didn't know what to say.

"Daphne's right," Roxie rambles, "we won't talk about this bizarre coincidence; how in all the streets in LA with all its millions of cars, we find ourselves next to a guy that doesn't even live here anymore. Someone who used to be your tag-along best friend back in college, the one who always swooned you when you would walk into a room and who always hung onto your every word?"

"Fine. Mum's the word," Roxie chortles. "But then again ... tell her, Daphne!"

My thoughts immediately shift to Paul's flirtatious remark at the Cialto.

I swallow hard. My phone rings. "Speaking of the devil... Hi, Paul," I answer flatly.

"That's no way to say hello to your best bud," Paul quips. "Did you get my text?"

"Yes. I was in the hospital. I couldn't answer—"

"Hospital? What happened? Are you okay?" Paul genuinely sounds concerned over the background road noise.

"I'm fine. Listen..."

"Ask him about the girlfriend," Daphne yells.

"I heard that," Paul responds. "Who's that? Doesn't sound like Roxie."

"I'm here too," Roxie screams into the phone and then slyly presses the speaker button. "That's Daphne, our little neighbor."

"Hi Paul," Daphne jumps in. "I hear that you're the best."

"Oh, who told you that?" Paul laughs.

"Chase," Daphne answers.

"When did I tell you that, you little squirt?" I interrupt. Daphne and Roxie break down into a fit of giggles.

"So..." Paul continues, "when can we get together and talk?"

I switch off the speakerphone. "How long are you here? Are you on business, or is this all about your new girlfriend?"

"A while. I just met her yesterday at a party one of my producers was throwing. She's okay. Just a morning breakfast."

"Just okay? Breakfast? Did you sleep with her after just meeting her? Roxie said you had your hand high on her leg. Oh. My. God, you've suddenly become a player, haven't you?" I counter.

"You know how Roxie loves to blow things out of proportion. Look, Chase, she's nothing—"

I abruptly hang up, but it immediately rings. I fumble to shut my phone down. I can't hear it anymore. My heart is beating so hard that it hurts. *Is this what jealousy feels like? Or rage? Or ... or ... I have no idea what I'm feeling right now.*

"Why didn't you an—" Roxie starts.

"Hi Roxie, and welcome back, little love," Gramps interrupts, swinging the door the rest of the way open. "What did you say your name was again? Daisy?"

"Daphne. Can I call you Gramps?" she asks candidly.

"Well, of course!" he bends over and gives her a big hug, motioning her in the den.

"You looked really handsome in your uniform," Daphne comments.

"How did you know I was in the Navy? Did the girls show you my picture? Back in the day," Gramps doesn't stop to hear answers, "I was quite the sailor. How about all of us move to the den so we can chit chat more? Oh, I almost forgot," Gramps turns around to talk to me, "your grandmother has a surprise visitor for you."

"I knew it! I knew she was up to something!" I exclaim. "What kind of visitor? Is this what she was talking about when she said she'd find me a husband?" I ask, my brows furrowed, pulling Gramps' arm. My grandfather gives a little shrug, and Roxie bursts out laughing. I look at her dead-on, narrowing my eyes into slits. "You knew about this and didn't tell me? Oh. My. God!" I ask, looking past her at my disheveled reflection in the hall mirror. "Maybe if you'd warned me, I would've taken the time to appear civilized. I look like a freight train just hit me." I run my fingers across my hair, securing my ponytail, brushing the loose strands into place, adjusting my pink-and-blue scarf around my neck. "Could you at least give me a hint about who's coming?"

"Oh, love," Gramps jumps in, "don't tell her anything. It'll ruin the surprise."

"Don't tell her what?" my grandmother chimes as she saunters down the staircase, martini in one hand, Lacy under her other arm.

"That it's a little early for cocktail hour," Roxie answers, looking aghast.

"Too early? It's never too early. Besides, I owe my longevity to extra-dry martinis and the love of my family."

"Notice that she said her martinis first," Roxie whispers in my ear.

"Nana?" I playfully scold.

"I still believe a double martini at lunch is a necessity," ignoring my comment. "When did that go out of fashion? They knew how to live in the fifties! Chase, take off that ridiculous scarf you insist on wearing every day. We're inside, for heaven's sakes."

I stare at her blankly, looking for any signs that she's had one too many already.

"Nana, happy Friday," Roxie shifts gears, pointing to Daphne, who steps forward, removes the box hidden behind her back, and hands it to her. "We brought you your favorite marzipan chocolates."

"My little darlings! You are so sweet. Thank you so much!" She takes two pieces and passes them around. "Please, help yourselves, but make sure you leave most of it for me to savor later." Nana laughs at her joke. The doorbell rings along with a loud knock on the front door. Nana pulls it open in one graceful motion, never worrying over her martini, which is now only half full. I don't remember seeing her take a sip. And how she pulled it open with Lacy still under her arm is another mystery.

While I try to process all of Nana's talents, in steps a guy who could be a GQ model with his cropped auburn locks, blue eyes, perfectly proportioned nose, and high cheekbones; my mouth drops open. He's a looker with a lean physique; he visibly lifts weights to keep in shape. He's decked out in brown suede loafers, tailored jeans, and a crisp, white collared shirt and accessorized with a shoulder pouch. Lacy begins to growl.

"What's wrong, girl? George won't hurt you," Nana says, holding Lacy a little tighter than usual. George's shoulder pouch begins to shift around, and out pops the head of a yippy, nippy, golden Pomeranian.

"Oh, dear! Chase, could you take Lacy into the kitchen? She doesn't get along well with other dogs." I dutifully scoop a wriggling Lacy and get her situated in the kitchen.

"Well, now," I hear Nana in the background, "Let's start this over again, shall we? Hello, George! It's been a long time." I return just in time to see Nana reach up on tippy-toes to plant a kiss on his cheek, lingering an extra second. She can be such a charmer.

"Twelve years, to be exact, Mrs. Morgan," George chuckles lightly.

"Call me Vivien, please! You remember my husband, Mitchell?"

"Call me Gramps!" my grandfather interjects, shaking George's hand.

"Gramps, good to see you! It's been a long time."

"It certainly has been," Gramps confirms.

"You remember our granddaughters, Chastity and Roxanne?" Nana jumps in. "And the little one is our neighbor, Daphne."

"Well, hello ladies," George says in a deep, manly tone. He steps forward and hugs us one at a time. "Chastity, Roxie." George smiles with such nostalgic charm; I'm immediately at ease around him.

"I'm so happy that your aunt called me yesterday, George, to tell me you were back in town, at least for the weekend."

"It's Chase these days," I say, ignoring Nana's annoying tendencies. At the same time, I'm madly trying to place him; I have no recollection of ever meeting this guy. Leave it to Nana, though, to find me a gorgeous husband.

"Of course, she remembers you, don't you, Chase?" my grandmother adds. "How could she forget her naked boogie boarding afternoons?"

"I swam naked?" I ask, mortified. "On a boogie board?" My eyes scan the room, hoping Roxie will rescue me.

"He used to push you naked around our pool on your boogie board back when you were a toddler and refused to wear clothing," Gramps chuckles.

I flash back to Charlie, Roxie, and me sitting on the edge of the pool; our feet are dangling in the water while we played Go Fish. A little boy walks in whose aunt and uncle lived five doors down from us in the pink Mediterranean house. He had his boogie board under one arm and a towel and a box of Oreos under the other. *"Deal me in,"* he'd laugh, always taking a seat next to Charlie. *"We'll play for Oreos this time."* From then on, we played for Oreos every time.

Roxie chokes out a laugh as my cheeks and nose turn a deep shade of red. "I remember that."

"I don't remember swimming naked, but I do remember the skinny little boy who loved to wear red suspenders and couldn't play Go Fish if his life depended on it," I chuckle. "That was you?"

"Guilty as charged," George answers, chuckling.

Daphne steps forward and lets the little dog smell her hand. "What's your doggie's name?"

The dog starts yipping.

"Shh, girl! It's okay," George says, rubbing her ear. "Bridget. Would you like to pet her? She loves people, especially children."

"Thanks!" Daphne pats the floor, and immediately Bridget jumps out of the pouch and snuggles up to her. George's pose strikes me funny like I've seen that somewhere before. Then suddenly, it hits me.

"OH ... MY ... GOD," I blurt out. "You're the streaker I saw from the upstairs window last night!"

"George is the naked car surfer with the sensuous body from last night?" Roxie looks George up and down with fascination. "Wow!" her face turning red as a tomato.

"Was that what you wouldn't let me see on our way home?" Daphne questions.

George blushes even more as all eyes turn to him. "Guilty as charged again. It was a dare from a friend who loves watching *Old School*."

"Told you, *Old School*," Roxie laughs.

"Roxie kept saying 'not for young eyes, not for young eyes,'" Daphne adds.

The adults, except for Gramps, erupt in laughter.

"Who's getting naked? Chase love, you're a little old to get naked in front of people," Gramps says, adjusting his hearing aid.

"By the way, where's Charlie? I haven't seen him in years," George asks. "And I have yet to meet Henry. My aunt mentioned he was coming too."

Roxie looks at Nana, who's gulping down her martini.

"It'll just be Henry today," Roxie jumps in. She looks at me and back at Nana, who wipes the back of her palm against her eyes.

"Henry's coming? That's news to me," I shrug. "He's in boarding school, Roxie, you know that."

"I'm just repeating what Nana told me," she shrugs back.

"He told me he would come. He should have been here thirty minutes ago. He's probably running late like he usually does." Nana looks worried. "Let's all go sit down," Nana motions for everyone to follow her into the den.

"So, Mr. Yummy, what do you do for a living?" Roxie takes a seat beside him on the old tweed couch and pats his knee.

George coughs. "I'm, uh, an entertainment lawyer. I also play keyboards in a band," he says, scooting over a few inches so he can reach Bridget to pet her.

"You don't look like the band type," Roxie says, surprised and inching closer, oblivious to his attempted retreat. "And you're not the lawyer type either. You are the..." she's checking him out like he's a shiny new toy.

"Runway-model type," Daphne says, picking up the little dog and cuddling her like she would one of her dolls.

"Oh, yes, Daphne's right, runway-model type, all the way."

Stop it! I silently mouth to Roxie when George's eyes are fixed on his dog.

"Wow!" I feign surprise, "You and my brother Henry will have plenty to talk about when he gets here; he wants to be a lawyer one day," I say, trying to ease the awkwardness.

"Does he? I can see that if he's anything like Charlie. He was such a feisty kid, always had to be right. Injustices bothered his young spirit. How's he doing these days?"

"Charlie's—" I start to answer, but I'm not sure what to say.

"You can ask Henry all about it when he arrives. I think you two will find you have a lot to talk about," Nana says, cutting in.

The doorbell rings, which sends me flying off the couch. Bridget yips like crazy.

"I'll get it." I practically run out of the den and fling open the door. "Thank God, you're finally here!" I whisper to Henry, who is wearing his tennis clothes, sweat dripping off his forehead. "You're late because you were playing tennis! Nana will freak!" I lower my voice again, "Things are a bit awkward with her neighbor friend, and Nana has already started with her martinis. We will have a word later about why you didn't tell me you were coming back into town," I playfully slap him on the shoulder. Bridget runs full force towards Henry. He picks her up and cradles her in his arms.

"Nana this, Nana that, sis. Get over it!" Henry waves me away and enters, looking a bit annoyed. "I'm just in town for a tournament. I didn't know if I'd have time to see everyone. You know, Santa Barbara's not that far. You and Roxie could come to visit me at Thatcher." I look at him like he's talking a foreign language. "Anyway, Roxie's been texting me. Where is George, and his little purse dog?"

"In the den." I puff out a sigh, defeated, as he scratches the little dog's ears.

Henry rolls his eyes. "You never listen when I call, anyway. Plus, Nana thought it would be fun to have this little reunion of sorts. Why she wants me to meet the infamous George is beyond me."

"Henry, dear, come meet our neighbor George," Nana says, standing up to take hold of his arm and lead him over to George.

"Hey, man." George gets up, giving him a firm man hug that is more patting than it is hugging. George looks up at Henry's six-six frame. "Man, you tower over me." George sits back down, taking his dog from Henry, asking him questions, ignoring Roxie and me. It's like we don't exist anymore. And he has this glowing look, almost like a twinkle in his eyes. "You look so much like Charlie," he keeps repeating. Henry looks over at Nana for help.

"Roxie, Chase, Daphne, why don't you gals go check on lunch," Nana coaxes us out of the den, her eyes wider than usual.

I nudge Roxie, and we excuse ourselves to check on lunch. Gramps follows suit, but heads upstairs instead.

"That was strange, right?" I open the refrigerator, perusing the containers of food Nana bought.

"Yeah, strange is a nice way to put it," Roxie replies, "What man with a body like his carries a purse dog? Just looking at how his clothes hug his body makes me hot all over. He's a dream. And Nana's a great matchmaker. Don't you want just to rip off his clothes and have your way with him? And bet you're picking out wedding venues as we speak."

"Roxie." I spit out, glancing over at Daphne, who's all ears. "Not going to happen."

"You. Think. He's. Gay?" Roxie continues slowly.

"Oh, my LORD! Why would you even think that?" I say a little louder than I had expected.

"Did you see the look he gave Henry?"

"I saw that," I admit. "But I think it's because Henry looks a lot like Charlie."

"It's weird because he's not flamboyant at all, but yet I have this itching feeling that he bats for the other team," Roxie adds, lost in thought.

Opening the refrigerator, I pull out a container of Greek meatballs on sticks, which smell divine.

"I'm hungry," Daphne raises. "Do you think Nana will get mad if I take one now?"

"Here. Call it done," Roxie hands her a stick. "What else are we supposed to bring into the den?" Roxie pulls out lunchmeat, a loaf of bread, a plate of deviled eggs, and a large pitcher of lemonade and hands them to me.

"Holy smokes! Something just hit me? Do you think Nana invited George here for Henry, not me?" I chuckle. "Nana couldn't think Henry's gay, could she? Plus, he's not even of legal age while George is thirty! If that's the case, what was Nana thinking? Or maybe it was the martinis talking."

Roxie bursts out laughing. "Here's the thing: Nana invited him here for you! She told me last night. She just thought you would act normal if you had us all here as wingmen. By the way, her gaydar is way off too. I guess it runs in the family."

"HA! So, I need wingmen now? Plus, Nana wouldn't know what the word "gaydar" means if her life depended on it. She's way too old school. You know that, Rox. And," I giggle, "George thinks Henry's gay and clearly likes him." I press my eyes together, grasping my stomach. I'm laughing so hard, it hurts. "Anyway, my love life is a disaster."

"You idiots!" Daphne cuts in, "Henry's not gay. He has a girlfriend. Just saying..." She says matter-of-factly before heading out of the kitchen with the bread and eggs.

"Girlfriend? Nah ... he would have told us if he had a girlfriend." Roxie says, whacking closed the refrigerator with her foot. Carrying the remaining items, we head back towards the den, but slow down when we overhear Gramps and Nana's conversation on the stairs off the hallway.

"Sorry, love!" his voice booming loud enough that we see George's and Henry's heads turn. "Chase isn't his flavor. Did you see the way he looked at Henry?"

"Henry? I brought George here to fix him up with Chase. She needs to get married, and he would make the perfect husband," Nana says. "Wait, did you just say Henry? I'm confused."

OH. MY. GOD!

266

My face must have turned five different shades of red as I make a beeline for the table in the den, deliberately avoiding eye contact with George and Henry. Flustered, I put the food on the den table and stay close to Roxie because I don't know what else to do. However, since Roxie appears to be no better off than I am, she aimlessly walks between the den and kitchen entrance with me trailing close behind, like a duckling. I spy George and Henry eyeing us like we just came in from Mars. "Let me turn up the volume on my hearing aid. What did you say, love?" Gramps's voice booms out again at top volume.

"Maybe you're right that Henry's gay. I'll play matchmaker for him instead," Nana shouts.

"I hate to foil your plans, love, but Henry's one-hundred percent not gay. I've seen him interact with women in a very romantic way. Just because Chase's fiancé turned out to be gay doesn't mean all handsome men are."

"Gramps is a bit senile and hard of hearing," Roxie says to George when she sees him collecting Bridget and heading toward the marble entryway.

"I'm sorry. I've gotta go," George whispers. "Chase, Roxie, it was nice to see the grown-up version of you two—clothes on and all. Do tell your grandparents, thank you. I already said goodbye to Henry."

"Stay. We can all still hang out," Daphne interrupts, "Grandparents can be really silly."

"Maybe another time when things are a little less—" George waves his hands around. We all stop momentarily to hear Gramps and Nana's continued chatter in the background. I roll my eyes. "Seriously," George adds, "I am flattered. I can't tell you how many times my straight friends have tried to set me up. I'm going to scoot now. I just feel ... odd. I hope there are no hard feelings," he smiles. "Oh, and please apologize to your grandparents for my hasty exit."

George turns on his heels and retreats through the front door, closing it gently.

"Talk about awkwardness." Roxie blurts out.

"Where did George go? It's time for lunch." Nana asks, sashaying down the hallway, sipping a fresh martini and looking clueless. *Does she have a rolling bar cart on every floor these days?*

"Well, he ran away when he heard Gramps' voice shouting 'gay' from upstairs," Roxie candidly announces.

"Girls, that's not nice." Nana scolds.

"What? Blame Gramps? Not us!" Roxie replies, kissing Nana on her cheek. "Sometimes the boy next door doesn't want the girl next door. He wants the boy next door."

"So true, dear," Nana concurs. "Sorry, Chase, better luck next time, I guess."

"What about gay?" Gramps asks, now looking at Nana from the second-floor landing.

"Never mind Gramps, and Nana, you need to lay off the martinis," Roxie says as she leans over, checking her martini glass.

"Do you want to be disinherited?" Nana says with brio.

"Ha, ha, Nana. Very funny!

"Are you going to announce to us that you like girls? I've never seen you with a man. And this bohemian, sometimes costume-Halloween look you insist on wearing would chase away any man," Nana asks, trying to change the subject.

Roxie bursts out laughing, "I'm a modern woman, Nana. Just because I don't need a man to fulfill a wild fairytale fantasy doesn't mean I'm a lesbian," she says, looking at me. "I don't mean that in a bad way, Chase. I was never glued to Cinderella, like you."

"And to set the record straight, I'm not gay," Henry jumps in. "I've been dating a lovely girl from Cate School."

"Told you," Daphne grins, tapping her Mary Janes against the marble floor. "You two never listen to me." Everyone looks at her.

"What?" she shrugs. "Why are you all staring at me like that?" My mouth is agape. "And ... hmm ... would you consider this a good or bad time to tell you the vase on the left side of your mantel is going to fall?"

Gramps bends down, eying the little girl. "Did I hear you say a vase is going to fall off my mantel?" Gramps chuckles. "Are you planning on pushing it over?"

She shakes her head.

"You know, um, I just got a text from Maria, and I need to get Daphne home," Roxie interrupts. "Chase!" her eyes speak volumes.

"Thank you for the lovely time Nana, and Gramps. I guess I need to go now." Daphne gives them each a hug and kiss, then promptly heads out the door. I follow close behind.

"But lunch..." Nana begins.

"Save it, Nana. We'll nibble on it later," Roxie yells before closing the door.

"I think you have some explaining to do, little miss," I brusquely say once we're outside.

"If you come back home with me," she says, unaffected, "I'll show you, but you have to promise not to tell my mom."

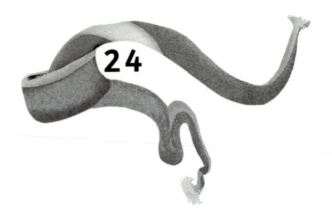

24

"This might freak you out, so sit down," Daphne warns, entering her bedroom.

"Whoa! I see what you mean." I blink several times, adjusting my eyes to the blast of floral pastel pink splashed on the wallpaper and bed duvet as Roxie and I take a seat on the giant pink pillows strewn about on the floor. More Teddy bears than I can count are lying around the room. My eyes gravitate to a small bookshelf near Daphne's bed, where I spot two bears dressed as a bride and groom. I guess no matter what age you are, you dream of weddings.

"You get used to it," Roxie chortles. "Frequent babysitting helps."

"You guys are silly!" Daphne interrupts. "That's not what I'm talking about." She reaches for an unmarked rectangular box under her bed. Flipping the top, she pulls out a board designed with the alphabet and numbers, a plastic spade-shaped object, a notepad, and places them on a bare spot next to the pillows.

"A Ouija board?" I raise.

"You can't tell my mom, okay? Promise me because she doesn't want anyone to know."

"That you own a Ouija board?" Roxie looks confused.

"Do you know why we moved here?" Daphne asks, changing the subject.

"Because your mom received a good offer at Huntington Hospital?" I assume.

"We had to move," Daphne looks left and right, "because our neighbor thought I was a witch," she whispers.

"WHAT?" Roxie and I screech at the same time.

"But that makes no sense," Roxie adds. "You're not a witch."

"This was my dad's," Daphne points to the Ouija board, changing the subject a second time. *And I thought Roxie was bad ... this kid tops her!* "He gave it to me when I told him that grandpa stood by my bed and smiled at me."

"Okay..." I clear my throat. "I assume your grandpa was ... dead?" I question as chills go down my spine.

"He died just before my fifth birthday," she confirmed. "Daddy hugged me and told me that he visited him too. He told me not to talk to Mommy about any of it because it makes her upset."

Daphne pauses, moving in front of the Ouija board. "Daddy said that I was lucky because I have a gift just like him, and he said that I'd never be sad or lonely, especially when he dies because he'll visit me, and we'll be able to communicate with each other through the Ouija board."

"He told you that?" Roxie blurts. "Weren't you creeped out?"

"A little. I was used to people visiting me since I was little, but I couldn't imagine my dad being one of them."

"You mean ghosts?" I add, "visited you?" I press my eyes together, pinching the bridge of my nose.

"Or spirits; they're the same thing, you know," Daphne says matter-of-factly. "So, last year, my dad got a brain aneurysm and died. He was playing golf when it happened. He came to visit me later that night by my bed and reminded me to use the Ouija board. We talked and talked while my mom cried herself to sleep. She was so sad that she wept for weeks. I thought it would help if I told her that Daddy was okay on the other side and that he wants us to be happy. When she asked how I knew all this, she freaked out. Thought I was making it all up."

"Oh, my God!" I blurt out. "You lost your dad? I didn't know. I'm ... I'm so—"

"It's okay," Daphne interrupts. "I mean, I miss him ... a lot. I can't give him hugs and kisses and play games with him, but I get to talk to him often, which unnerves my mom. She threatened to take me to a shrink, saying I need to stop making imaginary friends."

"Well, I'd probably freak—"

"Chase?" Roxie puts a hand on my arm.

"Look, I promise not to say anything. Admit it, though; this is something you don't talk about every day."

"It's okay if you get freaked out," Daphne calmly adds, smiling at us. "Anyway, she doesn't know that I'm talking to you about all this. Like I said before, when my neighbor called me a witch, that's when Mommy started looking for another job. That's how we got here. Mommy's still sad. I think she works a lot, so she doesn't have to think about him, to fill the void in her heart. People do that, you know?" She stares at me.

Silence.

I'm trying desperately to let all of this sink in. I glance at Roxie, who's staring into space.

"Anyway..." Daphne continues, "She's a non-believer."

"Who? The person who called you a witch?" Roxie finally speaks up.

"My mom," Daphne answers. She sits down and crosses her legs, putting two fingers on the object. "My aunt—she's my dad's sister—took my mom and me to a place called Lily Dale after Daddy died to prove that there are many people who are like me. She still freaked out and said it was all nonsense, like a circus show. Mom's a typical doctor; if you can't show concrete evidence of something, she thinks it's all fake."

"I heard of Lily Dale," Roxie chirps. "Isn't that a place for psychics?"

"Yes. They're also called mediums," Daphne responds, smiling widely. "Lily Dale is a place where people—kids, too— who have the gift of seeing and talking to spirits get together and talk about their gifts with each other. I thought it was pretty cool. I didn't feel all alone anymore."

"So..." I'm hesitant, but oh so curious, "What's your gift?"

"Okay," she nervously bites her nail, looking between Roxie and me. "I see things—people, things that will happen; they just pop into my mind at odd times. Before we moved and the mean neighbor called me a witch, I started my own reading business—you know, psychic readings, like a lot of the people at Lily Dale? I like combining the Ouija board with the other messages that I get; it makes it more interesting." She keeps one hand on the object while she scribbles on the notepad. "Anyway, I used the money to buy my bears." Daphne smiles proudly around the room. "But then that mean neighbor didn't like what I told her, and she told my mom and..." she glances down at the object again, which is picking up speed, moving across the board. "She wanted me to contact her husband. His name was George. So, when I tried to contact him, I got Arnold. She started screaming like a crazy person."

"Arnold?" I ask.

"She didn't tell me that she had four husbands, and the one who wanted to talk to her was the one she hated the most. After that, she called me a witch."

I burst out laughing. "I'm sorry, Daphne—nothing against you." My chuckles die down quickly when I see the object stop at letters. My eyes go wide.

I clear my throat again. "So, what are you doing?"

"I'm not doing anything. I'm just following where the spirits are directing me," Daphne calmly reports, like she's commenting on directions to a cake recipe, as the object glides across the board.

"Whoa!" I thought you had to have other hands on the object to make it move," Roxie blurts out, a look of complete surprise on her face.

"How do you know about Ouija boards?" I inquire, confused.

Roxie tells me about Carrie Fay, a girl who was in her first-grade class. She transferred mid-year and only stayed for a few months. She was a quiet girl who kept to herself.

"I barely remember her. Was she the girl who always wore her hair in braided pigtails?" I ask.

"Yep! That's the one; I made friends with her. There were a couple of times I went to her place. That's when she introduced me to the Ouija board. She said it took two or more people to make it work."

"Not so," Daphne interrupts. "Well, at least in my case. Most often, it is two or three people, but I guess I'm different."

"You have a gift," Roxie affirms. "Remember that!"

Daphne gives a broad smile as she continues to do her thing. We watch in awe as the object floats about, seemingly on its terms. I look around the room again at all the bears and wonder what her mom thinks of her collection. I asked Daphne, and she explained that since it was her dad that started buying the bears, her mom didn't think anything was out of order. My eyes revert to the object which has stopped. Daphne scribbles on her pad.

"So, when the object moves around, does that mean that there are spirits in this room? Now?" I ask, my eyes panning the room again. I feel the hairs on my arms stand up. "You're talking to gho—"

"Let me show you," Daphne interjects. The object starts up again, moving faster across the board as it briefly stops at letters.

"This is so cool, I used to read astrological charts for all my friends," Roxie randomly mentions, excitedly folding and unfolding her hands. "Not that I was any good or any of it came true."

Daphne lets go of the plastic spade and leans back against her bed. "I got a message from a man who says he was your grandpa. He said he was a pilot. He said that you have to stop worrying so much about flying. He said that he's with you on every flight. He said that he wants you to be brave when you travel the world."

Roxie looks at me, confused. "Gramps was a Navy sailor, not a pilot."

"She's not talking about Gramps, Rox. She's talking about my mom's dad—Pa on the Mountain. He was a World War II pilot. He died when we were really young. I can still remember visiting him up in Mendocino; he'd help collect silver dollars on the beach before taking us to a little diner. He'd let us have all the pie we could eat. You wouldn't remember him because you never came with us on those trips." I say, brushing a tear from my cheek.

I close my eyes. I can smell the sea air and see the old wooden house that sits on top of the point. There's Pa on the Mountain's giant red hound dog that bounds down the driveway to meet our station wagon. I see my mom, rushing to her father with his giant golly smile and a twinkle in his eye; she throws her arms around him. My mom lost part of herself the day she lost him. He was her rock. And then she lost— Daphne put her fingers back on the board. I watch as the plastic object starts moving again, stopping on letters.

"Chase, there are two guys in your future. I think they are trying to tell me that their names start with the letter L. Maybe it's his first initial. Anyway, I think one is good, and the other is ... odd. He likes to bite."

"Wait? What?" I can't keep up; Daphne is on a roll, doing her "Ouija board and psychic message" mix. I'm blown away. I've never experienced anything like this, especially coming from a kid.

She shuts her eyes again. "Oh, wow! You look like Cinderella. I hear you say 'yes' to the good one, and I'm your flower girl."

Roxie's phone abruptly rings out with a loud, distinct choo-choo tone. She dismisses it and sends a quick text before putting her phone down.

"You don't need my help in that department," Daphne winks at Roxie before she turns back to the board. "Weird! I see a third guy, Chase. He looks like a wolf ... dressed in sheep's clothes?" She cackles. "Maybe it's a Halloween costume."

"Do you mind if I write this down?" I ask.

"I'll give you my notes when I'm done, okay?" Daphne says, sounding like a businesswoman.

"Great... Thanks," I respond, feeling slightly diminutive.

"Oh!" Daphne continues, "you have to get Gramps to putty down his vase, or he will lose it in the next earthquake. I wasn't talking nonsense when I told him that."

"Earthquake? What earthquake? When?" I blurt. Maybe I should start preparing for said earthquake.

"One of your friends is in deep trouble," Daphne—new mistress extraordinaire of subject shifting—went on, shaking her head as her hand flies around the board. She follows the object, eyes watering. "I don't like to predict the bad stuff, but he's not doing well..."

"Girls, I'm home," Maria calls from downstairs. Daphne shoves the board under her bed.

"We were just finishing up tutoring, Mom. Chase is here too! She came to visit. Be right down." Daphne tears the sheet off the pad and hands it to me. She looks at the two of us sternly. "Not a word to my mom, got it?"

Roxie and I nod in tandem while I stuff the paper in my pocket.

Daphne grabs hold of my hand as I head toward her bedroom door. "By the way," she whispers, "I see a little blond boy running around in your pale pink living room. He has your eyes."

Roxie looks at me, furrowing her eyebrows. "I don't remember your living room being pink when we were growing up."

My mouth drops open. "It wasn't." I turn back towards Daphne, "I'm not sure what you're talking about. Back when we were kids my living room was sky bl—"

Daphne interrupts, "Life doesn't always have to make sense. I promise you; it's as clear as the light of day. I see a little blond boy running around your pale pink living room, and he has your eyes and is the spitting image of you."

"But the doctor told me I couldn't..." I trail off talking to myself as Roxie reaches into her purse for her wallet.

Daphne's eyes get wide, shaking her head vigorously. "You're my friend. I can't take your money. Can't I just hang out with you two, instead? It's lonely having no siblings."

"Kid, you're one of us now," Roxie answers. "Jesus, I sound like Brent, too," she laughs. We give her a giant hug. "Can we do this," Roxie points under the bed, "again?"

"Maybe, and remember..." She zips her lips before heading down the stairs.

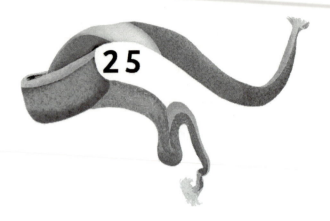

25

The last few months pass by in a blur with the ever-maddening cycle of school, teaching, lab work, research, and headaches galore. I always loved the sound of magpies arguing like angry children in the morning light just outside my bedroom window. I hear a familiar grappling sound—more arguing, this time from our local Scrub-Jays, the latter a warm-and-fuzzy reminder that spring is in full gear. But not today. Inside, I'm fuming enough to scare every bird in the area. My phone chimes, I pick it up on the first ring.

"Oh my God, Roxie. I'm convinced Alison is the devil reincarnated. Yesterday, she told me there was a meningitis outbreak, and I better not come down to campus to proctor the final exam; unless I've had the vaccine. Why the hell did she have to spend the entire quarter trying to sabotage me? She was semi-nice in Paris, but now she's gone back to her bat shit crazy and nasty ways."

"Yowzers! I was going to say 'Good Morning, Chastity.'"

Oops, I pull the phone from my ear, looking at the caller ID. It's Susan, Nana's trusty party planner, calling to firm up details about Nana's big birthday shindig she appointed me to throw at Lake Arrowhead tonight. Susan, who is perky, is the most organized person I know. She alphabetizes everything; color codes her underwear, and time stamps everything.

I let out an exhausted sigh. "Oh, I'm sooooo sorry about that," extending the o's longer than usual. "I thought you were Roxie. We're meeting up shortly. Ugh! It's been a really long spring quarter, and I'm more than ready for a brief vacation before summer school starts."

"Sounds like it! Anyway, I'm sure I'll hear all about this later. Right now, I need to go over the run-through for tonight," she rattles off, sounding like she just finished her fifth cup of espresso and a couple of Diet Cokes, a drink she's never without. "You said that you wanted every minute of your grandmother's eighty-fifth birthday celebration to be occupied so that your relatives don't have time to misbehave, so I've timed it all out." I rub my eyes, listening to Susan's directives.

"Just remember, no toasts, speeches, or karaoke. That will only lead to crazy relatives with a microphone and a captive audience," I grunt, picking at my glittery nail polish, ruining my perfectly good manicure I had a few days ago.

"Got it. Noted. We need to avoid chaos, hell, voices raised, wine glasses tossed, and, at the oddest moment, hair pulling." I can hear her scribbling over the phone. "And don't worry so much Chastity. This isn't my first rodeo, you know. Anything else?"

"We could have a stripper, one of those naughty officers," I say with a serious tone. "Maybe Nana needs a sexy man to give her a lap dance. She could pinch his buns of steel and spark dreams of her youth. That would lighten things up a bit."

There's silence on the line.

"You're joking, right? Are you trying to kill her, Chastity? I don't want to be the blame for the 'death by stripper' shock."

"I'm joking," I lightly chuckle. "Sounds like you've got everything covered. I can't think of anything else."

She laughs. "You just show up at five," Susan laughs, "flash everyone your winning smile, and be a great hostess. Chastity, enjoy yourself, enjoy the party. Nana will love it." She clicks off.

No sooner I'm off the phone with Susan; a loud tweet alerts me of an incoming email:

From: jacquesp@mera.fr
To: ChaseMorg@mylife.com
Subject: No Subject

Bonjour for me, bonsoir for you. I am sending you a video of me receiving an award tonight in New York. I garnered this award for the growth of my company. I am very shy, and to be on stage in front of people is really difficult: my brain is totally empty, and my heart beats so fast... What are your dreams? Je regrette de ne pas être etredans l'avion NY-Paris avec toi!

My eyes blink several times, rereading his email. *He suddenly reappears again after all these weeks?* I keep telling myself he could be THE ONE I've been waiting for. *Could he really be?* But his name doesn't start with the letter L like Daphne foretold. I shake my head, thinking back to her eerie connection with a Ouija board and wonder if my fairytale ideas aren't that far-fetched after all. I respond:

From: ChaseMorg@mylife.com
To: jacquesp@mera.fr
Subject: Re: No Subject

Is it bonjour for both of us now? You were in New York? You are not too far from California. Perhaps on one of your trips, you will head this way. You don't appear as if you would get nervous on stage. You hide it well. You seem very confident. It's lovely that they honored you for your success.
Chase

My phone emits an almost immediate loud tweet.

From: jacquesp@mera.fr
To: ChaseMorg@mylife.com
Subject: Re: Re: No Subject

I hope to be in California soon with you. By the way, I
am a bit drunk. I have spent a night with old friends in
a discotheque. So, you are smart, young, beautiful, and
delightful. Do you have an idea when I will have the
chance to see you? Your devoted fan, me, myself, and I.

Is he really coming? No, he couldn't really be coming? Could
he? This is crazy. People don't fly halfway across the world to
come to see a stranger. My thoughts run wild with the
possibility of seeing Jacques- Pierre in the flesh.

**Me: Roxie, call me! CODE RED! Jacques-Pierre
appeared. He said he's my devoted fan! WTF? And
he said he's traveling to California soon.**

SOON! Is he going to expect sex? You're right. I'm
diabolically programmed to have my happily ever after and not
a one-night stand.

My phone rings. "Listen, I'm in Starbucks, picking us up
coffee, so I have to be very quiet..." Roxie lowers her voice. "Do
you remember on *Downton Abbey* when Mary told the gorgeous
Mr. Pamuk, 'I think you're mistaken about me. I've never done
anything.' And he replies, 'Of course not. One look at you would
tell me that.' I think there's truth in that. Men can tell. He's not
going to fly to California solely to jump in the sack with you.
He's had years to sow his oats. Don't worry and psyche yourself
out about it now."

"But this is a much different day and age than *Downton
Abbey*." I try to sound calm, my hands still picking at my
glittery nails.

"Listen to me, Chase, just let it happen. He obviously likes
you. Please don't run from this one before he even gets close
enough to catch you. Like I said before, it's a lot less effort and
expense for him to just forget you—the girl who lives all the
way in LA but stood him up in Paris."

"Uh... Okay," I hesitate, feeling uneasy. I reach for the water bottle sitting on my bedside table and take a sip. "But his name doesn't start with the letter L. Daphne clearly said three men with names that start with the letter L."

"What if she's wrong? What if his name is Arnold, but he goes by his nickname, Lenny?" she puffs out an exaggerated sigh. "Chase, remember Goldilocks found the one that was just right after she tried every bowl of porridge. You have to try, or rather let him try because he's happy and eager to make the grand gesture that no other man in the world would make. You can do this."

"Okay... Yes ... I can do this," I reply robotically, not sure about anything, especially my abilities with the opposite sex. I grab a pen and pad and madly write down Roxie's tips.

"Think of it this way, like I have been telling you for years, it only takes one knight in shining armor. The others are all going to be some version of a weird frog. I suggest writing a list of all your mandatory traits —the ones beyond appearance and hotness—and then see where Jacques-Pierre fits into it."

"I'll think about it." Still not sure of anything.

"Don't think about it, Chase; do it. Then you can add your Amoremojis next to each one. 'Sense of humor' gets a laugh-out-loud Amoremoji," she laughs.

"I'm glad you find my love life so amusing."

"Admit it; you're having so much fun with my list and my Amoremoji stickers. I'll be over to pick you up as soon as this barista gets my order right."

She clicks off, and I glance at my scribble. I flip the pad to a new page and ponder Roxie's demands because she's right. It was one thing to strive for a hot guy when I was seventeen, but not now when I'm trying to find a life partner. *What do I want in a man, and could Jacques-Pierre indeed be the ONE? Can a lover be handsome, a witty conversationalist, and a true gentleman? What would make me happy?* I look at the ceiling and back at the paper. *Someone who...* The words start to flow:

· *Loves me for who I am despite my faults.*

· *Has the same sense of humor, and we can laugh at the same things. He can even take a joke at his own expense. Is honest but won't blurt out blunt truths if it hurts someone else.*

· *Is smart, but isn't embarrassed if he says something stupid.*

· *Comes home from a long day at work and is not afraid to throw on the apron, open the refrigerator, and cook.*

· *Sees life as the cup half full.*

· *Will be the only one on the dance floor, even if he has two left feet.*

· *Opens the car door, even if I'm driving and wraps me in his coat, even if he's shivering.*

· *Sits patiently and calmly on a hill while I learn how to use the clutch and the stick shift.*

· *Is my best friend; my companion. A relationship is teamwork, and that takes two.*

· *Embraces my family like it's his own, calling my mother "Mom" and feels comfortable enough to throw off his shoes, grab a drink from the refrigerator, and lie back on the couch.*

Done. I put the cap on my pen and jam the piece of paper into my purse.

Time to jump in the shower!

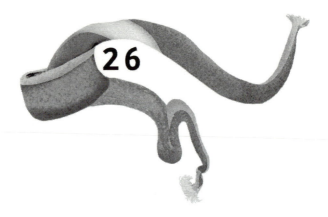

26

"That should do it!" Susan grazes the back of her hand across her perspiration-beaded forehead before she locks the main doors of the ballroom. "I'll see you both in a few."

Having worked the last hour or so on the finishing touches for Nana's shindig, Roxie and I look forward to a moment of repose. We walk through the main lobby of the lodge, which has a four-story, river-rock fireplace in the center along with Stickley rocking chairs, nestled in front of the hearth. There are a few Stickley couches and reading chairs in the middle of the room, too, with stained-glass floor lamps hugging the sides of the furniture. Hand-woven carpets add to the Craftsman-style lodge.

A group of preschool kids zoom past us, giggling, adorned with bathing suits and inner tubes that bounce off each other. We push open the stained-glass double doors and head down the hill along the path that weaves its way through the pine trees and out onto the wooden dock, which overlooks Lake Arrowhead. Fly fishermen cast their hand-hewn flies into the frothy waters. The scenery resembles an eye-catching postcard or an alluring photograph found in a travel magazine that includes crystal clear mountain water, pine trees, and men in fishing garb who appear to have reached Nirvana.

"If you fall off, grab the rope along the side of the raft, and yell 'Riley'..." The voice of the banana boat instructor, at the end of the dock, catches my attention. I notice the short but deep scar running underneath his cheekbone, accentuating his smile. I wonder if that's why he gives specific instructions. A chill runs up and down my spine as a flood of memories fill my brain. I'm grateful that Riley is drop-dead gorgeous; his buff body helps to interrupt my disturbing thoughts. One glance at Roxie lets me know that she's hanging onto his every word too. *Did I just see her salivate? Okay ... not going there!* I chuckle lightly.

"If we hit a big wave," he continues, "and you projectile out of the boat, make sure to turn your body as quickly as possible so that you're on your back." His eyes twinkle. His smile is brilliant, and his cocksure manliness is sexy as hell. *Oh, boy!* I'm smitten. He's flashy and dazzling like The Shard in London. *Bizarre observation, I seem to never leave the engineering behind, even for a night.*

"The most important thing is to remain calm and float on your back with your feet pointing towards the sky. Since the lake is not deep in some places, I wouldn't want your foot to get trapped underneath a rock. You don't want to hear the crunch of breaking bones. Believe me." I listen intently, gripping tight to the railing, feeling my anxiety take hold. "Any questions before we take off?" Riley pans the little group in search of an outstretched hand. "Well then, jump aboard!" he motions, taking a seat at the very front of the inflatable beast, waving to the motorboat driver to go.

"Hey, Chase, you okay? You look like you've seen a ghost." Roxie has that worried look in her eye.

"Sure," I lie.

"It's just a banana boat—nothing like—"

"AHHHH!" I scream. A ticklish poke at my sides catches me off guard.

"Doesn't that look like fun? Let's go join them," a familiar male voice says, his hands sliding under my stomach.

"WHAT the—" I blurt out, and before I realize what's happening, I'm being lifted in the air, cradled like a baby against the unknown man's chest. "Ahhhh..." I wail, kicking out and screaming even louder before I turn towards the man. "No ... way..." I gasp in shock as the man grabs me in his arms and jogs down the incline of the dock to the large rectangular portion jutting out into the water.

"Jaydon, what are you doing? She's afraid—" Roxie rudely cuts off as she tugs on his shirt, trying to slow him down.

"Oh, Chase, where's your sense of adventure?" he says, ignoring Roxie's plea as he nears the edge of the dock.

"Jaydon! Don't you dare drop me in!" I begin hammering him with my feet.

"Ouch!" he yelps, letting go. "What the hell? Those are my family jewels, not to be kicked at."

"If you would have paid attention, I was trying to say that she's afraid of the water, you idiot!" Roxie wraps her arms around my waist. Jaydon hears light sniffles and realizes that I'd been quietly crying. "Oh, man! I didn't think you'd—"

"Exactly," Roxie interjects. "You didn't think."

"Sorry, Chase! I didn't mean..." Jaydon smooths down my sundress. "I was just joking. I had no intention of throwing you in the water. I ... I had no idea... You must have had a pretty scary swimming experience or near-drowning experi—"

"I don't want to talk about it." I put a hand out to stop his blubbering. Giving my eyes a good wipe, I quickly compose myself. "It's fine, really. I'm fine. Just ... just don't do it again. Okay?"

"Sure." Jaydon pauses a second, putting his hands in his beige linen slacks. "I ... I hoped that you'd be happy to see me. Paul and I went to your house about ten minutes after you girls left. Your mom invited us to Nana's party tonight," he stutters, his eyes twinkling with sincerity against his crisp, white button-down shirt. He looks dashing; all dressed up. "Nice red knickers, by the way."

I look down at my feet, having forgotten what I threw on before leaving the house. I utter a weak "thanks."

286

"I would have guessed the only thing you'd be happy to see is another variety of condoms, Mr. Player," Roxie answers. "Does IT truly get lost in the dark—"

My eyes open wide, giving her a "boy are you snarky, girl" smirk. Yet I can't fault her perfect timing. Jaydon cuts her off. "You know those weren't just *my* condoms. I share that car with Paul. I'm not the only so-called-Player. You have me all wrong."

My mouth drops open as I see Paul approaching us in his relaxed way, wearing jeans, a T-shirt, and a tailored navy-blue sports coat.

"What does Chase have all wrong?" Paul asks rhetorically. "I'm so happy we flew into town a day early," he continues, wrapping his arms around me, engulfing me in an extra tight hug. "I never thought filming would end." He looks down at me. "You missed a spot," he says, rambling while rubbing in the blob of sunscreen on my forehead. "Luckily, we brought some party clothes along, so we're all ready for Nana's birthday tonight. Chase..." he pauses for a moment, taking hold of my hand, "are you sure you're okay seeing Grant, Brody, and little Maddy? Oh, and don't forget Mrs. Stevens. I hear that Nana thought it would be a way of extending an olive branch." My eyes widen. "Your mom likes to talk a lot."

"Actually..." I begin, leaning back against the railing, my eyes momentarily drifting out towards the lake and all the spring breakers. The banana boat is flying, the passengers bouncing up and down with a lot of hoots and hollers.

"It was my idea," Roxie interjects. "I was able to convince her that the past was filled with so many great memories. Why dwell on something unchangeable, even if Grant's acting like a deranged freak right now?"

"Yeah, but you have to admit that something just isn't right, Roxie. We both knew Grant would make an amazing husband and father one day. But it's like a flip switched in him, and now I see this whole new side I never knew existed, and..." my body suddenly gets fired up, "and that's not the rejected side of me being upset that he had to be gay and ... and ... not wanting me. It's weird..." I swallow hard, pushing back the screams within me. "He's turned into this unrecognizable ... ASSHOLE."

"Okay then, let's pretend for a moment that you're a duck who loves the water," Jaydon says brightly, laying a hand on my shoulder and trying to cheer me up.

"She is afraid of water," Roxie and Paul reply in unison.

"Why am I the last person to know this?" Jaydon throws his hands in the air, looking genuinely shocked.

"It's complicated," Paul answers.

"Right." Jaydon eyes Paul, Roxie, and me suspiciously. "So, did you know that they arrested three ducks last night?"

"God, you are so random!" Roxie shouts.

"Guess you've got competition," I add, chuckling.

"Shut up, Chase!" she says playfully, shoving my shoulder. "I didn't ask for your commentary on the topic. So," turning toward Jaydon, "what happened to the ducks?"

"Well," he drawls, stepping in close "they were in front of a judge this morning?" he says, smiling.

"Okay. So?" Roxie makes a circular motion with her hand, nudging him to continue with his story.

"So, the first duck gets up on the stand, right? The judge asks, 'What is your name and tell me what you think you did wrong?' The first duck says, 'My name is Quack, and I got busted for blowing bubbles in the pond.' The judge says, 'Okay, you go to jail for three days.' In comes the second duck. He stands before the judge. The judge asks him the same questions. The duck answers, 'My name is Quack, Quack, and I got caught blowing bubbles in the pond.' The judge sends him to jail for three days."

"Do you know where this is going," Roxie smirks, glancing at Paul and me. We both shrug our shoulders.

"Don't have a clue," I say.

"So, now we get to the third duck," Jaydon continues. "By the time he enters the courtroom, the judge jumps ahead of the usual questions and says, 'Let me guess! Your name is Quack, Quack, Quack?' The duck says, 'Nah, I'm bubbles.'"

The three of us burst out laughing.

The joke turns Roxie into a softie. "We haven't officially met. I mean, you were wasted when we dropped you off at the hotel. I'm Roxie," she extends her hand, as if hitting the reset button from the previous conversation, "and you must be the boy toy," suddenly looking at him with idle fascination. "Nice joke, by the way."

"Boy toy, now? What happened to Mr. Player?" he looks at her with fascination. "You forgot to introduce me to Righty and Lefty like you did at the theater," he says, giving her an exaggerated wink as he stares at her chest.

"Well, we may have gotten off the wrong footing," Roxie says shyly.

"Which one? The left or right?" Jaydon points to her feet.

"You are quite the jokester, aren't you? Has he always been this way?" Roxie directs the latter question to Paul.

"Never a dull moment," Paul laughs.

"Plus, many women think I'm a very nice guy." Jaydon grins widely, putting his arm around Roxie's waist, staring at her breasts again, which are protruding out of her tank top. "Maybe fate has brought us together. What do you think?"

"I think fate's playing a big role lately," Roxie beams. "In fact," releasing Jaydon's hold and turning toward Paul, "when Chase dated Grant, I read their astrological charts, and all signs pointed to them being soul mates, but I didn't see Chase ending up with him—well, before Grant came out and found his Prince. Paul, Chase's chart actually compliments yours," Roxie comments, giving Paul's cheeks a playful pinch. Paul glances at me, then down at his hands. He shoves them into the front pockets of his jeans. I can tell he's visibly uncomfortable. "You don't even know my birthday, Roxie."

"What? Of course, I do, you ninny! It's January 26, which makes you an Aquarius man. Aquariuses have an adventurous approach to romance, which often fascinates the very driven Leo, such as Chase, whose birthday is August 13. You two are a perfect match."

A perfect match? I feel flushed. *Really?* The mere idea of Paul and I as lovers is as far-fetched as me jumping ship and changing my sexual persona.

'We like what we like from a young age': Lady Gaga's mantra, my inner voice adds in, lamely. She says we're born this way, but now ... seeing as how I got so jealous, I'm not sure how I feel. Granted, this new information about the condoms belonging to Paul is just *gross!*

"But maybe that's not meant to be," Roxie continues, seeing my shocked expression, "now that you're with the mystery blonde you were all over in LA a few weeks ago. By the way, why isn't she here with you?" Roxie eyes him curiously.

"What are you even talking about?" Paul quips, chuckling nervously.

"Daphne and I saw you on Colorado Boulevard; you were in the Porsche. Who is she?" Roxie presses, following Paul as he walks up the dock back towards the lodge.

Paul looks at her, shrugging.

"You have no idea who she is? What? Did you just pick her up on your way to California? Is she a hooker?" Roxie interrogates.

"She's not a hooker. Do we have to talk about this now?"

"Yes."

"How 'bout later, Roxie?"

"Okay. Fine. Later." Roxie feigns deflation. "Gosh," changing topics, "it's getting hot! Time for more sunscreen." Roxie plops down on a boulder near the dock. Jaydon follows her. "OW!" she screeches, popping straight up. "Oh, shit! What a nasty little bee!" she yells, stomping on the dying insect. She tilts back and examines her bum. "I think the stinger is still in me."

"Let me see." Jaydon studies Roxie's hip, pulling her shorts to the side and inadvertently grazing her bum before pressing gently on her skin around what will eventually turn into a huge welt.

"Hey, I got stung on my hip. Hands off my ass!" She swats at him. "Where's a lifeguard when you need him? A big, brilliant Baywatch type with some tweezers?"

"You don't think I look like a Baywatch type? Shall I strip down and show you my manliness?" Jaydon purrs, tugging at his shirt.

"Chase," Roxie yells, "you saw him almost naked. Shall I have him strip down?" Her eyes twinkle with mischief.

I roll my eyes and shake my head. Paul walks over to study Roxie's injury. He pushes Jaydon away in a teasing, friendly way. "Here, let me try to pinch it out."

"Hey, you have a girlfriend. I should do it." Jaydon shoves him to the side.

"Oh, now she's officially your girlfriend?" Roxie playfully chides.

"I thought we agreed to talk about this later." Paul blurts. He briefly glances over to me as if to observe my reaction. "Hold still, I think I've got it," Paul says.

"OOWEE! SHIT! SHIT! SHIT!" Roxie jumps up, slapping Paul's hand away from her hip. "Man, Chase was right. You're such a Player, just like Jaydon. You two boys..." she shakes her head. "I wish I knew what to do with you guys," smoothing down her shorts. "Well, thank you both for coming to my stinger rescue." Roxie's mouth turns up into the biggest grin.

"We aim to please." Jaydon grins, slapping Roxie on her bum.

"I'm going to kill you!" She runs after him towards the water. "Payback's a bitch," she yells. "If I don't catch you now, mark my words, I will."

Thankful for the reprieve, I take my phone out of my pocket. I'm overdue with a response to Jacques- Pierre. I need something to distract me from this strange afternoon. My nerves and muscles suddenly feel so tense, and it has nothing to do with this upcoming party. *Does Paul have a girlfriend? That doesn't make sense. Paul always laughed about commitment, saying that he would never settle down and pick one girl.*

"Will this day ever end?" I mutter under my breath, typing out a response:

From: ChaseMorg@mylife.com
To: jacquesp@mera.fr
Subject: Re: Re: Dreams

You must have a bad headache. Poor you. I never would've expected you in a discotheque. Sounds like fun. I'm helping set up my grandmother's birthday party, feeling rather stressed. I should have opted for dancing like you.

"Someone looks dazed," Paul says, appearing at my side. I flinch, catching my breath.

"Someone snuck up quietly." I turn and smile at him as I hide my phone in my sundress pocket.

"I'm sorry about earlier, Jaydon pretending to throw you into the lake. I forgot that it might trigger bad memories." He looks at the ground, picking up my fallen scarf; he wraps it around my neck. "I feel terrible. I forgot how—." I shrug, cutting him off. I stare back at the lake. "And sorry," he continues, "that he keeps putting the moves on you. He's not used to rejection."

Silence. I'm thankful that he's giving me space.

"Penny for your thoughts, Chase?" he finally says. "You looked like you were in a different world."

"I was thinking about ... about how much life has changed in the last four months." I lean against the wooden dock railings.

"I have to admit that you picked the perfect spot to have Nana's party," he conveniently changes the subject, propping himself on the top of the railing. "Don't you need to be heading back to your room soon to change your clothes? In my humble opinion," Paul says, bowing, "you look good to go. I can't help but crack up. "By the way, I love your white sundress. And you look even more beautiful with your scarf," he laughs.

I look up and meet his eyes. "This old thing? It's my quick throw-on. Thanks, anyway."

"You do realize happy hour will start in less than an hour, which means..."

"That predictable Nana will most likely be the first person asking for martinis," I finish. We burst out laughing before my eyes stare back out at the lake again.

"Seriously, what's on your mind? Are you regretting Roxie inviting Grant, Brody, Maddy, and Mrs. Stevens?"

"No, it's not that," I state as I fiddle with my scarf. Paul scoots closer, rubbing my shoulders, working on the giant knots that have formed from all the party stress. My heart beats a little quicker at his touch.

"Are you sure it's not you still trying to plan your perfect life and control the outcome? Roxie's worried about you. No one will talk about your hospital stay with me, no matter how much I ask. She says your parents are worried about you, too. They say you're burning the candle at both ends: trying to finish your degree by summer and locking yourself in your room or at school; and that you're going on dates but coming back miserable."

"My dates seem to have a 'short shelf life,' as my dad likes to say."

"Well, you just need to find one that's not perishable."

"HA, HA! I've got to tell my dad that one." I can't help but laugh. "It's not that. Seeing Grant and Brody together, and now they have a baby girl. I want what they have." I rub my stomach, thinking back to what Dr. Patel told me.

"You will. Sometimes you need to wade through the pain and suffering to find love. And if you don't leave space, then there's no room to fill."

"When did you become so insightful?"

"Hey!" he protests, gently nudging my side with his knee. "I've always been insightful. You just never listened. "Chase," he interrupts, his eyes widening, "that's not funny."

"What's not funny?" I ask, perplexed.

"Don't move." He jumps down from the railing with no warning, inching closer. "Chase, whatever you do ... do ... not ... move," his hand, looming over my arm.

"What?" I gulp. "You're scaring me, Paul." My heart suddenly thuds. I feel a familiar trickle of alarm.

"Do ... not ... move," he whispers. His eyes are focused on my hand. Something large and black is resting on my wrist. Fear hits me like icy water.

"Ahhh!" I shriek, hands flailing and knocking the creature on the ground. I run, taking off in the opposite direction.

Paul stomps on the fast-moving spider. "Jesus, I thought you were playing a joke on me at first. But when I saw that the Halloween black widow bracelet lifted a leg..." Paul doesn't finish his sentence when he looks at my ashen face.

"I've had more than my fair share of uncomfortable things today, and I haven't even encountered my crazy relatives," I say, beginning to tear up.

"Come here." He takes out a handkerchief from his back pocket and lightly dabs the corners of my eyes. Grabbing my hand, he locks eyes with me. "Knock, knock."

I release a little laugh, preparing myself for one of his corny jokes. "Who's there?"

"Butch, Jimmy, and Joe."

"Butch, Jimmy, and Joe who?" I cock my head to the side.

"Butch your arms around me; Jimmy a kiss; and let's Joe the party." He wraps his arms around my torso, pulling me in tight.

"That was worse than your usual groaner," I swat his arm, bursting into laughter.

"I have a million of them," Paul says as he raises his arm for me to take. "I forgot to ask; will your little mischief-maker friend Daphne be at the party?"

"Yep," Roxie says, suddenly appearing by our side along with Jaydon. The four of us follow the path towards the lodge.

"She's such a funny little girl; she told me some bizarre things when we were heading down your driveway this afternoon," he laughs.

"Fascinating is more like it," Roxie adds, giving me a giant wink.

"She told me that 'we are the sum of all that has happened—good and bad—and, without going through both, we wouldn't be who we are, and we might not be open to our next great adventure.' When I asked her what that meant, she said, 'Life is filled with tests and choices, and positives arise from detours.' She said that I would fall in love with the one I least expect who's been right in front of me the whole time." Paul holds my gaze. "Whatever all that means."

"Seriously! Sometimes I wonder how that kid could only be ten. Do you think she's a prodigy?" Roxie looks between the two of us.

"Who's Daphne?" Jaydon interrupts.

Roxie, Paul, and I eye one another.

"The little girl in the driveway." Paul just looks at him.

"Huh? Oh, God! Don't tell me this is another one of those things that I'm left out in the loop?"

"Let me put it this way: it's for us to know and for you to find out," Roxie answers.

"I can hardly wait," Jaydon responds.

"Time for us girls to get all pretty. See you at the party," Roxie says as we head through the lobby doors towards our rooms.

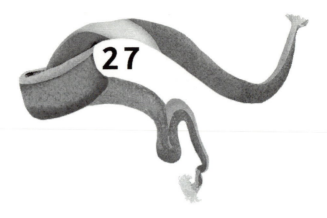

27

I am irritated that Roxie and I arrive five minutes late to the party. I wanted to be there twenty minutes earlier, but she got a call from her "secret admirer." Whoever the heck he is, he'd better be worth it because he's got Roxie so transfixed, it's unreal. I've never seen her fall for a guy like this—so unlike her. I compose myself the best I can, taking a couple of cleansing breaths before opening the door to the ballroom of the lodge. As miffed as I am, I can't help but smile when I gaze at the long rectangular tables. It's just what I envisioned. The tables are draped with crisply-ironed, white linens and adorned from one end to the other with miniature vases stuffed with roses. The brilliance of the hundred or so votive candles sprinkled about the room combined with towering three-foot-tall silver candlestick vases overflowing with baby's breath that glimmer in the spotlights is nothing less than breathtaking. A four-tiered birthday cake dotted with white flowers and brushed with shimmering gold dust with gold ribbon enhancing each layer sets in the far corner of the room. Topping it off is a large gold "85" to mark Nana's day.

"Chastity, thank you for including us in your grandmother's special day," Mrs. Stevens says, breaking my stare. She appears at my side, cocktail in hand. "I truly admire what you, Roxanne, and the party planner created here. And I was told even Henry, and your dad helped stuff the vases. Way to get the boys to work."

"Mrs. Stevens," finding my voice and hoping I sound genuine, "thank you for coming."

She leans forward, touching my forearm, briefly glancing at my un-jeweled hand. I notice her eyes widen slightly.

"Chase," she begins, her eyes welling up with tears, "after all these years, please call me Beth. I'm sorry for how you suffered post-breakup with my son."

"I assure you I'm fine," I respond flatly. Fine? What a joke! That remains to be seen, especially when I see Grant with his new baby girl. Considering the number of people invited who are on my personal "ditch" list, it will be a miracle if the party goes off without a hitch. And did I just catch her—Cruella de Vil, looking for my engagement ring—her family heirloom?

"I know you are, hon," Mrs. Stevens continues. "I just need to get this off my chest. I had no idea about Grant. That is to say ... that ... that..."

"He's gay," I finish.

"Yes. That my son is gay ... and, remarkably so, very happy. Oh, my! That's the first time I've acknowledged this out loud. Otherwise, I don't know how I could have told you if I had a clue." She rests her hand on my forearm a second time, glancing at my naked ring finger and lingering an extra second. "Please forgive me."

"I already have," placing an assuring hand over hers. "I also have your ring. It's just not with me right now. I know you're just cordial because you want it back." Her mouth drops open as I look beyond her and see Brody and Grant coming through the doors. Brody has a baby wrapped in a pink blanket in his arms. Mrs. Stevens looks as pale as a ghost as I walk away from her and head toward the large punch bowl in the hopes of not attracting their attention. I fluster when I see the trio head straight towards me. "Hi ... um ... you three," I blurt out awkwardly.

"Chase, this party is spectacular," Brody pans the room before engulfing me in a side hug. "This little angel is Maddy. Maddy, meet Chase, your Godmother, or at least I hope she'll be." Brody manipulates one of Maddy's little arms like a puppet, making her wave to me. I wave back, smiling weakly.

"Godmother?" I squeak.

"Mind if I steal her away for a moment?" Grant looks at his husband, who gives him a little nod.

"Go, he's okay," Brody whispers to me, topping it off with an encouraging smile.

Grant pulls on my arm, leading me to a quiet space in the corner of the room. "Chase," he begins. I steel myself, not sure what's going to come next. "I'm ... I'm ... sorry; sorry for how I acted the last time I saw you. After everything you've been through ..." another long pause. "You didn't deserve to find out the way you did. I was childish and cruel. I just ... I've been hiding who I really am for too long, and then the day I met Brody ... well, something snapped in me, and I wanted to shout out to the world who I am. I never cheated on you, Chase. I loved you then; I love you now. Things just happened..."

My hands automatically ball into fists; heat rises at the nape of my neck as visions of the last time I saw him in his drunken state flash by me. "You ghosted me!" my voice low but acerbic; my eyes fixed angrily on his. "You pretended like everything was fine to all of our friends and family for an entire month. They thought I was nuts when I said you went MIA. YOU. MADE. ME. LOOK. LIKE. A. FOOL." A small gob of spit lands on his pants for good measure. "AND ..." I stop briefly, recognizing that I've raised my voice enough to see a few heads turn. "And after that? You've become the biggest asshole on the planet." He flinches, pressing his eyes together. "Look, all I can say is that I was ashamed. I ... I couldn't face you and tell you who I truly am. I wanted you to love me as a friend still. I didn't want—"

Grant cups his mouth. His eyes start to get moist. I don't know whether to believe he's telling the truth or putting up a big act to cover his shady self.

"I didn't want to let you down. I need you in my life, Chase. We're the five—I mean—four musketeers. We're best friends. Forever. Remember? I can't lose you too."

"You have a weird way of showing it. You show up drunk to my school, you demand your ring back, you act all snippy," I release a little chuckle. "You have no idea what I've been going through since—" It's my turn. I muster up the strength to keep myself from crying. "Part of me wants to ditch my career and just be my 'hopeless romantic' self, but at the same time, part of me wants to chuck my 'hopeless romantic' self and be a career woman. I fight these feelings daily, Grant. Do you understand?" I nervously giggle lightly again, "I'm confused, I'm a mess, I'm sad, I have this new pain I have to manage, parts of my future have been squashed, but I don't go around getting wasted and acting like a creep to the ones that love me."

He reaches out, taking my hand in his. "You and I shared a bond during a rough time, and I thought the bond meant something more than it did. It wasn't fair for me to think that I could ... fill his shoes."

"Attention, everyone!" Nana's voice booms through the cordless microphone. The great room is abuzz with people trying to locate their seats. The room grows quiet as Elvis Presley's rendition of "Falling in Love" plays through the stereo system.

SHIT! I told Susan to hide that thing!

"I would like to thank all of you for coming to my birthday party this evening! I appreciate all the traveling, whether near or far, to join me on this extraordinary night at this beautiful lakeside retreat." There's a loud round of applause. "The song you're listening to in the background is the one I walked down the aisle to when I married the love of my life. Mitchell, I'll love you forever, dear."

Nana blows Gramps a kiss as she stands tall, still looking like she stepped off the cover of Life Magazine, which she did years ago when she was a runway model. She's wearing a long-sleeve, sky blue chiffon dress that beautifully falls to the floor. The color highlights her eyes, giving them an extra shimmer tonight.

"I want to take a moment—" She turns away from the mic to hiccup, steadying herself on the little table that holds her four-tiered birthday cake. "I want to take a moment to thank my grandchildren for organizing this lovely party." She pauses, closing her eyes as she gulps down her martini. "Roxanne, Chastity, Henry, raise your hands so that I can acknowledge you." We obediently do as we're told. The room breaks with a round of applause. "Thank you, little loves!" Nana says over the clapping. "It couldn't be more perfect if I had planned it myself. I would also like to thank Susan, my extraordinary party planner who helped the kids with every detail." Another round of applause erupts as Susan stands and takes a light bow.

"Chastity, love, where are you? I'd like for you to come up here."

Oh, boy! I have no idea what she has in mind, but I can tell that she's gung-ho, holding her empty martini in one hand and the microphone in the other. I sidle up to Nana. She takes my hand in hers, giving it a little kiss before she returns to the mic.

"For all the eligible bachelors out there—"

"Nana! What are you doing?" I protest loudly, reaching for the microphone, but she dodges me, grabbing my wrist instead. Uproarious laughter fills the room. I feel the heat on my neck and face.

"She's single, and past due to get married."

I try to break free from Nana's hand, but for an eighty-five-year-old gal, she's got some grip. Realizing that I'm trapped, I decide to play along even though I'd rather crawl in a hole somewhere and die. "When I was her age," she drawls lightly, "my handsome, darling Mitchell, and I were expecting our first child. Mitch, you make me glow with happiness every day. I love you. So, please, for all you single "Mitchells" out there, come find Chastity, and marry her while I'm still alive. That would be the most delightful birthday present I could ever ask for."

My jaw drops open. *WHAT????????* *What the hell is happening?* Realizing that I must look pretty stupid with my mouth open, I pretend to take it all in stride, releasing a laugh while I embrace her and plant a big kiss on her cheek. I need to escape. Letting go of her hand, I can hear Nana's closing remarks fade away as I make a mad dash for the ladies' room.

"On that note, may you always savor the warmth of good gin, good friends, and good memories, let's all enjoy this party!"

"Oh. My. God!" I yell at my reflection in the mirror. "IS SHE MAD? What kind of harebrained idea is this? Next, she'll be lining up the bachelors in single file to check their resumes!"

"Chase?" Roxie barges in the bathroom "Are you okay? I can't believe—"

"I'm going to kill her!" cutting her off. "I swear I'm going to kill her! She's gone loony," I continue to yell.

"Shh ... Calm down, Chase! She's Nana. What do you expect? She only wants the best for you. She wants to see you married."

"Ee-yeah! I'd like to see me married too, but that's not happening, is it?"

"Well, with Nana's little stunt, you'll soon find out who's single and available. You have to admit, it was kind of funny."

"Excuseeee meeee, everyone!" an obnoxious but scarily familiar voice bellows from the great room.

"What the f—" Roxie blurts out as the two of us run to the door, opening it just enough to get a good view of who's at the microphone. We see Nana trying to grab it away, but a redheaded gal pushes her aside. I can only see the back of her until she turns. My eyes go wide.

"IT'S MEDUSA!" I whisper. "How the hell did she get in?" I ask rhetorically. Nana would never invite her or her family after what happened at Aunt Kate's Christmas party.

I watch as Medusa madly scans the room, looking for someone. "Where are you, Graaaannnnnt?" her eyes continuing to pan the room. "Oh, there you are ... you devious scumbag. She's myyyyy baby. Yes, I had a brief moment where I didn't want to be a mother, but you had no right just to take her into your perfect little world. But," she belches loudly, "you're not so perfect, are you?"

"Susan, do something!" Nana yells, looking helpless.

"OH, FUCK!" Grant's voice carries as he bolts towards Medusa.

"Ahhh..." she belches a second time, "here comes Mr. Perrrrrrrfect now. Want to take a bow, baby snatcher? Or do you want to knock them up and steal their babies? You told me you loved me. LOVED MEEEEEE!"

"Stop, you bitch!" Grant snatches the microphone. The sound goes dead.

"Holy shit! He didn't just call her—"

"He did," I finish. Roxie and I stand transfixed. I'm elated that I'm not a part of the audience.

"BITCH?" she yells. "Did you just call me—." Julie lunges forward, pushing him right into the cake, and in a surreal moment set in slow-motion, I watch in horror as frosting pelts the front-row guests. A resounding "OH" fills the room.

Susan grabs the mic, which lands next to the "85" cake topper while two burly waiters quickly surround Julie and Grant and escort the frosting-covered duo outside.

"What do you mean, BITCH, you, you gay ..." she rants as her voice trails off in the distance.

With Julie and Grant out of the way, Roxie and I rush over to see how Nana's doing when someone taps my shoulder.

"Not quite what you had in mind for your grandmother? I'm so sorry for the rude interruption. Your grandmother is a pretty feisty gal, though. She'll be fine. Trust me."

"Mrs. Adelman?" I blink a few times, wondering if I'm seeing things, my mind grappling with her supposed prophetic message about Nana's well-being.

"Yes, darling." She spins me around, "Look at your Nana. She's back to her old self again."

I glance at her signature bedazzled jacket over a beautiful tea-length pink organza dress before eying Nana, who, without a hitch, is laughing and drinking another martini, as if nothing happened. A fight breaks out, a beautiful cake ruined, and she's too tipsy to remember what happened.

"Oh ... I ... see..." I stutter.

"I see your grandmother is ready for you to meet the perfect man. Like I mentioned when I first met you." My mind quickly shifts back to me, bent over the toilet.

"It was a strange first encounter at Aunt Kate's Christmas party," I add. "And a strange second ambush in New York at the rooftop bar."

"To be sure," she responds matter-of-factly. "But the bottom line is that I found your soulmate, and he's perfect. He embodies the whole package—brains, looks, sense of humor, love of his family. I'll set you up when you're back in LA," Mrs. Adelman says.

"Oh, God! Not to sound ungrateful, but ... but I can't handle this right now, Mrs. Adelman. Spring quarter starts at the end of the week. I only have one class to finish for my degree, and I want to focus on it and my research, not on men. And now I have to fix the cake situation. Pronto," I rattle off quickly as I head for the cake table, hoping I can shut her up. "Anyway, I can't pay your fee. I don't have that kind of money."

"I will not take no for an answer. Call it a birthday present for your grandmother."

"AUN-TEE JOSIE!" I turn midway and stop dead in my tracks when I see Daphne in a matching pink organza dress with her hair in a French braid with a pink ribbon tied at the end, running up to embrace Mrs. Adelman in a giant hug.

"Auntie? Mrs. Adelman is your aunt?" My eyes go wide, looking between the little girl and the pushy lady. I'm confused. "No way. She couldn't be."

"Josephine is my late husband's sister," a voice says. It's Daphne's mom, Maria. "Has she been trying to fix you up?" She releases a little chuckle, shaking her head. "You might want to think about that..." She's interrupted by Mrs. Adelman rattling off a diatribe to her sister-in-law.

Everything is happening too fast. I cup my head with my hands, a look of panic on my face.

"Well ... uh..." is as far as I get when the DJ plays "Save the Last Dance." Someone grabs my hand. I'm surprised when I look up and see Paul.

"I need to borrow her if you don't mind," he nods to Maria and Mrs. Adelman. "Hi, Daphne!" He hugs her before pulling me across the room to the dance floor, his bushy beard pressing into my cheek as he draws me closer. "You looked like you needed saving," he whispers in my ear.

"Thank you. My mind is in a tizzy. Dare I ask what the hell just happened with Grant and Medusa?"

"Medusa?" he chuckles, "from the sea witch from Little Mermaid? You must fill me in on that one."

"*The Rescuers.* Ursula is a different person, she's the sea witch from *The Little Mermaid,*" I say, matter-of-factly.

"Ursula?" He looks at me blankly.

"Never mind ... um ... long story."

"Well, same here. I don't even want to explain what just happened."

"Don't want to explain what?" says a familiar voice. "May I cut in?"

"Uncle Mason! When did you get back?" The look of shock on my face couldn't have been more obvious. *I could have sworn Roxie said he'd be in England for another month.* He's decked out in a beautiful three-piece, navy pinstripe suit—nothing like my dad's ensemble: a beige suit with a beige cowboy hat and boots. I get that they are twins and look identical, but they sure are polar opposites in the wardrobe department.

"Yesterday morning. My last deal fell through, so I came back."

"I'll let you two play catch up," Paul interjects. "I need to do a little, let's say, reconnaissance..." He plants a light kiss on my cheek before heading to the other side of the room. Uncle Mason escorts me back to his table and pulls out a chair for me. I give it a cursory glance, half expecting to find a whoopee cushion. He's such a jokester. I never know when he will pull a fast one. The short-sheeting and itching powder were the worst of them. Thank God that my mother is sitting across from me, so she can play referee if he gets out of hand.

"So, I understand that you are the most eligible bachelorette in the room. How lucky is that? You wouldn't perhaps be in this position because of your fiancé, Gray, who is sitting across the room and not at our table? And it only gets better now that he's in a shitload of hot water, right?" Uncle Mason asks, blatantly. When he talks snarky like this, all I can think of is Melvin, Jack Nicholson's character in *As Good as It Gets.*

I throw my hands in the air. "Grant. His name is Grant, Uncle Mel—, Mason, I mean. You know that, you cad! And whatever happened to 'Hello, Chase! It's lovely to see you,'" I say with an awkward laugh.

Uncle Mason pinches my side. "I'm not rude, and you're not exactly married. Look at it this way: Nana just elevated your status." He gives me an exaggerated wink.

"Oh. My. God, give it up." I place the napkin in my lap, disregarding his stare.

"Give up what? Sweets?" he says with a flourish, spreading his arms wide.

"Fine." I slam my hands on the table. "Here it is, short and sweet: Grant eloped to Vegas before Christmas. And yes, he left me for a man." The words tumble out in a rush, my voice falling flat. "The thought of our engagement dissolving never even crossed my mind. And I never, ever, thought he was gay. Sure, he was a good dresser, wore sharp suits well. Plus, he's excruciatingly handsome, and yes, Uncle Mason, he never wanted to sleep with me, so that was bizarre too. But now we are trying to be friends. Thus, why Roxie invited him and his family to our party. So ... that about rounds it out. Anything else you so desperately need to know?"

"I know sweets. Roxie filled me in the day after it happened. I just wanted to hear it from the horse's mouth," he chuckles smugly.

"WHAT IS WRONG WITH YOU?" *God, why do I have to have such a dramatic family?* I raise my voice, shaking my head indignantly. "You could have just walked across the street and asked me yourself."

"When would I have done that? I've been in Vegas and London making deals, so it's time to play catch up. But now the million-dollar question is: if he's gay, how did he have a child with that redhead train-wreck who just ruined a perfectly good cake?"

"Beats me. I'm just as confused as everyone else. By the way," I shift gears, trying to find a way to jab back at him. "Brent left for an art exhibition and couldn't make it tonight. Did you scare him off?"

"Dad, do you always have to be so blunt? You're hurting Chase's feelings." Roxie appears. She stands behind her father, wrapping her arms around his neck. "You can be such an ass, you know? And don't worry, Chase. He didn't scare Brent off. The two of them get along well, all things considered."

"Pull up a chair, sweetheart. Why aren't you at our table?" Uncle Mason asks Roxie.

"Because Nana wanted me at hers." She pushes next to me. "Can I squeeze in with you?" I scoot my bum over.

"Is Maria single?" Uncle Mason questions to no one in particular as he stares with lustful eyes across the room at our neighbor just as Aunt Kate saunters over to the table with Herb following close behind. "Oh, Kate, Herb, lovely to see you. I heard your Christmas party was where all the action went down. I'm sure it will make for some great stories."

"Mason, you never change, do you? You were always the troublemaker. Why don't we talk about something else? A toast to new beginnings, and good riddance to bad memories," Aunt Kate raises the glass of champagne she's been sipping. "Nothing a little alcohol can't make us all forget." She finishes her drink. "We'll come to find you in a bit, Chase. We're going to make the rounds first." The two mosey across the room, hand in hand.

"She's quite the cougar, isn't she? Look how her dress accentuates her beautiful figure and look at how her husband follows her in awe. Maybe that's the key, Chase. Maybe you're looking at the wrong age group."

"What? I will not be a cougar! What are you thinking? Thanks for whittling me down to whore status. And Aunt Kate is not a cougar; she's a very respectable—"

"Suit yourself," Uncle Mason cuts me off. "Where's your little brother? He will be a senior this year, right? I want to hear all about his love life too."

"Good luck with that one; Henry's an introvert," Roxie laughs. "But you can go ask him, he's sitting with your brother," she points, "and some relatives in that far corner. There was a moment not too long ago when Nana thought he was gay. But then he informed us that he has a girlfriend. So, who knows?"

"Gay?" His eyes widen. "Nah. I could have told you he's not gay. How's your dating life been post-breakup?"

"It's been ... interesting. I'd rather not talk about it." I'm still miffed with his boorish mannerisms.

"Oh, it's been *really* interesting," Roxie volunteers, clapping her hands like a schoolgirl who has a dirty secret.

"Roxie, please..." I quip, my eyes scanning the room for help, but to no avail. The room is in full-party mode with a third of the crowd on the dance floor, while a handful of waiters walk around serving appetizers.

"Really?" Uncle Mason looks to be all ears. "Tell me more."

"Where do I begin?" Roxie taps her cheek. "Well, she accidentally told her handsome Swiss seatmate en route to France about her nonexistent sex life..."

"Roxie!" I swivel back in my seat.

"And then told a gorgeous conference leader that she was horny by mistake, and in bad French, no less, said she had an orgasm!"

"Dear God!" I yell out loud. The acorn doesn't fall far from the tree!

Uncle Mason spits out his drink. "On purpose?"

"Seriously? When's the last time you remember Chase doing something embarrassing on purpose, Dad."

"Okay, you proved your point. Go on." Uncle Mason moves in closer to hear better. A burst of laughter erupts just behind our table.

"I need to leave," I blurt out. Add to that, from one asshole to the other! Jesus, help me!

"So, *Je suis* means 'I am.' Right? And *J'ai* means 'I have.' Well, she got confused with which one to use. I mean, I can understand. It's an easy mistake. Who would ever remember to say 'I have heat'? Doesn't it make more sense to say, 'I am hot?' Anyway, the conference leader thought it was so funny that he sent her and Auntie Olivia to the largest penis art show on the planet, instead of Monet's Water Lilies, where Chase's Swiss seatmate was sponsoring an art exhibit."

"It's true. We did," my mother laughs. "It was, to say the least, educational."

"And the story only gets better while we were in New York."

If looks could kill, Roxie would be pushing up daisies at this very moment. I am so angry that I begin stomping my foot uncontrollably under the table. Of course, no one can hear because of the loud dance music. So, I sit and fester because a part of me needs to see how far Roxie will take this.

"So, Chase and I take in a nightclub," she continues. Everyone around the table is engaged in the storytelling, except me. Does anyone care that they're making a fool out of me? It's the same ole, same ole "let's have fun with Chase." I hate my life right now.

"And she meets this hot Costa Rican, who, it turns out, runs a drug trafficking ring. Personally, I thought he exported bananas, but that was his secondary "cover" business ... his friend dubbed him Banana Man. And he drugged Chase with the sex drug, ecstasy, to be exact." Mason's eyes go wide as he silently mouths the word ecstasy several times.

"I met a nice pilot named Vincent on the way home from Idaho," I suddenly announce. All heads turn, giving me the "deer in the headlights" look. "But he lives in Maine, and he told me only to call when I was totally over my ex."

"So..." Uncle Mason exaggerates, "are you over Gray?"

"Grant. His name is Grant, Uncle Mel—, Uncle Mason."

"Oh, don't forget to tell my dad about the boy toy and his variety packs," Roxie beams. "So, I guess Chase was momentarily a cougar."

"Ugh! I give up!" I yell, throwing up my hands.

"Boy toy?" Uncle Mason questions, downing his drink.

"Well, all I can say is that guy knows how to find his penis in the dark!" Roxie guffaws obnoxiously. "Chase, show my dad your sticker chart. She made an Excel spreadsheet out of my post-breakup resolutions list. I gave her Amoremoji stickers to fill in for good and bad outcomes. I'm dying to see the list you made up of qualities you want in a man. Hot better not be on there."

"Roxie, stop!" I hiss. I see Paul and Jaydon heading towards us. "That's enough!"

"You promised me, Chase."

"That's personal, not something to share with the entire world!" I shout.

"No problem, I took a picture."

"You WHAT? WHEN?" I shriek.

"Oh, calm down, I'll just show it to my dad." She pulls out her phone and enlarges it. "Hey, when did you add the little flames?"

To-Do List (Week by Week) Completed by: Chastity Morgan Get Married: God Only Knows D = Date A = Amoremoji SR = Success Rating								
Meet a bunch of hot guys			Have lots of sex			Fall in love		
D	A	SR	D	A	SR	D	A	SR
Brent	😐	😐	Jacques-Pierre	🔥	🔥			
Boy Toy	😀	😀	Jacques-Pierre	🔥	🔥			
Banana Man	😵	😵	Jacques-Pierre	🔥	🔥			
Jacques-Pierre	😋	😋	Jacques-Pierre	🔥	🔥			
			Jacques-Pierre	🔥	🔥			
			Jacques-Pierre	🔥	🔥			

"The what??" I snatch the phone from her. I totally forgot the stickers I placed for all the times I had hot- and-heavy dreams. "Oh, SHIT!" I say a little louder than expected. I hit the delete button and hand it back to Roxie.

"What the hell did you do that for? You've been keeping secrets from me, haven't you, Chase? I didn't know you've been having sex. With whom? When?"

"Sex?" Jaydon raises. "Not with me, but we were close."

"Oh, it's Chase's boy toy," Roxie says off the cuff.

"Boy toy? Now, I need to hear about this one," Uncle Mason's eyes grow wide.

"Not I, said the cat," Paul adds.

"WHAT?" I yell. "Not even ... What the heck, Paul. It's a conspiracy, I swear!"

"Oh, don't let Nana hear this," my mom adds.

"MOTHER!" I'm red in the face now.

"Oh, I love it when you turn that color. Brings out the best in you," Uncle Mason smiles widely.

"Jaydon, why are you even here?" I ask him.

"Your mom invited me, remember?" Jaydon arches his eyebrow. "Besides, I'm here to ask Roxie for another dance. Oh, and at your first available bachelorette moment, I'd love to finish our ping-pong game," he winks.

"That's it!" I stand up. "I need to check on the cake situation." I turn toward the station, but I decide to head towards the ladies' room instead, which these days seems to be my new sanctuary.

"Chase, little love..."

Oh, no!

"This handsome fellow found himself alone at his table." I turn around to find Nana by my side. "You're the hostess, and I did not teach you ever to do such a thing. You are supposed to circulate the room." She smiles and gives me a wink, turning back to Brody with her gin martini in hand. "You are the most handsome little devil I've ever seen," she drawls. "I could..." *Wait for it!* "I could park my slippers under your bed any night of the week." Nana finishes. I roll my eyes. *Nana loves that line!*

"Handsome, are you Roxie's new boyfriend?" Nana says, leaning slightly against Brody as she sips her martini.

Roxie bursts out in laughter.

"No, Nana. He's Grant's husband," I say, rubbing her forearm. She takes a step back in shock, before cackling with laughter. "Remember, from Aunt Kate's Christmas party?" I add.

"Well, dear, no offense to you, Chastity, but Grant sure did pick a looker."

"Nana!" My eyes widen.

She takes another sip, "Oh, love, he would have turned me gay too." She links arms with Brody, clinking martini glasses.

"Oh, Nana!" She did not just say that. This is so embarrassing!

Everyone at the table seems taken over by Nana's antics. I seize the perfect opportunity to slip away into my little haven.

"I knew you'd eventually show up," a voice calls out from one of the stalls.

"Is that you, Daphne?"

"Yep! Crazy night, isn't it?"

"You could say so," I reply, letting out a huge sigh.

"Well, it's only the beginning," she pops out of the stall, heading directly to wash her hands. "So, as they say at Disneyland, hold onto your hats and glasses."

"What? Please don't tell me there's more to come tonight. I can't take much more of this. It's been a nightmare already! Please don't tell me you had another one of your visions."

"In pieces. There's definitely some 'not so nice things' coming up mixed in with some super good things," Daphne says.

"Oh, God! I don't know if I can handle this, Daphne."

"Really. You'll be okay. The best part is that you'll finally fall in love." Daphne pulls out a handful of paper towels, wiping her hands thoroughly.

"You saw that? With whom?"

"Not sure! It was kind of dim. But I have a hunch." She shrugs, tossing the wadded-up paper towels into the trash can.

"Who? Who? Tell me."

"Nope. That's not how the psychic world works. I'm sorry, you have to be patient," Daphne says as she promptly walks out of the bathroom door, leaving me standing there in the middle of the room thunderstruck.

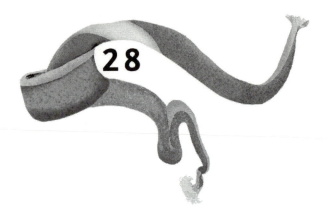

28

"Walking to New Orleans" by Fats Domino rings out through the speakers, followed by the roaring sound of a nine-piece brass band. Susan mentioned to me that Nana specifically requested the New Orleans getup since it reminded her of her honeymoon. I peer out of my sanctuary again, watching the ballroom become ablaze with enthusiasm. I notice some standing to clap and others waving their hands in the air while the remaining and most enthusiastic guests jump up and down, shouting "Dance On!"

"Chastity, it's so lovely to see you." The voice makes me jump as I carefully exit the ladies' room. Mrs. Walters, my grandmother's dear friend, appears out of nowhere; Mr. Walters snuggly tucked behind her, leaning on his cane for support. She embraces me in a little hug.

"Hello, Mr. and Mrs. Walters. I'm so happy you could come," I murmur, my heart still pounding from Daphne's mixed message of adversity and amore; my mind stuck on the former.

Why did she have to tell me that shit is about to hit the fan? Again?

"We wouldn't miss it for the world," Mrs. Walters pats my arm. She's very prim and proper with her hair-sprayed gray hair that flips under at the end, and it almost looks like a helmet. She's wearing a two-piece, bright yellow tweed suit with matching yellow shoes and thick stockings. "We were just on our way to find your grandmother. I still can't believe she's eighty-five today. She looks so young," she adds.

"'This is the first birthday in fifty-five years that I've spent somewhere new and not in Sun Valley, Idaho. Can you believe it?'" I parrot. I'm relieved to have remembered Nana's comment since I'm feeling brain-dead and not in the mood to converse.

"Yes. She told me that too. She was so worried that all the out-of-towners, who were many, might not make their flights over here. Spring weather can be unpredictable. They might have a snowstorm that shuts down the airport. Did she ever tell you about Gregory Peck?" abruptly changing the subject.

I move to her side, trying to head towards the cake that now resembles a flattened pancake of batter and frosting.

"Gregory Peck?" I try to look engaged, taking one step in the other direction. "She loves to tell that story."

"Yes, and he remembered her from Paris. Isn't that—"

The band drowns her out as it passes us and spreads out, weaving around the tables and continuing to fuel excitement among the crowd.

Clapping, I pretend to be okay when all the while, I am itching to make a run for it. I turn back to Mrs. Walters and notice her mouth still moving. I lean in to hear her ramblings.

"Nana was visiting your dad and uncle in Paris in the 1970s when they were living abroad. The three of them went into an American bookstore on the Rue de Rivoli, where she spotted him. She marched straight up to him, outrageously flirty, and told him that he could park his slippers under her bed any night of the week. It sent your dad and uncle flying out the doors in embarrassment."

I genuinely laugh, recalling the tale. The trombone bellows out a final note.

"But lo and behold," she continues, "the following Christmas, they were walking into the bookstore at the Sun Valley mall when they bumped right into him. Your Nana was surprised when he turned to her and said, 'Virginia, what a pleasure to make your acquaintance once again.'"

There's definitely some 'not so nice things' coming up. I hear Daphne's voice clearly as if she is standing next to me.

"But why?" I suddenly blurt out, responding to my mental meanderings. Suddenly embarrassed, I feel the heat rising on the sides of my face.

"Why?" Mrs. Walters, considering my question as natural, has a quick comeback. "Probably because your Nana is an unforgettable and remarkable woman, that's why, darling. And now still a spitfire at eighty-five, I don't know how your poor grandfather keeps up," she jokes.

"Hearing aids," I exclaim, wondering where I conjured the prompt answer.

"Hearing aids?" Mrs. Walters gives me a curious look.

"Yeah. He takes them out half the time." I guffaw at my dumb response.

Mr. Walters bursts out laughing. "He's a genius! Why didn't I think of that?" he coos to his wife, winking. Disdain written all over her face, Mrs. Walters puckers her lips for added effect.

"By the by, Chase," she shifts topics again, turning towards me.

By the by? What era is this? Who says stuff like that anymore?

"Have you met our grandson, Dean?" Mrs. Walters jerks her finger toward the corner of the room.

"No ... No, I haven't," I stutter, following her aim. I stand transfixed.

Oh. My. God. It couldn't be him, could it? Visions of freshman year of college and a sea of virility and testosterone dance in my head. Right in front of my eyes is my college fantasy guy, the unattainable senior football god whose image was plastered on billboards. He was, back then and still is, like a brick masonry building—heavy and stiff but with a remarkable façade.

314

There I go again, always having to relate men to buildings! I would think my engineering mind would take a break sometimes. I shake off the thought as my heart swells with glee. Holy smokes! Is this who Daphne was talking about? Could he be the one I'll fall madly in love with?

But then again—

My happy thoughts come to an abrupt halt. Dean wouldn't give me the time of day back then. Why would he even consider me now? Plus, his name doesn't start with the letter L.

Before I can even begin conceptualizing resistance, Mrs. Walters beats me to the punch, placing her hand on my arm and leading me towards their table.

I exhale and inhale quietly and roll my shoulders back. *Okay, I can do this,* I convince myself. I keep my eyes on Dean as the gap between us closes. He stands up, running his fingers through his cropped, dirty blond hair. It's perfectly coiffed in place, and no longer long, messy, and wind tousled like how I remembered it looking when he'd pull off his helmet. He looks even taller in person, with his broad shoulders and golden skin. His chin is lightly stubbled, which makes him look even more stunning. He's wearing a pale beige linen suit with an electric-blue, buttoned-down shirt. A delicate yet manly silver cross dangles around his neck. He brushes something out of his eyes and looks up to meet my staring gaze.

"Uh … hi," I say weakly, smiling like a loon and at a loss for words. He's big, powerful, and more than a bit intimidating.

"Dean, I would like you to meet Virginia's granddaughter, Chastity." He stands, his six-foot-six stature towering over me. He grasps my hand in his. I feel mesmerized, touching the giant hand of my fantasy man.

"I'm afraid I'm a bit of a party crasher, but thank you for having me. It's been an incredible night."

"Glad you're enjoying yourself," finding my voice again. My palms feel sweaty. *Why does that happen every time I meet a new man?*

"I am curious about one thing, how in the world did your grandmother get a New Orleans band to come to play at her birthday party?" he says playfully, a huge smile lighting up his face.

315

"My, my," Mrs. Walters interrupts. "I see you two have a lot to talk about. It was very nice to see you, Chastity. Come on, sweetheart," she says to her husband. "Let's leave these two to get acquainted." And just like that, Dean's grandparents vanish as they blend in with others on the dance floor.

"Subtle, aren't they?" Dean says, pulling out an empty chair beside him.

"Like a train wreck," I say under my breath.

"Excuse me?" Dean leans in to hear me over the dance music.

"Oh, I was just saying right as a check."

"Never heard that maxim before." Dean screws up his face.

"Oh, Valley Girl talk ... from the '80s," I conjure up. "Meaning that I agree with you." I end with a girlish grin.

"Valley Girls? Now that goes way back. Why don't you sit down and have a drink with me?"

As I settle in, I begin to make a tally on the "Gentleman List" I'm creating in my head.

"Do you take after your grandmother with her flirtatious charm?" Dean spouts brazenly.

"Good question!" I flash him what I hope is a winning smile because right now, I feel like I've won the lottery.

He hails a nearby waiter. "Two champagnes, please, and a 50-50 martini." 50-50? What's that? Maybe it's like my odds that this could go well, just like Daphne said.

"My grandmother was telling me that we went to the same college. I played football there. Did you ever attend any of the games?" Dean poses.

My mind wanders to a flashback of him in his tight, sparkly golden spandex pants. Dean pulled off his helmet, sweat dripping from his golden locks and running down his cheeks. He sat, resting his elbows on his knees, sipping a Gatorade as his biceps contracted with exhaustion, and the only thing I wanted to do that day was climb onto his lap and plant a giant kiss on those gorgeous lips.

"Chastity? Earth to Chastity?" Dean is waving a glass of champagne in front of my face. "Champagne?"

"No, thanks," I say, robotically. I will never take alcohol again from a man after the New York incident. I accept the water glass in front of me instead and begin gulping madly, trying to erase the lustful image I fabricated. *This is not a good start. I'm just out of the gate, and I can't get myself to answer a simple question. Focus, Chase, focus! What was his question again? Oh yes, did I go to any of the college football games?* "Yes, I'm well aware that you played football." I can't help grinning like a loon again. I chuckle lightly.

"What's so funny?" Dean rests his left elbow on the tablecloth and leans in, eyeing me with such intensity that it feels like he's about to hypnotize me into telling him all my deep, dark secrets.

"Oh, just silly college memories. Back then, you were like a superhero. Every girl I knew wanted to date you, and every guy wanted to be you." I blurt out the words without thinking, casting a downward glance at my water. *Why do I have no control over my mouth? I don't need a repeat of the plane incident.*

His brow creases with surprise, "So, you watched me play? I never pegged you as a football fan."

"Guilty," I confess, lowering my voice. "Actually, my cousin and I watched you through my binoculars. Who would think binoculars would be so useful, right?" I giggle girlishly. *Okay, Chastity, STOP! Bite your tongue and think before you answer him.* I take another sip, to give myself a moment to compose my thoughts. "I heard you went pro."

"For a few years," he mumbles with a bit of sadness added. *Uh-oh, did I say something wrong?* His martini arrives, and he immediately drains it. I feel my jaw drop. I seem frozen in place, staring at him. I'm speechless. I watch as he returns the empty martini glass on the table behind him. "Now I," he abruptly belches, the stench of alcohol wafting in my face, "work for the government. I just got back from being in the woods."

"Oh! A forest service park ranger, right?" I query.

"No. Desk job in D.C. From time to time, they send me into the woods."

He said it again! What type of lingo is that?

I watch as Dean shifts his gaze around the room. A waiter appears, depositing a plate of mashed potatoes topped with a hanger steak, and Brussel sprouts in front of us both.

"Martini, please!" he yells to the waiter.

"Sir, that's your—"

"I know damn well how many I've had, thank you very much! Now, would you pleeeeeease get me another one?"

I watch the waiter walk away, shaking his head. In a moment, he returns and hands the drink to Dean, who downs it in a matter of seconds. My eyes widen. I blink a few times to rid the martini scene so I can return to his cryptic job.

"Uh ... that ... makes ... no ... sense."

"What doesn't make sense?"

"Why would a desk job ... require that you go into the woods?" I sputter, hoping that I don't sound like an idiot. He shrugs and says nothing, looking about the room. Again, I can't help but stare, this time out of pure curiosity. I muster up boldness.

"So, you're a spy, aren't you?" I grab my fork and dive into the potatoes before me, realizing that I probably crossed the line. I'm surprised when he looks back at me with a sexy smirk on his face.

"I mostly translate documents, but as I said, they send me into the woods," he laughs.

I nervously giggle, muffled with a mouthful of food. *He must think I'm a dweeb!*

Without warning, Dean takes my hand and runs his fingers along my ring finger. "I see no ring, so you're not married or engaged. How about a relationship? Are you in one?"

I sit up straight, tilting back in my seat as my stomach clenches for the second time tonight. "Uh..." I stammer. "I ... assume you missed—"

"I saw and heard the whooooole thing, sweetie." Dean's slyly smiles. "You're very single, so much so that your Nana would hogtie anyone into marrying you, wouldn't you say?"

I give him a hard stare.

"And your point?" I say with an edgy voice.

"How important is sex in your relationships?" he asks, scooting his chair closer and studying me with even more curiosity.

"Huh? If that isn't a dumb question—" I raise my voice, wondering from which boat he just got off.

"Hello! What do you mean 'how important is sex in your relationships?' Isn't sex everything to a man? Well, duh! Okay. Don't answer that," I say, all in one breath. *Oh boy, this could go bad real fast. If I tell him I've never had sex, he'll think I'm a prude. If I lie, he'll quiz me and soon find out I'm the former.*

"Actually, I will." He runs his hands through his hair before leaning forward and whispers, "I have ED."

"ED? What's—" I say louder than expected.

"Shh!" He cups my mouth with his hand.

"What's that?" I whisper.

Dean pans the room before cradling himself in my shoulder and cups my ear. "Erectile dysfunction."

I jump back in my seat, chair legs wobbling. "Excuse me?" My college-fantasy image suddenly bursts. I scoot my chair away from him a bit. I can't look at him. I don't know what to say. *This guy is KOOKY!*

"I have erectile dysfunction, but I take medicine for it," Dean blurts out, followed by a massive burp. "Look, I don't make a habit of sharing my problems, but you seem like an honest and frank person, and if we're going to get personal—"

"Personal?" I yell.

"Shh!" he cups my mouth again. I slap his hand.

"Hey, no need to get so frisky, little lady!" throwing his hands up in surrender.

"You can't be serious? Are you telling me that you take those penis-helper drugs you see in commercials for older, horny couples?"

"I'm just saying that someone like you must need a lot of sex to satisfy your most obvious nymphomaniac leanings. You might be the most beneficial thing for me, and the answer to my problem," he bluntly remarks as he reaches over to take a sip from my champagne glass. With lightning speed, I swipe my glass from him. I look around his shoulder and notice the collection of empty glasses on a tray that are set on the table behind him. *Now it makes sense.*

"You're drunk, aren't you?" I counter an octave too loud. People turn to look at us. I feel like screaming but will myself to remain calm. In the process of taking a deep breath, I accidentally swallow saliva and erupt into a coughing fit. I can feel his eyes boring into me as I hack away in a table napkin.

"Get the little lady a fresh napkin and a glass of water. Pronto," he orders the same waiter.

"I'm ... not ... a ... nymphomaniac!" I croak, coughing between words once the waiter is out of sight.

"Look at you! You're smart, beautiful, and confident. You've most likely been with a lot of guys by now. What are you? Twenty-eight, twenty-nine? And from what your Nana said, you're a player who doesn't want to settle down. I imagine it would take a lot to satisfy you." Dean looks at me, his face intrigued. The waiter returns just as Dean finishes his weird explanation, and quickly attends to my needs, periodically glaring at Dean while lightly patting my back and offering me water.

"Thank you. I think I can take it from here," I nod to the waiter, supplying him with a weak smile.

"I'm not a nymphomaniac!" I say, gritting my teeth once the waiter is out of earshot again. I feel the heat rising on my cheeks; they have to be blazing red. "And you misinterpreted what Nana was saying. I may have been out of the dating world—"

I stop dead, realizing that I'm about to divulge my virgin status. The last thing this wacko needs to know is about my lackluster sex life. I'd be damned if I—.

I turn and notice that he's staring at the ceiling—totally oblivious to my flustered state.

"Dean!" I yell, making him flinch. "This is all a joke, right? The ED? The medication? Right?"

Before I know what's happening, he wraps his arms around me in a tight hold and passionately kisses me. "Whoa!" is all I can say after he releases me. *What a kisser!*

"And to answer your question," he leans in for a whisper, "It's called too much porn!"

"WHAT?" I scream, reaching my limit. "That's it! I'm—"

A hand gently squeezes my shoulder.

"Sorry to butt in on your romantic moment, Chastity," Susan smiles.

Speechless, I give her a look of incredulity.

"Can I borrow you? Your family wants to take a few pictures, and we need to fix the cake situation."

"Ah ... sure! I'd be glad to! Let me just get my..." I scan the table, madly searching for my phone when I see Dean thumbing on his phone, mine sitting right in front of him.

"Oh, don't tell me!" I begin to raise my voice.

"We'll be in contact, little lady. Good playing catch-up with you!" he shouts as he heads for the men's room.

"I don't believe it!" I say aloud to no one in particular.

"Come on, dear. The photographer is waiting." Susan lightly pulls my arm as I follow her mindlessly.

* * *

Picture taking goes on for what seems like an eternity, which is fine by me. I need a reprieve. Somehow, I keep my composure during the photoshoot even though my mind keeps replaying the evening's objectionable events. And thankfully, the chef had a few sheets of cake already prepared in the back as extra, which took care of that problem. Why I choose to sit back down afterward with Uncle Mason is beyond me. I plop myself down between Roxie and my mom this time, hopefully as a safety cushion.

"Happy Birthday" rings out, and I barely glance over the crowd to see Nana blowing out her candles on the sheet cake. I can't bear seeing another disaster.

"Hubba-hubba. He looked so oddly familiar, right?" Roxie queries, throwing her arm around me for good measure. "Did you have a fun time conversing with the handsome stranger?"

"Who? Dean?" I counter.

"Dean! That's it!" Roxie exclaims. "Who's Dean?" she says, looking confused. A waiter passes by, depositing plates of cake on the table. "We went to college with him."

"He was in our dorm? I'd remember a hunk like that," Roxie states, slapping her hand on the table and nearly toppling over her dessert. "Hey, who ate half my cake?" She yells as she pulls out a piece from a luscious-looking coconut concoction with her fork. She looks over at her father, who has a mouthful of the delectable treat. "DAD! Eat your own."

"No. We stared at his amazing buns of steel with binoculars every football game. He played wide receiver. Ring a bell?"

"Oh, my God! I never looked at his face." Roxie bursts out laughing. "Ooh-la-la, to think we get the opportunity to see his tight ass up close and personal. This birthday bash just got a hell of a lot better."

"Well, he's all yours!" I announce.

"Really?" she pauses a second. "Oh ... nope. One man is enough for me. I've turned a new lease on life. But I can still window shop!"

I roll my eyes as Roxie gets out of her seat and anxiously pans the room for Dean.

Seizing the moment, Uncle Mason replaces Roxie and scoots in closer to me. "You two did look rather cozy, Chase."

"I'm really not interested—"

"Enlighten me," he interrupts. "How's his ED?"

"ED?" my mom asks. "It's not what I think it is?"

"Yep! Erectile dysfunction," Uncle Mason blurts out rather loudly.

"How did you—" I begin.

"Know? Jesus Christ! The guy was about as quiet as a moose in heat. I could hear him across the room." I slowly sink in my chair, hoping that by some great miracle, I'll fade away.

"Oh, the poor guy..." my mom expresses sorrowfully.

"Oh, poor guy, my ass!" Uncle Mason spouts. "They've got meds to take care of that kind of thing nowadays. He's probably having a heyday fapping away."

"What's ... what's fapping?" My curiosity gets the best of me. I sit up straight again.

"Well, it's one of those things that go hand-in-hand, so to speak," he chuckles at his joke, "when you watch a lot of porn."

My mom and I look at each other, clueless. Suddenly, it hits me.

"OH. MY. GOD! It's not what I think it is?"

"It's EXACTLY what you think it is, sweets." Uncle Mason grins from ear to ear, still laughing.

"Oh!" my mom blurts. "That's gross! I'm done with this conversation. I think I'll go find your father." She gives me a light peck on my forehead before walking across the room.

"So," I continue, "Why would anyone that looks like him need to jerk off a lot? I mean, why does watching porn cause a guy to need erectile dysfunction medication?"

"Online porn has become an addiction for some people."

I turn to look at my uncle who, for the first time that I've known him, is actually serious.

"I think guys find it so easy to log on and see something sexual and whack off," he says. "The problem begins when guys try to sexually interact with real-life human beings, which causes them anxiety. And when guys have anxiety, they can't get a proper stiffy. Even if this kind of porn-addicted guy is sexually excited, it's not necessarily enough to keep it up. Performing well becomes but a dream. Thus, the need for medication."

"Huh," I ponder. "It sounds like a vicious cycle."

"Bingo!" my uncle yells.

"How do you know all this?" I look at him straight on, folding my arms and wait for a confession.

"One of my college roommates had, let's say, issues. I tried to help him, but he kept pushing me away. I finally went to talk to the health center about it. It was eye-opening, even for a cocky asshole like me."

I am visibly shocked at his admission. The Student Health Center has porn discussions? I remember them distributing fruit-flavored condoms to all our dorm rooms, wondering what they were for. But porn?

My phone vibrates.

```
Dean: Want to see my tattoo?
```

I scroll down to see an undefinable picture. I realize what I'm looking at as soon as I enlarge it.

"SHIT!" I throw my phone, which flies across the table and promptly lands on the floor with a resounding splat.

"He did not just send me that," I mumble behind the cupped hands on my face.

"It happened, didn't it?" Daphne appears out of nowhere, handing the phone back to me.

"What's wrong?" Uncle Mason asks.

"Daphne, don't look at it!" I yell. "Show it to Mason." I'm relieved that she dutifully obeys.

"Be warned, it's scary!" the little girl laughs. "I told you, bad would happen."

"Daphne! I told you not to—"

"I didn't, Chase."

"Hey, is your mom single?" Uncle Mason asks Daphne.

She stares at him intensely, as if looking into his soul. "Aren't you already in love with someone else? I don't think you have room in your heart for two."

His eyes go wide as he looks across the room. Daphne smiles as she turns and walks away.

"What just happened?" Uncle Mason genuinely looks stunned.

"You know, kids these days," I laugh nervously.

"No, I don't," my uncle responds, deadpan. "Okay, whatever!" He returns to the phone in his hand.

"Oh, interesting!" Uncle Mason comments.

"What?"

"The tattoo by his privates." He moves the phone in my direction.

"God, no!" I shut my eyes. "I don't want to see it again. Just tell me what it means."

"It's a black diamond. Hmm ... I'm guessing he's trying to say that his package is for experts only. Clever. I wish I'd thought of that when I was young." He lets out a deep belly laugh.

"O ... K..." I say mechanically. "So, is this supposed to be the new trend of dating? Pictures of your private parts, discussions on sex life, and porn? What happened to good old-fashioned romance and wining and dining a lady? I feel like I've just woken up in *The Twilight Zone*."

"I keep telling you and Roxie, you both need an all-American cowboy. A stud who wears Wranglers, a Stetson hat, a huge silver belt buckle, and kick-ass cowboy boots," Uncle Mason says, taking a sip of his wine.

324

"Don't tell me—like John Wayne, right?" I ask. "Because Dad beat you to it."

"Absolutely! The 21st-century version of him."

I guffaw. Maybe Dad and Uncle Mason are right.

"All right, let's get back to this wacko. What do I text back?" I ask him.

"Say, if that's all you've got to impress me, then I'm moving on."

"Oh God, that's something a guy would say." I shake my head.

"Well, I am a man, and you asked for my advice. How about this … say that you're still on the bunny hill, but maybe one day. Dot. Dot. Dot. That will make him believe there's still hope," he laughs.

"Got it." I chuckle, thumbing the response on my phone. "When it's time for me to get married, I want a man to profess his love for me, not show me his junk. Is that too much to hope for?"

"No, sweets, it's not," my uncle pats me on my shoulder. "You know, I may be one hell of an asshat, but you will *always* be my favorite niece."

"Really? I'm also your *only* niece, asshat!" I blush. "But I'm still very flattered, Uncle Mason. This is a side of you that I've never seen before."

"Yeah, I know, so don't go blabbing to the world, okay?" He gives me a big bear hug. "Now that we've got that out of the way," he leans in to whisper. "Can I see your Excel spreadsheet again? That was quite a marvel."

"NO!" I slap him playfully on the arm. "And forget you ever saw that," I add.

29

"I can't believe I'm doing this!" my new mantra as I cross the skywalk to my spring-quarter class in the Math Sciences Building. The last course I will ever take in my engineering career. Claustrophobia hits me when I open the entrance; students clustered in the hallway wedge so tightly I can't find a clear path to my assigned room.

Someone behind me pushes me towards the opened door to MS 101. The welcomed kinetic energy boosts me to where I want to be: in the back of the newly designed classroom. It takes a few seconds for me to adjust to the brightness of the yellowed walls against the morning sunlight. A cursory glance toward the front catches the professor, scrolling his name in giant capital letters across the horizontal-sliding chalkboard. Spotting the farthest green swivel seat, I speed up my steps and plop down. My phone immediately vibrates in my pocket. I barely swipe over to my email when I hear my name.

"Hi, Chastity," the professor shouts, striding towards my desk. I pan the room, noticing the turned heads of the other students.

"Oh shi—" I whisper too loudly.

"I heard that," the professor says, chuckling lightly.

"We had this discussion this morning," I whisper more quietly this time while sinking lower in my seat. "Remember? You're supposed to pretend I'm just another student in your class. I'm only taking it because I need to know how to design a timber and a masonry structure, and it's the last class I need for my degree; otherwise, I would have opted out."

"Chase, my class is not a nightmare," he says loud enough to turn some heads again in the room. "SHH..." I blurt.

"It's actually one of the students' favorites," he continues, lowering his voice considerably. "Everyone's going to find out sooner or later. It's not like you can hide the fact—"

"SHH..." I repeat. "PLEASE..." I mumble through clenched teeth, "for the time being, let's stick to the plan."

He shrugs his shoulders and walks to the front of the class. "Oh—" he bellows once he gets to the chalkboard, "what time is your mother expecting us home for dinner?"

A look of horror plastered on my face; I give my dad a hard stare.

"Oh, right. Sorry," he mumbles. "You're just another student in my class." The room turns eerily quiet as all eyes stare at me. *Oh, fuck me! It's going to be a really long spring quarter.*

"Welcome to Advanced Structural Design," Dad announces in a booming voice, which fortunately breaks up the awkwardness. He's wearing beige slacks and a pale blue long-sleeve collared shirt, looking like a real professor and not a wannabe cowboy. "My name is Dr. Preston Morgan, and I will be your professor for this class. Advanced Structural Design is the study of..."

My father drones on. He has rehearsed this introduction so many times at home that I can practically recite it word for word. I turn to look at my email.

From: jacquesp@mera.fr
To: ChaseMorg@mylife.com
Subject: Dreams

Last night I had a dream where I took a plane to come and see you. I think you are in my dreams now. I hope to be in one of them. Have beautiful dreams, ma cherie. Je t'embrasse.

Jacques-Pierre had dreams about me?? OH. MY. GOD. I was right when I said he's the ONE! Forget all the rest of the idiots I've met because Daphne must mean him! His email is enough proof.

I forward the email to Roxie with a subject heading: Look what he said. I flinch, nearly dropping the phone when it begins madly vibrating in my hand. Roxie's name shows up on the screen.

"Hey, I'm in class," I whisper, sinking in my seat to hide.

"Isn't that the coolest thing, Chase," Roxie screams into the phone. I try muffling the sound with my scarf, but it's too late; all the heads in the back of the room turn in my direction.

"Excuse me," my dad directs at me. "Is everything okay in the back of the room?"

"Um ... I ... need..."

I don't finish my reply. Instead, I rush out the back door of the classroom and head to the hallway. "Geez, Rox, did you have to—"

"Holy shit!" she chokes out. "Can you believe he's coming to visit you?"

"No, it was in his dream," I state, matter-of-factly as I stand against the wall, allowing for the crowd to scurry by me as they rush to get to their classes on time.

"Same thing. That's his way of running it by you first to see how you'll respond. All of your issues don't alarm him because he witnessed it upfront, and now he's in hot pursuit. Whoa! I

328

just walked past a local French bistro on 73rd and Lex. It's a sign!"

"It's a sign? Wait! Are you in New York again? When did you leave for New York? We just got back from Lake Arrowhead."

"Um ... uh," Roxie stumbles on her words. "Red-eye. I'm scouting wedding locations for another client. I'll tell you about it when I get back."

"Wow! Really? Congratulations. I'm sure you'll find them the most romantic spot—"

"Babe, let's go." A deep voice bellowing in the background catches me off guard.

"Who's—"

"Got to run, Chase! Miss you!" She hangs up.

I stare at the phone, playing back the awkward few seconds of the conversation. "That has to be Roxie's new man. Did I hear the sound of a kiss, a smacking sound before we disconnected? I'm sure I did," I say aloud, listening to the reverberation of my voice as I stand alone in the now deserted corridor.

I find the back door to the classroom and enter quietly. I hear a hissing sound just as I slide into my seat. "Didn't you just hear your dad's 4-1-1 phone policy?"

No. Please not her. Could this day get any worse?

I turn to my left slightly and notice the signature pencil-thin black skirt and red kitten heels. I feel the hairs on my arms stand up. Just when I thought this class couldn't get any worse. *It's ASSon.*

Ignoring her, I type out a response to Jacques-Pierre. I can hear her making a huffing noise.

From: ChaseMorg@mylife.com
To: jacquesp@mera.fr
Subject: Re: Dreams

I did have beautiful dreams. They were wonderful. Je t'embrasse.
Chase

"Kudos, by the way," she adds, her words dripping with sarcasm. "Since your father is the professor, that's a guaranteed A."

"Ahem," my dad clears his throat loudly, getting our attention; his glare meets our deer-in-the-headlights look.

"Later," ASSon mouths to me.

* * *

I blast out to the building, trying to avoid ASSon, determined not to let her get the best of me and haunt me as the Prissy Posse did during high school.

"Okay, it's later," she yells to me as I approach my car. I want to unlock my door, slam it shut, gun the engine, and run her over. That would make my day. Instead, I turn around slowly.

ASSon smiles at me innocently. "I thought you'd like to know that your advisor is senile; he's at the beginning stages of Alzheimer's. They want to force him into retirement, so it looks like you might not have an advisor for the rest of the quarter."

"Senile?" I echo. Not following, I picture the quiet gentleman who is not a day older than sixty that likes to sit at his desk and eat anything chocolate.

"Exactly."

"That doesn't make any sense."

She hesitates, flipping back her hair. "He couldn't remember where he was or what class he was teaching."

"You're so full of nonsense, Alison, just like when I came to school to proctor the final, and you said that if I stuck around, I'd pick up meningitis." I've had enough of her. I turn on my heels to open my car door. ASSon lets out a guffaw.

I feel my anger rising. Taking a cleansing breath, I set my bag of class materials on the ground, turn back, and crack my knuckles loudly as Charlie taught me during our 'how to intimate jerks' lesson. ASSon visibly gulps.

"Alison, I will say this once, so pay attention: I'm sick and tired of your constant harassment, and how dare you sit next to me in class, like we were best friends, only to undermine me the whole time. Who taught you how to act this manipulative? You were so sweet and shy back in high school. What happened to you? Was it Medus—" I stop myself, "I mean, Julie? Joan? Lizzie?" I throw up my hands as she makes a tsk sound. The words are coming out of my mouth, and I can't believe I have the gumption to say them. I have this sudden overwhelming confidence.

"UGH!" I let out, exasperated. "And what is your problem anyway, trying to sabotage the final I was proctoring? And if you were looking to give out kudos, you should have used them to congratulate me on finishing all but one chapter of my dissertation. Plus, I received the highest marks in my winter-quarter classes, *and I* managed to get better teaching-assistant ratings than you. What does *that* say about your character? Yeah, you're a character, all right!" I am definitely on a roll. I inadvertently slap her across the face when I throw one end of my scarf across my shoulder for effect. ASSon's smile morphs into a frown, her face growing paler by the second.

"All that's left for me now," I continue, "is to finish this class and defend my dissertation. I'm on the home stretch. It's too late, Alison. Your time is up because nothing—NOTHING IS GOING TO GET IN MY WAY, so FUCK OFF, BITCH!"

And just like that, I pick up my bag and get into my car. ASSon is still standing in the same spot, looking dumbfounded as I pull away.

I jolt when the car speakers ring out loudly. Yesterday, I finally synced my phone to the car but never had a chance to use it. Until now. I press the phone button on the steering wheel. Brent's voice comes through louder than I expect. I flinch again.

"Hello!"

"You're late! Daphne and I have been waiting ten minutes already, and our stomachs are growling. The food truck is going to take off by the time you get here. Where the hell are you?" I hear Daphne giggling in the background. "We put in our order. What do you want?"

"I know. I'm sorry. I had ... to tie up some loose ends after class," I respond, thinking back to my moxie. "I'm driving. Order me two large slices of the Vegan, gluten-free pizza."

"God. How can you eat that stuff?"

"No questions, Brent. Just order it. I'll be there in a few minutes with my tennis racket in hand." I can't help but smile. I've actually missed the mischief-maker, pseudo-sex coach.

"Well, chop-chop! We're starving and ready to kick your ass!"

* * *

I pull alongside the park and see Brent and Daphne on a patio table with a brightly colored umbrella near the tennis courts, waving madly. A dull pain suddenly radiates across my abdomen, which momentarily takes my breath away. I slowly breathe a couple of times while lightly massaging my stomach. The pamphlet Dr. Patel gave me warned me that I could not get stressed out, or it can lead to pain attacks. I do a couple of long deep breaths, taking my time walking towards Brent and Daphne. It's 90 degrees out today, but with the sun beating down full force, it feels more like a sweltering 105 in this heat.

"Bout time," Brent drawls, grease running down his face. I take in his crazy attire—white short shorts, a white polo shirt, and a white fedora. Very Wimbledon-esque. My mind wanders to him on the grass courts, sauntering up to the lady referee, trying to charm her into giving him an extra point. *Don't you look divine, like you just got off the beach with your sun-kissed skin and perfect smile? I could douse you in whip cream and lick you all day long.*

"Your stuff should be out soon," Brent says, nearly shouting and snapping me back to reality.

Daphne runs up next to me. She's wearing a bright yellow tennis dress with her hair in pigtails and playfully swinging her racket. I guess I didn't get the memo on the crazy tennis attire.

"Chase! Yay! We get to hang out with Paul before he leaves. I really like him." She gives me an exaggerated wink.

332

"Paul's joining us?" I question. Daphne smiles at me.

"Like who?" Brent abruptly stands up, slapping me playfully on my rear end.

I winch. "Ouch!"

"You okay, Chase?" Daphne asks. "You look like you're in pain."

"I didn't smack you that hard. What the hell?" Brent quickly defends himself.

"It's not that," Daphne comments.

"What do you mean? How do you know, Daphne?" Brent blurts out.

"She knows," I answer, taking a seat in one of the chairs.

I pan the park; it is full of people with kids, wildly running around the jungle gym, zooming along the paths on scooters, and playing frisbee.

"Besides," I add, "it passed as soon as I got out of the car, so I'm good."

"Don't get yourself so stressed out," Daphne offers.

Daphne and I give each other a knowing look. It's eerie how this kid knows everything ... and I mean everything.

"Thanks!" I say, smiling weakly.

"You're welcome!" Daphne returns, holding my hand.

"And I'm clueless," says Brent, passing me a bottle of water, "again!"

"Don't worry about it," I say after unscrewing the cap and taking a long sip. I change the subject and look down at Daphne. "So, what do you think of Brent as a babysitter? Is he better than Roxie?"

"He's cool! He even lets me tell him his horoscope." She grins widely.

"Really?"

"Really," Brent answers. "And she's pretty damn good at it too for being a kid."

My eyes pop open. "So, what did she tell you?"

"I ain't gonna—"

"His love life sucks," Daphne answers, emphatically.

"Daphne!" I screech.

"Well, that's what the stars say. I'm just saying."

Brent sighs. "She's right."

"But it will get better," Daphne interjects, smiling from ear to ear.

"Oh, really? When?" I feign interest. *This ought to be good!*

"Well, that's up to him," she says, crossing her arms.

Daphne and I turn to look at Brent.

"I have to get some sh—" quickly cupping his mouth. "Sorry, 'stuff' for that to happen. It's ... it's a long story," he stutters. He pops up from the table and walks to the food truck to get my food.

"Two large slices of Vegan, gluten-free pizza?" He says, looking at me for confirmation that he got the order right.

"That's it!" I respond, raising my hand like I was still in class. Brent's eyes widen as he dutifully sets down the food. Daphne lets out a giggle. I didn't realize how hungry I was until my stomach growled after taking in the luscious aroma. I stuff my mouth with a huge bite.

"Geez, Louise! You attacked that piece like you haven't had food in days," Brent roars, his eyes even more prominent.

"I'm a growing girl," I muffle between bites. Brent and Daphne immediately erupt in laughter.

My phone dings with a text. I wipe my hands thoroughly before swiping:

Mrs. Adelman: Can you meet my bachelor for drinks at 8 pm tonight at

Tap Room? His name is Shorty.

"How random is this?"

"How random is what?" Brent asks before taking an extra-large bite of his pepperoni pizza.

"This text from Mrs. Adelman." I shove my phone in front of his face.

"Oh, Auntie Josie!" Daphne starts to bounce lightly on her chair. "What does she want?"

"Well, she wants me to meet up with a guy she thinks is a perfect match for me."

"Seriously?" Brent asks.

"What's his name?" Daphne adds.

"Shorty."

"What type of 'perfect match' name is that, Chase? Sounds like a real winner if you ask me," Brent chuckles, giving me a giant dramatic eye roll.

"Daphne, this is your aunt we're talking about," ignoring his comment. "I don't think she'll steer me wrong, right? Besides, what do I have to lose by saying yes? I want to get married, and she thinks he's the perfect candidate for me."

"Oh, boy! It doesn't sound good. I don't kn—"

"Come to think of it," Brent cuts Daphne off. "I used to know a guy named Shorty."

"Yeah?" I respond blankly. "Here, let me text her back."

> **Me: Sure. How will I know it's him? Is his name really Shorty?**

A moment later, my phone pings.

"Okay. This is what she says: He'll find you, and yes, he's really tall. It's a nickname, but he likes to go by it."

My mind wanders as Brent and Daphne start up a running commentary, their conversation quickly fading.

"So, you're the stunning Chastity Morgan everyone keeps telling me about."

"In the flesh." I'm surprised at my brazen response. "And you must be Shorty."

"Here, at your service," he replies, winking.

"How did you end up with a name like that? You've got to be six foot—"

"Six-four to be exact," he finishes. "Alexander is my real name. Alexander Dominica."

"Wow! What a beautiful name!"

"It's Grecian." Alexander walks over and takes my hands, kissing each softly. He stares into my eyes while slowly wrapping his arms around me. "May I kiss you?" he whispers into my ear.

"Uh—"

Not waiting for my answer, he bends slightly and kisses me. Passionately.

HONK! HONK! HONK!

"Sweet Jesus!" I yell, the chair rocking back. I grab the table to steady myself.

"Oh, man!" Brent drops his phone just when he presses the side button to take a video. "That would have been good. Where the hell were you, Chase?"

"It's Paul!" Daphne screams, running over to the car to greet him with a big hug. "Good timing! We just finished eating."

"Awesome!" Paul says, walking toward me, flashing his winning smile while spinning his tennis racket. "I saw you jump. You looked surprised to see me." He reaches forward, pressing his lips against my cheek and embracing me in a tight hug. My heart skips a beat as my body reacts to this sudden closeness. "Daphne told me you invited me. At Nana's party ... she arranged it all..." he stops to look at the little girl. She's smiling, spinning around like she just got away with something clever.

"Yeah, you missed it! Chase almost fell off—" Brent guffaws while chewing his last piece of pizza.

"Brent!" I give him a dirty look.

"Whatever!" Brent waves me away before extending his hand to Paul. "Good to see you again, man!"

"Good to see you too," Paul replies, shaking Brent's hand heartily.

"How ... do ... you two know each other?" I stutter, staring at them inquisitively.

"While you were in New York," Paul provides. "I stopped by your place to take you out to dinner, and he popped his head out of Daphne's front door to tell me that you weren't home. Before your dad filled me in, of course."

"Ah..." I begin to fiddle around with my scarf.

"God, aren't you hot wearing that thing?" Paul scrolls through his phone to answer a text. "It's fucking 105 out."

"It *feels* like 105; it's on ... ly ... 90," I spout, looking at the weather app on my phone. "I'm just fine. It's a thin material, not as heavy as it looks," I say between sips of water.

"Well..." Paul claps his hands, "on that happy note, are you all ready to play ball? It's not going to get any cooler." His voice gets smaller as he heads over to the courts.

"Ready!" Daphne smiles, running to his side.

"Do you mind if I pick Chase to be my partner," Paul wraps his arm around the little girl.

"Cool! That means I can play against you. I'll beat your socks off," Daphne says snarkily.

"Whoa, that's a load full from a kid," Paul feigns a look of surprise.

"I've been playing since I was four. Give me a break!" Daphne giggles as she walks toward Brent on the other side of the court.

"She ain't lying," Brent offers. "I've seen her in action."

Paul lets out a hearty belly laugh as he places his arm around me, and we head in the opposite direction. "So, you're probably wondering what happened to Grant and Medusa, the witch..." Paul says out of the blue.

"Now you're going to answer me? I sent that text a week ago," raising my voice, slightly annoyed.

"I know, but I wanted to have this discussion in person. I hope you don't mind." Paul reaches out to hold my hand. I suddenly feel tingly all over again. *This is odd! What is wrong with my body?*

"Uh ... uh," I stutter. "Fine. So?"

"Well, Medusa tried to slap the burly waiter who escorted them out of the ballroom. He caught her arm just as a cruiser showed up. In a matter of minutes, they were in the back seat. Grant told me to tell Brody to meet him at the station before they drove away. I sent several texts to Grant since. He hasn't returned any of them."

"Oh. My. God! What about Brody?"

"Couldn't tell you. I haven't spoken to him since I relayed the message."

"And Medusa?" I ask, grabbing my ankle to stretch my hamstring.

"Clueless."

"The whole thing appears to be a mystery. The sad part is that Medusa has been such a shady character since high school; it's hard to know when she's telling the truth. And, to be honest, I'm worried about Grant."

"Me too." He gives me a long stare.

"Why?" I question, breaking the awkwardness, sitting down on the rickety bench near the court. I lace up my tennis shoes.

"He hasn't been himself lately. I can't put my finger on it. It's just a feeling. Anyway," Paul waves his hand, erasing the last thought midair, "that's all I have to report. I wish I could tell you more."

"Can we play? We're waiting," Brent yells, flipping around his racket while stretching from side to side. I have to hold back a fit of giggles; his shorts are WAY too short.

"You're asking for it, bud," Daphne spouts, spanking his bottom with her racket.

"What do you mean?" Brent looks at her incredulously. "I've been an awesome babysitter."

"You'll see," Daphne smirks, taking her place at the net while Brent trots to the service line.

Paul and I give each other a knowing look.

"Ready?" Brent says, bouncing the ball in preparation to serve.

"Ready," Paul winks.

* * *

"Can you just give Chase a few more groundstrokes and then we can play a set," Brent says as he draws away slowly, trailing a hand down my back before jogging to the side of the court and taking a long sip from his water bottle. Paul fires ball after ball until I'm completely out of breath and barely moving.

"Slight change of plans," Daphne announces. "Chase and I are going to take you two little boys on, and we will show you no mercy," Daphne beams, tossing the ball in the air and giving me a back-handed low five. "We'll play the best of five points."

Paul moans, but he follows Brent to the far side of the net.

"Daphne, what have you done? We're going to get creamed," I murmur.

"Trust me; this will be fun. I wasn't showing you my best tennis yet. I'm really good at the net when I hit volleys. Brent thinks he's the king of the tennis court, and no one knows how

338

to do anything better than him. We need to show him who the boss is. How good is your overhead these days?" Daphne asks, winking.

I smile broadly, and the battle begins between Paul and me as Daphne and Brent stand at the net. Balls are flying at us fast, and I don't have time to think.

"Are you ready, Chase?" Brent asks, positioning himself in the middle of the court but closer to the net a few feet in front of the service line. "The next point wins."

"Yep, I have this. Serve it up, Paul," I laugh, giving Daphne a wink as I stand at the net opposite Brent, waiting. Paul takes out the ball and serves it right at Daphne. She hits it deep in the court, returning it past Brent and rocking Paul back on his heels so that he pops up what I expected: a short lob.

I am grinning with such malice, waiting for the overhead. I smash it, hitting Brent.

"Bull's-eye!" Daphne yells. Brent drops to his knees, clutching his groin. "Target down!" Daphne laughs, running to high five me.

"Chase, you have a mean overhead," Brent moans, lying on his side.

"I'm sure it's not the first time you've been clobbered in the jewels," I exclaim.

"So much for jewels after that hit," Brent mumbles. "They may never work again."

"You know that was a match point, right? Chase and I win!" Daphne cheers, high-fiving us both.

"Ow," Brent grunts in more pain.

"Poor baby has an owie. Do you need some ice?" Daphne asks, patting his shoulder.

I smile, extending my hand to help pull Brent up. I can't stifle my laughter any longer; it erupts, and I double over, clutching my stomach.

Paul comes around the net. "I guess I should have warned you that Chase has a lethal overhead when you piss her off. Better wear a cup next time."

"That's IF there's a next time. What the hell did I do to piss her off?" Brent's voice trailing off as Paul extends his hand.

"Good game, guys," Paul says, ignoring Brent. He looks over my shoulder. "Ah! The next group is here to play. We better get a move on," he says, grabbing his stuff from the bench and heading off the court.

"Oh, well, that's—." My phone buzzes as I sling my purse over my arm. "Let me check this. Oh, it's Mrs. Adelman!"

"Daphne's aunt? From the birthday party?" Paul gulps down his energy drink and abruptly stops. "The bedazzled lady?"

"Yes," I smile, looking down at my phone.

Mrs. Adelman: Could you meet my bachelor right now? He's waiting for you.

"Seriously?" I yell again, surprised. "Now?"

"What?" Paul leans over to see my phone.

"Mrs. Adelman wants me to come right now. She says he's waiting. How do I look?" I start fingering my hair, sweat pouring down my temples. "Is my mascara running? Does my hair look gross?" I pull up my elbow, sniffing my underarms. "Do I smell?"

"Who's this bachelor guy?" he inquires, wiping sweat from my forehead.

"Some guy nicknamed Shorty." I retort as I reach my car. I squat down to look at the side-view mirror.

"You've got to be kidding!" Paul guffaws. "Why would you, of all people, pick a little man?"

"Hey, Mrs. Adelman is a professional. She hand-picked this guy for me," I counter, rummaging in my purse for a hand mirror and lipstick. "And supposedly, he's tall."

"Yeah, but Shorty? Something doesn't sound right. You don't need a matchmaker, Chase." He puts his arm on my shoulder, looking into my eyes. "There are plenty of men who would love to spend time with you."

"Why does everyone keep saying that?"

"Because it's true," Brent spouts, looking concerned while wrapping his arm around my waist. "You just never listen to us men."

My phone buzzes again.

"Who is it this time?" I say, annoyed as Brent grabs my phone and swipes.

Mrs. Adelman: Is that a yes?

"Don't go," Daphne shouts, grabbing my phone from Brent.

"Daphne, why not? Your aunt's a professional," I scold, unlocking my car and taking my phone back. "She said he's my perfect match. Perrrrfect!"

"She's not what you think," Daphne counters.

"What do you mean?" raising my voice as a boisterous crowd of college girls approach the court, which quickly drowns out our conversation. "Listen, I need to head out, or I'm going to be late." I open the door and throw my purse inside. "Nice playing with you all. Paul?"

"Instagram. I'm on Instagram," he shouts, his voice bellowing over the cackling girls and trying to get my attention. I shake my head as I jump in my car and slam the door shut.

"She's not—" Daphne runs towards my car near my passenger window. I see her mouth move, but can't make out what she's saying.

"I can't hear you, sweetie! Talk to you later," I yell as I roll down the window before pulling away from the curb.

Daphne cups her hands around her mouth and screams, "like me."

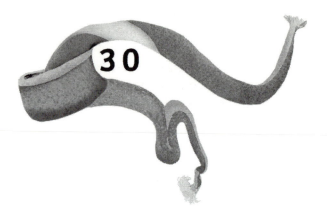

30

"Second time's a charm, right? God, I hope so! Drinks have to be better than that tennis battle in the scorching heat." I deliberately speak out loud, making sure my voice is prepped for conversation. I look in the rearview mirror, touching up my once-smudged face with a cover-up stick. "The last thing you need, Chase, is to squeak like a mouse." I retie my security-blanket scarf around my neck and hold on to the ends for a few extra seconds. My eyes briefly close; a flood of good memories fills my heart, giving me the confidence to get out of the car and head into the Tap Room.

"Chastity?" a man asks, waiting for me at the entrance to the bar. He's wearing jeans, a white T-shirt, and navy-blue sneakers and he's anything but short, towering at 6'6. Mrs. Adelman assured me that he's everything I could want in a man. He doesn't drink or smoke. He's clean-cut, brilliant, kind, loves his family, a Princeton grad, and he owns a successful tech company. I slow my steps and turn to take in my future husband. My engineering mind immediately engages. He reminds me of the Eiffel Tower. *God, I can see right into his skeleton; the steel beams showing every nut and bolt without a pretentious façade!*

His mouth turns into a giant grin, perfect white teeth gleaming against his peaches-and-cream complexion.

"I'm Shorty. It's nice to meet you," he grins, his eyebrows purse together as he extends his hand and guides me towards a small corner table. A hasty glance around the room makes me feel like I've just walked into a scene straight out of a James Bond movie: dark mahogany paneling dotted with gorgeous oil paintings, and at its center, curved-shaped couches flanked with mini tables.

Shorty eyes me again. *There's something oddly familiar about the way he just looked at me, but I can't put my finger on it.* "I took the liberty of ordering you an Arnold Palmer. I hope that's okay." He pushes the drink towards me along with some mini snacks as I take a seat across from him. He talks about his work but keeps it brief, quickly turning the conversation to me. He prefaces his questions with a comment. "I want my future wife to pursue her dreams and achieve her goals. That includes having a family, if that's what interests her."

His words wrap me like a warm blanket; He wants me to pursue my dreams ... I'm beguiled.

I see his mouth moving but hear nothing as I flash forward to my fantasy wedding. It's Christmas time; the room is decorated in festive trimmings. Carolers are singing as I step, one foot in front of the other, down the white catwalk towards Shorty. I look up at my goofy father, who's wearing a tuxedo, cowboy boots, and a black Stetson hat. My feet start to slow down as snow piles up to my knees. Struggling now to lift a leg, I feel my foot disengage from its glass slipper. I suddenly lose my balance and start to topple forward...

"Hey, kid! Funny running into you two here."

I shake my head lightly, confused with the off-color comment, and flinch when I see Brent exchanging hugs with Shorty.

"OH. MY. GOD! YOU FOLLOWED—"

"You two know each other?" Shorty interjects, looking between the two of us.

"The kid and I go way back, just a few minutes ago we were—"

"Don't call me that! How many times—"

"Could you bring some extra slices of lime for my cranberry juice?" Shorty waives a waiter passing through the room. At the same time, Shorty's phone vibrates; he pulls it from his pocket, swiping it a few times. "Could ... you ... excuse me for a second?" he stutters, exiting quickly without waiting for my response. My mouth drops open.

"You seem a little, uh, stiff," Brent chuckles now that Shorty is out of earshot. I start to protest, but he draws my lips together. I lightly slap his hand. "I thought you might need a wingman," Brent says, grabbing a chair from an adjacent table and pulling it over to me.

"Whoa! Who invited you to my date? And how do you even know Shorty, by the way?"

"We worked on a project together a few years back," he says, scooting closer to me. He tucks a loose strand of hair behind my ear.

I playfully push him away, pulling my hair out of his grip. "Why are you acting so bizarre today?"

"Let me give it to you straight, Chase. Run! Grab your purse and RUN!"

"Brent, knock it off. I finally found Mr. Perfect. Can't you at least be happy for me?"

"Mr. Perfect," he scoffs. "He's anything but ... I tried to warn—"

"Warn me?" I cut him off. "When? All I've heard from you and Daphne is that dating a guy named Shorty is weird. *That* is not what I call a warning."

"He goes to invitation-only sex parties in luxury penthouse suites." Brent leans into my ear to whisper. "Sometimes people watch him having sex; sometimes he likes to do the Eiffel Tower—"

"The WHAT? That sounds like an architectural game. I'd be down for that! Actually, it's funny; you should say that. I was just thinking that if he were a structure, he'd look like the Eiffel Tower, right? And, so—" I catch Brent, making a face as he stares at me. "What? What did I say?"

"It's what you *didn't* say. You have no idea what I'm talking about, do you?"

"The Eiffel Tower. Sure, I d—"

"It's a threesome—two guys and one gal. One gets her from behind while she gives the other a blow—"

"Enough!" I yell, covering my ears. "That's DISGUSTING, Brent! It's not even funny. How can anyone do something, something so vile? I've heard enough!" I push back my chair. "You're so gross. I'm going to go freshen up in the ladies' room and try to erase these disgusting images you conjured up. When I get back, make yourself scarce. Got it?"

"Listen to me, Chase," grabbing my arm, "the whole ride home, Daphne kept going on about your date being a scary bird."

I've never seen Brent look so serious, but he is dead serious. I can see it in his eyes. We stare at each other for a lot longer than I would like before his eyes shift over my shoulder to where Shorty is standing in the distance. "Anyway, she told me to come check on you. Believe me, he's not your fantasy guy. I'm not making this shit up."

"Brent ... I don't know what to say, except that it's best that you ... leave," I stutter. "I need to wrap my head around all this."

I scurry off to the ladies' room. Finding solace in my little sanctuary, I look at the reflection in the mirror and grasp my scarf. "Charlie," I whisper, "please give me the strength to continue on this wild journey of finding my soulmate." I splash a little water on my cheeks. "Why does it have to be so hard to find a husband?" I mutter.

"Men, you can't live with them, and you can't live without them, honey?" A woman in her late 70s says, exiting the stall. I flinch. Her bright blonde hair is teased, and she's wearing a little white pantsuit, making her look super chic. She smiles as she washes her hands. "Did you know 80% of women are against marriage? Why, you may ask? Because women realize it's not worth buying an entire pig just to get a little sausage." And with that, she winks and leaves.

The comment stuns me for a moment. I chuckle in the mirror as I fix my makeup. I decide that it's best to peek my head out to see if the coast is clear. I spot Shorty, sitting happily alone at our table. Brent is nowhere in sight. *Thank goodness!*

"Ah! There you are," Shorty stands, pulling out my chair.

"Mind if I have your drink instead?" I ask. He watches wide-eyed as I slide the cranberry drink towards me and quickly take a sip. "I'm rather partial to cranberry juice."

I feel like I'm under a trance as he smiles again. Continuing where he left off, he animatedly talks about himself and his community involvement with Habitat for Humanity. His silky-smooth voice captures my attention. I'm pleasantly surprised that we have a connection when he mentions spending his Christmases in Sun Valley, Idaho. *Hmm ... I wonder if he knows Aunt Kate?*

My mind quickly puts together a laundry list of good qualities—sweet, attentive, thoughtful, loves his family, works hard, exercises regularly, a full head of hair. *I guess that's why Mrs. Adelman thought we would be perfect. So, why is he making me feel uncomfortable? Maybe it's because he's too perfect. God, there's something so oddly familiar about him. And if what Brent says is true? Kinky sex? I can't have kinky sex! I don't want someone watching me! Eeeeewww!*

"I know I'm moving fast," finishing my Arnold Palmer, "but I can feel something between us." He grabs my hand in his. "Chastity?" He shifts his eyes, slouches in his chair, and begins whispering. "Do you see my ex-fiancée? She's sitting on top of the bar counter like a gargoyle, licking her claws."

I turn in my chair and look towards the long, mahogany countertop bar; there's only a bunch of men watching a tennis tournament on the large-screen TVs.

"Ahhhh ... I don't see anyone."

"You don't see her? She has black wings like a witch, and she's smirking at me." His eyes shift back and forth, and his head is practically on the seat of the chair; he's slouched down so low.

My eyes widen. He's hallucinating!

Shorty pushes back in his seat, screeching his chair against the wooden floor. "I have to leave before she descends upon me," he babbles before bolting out of the bar.

"Wait, stop!" I toss a twenty on the table and run after him.

He's screaming at the top of his lungs as he heads straight for a white U-Haul truck in an adjacent parking lot. "I'm going to be free of clothes, possessions, free of her, and commitments."

I watch in horror as he climbs on top of the truck and begins undressing. He's ripping off his clothes piece by piece. "I can be free like Superman and jump."

Holy shit! Is he trying to kill himself? I speed dial 9-1-1. "There's a guy, he must be tripping out on drugs," I stammer frantically "He's seeing things—witches, giant blackbirds, stuff like that, and he's stark naked and about to jump—"

"Some things never change."

I hear a distant but familiar voice coming from the backside of the Tap Room. I turn to look as I hear the dispatcher's voice in the distance: "Ma'am, we have your coordinates. We're sending help. They should be there shortly."

"Thank you," I yell, mindlessly disconnecting. I turn to see Brent walking up to me. "Brent!" I scream, grabbing one of his arms. "Holy shit! Help me, this guy, Shorty, is about—"

"This guy happens to be Stephan," Brent says, laughing. He's unaffected by the display of hysteria.

"Shorty. And it's not funny! He's trying to kill him—"

"No," Brent butts in, "his name is Stephan. Stephan Dukas. Shorty is his nickname."

I let go of my phone and hear a splat on the blacktop.

"Holy shit! Not the Stephan Dukas from—"

"The plane?" Brent finishes. "Yes." Brent walks over to pick up my phone. "One and the same," he says, handing it back to me. "I just tried warning you. How did you not know that?"

"Oh. My. God! I didn't recognize him ... him ... without..."

"The long hair and beard. Right?"

"Yes," I answer, weakly. "Oh, my God! It all makes sense now. When Mrs. Adelman said she found me one with the same interests and vacations at the same place, I never thought it would be him! Wait. How did you know that Short—, I mean Stephan, was on the same plane with me?"

"Guess?" Brent pauses, waiting for my response.

"Oh, no. Roxie. Has to be," I blurt out.

"Ding, ding, ding! Corrrr-RECT!" Brent imitates Alex Trebek. "The one thing you don't know is that the judge was lenient and sent him to rehab instead of jail."

"He what?" My mouth drops open.

"Oh, and please don't tell me he drank your Arnold Palmer?"

"Actually, he did. I'm not a fan of the lemonade, iced tea combo. Why?" I glare at him.

"I saw him slip something into it," he says matter-of-factly.

"When? I thought I told you to make yourself scarce?"

"I did. I stayed in the next room, where I could get a clear view of what was going on."

"Brent!" I yell.

"He was clearly going to roofie you or slip you a Molly. Either way, he ended up taking his own weird shit instead."

"Oh. My. God. Like a repeat of New York." I slap my hand against my forehead. "What is it with men wanting to drug me? Wait. How do you know Ste—"

"I've been around, kid. Circuits tend to cross over. After a while, some stand out over the rest, and the rest is history."

I overlook his "kid" comment and mull over his explanation just as a series of sirens wail in the distance. Stephan takes out his keys, pointing them at his chest. "I'm going to rid myself of my black heart." He plunges the metal object into himself. A police car and ambulance show up just in time; officers jump out of their vehicles and surround the truck.

"Sir, don't move!" commands the officer. "Take the weapon and put it down."

Brent quickly skirts over to the officer in charge and talks with him. The officer nods and walks back to the truck.

"Sir," the commanding officer yells, "Ellie is gone now. There's nothing to worry about. Please come down." The other officers look cluelessly around for Ellie.

Stephan surprisingly lays down his keys and obediently slides down the truck. He extends his hands to be cuffed. The remaining officers wrap a blanket around him and escort him into their car.

"I love you, my Fair Maiden. I want to marry you," Stephan yells to me before they close the back door. My eyes bug out.

When I declared to the universe that I wanted to get married and have a man profess his love, this was not how I envisioned it.

"So..." Brent says as the cruiser and ambulance ride away, "do you want to go out? Like a proper date? Once and for all? I mean, seriously, if you're looking for quality stock, look no further. I'm the real deal. And Daphne said that I would find love."

I look at him, shaking my head incredulously. I take out my keys from my purse while walking toward my car.

"Look. I don't know what's gotten into you, but can't you see that I've had enough for one day? Besides, now I'm going to be wondering what will happen—"

"He'll be fine," Brent cuts me off. "The worst that could happen is that they'll put him in 72-hour lockdown. It's his own fault for putting something in your drink."

Brent, who is jogging to keep up with me, doesn't see me roll my eyes.

"Chase, think of it this way: You dated a drug dealer who sold drugs to Stephan—not to mention many others in your neighborhood. I wouldn't expect this to scare you off from dating altogether. Granted, the idea of Stephan taking part in sex parties should have scared the hell out of you!"

"What do you mean I dated a drug dealer?" I yell from inside my car. "I never dated a drug—"

"Oh, yes, you did." Brent points his finger at me as I roll down my window.

"You're unbelievable. I'm not buying into any of your bullshit," I yell, shifting the gear stick to reverse.

"Is that a yes?" Brent smiles widely.

"WHEN PIGS FLY, mister! And for your information, that means NEVER!" I zoom off.

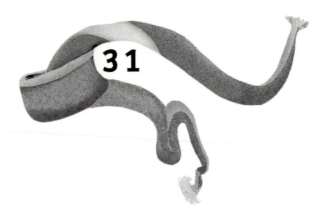

31

The doorbell rings for a second time. It's 7:30 in the morning. Who the heck—?

"Mom, are you available to get the door?" I yell from upstairs, interrupting my thoughts.

No answer.

I charge down the stairs; a backpack slung over my shoulder. I hear rustling in the laundry room; my mom is folding clothes while the dryer hums loudly. *No wonder she can't hear the doorbell!*

"I'm off to school, Mom," giving her a peck on the cheek.

"Good luck on your defense, honey. I'm sure you'll pass with flying colors and be Doctor Chastity Ann Morgan when you get back home."

"Thanks," I yell as I rush toward the front door.

I notice a familiar figure through the window slits. I fling open the door.

"WHAT ARE YOU DOING HERE?" I say through gritted teeth. It's Brent; he smiles widely, tipping his signature fedora hat. "I told you, I'm not going out with you, Brent. Your efforts this week have been a waste. But I have to say that I loved the pink roses and the basket for my bike. Excuse me," I shuffle by him, shutting the door behind me. I hear a low rumbling above as I notice the fully bloomed white roses, sprawled across the little front walkway. I take in the last bit of the sun's warmth before it disappears behind ominous clouds.

He's on my heels like a little puppy dog as I dodge thorny branches on my way to the car.

"Ta-da!" He announces loudly, standing in the driveway with a freshly made dessert in his hands. He shoves it in front of my nose; I can see steam rising from the crusted slits. "I brought you your favorite dessert as a peace offering, not a date offering. I've given up on that idea. Roxie says that you'll never say no to apple pie." I can't help but burst out laughing as I get into the car.

"You're too much, Brent." I roll down the window before shutting the door. "You just don't give up, do you? I'm off to school; it's Double D-day, Dissertation Defense day. Could you leave the pie with my mom?"

"Do you forgive me for crashing your date?" overlooking my question. "Gotta admit it was pretty funny."

"Funny? I didn't think it was funny. Shorty called me from the psych ward, telling me he was Han Solo, and I was Princess Leia and asked if I could get Chewbacca to come break him out." I begin backing down our driveway. "I'm still traumatized. I will never forgive you, but thank you for the pie."

He stabs at his heart with an imaginary knife. "Ugh ... You're killing me, Chase. You should be upset with Mrs. Adelman, not me. Can't you find it in your heart ... to stop being mad at me? I'm going ... out of town for a bit again. Maybe, you will forgive me by the time I get back," Brent runs alongside my car, struggling to catch his breath in between his pleas.

"Bye!" I wave as I take off down the street. "Peace at last," I blurt, looking in the rearview mirror and seeing Brent with a deflated ego walk across the street to Roxie's house. I hear my phone "ping" just as I approach a red light. *Do I even dare look?* Of course, I do. It's a text from Brent:

```
Brent: You know you'll miss me, kid. I saved
you from your naïve self.
```

Imagine if you would have ended up at one of Stephan's sex parties. You could have been Princess Lei chained at the neck by Jabba the Hutt. Bad. Very bad. Wouldn't you say?

"OH. MY. GOD! He doesn't give up!" I yell, muting my phone before tossing it in my purse. "The last thing I need to think about right now is having kinky sex with Stephan Dukas. Chase, focus! Focus!" I'm actually thankful for the bottleneck on the way to school; it bought me enough time to calm down and get my mind redirected.

I pull into a parking garage, cut the engine, and take a couple of cleansing breaths. "Chase, you can do this!" I say aloud while giving a last look at my makeup in the sun visor mirror. "Remember, you have one more challenge to go—your oral defense. If you pass that and pass Dad's class at the end of the quarter, then you'll earn your PhD in Earthquake Engineering. If you fail, then there's no degree, and you've just wasted years of your life. Chase, you can do this!" I say once more before exiting the car.

* * *

"Good luck today!" my father says, popping his head into the little conference room, where I'm plugging in my laptop at the podium in front of the blackboard. "Remember to breathe, speak slowly, and relax. You can do this!" I notice him carrying a copy of a Peruvian Paso horse magazine. He's all gung-ho over this new breed of a horse since he claims their gait is smooth, and he won't come home with blisters and bruises—something that comes along with riding a horse, apparently.

"Thanks, Dad. I'll see you at home," I say, pulling down the projector screen. I test the laser pointer once it's connected. My phone buzzes. I have a few minutes before my defense begins, so I grab my phone, curious to see who contacted me this time.

Paul: Good luck! Jaydon and I are heading to Portillo, Chile, for filming. Be back in Idaho very soon. You and Roxie better carve out some time to come see us. And I don't mean another tennis match.

Hmm ... I haven't quite figured out what to make of him. I feel a tinge of jealousy that he has a girlfriend, which means I must be into him. *Maybe I need to see Dr. Brennan. I think he was onto something with his psychobabble mumbo-jumbo about me winning at relationships, even if I'm losing. And I'm clearly losing since I have no boyfriend and keep meeting these deranged men that want to drug me.*

I flinch when my phone buzzes a second time. This time it's an email:

From: jacquesp@mera.fr
To: ChaseMorg@mylife.com
Subject: Dreams

I think about you. Can I call you? For this, I need your phone number.

Jacques-Pierre wants to pick up the phone and call me??!! OH. MY. GOD. He's GOT to be the ONE! A man wanting to speak to a woman on the telephone is a far-fetched idea these days. They text, they email, they Facebook, they even Snapchat, but picking up the phone and having a conversation? NEVER! At least in my world, they don't.

My heart pounds as I reply:

From: ChaseMorg@mylife.com
To: jacquesp@mera.fr
Subject: Re: Dreams

My number is 555-555-1212. Je t'embrasse.
Chase

The little conference room starts to fill up with my committee members. I stash the phone in my bag and resume my spot at the podium. Beads of sweat form at my temples; my skin is flushed, and I'm sure my nose is crimson enough that people may begin to think that Rudolph the Red-Nosed Reindeer and I are related.

"Thank you all for coming to my dissertation defense, which I have called The Response of Reinforced Concrete Structures During an Earthquake on Various Surface Topographies." I clear my throat lightly, swallowing down a lump that has formed. My eyes dart around the small conference room. I see my advisor, Dr. Wang, the head of the department. Dr. Wellington smiles brightly, except his new toupee looks just as bad as his previous one. There's also Professor Feldman, looking more relaxed than I have ever seen her, with her hair dolled up in springy ringlets. *She's wearing lipstick. That's a new one!*

I recognize Professor Reynolds. Even though I've never studied under him, he's widely known as an expert in Fortran Analysis. Other than that, I've never heard an unkind word against him. Maybe it's because he is a man of few words, and when he speaks, everyone pays attention because of the many gems he leaves for his audience to ponder. *Hmm ... THAT is an outstanding quality I need to include on my future-husband list!*

In the distance, I hear a hurried and all too familiar clip-clop of spiked heels, heading in the direction of the conference room. *Oh, God, no! Why did they have to pick her as the student committee member?* In comes none other than ASSon.

SHOOT ME NOW!

There's another set of footsteps, undefinable. I wait with bated breath, wondering who else will attend my defense.

"*Je suis désolé.* So sorry I'm late," a man runs in, grabbing the last seat. He's sipping on a cup of coffee while passing another one to his committee members.

"Dr. Milton?" I ask, surprised. The last time I saw him was in Paris when I accidentally said he had a nice ass. *God, please, don't let me embarrass myself or him by putting my foot in my mouth!*

354

"Oh yes, I wouldn't miss this for the world. I'm in town for a conference in Santa Monica." He lets out a loud chuckle, snuggling in closer to Professor Feldman. I glance over at ASSon; her shocked expression says it all. *They are definitely "special friends."*

"I'm assuming your defense will be in English?" He gives me a little wink as my cheeks flush.

"Oui. Je suis fou de toi." I say with gusto.

"You're crazy about Dr. Milton?" ASSon gasps.

Oh, God, just shoot me again! "I ... no..." letting out a nervous laugh. Fortunately, no one else gets the mix-up as they open copies of my dissertation, waiting for me to begin.

I take a slow, deep breath to collect my thoughts before I click on my PowerPoint presentation.

"Good morning, everyone, and thank you for being a part of my presentation. I'm first going to talk about the Response of the Reinforced Concrete Structure when it's located in a semi-circle, canyon-like sur—." I glance at my computer and notice that the screen is blank.

"Uh..." I reach for the cord, making sure it's still plugged in. "I'm so sorry. I have to reboot. I've never had this happen before. I rehearsed this so many—"

I turn quickly to see ASSon, smiling smugly.

Shit! Shit! Shit!

"Sh—So sorry!" I can feel the heat rising on my cheeks at my near mistake. My hands are visibly shaking. I grab my hands into a fold against my stomach; pain radiates through my abdomen. I turn away from my audience to steal a drink of water, pinching my eyes shut. *Chase, you can do this! Remember what the doctor said, that stress would cause episodes. Just breathe through them!*

A few gulps and breaths later, the screen glows to life. I feel for my scarf wrapped around my neck, needing an extra boost of confidence along with my mental "I can do this" mantra.

I take a final cleansing breath before resuming my presentation. "So, as I mentioned before, I developed a computer program to calculate the displacement results for a reinforced concrete structure on different- shaped surface topographies during an earthquake..."

* * *

"Well, if there are no more questions," I say fifty minutes later, surprised that my presentation appeared to flow naturally. "I want to thank—"

"I have one," interrupts the unmistakable voice of ASSon. "How do you know your calculations are correct? What did you compare them to?"

"If you turn to page forty-three, you'll notice that I compared my semi-circle program to Dr. Wang's Fortran boundary problem. And if you are referring to the alluvial-filled valley, I first emptied it and made it a blank valley—meaning an empty semi-circular canyon—and then compared it back to the same solved semi-circular Fortran boundary problem. Dr. Wang made sure my program was spitting out the correct results." I grip the podium.

"Yes, but how do we know for sure? Didn't that coincide with your academic probation when you were kicked out of school?" she sneers.

She just won't quit. "You should have run her over with your car when you had the chance," the little Chase Angel snickers, turning a bit devilish.

"Yes, I'm with Alison on this one," Professor Wellington pipes up. "I would like to hear your explanation. I was also wondering why you didn't take into account the SH earthquake waves. I would like to see you go back and analyze your different topographies for an incoming SH earthquake wave."

My mouth is agape. He can't be serious. That's another year of work.

"My dissertation was solely on P- and SV- wave propagations for a reinforced concrete structure, not for SH earthquake waves."

"Yes, yes," Professor Wellington pushes back his chair. Grabbing a piece of chalk, he begins scribbling on the chalkboard. "Can you tell me what the resulting waves would be if the incident wave is an SH wave? Would they be a combination of a sine wave and a cosine wave?"

"I'm not sure. I would have to calculate the Fourier Series—"

"That's enough," Professor Feldman interjects. She walks over to my side.

"I am in my right to ask her any question I see fit," he says, putting down the chalk while adjusting his toupee ever so slightly.

"CHAS-dah-dee completed all dat vee asked her to complete, and I vood like to be the first to congratulate you, Dr. CHAS-dah-dee Morgan. You passed with flying colors, and vee look forward to having a vooman like you join the teaching profession. You made me proud today."

"Excuse me," Dr. Wellington belts out. Steam seems to be coming out of his ears as his face turns a deep shade of red. "Might we have a word outside, Professor Feldman? I'm still the head of this department." His eyes are blazing. Professor Feldman follows him into the hallway. I can hear words flying around: *"chauvinist," "picking on my student," "a bone to pick," "didn't get the grant."*

I stand perfectly still; my eyes nervously glance from one committee member to the next, hoping for an added assurance from at least one of them that Professor Feldman isn't full of hot air and that I've successfully passed. The sound of crinkling paper from Dr. Wang gets my attention.

"Don't worry," he says in between chews on a caramel candy bar. "You've ... earned every bit ... of your degree," he says, swallowing hard. "Ignore what's taking place in the hallway. Those two have had a bitter rivalry for years, which has nothing to do with you. So, as far as I'm concerned, you've passed."

Except for Dr. Wellington's muffled yet disgruntled hallway comments, the room grows eerily quiet. An incessant buzzing noise appears from nowhere. I notice heads oddly turning, trying to locate the annoying sound. It takes only a few seconds for me to realize that the buzzing is coming from my purse, which sits among a pile of bags behind the desk near the room's entrance.

Shit! I bet that's Jacques-Pierre. Lousy timing, Romeo! I force myself from rolling my eyes.

"Congratulations, Miss Morgan!"

I flinch, dropping my laser pointer. Dr. Wellington reenters, followed closely by Professor Feldman. They're walking directly toward me. With his lips tightly pursed, Professor Wellington extends his hand. He looks resigned. "Thank you, Dr. Wellington."

"We'll see you around the halls, Professor Morgan." Dr. Milton jumps out of his seat as he approaches me, grinning widely. He hands me my pointer before patting my back. "You impressed them all. *Toutes nos felicitations.*"

"*Merci beaucoup!*" I confidently respond, knowing full well that I wouldn't mess up that phrase. Again.

"You surprised meee," Professor Feldman whispers as she helps me collect my materials before heading out. "I took a chance on you, and you outperformed. Go celebrate before that old grump changes his mind."

I can't help but stare at her genuine smile—something I've rarely seen during my time at the school. *There is hope after all! People can change.*

I sneak a look at my phone before heading out. *Six calls? Jesus!*

* * *

"You lucked out. I would have failed you," ASSon hisses as she pushes her way past me in the parking lot. She gets into her car, which is next to mine. "This isn't over yet," she yells before slamming her door. Still on a high from my recent accomplishment, I look at her unperplexed, rolling my eyes as I unlock my car with a beep. Just as I place the last item in the back seat, my phone buzzes again.

"*Bonjour*, Chase! It's not too early that I am calling you?" the voice says in a husky French accent.

"*Bonjour*, Jacques-Pierre," I scurry in the car, thankful that I made it to the garage without getting wet. Lighting flashes, followed by a loud crash of thunder before I continue talking. "I'm so sorry I didn't pick up earlier. I was defending my PhD dissertation."

"Ah! And how did you do?"

"Well, I am now officially Dr. Chastity Ann Morgan. Can you believe it?"

"Believe it? You have no idea, *ma cherie*. I can't stop thinking about you because you're absolutely amazing!"

I giggle nervously over the phone. This feels too unreal for words. Like something that happens in the Hallmark movies I watch, but not in real life.

"Oh, *ma cherie*, I cannot tell you how happy I am that you emailed me and that we've been in touch. Do you know that I waited hours that day at the restaurant? Hours. I thought you would show up."

I gulp in horror. "I—"

He continues without letting me explain myself. "Then I waited at the exhibit. It was almost closing time when my friend told me that I needed to give up and face that fact you weren't coming. He suggested I leave you a note. *Oui monsieur. C'est assez. Merci beaucoup,*" Jacques-Pierre says.

"What are you doing?" I ask.

"My car needs petrol."

I laugh. I can't picture him in a handsome suede jacket with a nozzle in his hand, filling his gas tank.

"Do you have one of those mini European cars?"

"Oh, no. I drive my Ferraris," Jacques-Pierre says matter-of-factly.

I choke out a little laugh. "As in more than ... one?" I sound bewildered because I am.

The moment I crank the engine, his voice booms through the speaker system. "Yes, at least a dozen. Most are classics, but there is a special one for racing in the country," he answers so nonchalantly that I want to yank him out of the phone and slap him silly. *Having a Ferrari is not an everyday thing to own like a refrigerator. And owning more than one is absurd.*

"Let me be clear. I have absolutely no interest in a man who is a Ferrari-driving womanizer," my voice now high-pitched. "I can't believe you're one of those guys: Ferrari equals coochie-chaser." I'm gripping the steering wheel so tightly I'm surprised it hasn't snapped in two. *This isn't good! The happy images I've conjured up begin cracking at the seams just like my reinforced concrete column did when the pressure got to be too much.*

"No, you have me totally wrong." The words stumble out of his mouth as he rushes on. "I buy a Ferrari at the end of each year to remind myself of my hard work and success, not to chase after women. I don't need a pretty car for that," he laughs. "And, I promise you, I am a humble man from the modest of childhoods. Here, I want you to listen to a song, 'What Becomes of the Broken Hearted' because then you will understand who I am."

My eyebrows rise in surprise, as I scribble the title on a napkin that I find, madly rummaging through the glove compartment.

"I think about you all the time, *ma cherie*. I go to bed thinking of you. I wake up thinking of you. *Merde!* Oh, darn! My other line is beeping. I have to take this. We will talk soon. I promise. In the meantime, listen to the words of that song."

Before I can get a word in edgewise, the phone disconnects. I quickly search for the song on YouTube. Listening intently, I scrutinize every word, looking for a secret message from Jacques-Pierre. The inspector in me deciphers the gist of the lyrics: It's about a man who lost his wife. It's about lost love. *Was he once married? Did his wife die? If that's true, then maybe he's not a womanizer. Perhaps he just likes fast cars.*

"Well," I say in the confines of my car in the parking garage, "there's one way to find out." I cut the engine, lock the doors, grab my laptop, and pull out a bag of mixed nuts and a banana from my backpack. Thunder crashes, followed by even more torrential rain that pounds against the garage's metal beams. "I might as well settle in. I'm not driving in that stuff," I say, laughing at my snarky commentary on the mid-May weather. "Now, let's see," I continue aloud. "He was introduced as an internationally acclaimed speaker at the conference, which means I should find info on him easily enough on the internet."

It doesn't take much for my laptop to boot up. I click on the Google icon and begin my search for Jacques-Pierre Beaumont. His company, JPB International Roofing, is the first hit in Wikipedia. I scan through its bio until I read a line, indicating that Jacques-Pierre is fifty-three-years old.

What the f---?

"He's twenty-three years older than me," I blurt. "Jesus! He could be my ... my ... father!" I screech. There's a "Relationships and family" link under "Personal Life" in the table of contents; I click on that. A couple of sentences catch my eye:

"In 1991 Beaumont married actress Loretta Lyndale. Lyndale gave birth to fraternal twins, Coby and Ben, in 1992, and died moments later."

"Oh, how sad," I mutter; tears begin to blur the text.

So maybe I have it all wrong, tagging him as a womanizer.

I can't dismiss the fact that his emails and brief conversation reflect a man who's smart and confident, but not at all arrogant. I realize that he's trying to be honest with me, which is a profound change from the liar Grant turned out to be. But at the same time, it's nerve-wracking.

What if he's not the one and just some big fantasy I've created?

This will go one of two ways," the little Chase Angel says, whispering from her spot on my shoulder while poking her finger in my cheek to get my attention. "Either Daphne will be right, and you finally find your true love after all of these disasters, even if his name doesn't start with the letter L, or you're going to be dead wrong and laugh about this later with Roxie. Either way, you're screwed!" I swipe the image and smack my shoulder hard.

"OW!" I yelp. "Dear Lord, I think I'm losing it!"

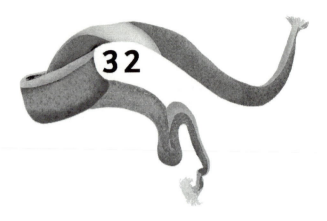

32

I shudder slightly. Another impending storm is brewing, dropping the temperature a few degrees. I take one last look at the foreboding sky as I unlock the backdoor.

"Mom, I'm home!" I yell. The teakettle's whistling in the background at full volume while I deposit my bags in the den. "I passed. I'm now Doctor Chastity Ann Morgan! It has a nice ring to it, don't you think?"

"Honey, I'm in the kitchen," she shouts. I run in and repeat the good news, figuring that she didn't hear me the first time. I take the kettle off the stove before embracing her in a giant hug. "I knew you could do it!" she says, raising her voice a little louder. "You can be anything you want, sweetie. Shoot for the stars! You look chilled," changing her tune. "You're just in time for tea. Sit down." My mom pulls out a kitchen chair. I'm more than willing to settle in, wrapping my scarf around my neck a second time for warmth. She pours me a cup of tea. "Charlie would be proud of you that you didn't give up."

Tears well up in my eyes, "I know. I just wish..."

"He was here?" my mom finishes. "He's still here, Chase. He hasn't left—"

"I know, I know, Mom," cutting her off abruptly. "He hasn't left my side for a moment. You've been telling me that since—"

"But it's true! You just have to believe."

"Mom, no offense, but I don't know what to believe anymore, especially since Grant dumped me."

"Look!" my mom takes hold of my hands. "I'm not sure why things went how they did, and I know you're upset. I would be upset if I were in your shoes too. I have to believe that it happened for a reason, and granted, we may never find out why. Second, you're a lot stronger than all of that. It's like the storm that's brewing outside; it may be nasty for a time, but it will pass. Look at all that you've gone through, and here you are today, Doctor Chastity Ann Morgan."

I chuckle lightly. "You always make sense even if I don't understand it all."

"It's called faith, sweetie. Believing in the things that can't be seen."

"I'm trying, Mom." I take a sip before continuing, "Which reminds me, I could use some advice."

"Like what?" my mom inquires, still holding onto one hand.

"Jacques-Pierre," I mention hesitantly. I fiddle with the end of my scarf.

"What about Jacques-Pierre?" she takes a sip of her tea, looking me squarely in the eyes.

"Well, he called me today, and—"

"He called you? All the way from France?" Her eyes go wide as she nearly drops her cup.

"I think he called from somewhere in Switzerland; he was getting gas for one of his many Ferraris."

"Ferraris? Oh, my!"

"Yeah, more than a dozen, he says. He claims he buys a Ferrari at the end of each year to remind him of his successes."

"He must be a hard worker and—"

"Probably a womanizer too. But then he said that I was reading him all wrong. He told me to listen to the song 'What Becomes of the Broken Hearted.' He claimed it would help me understand who he really is."

"Oh, that's such a sad song," my mom chirps.

"Right? So, I googled him and found out that he's fifty-three and that his wife died in childbirth—Ouch!" I yelp, doing a simple stretch to touch my toes. A tingling burn suddenly overwhelms my body, cramping my legs. I don't know if it's from standing for close to an hour during my defense or the effect that Jacques-Pierre's personal experience has on me.

"Honey, are you okay?" my mom runs to my aid. "Maybe you should go for a small run. Think about all this later."

"In this weather? It could rain any moment now."

"It may. It may not. If anything, the sky has been making an awful lot of noise for the last twenty-five minutes without releasing a drop. A little fresh air should do the trick to help loosen you up. At least go out and do some stretches."

And just at that moment, I spy Uncle Mason across the street, watering the garden Roxie started for him while he was away. *Hmm...*

"Sounds like a plan. Thanks, Mom!" I yell, racing up the steps to my room so I can quickly change.

* * *

Donned in a dark T-shirt and matching jogging shorts, I open the front door and survey the ever-threatening sky with periodic flashes of lighting zigzagging the billowing clouds. Uncle Mason is now bent over, his face close to the ground.

"Here's your chance, Chase," the little Chase Angel says. She flicks my ear with her scarf and screams, "It's now or never! Scare the crap out of him! He deserves it."

"Am I hearing things?" I mutter out loud. "Maybe I should tell Dr. Brennan about this."

I feign a jog and skirt over the next-door neighbor's yard, following the line of arborvitaes to the break in-between the tall trees that cut into Uncle Mason's yard.

"Forget that last idea. This is my chance," I say, still muttering. A loud crack of thunder allows me to noiselessly maneuver around his rose bushes to my uncle's backside.

"Roar!" I yell, grabbing his shoulders.

He jumps, reflexively yanking the hose straight up in the air, a look of shock written all over his face when he realizes that the water's been turned off.

"Chastity! Do you realize payback's a bitch? Whoops! What does karma say?"

"I'll be ready," I guffaw loudly. "Just try to prank me!"

"Better watch your threats, little lady. I'm the one holding the hose!" He scoots over to the valve, cranking it on as he raises his eyebrows, taunting me as he's done throughout my life. When Roxie and I were kids, we'd surprise him with squirt guns, and he would retaliate with a giant super soaker. He always had to one-up us with the pranks.

"Okay, truce. For the next month, I won't jump out of any closet or from behind any of your rose bushes. Promise. Pinky swear!" Uncle Mason looks perplexed. I hold out my hand; pinky curled up to shake with his pinky. "On second thought," pulling my pinky away, "what's the fun in that?"

"What am I going to do with you?" he laughs, going back to watering his garden. "I thought you would have learned by now I always win no matter what."

"You look pretty dumb watering when it's been raining most of the morning, and there's probably still more to come—"

"My tomato plants are under the overhang, which makes it difficult for the rain to reach. If I don't water them, they will die."

"Fine. You're exempt," I respond, rolling my eyes noticeably.

"Okay. Shifting gears, I have a question for you. There's a guy who's crazy about me, but the thing is that he's twenty-three years older."

"Older. Hmm ... I don't know about that."

"Why do you say that?"

"Well, some guys can be ... let's say, unpredictable."

"You wouldn't perhaps be speaking about yourself by any chance?"

"Now, hold on a minute, little lady. Isn't that getting personal?"

"Yes." I look him straight in the eyes. I was taught to always t respect my elders. I would never dream of stepping over that threshold. *I wonder if my experiences are catching up with me!*

"Oh, aren't we brazen? Okay. So, I haven't been Mr. Perfect. I will admit that. Happy now?" He gives me a strained look, one that reflects pain. I can't help but melt.

"I'm sorry, Uncle Mason. It's just that—"

"It's just that no one wants to talk about the hard things, right? How about you and Charlie?"

I cower. "Okay. Truce."

We stand in silence, listening to another crack in the sky, a few water droplets hitting us on our faces. "How do I know if a guy is truly a good person and not a womanizer?"

"Well," he bends over to shut off the hose, "if he's after one thing, then he couldn't care less about you. That goes for all guys. Respect. It's all about respect. But you'll never find out if you don't even try." I stand, staring at my uncle, astounded by his brilliant words.

"Wow! I've never heard you say anything like that. That was … profound."

"I surprise myself sometimes too."

"I can't tell her yet: it'll freak her out. Why do you have to be so annoying, anyway?"

Uncle Mason and I turn at the same time, spotting Daphne decked with headphones, flying by on her scooter towards her house.

Huh! Maybe Maria got her a cell phone with a headset. That has to be it. How else would she be talking to an imaginary person?

"Hi, Daphne," I shout, hoping my voice will carry over her conversation.

"Oh, hi, Chase! Wanna see what my aunt gave me?" she screeches to a halt.

"Time for me to get inside, you two better think about going indoors. Later, Chase, Daphne!" And with that, Uncle Mason leaps across the lawn into his garage.

"What's up?" I walk across his front lawn to the sidewalk. "Your aunt is a bad matchmaker! Your dad had psychic powers, and you clearly have them, but what happened to her? Plus, Shorty, I mean Stephan Dukas, is crazy."

"I tried warning you. Somehow the gift skipped her. She's really sweet and means well." Daphne pulls out the antiquated object from her back pocket. "Like this Walkman she gave me. Isn't it cool?"

"Oh, wow! I haven't seen one of these things since I was a teen. I can't believe it still works," shaking my head, my eyes wide open.

"She gave me a bunch of cool cassette tapes with it too!" Daphne grins from ear to ear.

"What are you listening to?" I ask, genuinely interested.

"TLC. Ever hear of them?" Daphne replies, now pushing her scooter across the street towards her house.

"Hear of them? They were one of my favorite groups. What song?"

"Don't Go Chasing Waterfalls. Sorry, I know that song makes you sad."

I gulp hard, holding back tears.

"How..."

"Someone told me," Daphne says, grabbing my hands. "It's all good. Gotta go! Play some Tom Petty! Gotta love 'American Girl.' See you later!"

Tom Petty? How did she know...

Daphne takes off on her scooter and suddenly stops. "Oh, and the guy with all the cars? He's going to give you a pretty gift. If you don't want it, I'll take it," she yells. "Words are meaningless. Seeing is believing."

"What?" I stand there; my jaw dropped, totally flummoxed. *What is it with everyone telling me to believe?*

How the heck is she just a kid? She's more perceptive than my shrink. "I need to go for a run," I blurt out loud, disregarding the ominous sky.

* * *

I am completely drenched by the time I get back. I towel off as the rain pounds down against the roof for a second time. *Could Uncle Mason be right that it's all about respect?* I do a review of all the men who have encompassed my so-called love life. *Grant. What was I thinking? I probably wasn't. He was the first one to sweep me off my feet and teach me about love—or so I thought. How can someone give love and then suddenly cut it off?*

I ruminate on this last thought as hot shower water rushes down my head. "And then there's Jaydon," I blurt out. "He's an interesting piece of work!" My mind continues to wander as I think of Vincent and Jacques-Pierre. *No, Banana Man and Stephan Dukas are most definitely NOT going on my love list. No, no, no!* I shake my head while attempting to wrap a towel around my dripping hair. "But I certainly know how to pick them, don't I?" I blurt out again. "What the hell is wrong with me? Can't I see the forest from the trees?"

And why does Paul keep popping into my brain? He's got a girlfriend already. I think I need to see Dr. Brennan again. My mind shifts to Jacques-Pierre and Daphne's mysterious message about him, giving me a gift when I hear my laptop ping.

From: jacquesp@mera.fr
To: ChaseMorg@mylife.com
Subject: Re: Re: Dreams

Youpee!

What the fuck? Does he have psychic powers too? my voice echoing in the bathroom. I know I was just thinking about him. But this? Maybe unbeknownst to me, I was sending him telepathic messages. For whatever reason, his email freaks me out. I forward it to Roxie before calling her.

"Check your email," I shriek over the phone, not giving her a chance even to say hello.

"Okay, hold on, hold on! Why the red alert?" she says.

"Just read the email I sent you. I also included a Wikipedia link. Jacques-Pierre's fifty-three. That's twenty-three years beyond me!" My voice is an octave too high. "And what the fuck does 'Youpee!' mean? Seriously! Like 'you pee'? Plus, he told me to listen to the lyrics to 'What Becomes of a Broken Heart.' I included a link to that too." I feel my heart racing.

"Whoa, whoa! Chase, slow down!"

"You don't understand. My day started out great, but it's turned bat-shit crazy."

"Chase, are you sure your Defcon alert is warranted because …"

"Because what?"

"Well…"

I hear a man's voice in the background.

"Are you with—"

"I'm enjoying an afternoon siesta," Roxie interrupts, "and I don't want to get out of bed."

"Oh, come on, Roxie. This is important, especially since Jacques-Pierre is planning to give me a gift—at least that's what Daphne says."

"A gift? What kind of gift? Like a ring?" she gasps.

Suddenly I'm transported to the Luxembourg Gardens in Paris. I'm strolling hand in hand with Jacques-Pierre admiring the springtime flowers. He stops me, dropping to his knee, pulling out a little red box. "Oh, ma cherie—"

I hear ticking on Roxie's end, which snaps me to and lets me know that she's on her laptop.

"Don't know. Listen, click on the Wikipedia link and keep scrolling down to the last paragraph where it says he has kids, as in more than one—more like twins. He hopes that one day his sons will take over his company. I'm not ready for kids, Rox! I don't want to be an evil stepmom. I'm still a kid myself," I whine while Roxie laughs.

"He hasn't even proposed to you. Would you quit fretting? You're driving me nuts! Okay? Wow! He certainly has had an interesting career. Oh. Found it! Cody and Ben. Oh, and his wife died during childbirth? How sad!"

I hear a mumble, a male mumble, responding to Roxie's last few words.

"Rox, are you with your mystery man?"

"Of course, I'm not. I've got the TV going in the background. Well, if it were me, I'd say go for it. Life is too short. Follow your heart, Chase." She whispers.

"Do you want butter on the popcorn?" a man's voice asks.

"That was NOT the TV! That is totally your mysterious boyfriend. I knew it! Who is he? The voice sounds so familiar."

"Um ... Got to run, Chase! We'll talk more later. Love you." Click.

"Wow!" I say out loud, shaking my head. "That was a warm-and-fuzzy. I feel like I'm back at square one!"

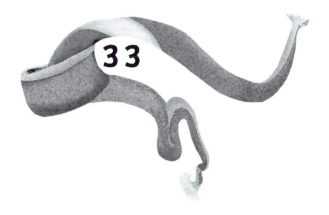

33

"Oh, Oh, Oh, to touch and feel exquisite velvet, AH!" I repeat aloud while lightly rubbing my temples. Why I would recall the strange mnemonic Roxie used to help her remember the twelve cranial nerves when I massage my aching head, I have no idea. I lay on my bed with my eyes closed and allow a flood of memories to pour in.

"Pre-med is killing my creative brain cells, Chase. If I don't get out now, I'm going to burst. I'm taking a break–like forever. Sun Valley, here I come! Why don't you come, cuz? You look like you could use a break too."

I see in my mind's eye Roxie tugging at my arm. It feels like it was yesterday.

"I'll go if we can drive." I see myself rubbing my temples.

"Chase, you've got to get over your fear of flying. It's not that bad."

And here I am again, mentally preparing myself for another visit to Sun Valley. No matter how many times I force myself to fly, just the mere thought of being hurtled through the air in a thin metal tube leaves me ... unnerved. I'm a thousand times better after our New York helicopter ride, but I still get uneasy. Ironically, one would think that the many happy memories attached to that place would override my fears, but they don't. Plus, I'm not sure what to make of this next visit. I can't help dismiss the intuitive unease that creeps into my thoughts when I grasp the reality about Paul: He's getting ... MARRIED?

Why didn't he call to tell me first before sending out the invitations? He mentioned that Roxie and I should come hang in Idaho soon, but I never imagined this is what he meant by "hang out." "Hang out" is not code for "Hey, I'm getting MARRIED!"

I pick up the invitation. Reading it for the umpteenth time, I find that all the hyphenated names amuse me.

SHE SAID
"YES"

Please join us for an engagement party in honor of

Elizabeth Fairfax-Worthington & Lynn-Ashbury Paul Maxson

on Saturday, the twenty-ninth of May,

at seven o'clock in the evening

Trail Creek Cabin, Sun Valley, Idaho

I flash back to the day I took my GRE. I remembered being so nervous, worried that I wasn't graduate material. To my surprise, I breezed through the exam, finishing fifteen minutes earlier than the time I told Grant. Waiting near the building's entrance for him to pick me up, I shook my head when I saw Paul's brand-new black truck approach.

"Get inside, sunshine. Grant got tied up, so you're stuck with me."

I remembered his warm smile as I got into the truck. "Don't You Forget About Me" by Simple Minds was playing on the radio; Paul hummed to the catchy tune.

"Hey, how 'bout a trip to the ole 31 Flavors?"

Who could resist an offer to Baskin-Robbins? He waved a hand, indicating that he was in charge of ordering. Shrugging my shoulders, I looked for an available booth and settled in. Moments later, Paul brought over a tray with two large dishes.

"I couldn't decide, so I got one of each."

He gave me another one of his winning smiles. We giggled like school kids, tasting each flavor. My heart beats a little faster, replaying this scene, replaying him feeding me bites from his dish.

"Holy shit!" I say louder than I expected, looking away from the invitation. "Don't tell me that I've been secretly in love with Paul this whole time? And all this Jacques-Pierre stuff has just been a distraction?" The doorbell rings. I jolt, dropping the invitation. I hear my mother's voice, muffled.

"Chase, Daphne's here to see you," she hollers from the front door. A series of rapid steps up the stairs follow. There's a knock at my door.

"Come in," I yell.

"Hey!" Daphne waves as she walks into my room with her backpack.

"Hey," I respond. "Sorry, I haven't been available to tutor you. I've been so busy," I prattle off nervously. "My advisor wanted me to add one more chapter to my dissertation because he thought the information would make a good journal article. And then I leave for Idaho tomorrow morn—"

"I'm not here for that," she whispers. She scoops up the invitation from the carpeted floor and hands it to me before climbing onto my bed with her backpack. I set the invitation on my desk and join her, only at the opposite end. I try not to show that I'm growing uncomfortable, but I'm doing a horrible job at it.

"I came to cheer you up," she continues, smiling; her sky-blue eyes fixed on me. I visibly gulp.

"I've been around you long enough to know that you have thi uncanny ability for not missing a beat. I'm not surprised—"

"But I scare the shit out of you sometimes, right?" Daphne finishes.

My look of shock is short-lived as I burst into laughter.

"Don't tell my mom—"

"Mum's the word," I offer her my hand. We pinky swear.

I suddenly feel relaxed, watching her unzip her backpack. She pulls out her Ouija board.

"You remember me talking about that TLC song a few weeks ago?"

"Eh ... yes," I respond slowly.

"Well, that's you," Daphne says bluntly.

"What do you m—"

"Chase, stop chasing and let them chase you!" she interrupts.

My eyes widen. A single tear cascades down my cheek. I feel for the pink-and-blue scarf wrapped around my neck.

"Where ... where did you hear that?" I stutter.

"I'm sorry." Daphne's eyes begin to well up with tears. "I didn't mean to upset you. It's just that he's so annoying. He won't leave me alone. Are all boys like this when they get older?" she babbles like she does when she's uneasy.

I stare at her, trying hard to decipher her cryptic message.

"He looks so much like you," she continues. "It's weird. He told me to tell you that it's not your fault. It was his choice. He also told me to play this song." She rummages around in her backpack and pulls out her phone. After a few swipes, she presses an icon; "American Girl" blasts through the phone's mini speaker.

The song takes my breath away momentarily as I flash back to my twenty-eighth birthday at Newport Beach. It's the crack of dawn. Sunlight hasn't yet peeked through the windows of the house we rented for the weekend as I sat around the breakfast room table with Charlie, Roxie, Uncle Mason, Grant, Henry, Nana, Gramps, Aunt Kate, and Uncle Herb. My mom and dad were upstairs sleeping. Charlie was pulling a giant tub of jamoca almond fudge ice cream out of the freezer. "American

Girl" played softly in the background while we ate. He made that our song back when we started high-school, and since I needed something to wake me up every morning, it became the perfect solution to my teenage conundrum. *"And when you finally do hog-tie a man into marrying you, let's buy houses next to each other. We'll have a bridge you've designed, connecting the two, so we can always see each other–kind of like Dad and Uncle Mason; they had the right idea, buying homes across from each other."*

"You sound like such a goofy dork; you know that?" I laughed.

He suddenly sprung up from the table singing along with the song before he said, *"I want to see the sunrise. Come kayaking with me."*

"I can't swim well enough. You go. I'll walk down to Main Street and round us all up some cinnamon rolls for when you get back. I still can't believe we're twenty-eight. That was the perfect birthday on the beach yesterday with the whole family," I said. He kissed my cheek and headed out the front door. The kiss felt different. I couldn't put my finger on it, except to say that I had this immediate sinking feeling in the pit of my stomach. I had no idea that that would be the last time I'd see him.

"He keeps saying twin," Daphne whispers, gently slipping her hand around mine.

The dam breaks as tears begin to pour down my cheeks.

"I'm so sorry, Chase. He says his name is..."

I silently sound out each letter as Daphne lets her fingers glide across the Ouija board.

"Charlie," I gasp. "My twin brother ... is..."

"My imaginary friend who I've been talking to," she finishes.

I'm a mess, sobbing uncontrollably now. I let the lyrics to "American Girl" wash over me as I grab a handful of tissues. I think back to that dreaded morning. An hour after Charlie left to go kayaking, we were sitting around the kitchen table eating the cinnamon rolls when my dad got the call that a wave flipped the kayak, and Charlie wasn't able to right the boat; it trapped him inside. Some locals walking on the beach noticed the boat and contacted the police. We were told that he had been dead for several minutes by the time the paramedics arrived.

Daphne gives my hand a light squeeze. "He told me to tell you that he loves you, Chase. He said that it's time for you to let go and be happy and to stop trying to fill the void. There is no void. He's around you every day. And you'll get your fairytale ending, but please stop chasing love and let it chase you instead. He always laughs when he says that because he thinks that the last part is hilarious."

I can't help but let out a guffaw because it was like Charlie to play with words, especially with a name like mine. I look up to see Daphne smiling at me.

"There's more when you're ready. I can wait."

"I think ... I'm ... ready," I say between sniffles. Daphne hands me a couple of tissues to dry my eyes before she grabs a notebook from her backpack. She shuffles through a few sheets, then looks at her notes.

"Okay. Are you ready?"

I nod affirmatively.

"He wanted me to give you some messages."

I notice that she's got them numbered.

"Here's the first one: something about why mom doesn't have hens that lay blue eggs anymore. He said that that was so cool. He thinks the beige ones are too boring."

"What the— How did he—"

"Two," Daphne continues, giggling. "Ask dad why he served Thanksgiving and Christmas for dinner on their respective days? That just wasn't funny!"

"Ha! That's perfect!" my eyes widening again. "Dad thought you would never know. He hated those "damn" turkeys, as he used to say. They would bite him every chance they got."

"Here's a good one: stick a French fry in Nana's hair; she'll get the joke. Number four..." Daphne catches me shaking my head, shocked. "Kid with Gramps and tell him that you will swim naked in his pool again."

"Oh, no, not that again!" I shout.

"Tell Henry," Daphne continues on number five, "that just because he moved into my room, it doesn't make the room his. Pull up the rug in the far corner of the room and show him the

376

carvings I made on the floor." Daphne carefully makes a crease on the perforated lines before tearing out the sheet and handing it to me. "There's more. Little things that happened over the last two years, to show that he was here watching you." I scan over the paper to make sure I can read her elementary cursive and set it next to me once I realize that everything is legible.

"He's proud of you—that you finished your degree." She zips up her backpack after returning her notebook and popping off my bed. "He just wants you to let go of your sadness. He doesn't want you to grieve for him forever."

My mouth drops open as I sit rooted to the spot on my bed, stunned. "Is ... is he here ... like in the room? Now?"

She nods her little head, pointing at my desk. "He's at your desk, touching the watercolor painting he made for you. You two look so much alike. I'm surprised I didn't see it sooner."

"Then ... why the Ouija board?" I inquire gently.

"He didn't think you'd believe me if you didn't see his name spelled out." She lets out a long sigh. "Boys! I told you he was bossy and annoying."

I feel my body crumbling again. More tears appear. "I love him so much. I miss him every single day. It's been so hard for me. I haven't known how to function without him. I've tried. It's just so hard."

Daphne wraps her small arms around my neck. "He knows how much you love him, Chase. He's happy you love the scarf so much." She takes the ends, gently retying it around my neck.

I flinch when her phone lets out a weird screech.

"What type of ring tone is that?"

"It's an owl," she answers without batting an eye. She walks toward the door. "I fell in love with them after watching the *Harry Potter* movies. Anyway, that's used for my mom; and if I don't get back soon, she's going to send the search-and-rescue squad out for me. Oh, by the way," she turns back to me, "I'm not sure a game of tug-of-war is the best idea."

"Tug-of—" I mutter silently. "What—"

"Ciao!" Daphne clip-clops down the stairs, yelling "goodbye" to my mom.

"Go visit Chase. Okay?"

"Sure thing! Bye, sweetie!" My mom shouts as she heads up the steps and suddenly stops when she sees tears pouring down my face.

"Oh, honey... Are you okay?" My mom wraps her arms around me.

"I don't know ... if ... you would believe me ... if I told you. Mom, I miss Charlie. He was my best friend, my other half. How will I ever find someone to fill his shoes?"

"You don't," she responds, releasing me to look into my eyes. She quickly pans the room. "Charlie's been in the house again, hasn't he? Our little neighbor talks to him, doesn't she?"

I look at her incredulously. "You ... You believe in all that stuff?"

"Oh, honey, more than you know. A psychic once told me I would marry a man born on May 24, a Gemini, which means 'twin,' and he would be a twin and give me twins—three beautiful children to be exact." I look at her. "I guess what I'm trying to tell you is that your destiny is written for you already. Charlie's destiny was his destiny. It would be best if you found yours now. I know he left a huge hole inside of you, but you need to move forward. All of us need to move forward. He wouldn't want you to stop your life for him. He's still the little devil; he'll flip over his picture next to my bedside in the middle of the night, reminding me he's still with us," she laughs. "Even though he's gone, he's still my little prankster."

"Oh, Mom," I wrap my arms around her in a giant hug, letting more tears pour down my face. My mom gazes at my bed.

"What's that?" pointing at the sheet.

"How 'bout ... you make us ... some tea," I muster between sobs. "You're going ... to need to sit down for this one."

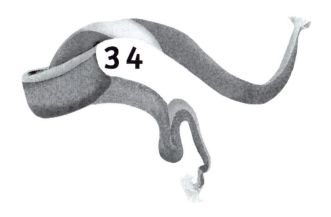

34

"Okay, but this might scare you," Roxie randomly blurts while we walk through the airport terminal. "Last night, I was at the store on errands, and a mom and four tweens got in line behind me."

We spot two seats in a corner near our departure gate. Roxie looks preoccupied as she plugs in her laptop and phone at a charging station. She promptly sits down and begins swiping on her phone.

"And?" I grab her phone away.

"Hey, I was in the middle of texting," Roxie slaps my hand before taking it back.

"Yeah, and you were in the middle of telling me what you thought would be a disturbing story," I raise, staring at her, annoyed.

"Oh, right. So anyway, she must have been taking—the mom, that is—the girls somewhere. They all had braces, so I'm figuring maybe sixth or seventh grade. They were talking a mile a minute about some boy who likes one of them," Roxie says rapidly while madly texting. She sets her phone down when she sees that I'm glaring at her. "And the mom was funny, too. She rolled her eyes at me, shaking her head. An older woman next to them who was also watching leaned into us and whispered, 'I remember those times. Aren't they adorable?' I said, 'Remember? What do you mean by remember? I'm twice their age, and they sound just like my cousin and me; we're *still* talking about the same type of thing: waiting to find out if guys like us.' The mom and the older woman cracked up. Then the older woman said, 'Oh well when you get to be my age it's wonderful. I have a male friend who comes over on weekends, and it's simple— we just spend time together. The expectation is evident: companionship.'

"So, the moral of the story is this: the prospect ahead of us—of at last arriving at boring companionships in twenty years—has scared me, and it should scare the shit out of you," she states like she was relaying an Aesop fable. I give her another hard stare as she situates her bags, so they double as a footstool. She rifles through a stack of magazines. I watch her nonchalantly lean back in the blue airport seat like she doesn't have a care in the world.

"Okay." I tap my fingernails vigorously on the empty chair next to me. "Is that a sign that maybe ... we're not supposed to go?"

Roxie acts as if she didn't hear me.

I hear the flight attendant announce boarding. I drop my head into my hands, suddenly stressed. I do the deep breathing exercises I've been practicing with Dr. Brennan. *"You conquered your fear of flying in NY, Chase; you don't need an anti-anxiety pill now. You can do this!"*

"This day has been really—" I stop short of mentioning Daphne and what she told me about Charlie earlier. *A, she won't believe me and, B, if she does, she'll freak out.*

"I don't believe in signs," Roxie abruptly laughs. Her delayed reaction makes me flinch. "Maybe it means that you should finally look up that hot flight attendant, Vincent."

Vincent. Where the hell did that come from?

"Right," I reply, feigning that I had the same thoughts. "Well, I think I should focus on my work right now. I know we're only going to Idaho for one night, but still. I have a few things to tweak on my dissertation before it gets bound for the library."

I clear my throat when I hear the flight attendant boarding our seating area. We quickly collect our belongings.

"What if we get caught in a freak snowstorm, and we can't make it back for graduation? I've waited a long time for this day." I zip up my bag, stuffing my fan and iPad back inside before getting in line.

Roxie turns to stare at me hard. "That's. In. June. Chase," she says with emphasis.

She looks at me again. "What? Don't look at me like that. It's Memorial Day weekend, and freak snowstorms are known to happen," I say a little louder than expected. A few heads in front of us turn, guffawing.

"Stop!" She stomps her foot, her finger pointing at me like a stern teacher. "You are not going anywhere, except on that plane. Do you understand me?"

I gulp hard, drawing my possessions close to me for comfort. I hate to admit that she's right. It's time for me to buck up and get on with my life. *I'm doing this for you, Charlie. Do you hear me?* I take a cursory glance around the terminal, half expecting that I'll see him sitting in one of the empty chairs. I don't feel or see anything. *Faith. Gotta have faith, Chase!* I mentally replay the last statement, praying for a miracle.

* * *

"Did you read the invitation carefully? Paul's proper name is Lynn-Ashbury," Roxie says as we settle into our seats. I'm so concentrated on deep breathing that I only catch the last part. "The name sounds like something out of *Gone with the Wind.*"

"*Gone with the Wind?* What ... are you ... talking about," I reply in between breaths.

"Paul's proper name," Roxie robotically repeats, busily thumbing on her phone.

"Oh," I mention flatly. I'm not sure I want to get started in another conversation. It's taking everything that I've got and then some to focus on keeping calm, anticipating that the plane will begin taxing any minute now. I watch Roxie as she puts her headphones on. She starts to play with the seat-back screen in front of her.

The phrase "scared shitless of flying" said with a British flair catches my attention. I glance across the aisle at the tattooed guy with an atomic red Mohawk and beard that are exquisitely braided. I can't help thinking of Boss, the rooster, that struts around our backyard showing off his wattle. I rub my eyes, hoping to wipe away the similarity. The two guys next to him— clones, except for their black Mohawks and beards, are out like lights. It must *be nice!* I shake my head lightly. The people in front of them don earbuds; their eyes glued on the seat-back screens. I feel movement against the back of my seat. I glance between the crack separating our seats and see a mom and her daughter snuggle under their blankets. *Amazing! Like they don't have a care in the world.*

"Can you bring me two gin and tonics to ease my nerves?" Rooster Man gets my attention again as he talks to the flight attendant, holding cash in front of her. "And one more once we are in the air. I'd appreciate it. Thanks!"

I see her whisk away, money in hand.

"Excuse me," I whisper, once the attendant is out of earshot. "Sorry, I couldn't help but overhear your conversation. I saw your tattoo. Is that some corny saying, or are you terrified to fly?" I ask, halfway leaning across the aisle. He nods. "I can solve that." I signal a momentary pause, displaying my pointer finger before turning back and reaching for a little orange bottle in my little pink mesh bag. I notice Roxie staring at the screen in front of her, totally oblivious to my interaction with Rooster Man. "I don't like to fly either. I'm much better now." I hand two of my anti-anxiety meds into his outstretched hand. "These little pills work miracles to where you may start singing 'Happy Day' while flying 30,000 feet above the ground."

"Thanks!" he genuinely smiles. "Isn't this ille—"

"Here are your drinks, sir." The attendant returns with a tray.

"Thanks," he replies. "And thanks for the meds," offering a nod to me. He opens his hand and pops the pills in his mouth. The stewardess looks down at him in horror.

"Excuse me, sir. Did the lady just give you these?"

"Huh?" I give her a quizzical look. She leans over my stomach, looks at my bottle of pills, and promptly picks up my little pink bag.

"What are you doing? Are you crazy?" I'm tugging on the bag, playing tug-of-war. "Give it back to me. That's mine!" I'm screeching at the top of my lungs, holding on for dear life.

Our tussle appears to have awakened the dead, so to speak as I hear an undertone of mumbling among the once-unconscious passengers.

"Mommy, what's going on?" I hear the little girl behind me speak for the first time.

A light chorus of "Whoop! Whoop! Whoop!" from the Black Mohawks is short-lived with Rooster Man's resounding "bugger off, you wankers."

Amid the cacophony, Daphne's words instantly scream in my head: *playing tug-a-war is a bad idea.* "Ah!" I screech, letting go of my mesh bag. The stewardess flies backward, arms flailing. As quick as a flash, Rooster Man jumps out of his seat, grabs the flailing flight attendant's arms as well as my bag and tosses it back to me before righting her.

"Hey, it's illegal to share medical prescriptions," states the stewardess, who is clearly on a mission by yelling at me.

"Oh, for God's sake! They're anti-anxiety pills," I retort. "It's not cocaine. It's a health aid." The words escape my mouth. One look at the now-disheveled stewardess' deeply reddened face is a clear indication that I should not have raised my voice. "Uh ... Fffffredrick!" I produce, remembering the little girl behind me. Roxie looks at me like I just got off the boat before turning back to her movie.

"I witnessed you distributing illegal drugs," she says with weary surliness while smoothening down her jacket and skirt.

"I don't understand." Because—the thing is—I really don't understand. "Are you implying that I'm a drug dealer?" I scrunch my face up, in shock. *This has to be a joke.* "Are you mad?" I screech. "It was a prescription pill for anti-anxiety, not drugs. Check the label; it's quite legal, and it's legally my prescription."

"Miss, I understand. But it's illegal to give another person prescription medication. This is against FAA regulations." The flight attendant mumbles something into her walkie-talkie. "We will have to escort you off the plane. Please collect your bags and follow me."

"YOU'RE KICKING ME OFF THE PLANE?" I can't help but screech.

"Honey," Rooster Man's eyes widen as he looks at me. "Thanks for remembering to grab my meds before we left home. I don't know what I'd do without you."

"Honey?" the stewardess repeats, dumbfounded.

I'm equally dumbfounded at the turn of events, but I keep my composure and play along.

"No problem..." I glare at him. He mouths his name.

"Sssam," I say, sounding more like a snake.

"Oh, how uncouth of me," Sam says with a flourish. "This is my fiancée—"

"Chastity," I interrupt, knowing full well that there's no way in hell that he'd be able to decipher my name if I mouthed it to him. I extend a hand to the steward. She shakes it weakly.

"Chastity," he repeats. "My sweet Chastity. We're on our way to get married."

"Yes, yes," I blurt, turning red in the face. *I can't believe I'm doing this! Despite the crazy Mohawk, I have to say he's cute!* "And he's nervous, you know—wedding jitters?" I reach out to Sam, where we hold hands across the aisle. He rubs the top of my hand fondly.

"I'm soooooooooo sorry for the confusion," Sam announces to the flight attendant, a little heavy on the adverb. "You're only doing your job. I understand."

"And you're not sitting together?" She adds, confused.

"Oh, I'm with my maid of honor." I point to Roxie, who is in another realm; her eyes still locked on the screen. The flight attendant waves to her stupidly.

"And ... and these are my best men," Sam interjects.

I let out a snort when I see both clones leaning heavily to the right with their mouths wide open. The stewardess nods awkwardly, scratching her head as she returns to the cabin to prepare for taxiing. "Thanks," I whisper to Sam. He shushes me and points down to the pen and paper on his lap. I nod understandingly. Seconds later, I hear a low whistle. I turn, grab the note, and promptly open it:

"Would you fancy having a cup of tea at my hotel tonight around midnight? I have to play a show when I land, but afterward, I'd love for you to come and see me. As a thank you."

I write a quick response:

"That's very kind of you. Unfortunately, I'm going to have to take a rain check since I have plans for the rest of the day and evening."

I feel like I'm in high school again as I fold and pass the paper back to him. I hear another low whistle and retrieve the multi-creased sheet.

"Call me sometime. I live in LA."

He ends with his phone number. I turn, giving him a smile and a thumbs up. I see him gulp down his second drink.

The pilot's voice comes over the loudspeaker. "Welcome aboard, please sit back, relax, and enjoy this two-hour-and-forty-five-minute flight to Sun Valley, Idaho."

Feeling the medicine finally kick in, I snuggle into my seat and buckle myself in securely before closing my eyes just as the engine begins to roar. In a matter of seconds, I'm out cold.

* * *

"Why didn't he tell us he was getting married? Grant's MIA, and now Paul isn't answering either. What is it with these men?"

"What? Where did that come from?" I respond to Roxie after returning from the bathroom. A couple of sips of water satisfies my dry mouth, a side effect from the pills.

"Shit, Chase. It just hit me!"

"What now? Did you suddenly see a unicorn?" I joke, taking out my mini fan now, waving it around my face.

"Lynn. What does Lynn start with?" Roxie pauses, leaning over to look me straight in my face. "An L," she says, not waiting for me to respond. "It starts with an L, Chase, just like Daphne said."

"Okay," I say flatly, not making the connection until I remember the scene with Daphne working the Ouija board. "OH!" I blurt. "Oh, my God, Roxie. Do you really think he could be … THE ONE? Every time I hear from Jacques-Pierre, I think that he may be the one. But when that invitation arrived, it hit me like a ton of bricks. God, I can't believe that I've been missing what's right in front of me—Paul."

"You better figure out how you feel because, in a few short months, he will say 'I do,' and it won't be to you."

I gulp hard. Tears begin to well up.

"Sorry, Chase. It's just that it's—"

"True," I finish.

"Well," Roxie claps her hand, "since that's settled, I found a new resolution on Pinterest today called Seven Cardinal Rules for Life. I know you're tired of trying to fall in love and have sex. So, maybe these should be your new resolutions to strive for." Roxie brings up the pic on her phone and reads from the list:

- Make peace with your past, so it won't disturb your present.
- What other people think of you is none of your business.
- Time heals almost everything. Give it time.
- No one is in charge of your happiness, except you.
- Don't compare your life to others and don't judge them. You

have no idea what their journey is all about.

- Stop overthinking. It's okay not to know the answers. They will come to you when you least expect it.

- Smile. You don't own all the problems in the world.

"Make peace with your past, so it won't disturb your present," I repeat. "Yeah. That's number one," Roxie confirms.

"Daphne came over last night," I announce suddenly.

"Oh? And?" Roxie shifts her body to face me directly.

"She talks to Charlie." I look at my hands before glancing at Roxie, her mouth agape. "I knew you wouldn't believe me," I say, throwing my hands up in the air. "That's why I didn't tell you earlier." I fidget around my neck, realizing that I don't have my scarf on.

"Your scarf?" Roxie yells.

"What... What about it?"

"It's not around your neck! Where'd you put it?" Roxie fumbles between the seat cushions and stares around at the floor. "Did you drop it somewhere? You go never go anywhere without—"

"It's at home, Rox. I left it at home. I made peace with my past."

Roxie stops dead in her tracks and looks at me as if she didn't hear me correctly.

"She knew things, Rox. The blue eggs. The French fries Charlie would stick in Nana's hair. What he always used to say to me: 'Chase stop chasing and let them chase you.' She knew exactly what Christmas presents we got each year." I included the additional list Daphne gave me the next morning. "Even the silly gag gifts like poo-pori your dad stuck in our stockings. He even knew we ate Thanksgiving and Christmas last year!"

Roxie stares into my eyes like she's trying to read my mind before bursting into full-on laughter.

"I believe you. No one knew his pets were named after the holidays! To think your dad finally cooked them. Morbid! It turned me into a vegetarian for a bit. But still..."

"See what I mean? Daphne telling me he's happy gave me closure. I don't need to wear the scarf he gave me for my twenty-eighth birthday—our twenty-eighth birthday—to remind me of him anymore."

Roxie lets out a prolonged "wow." We stare at each other for several seconds, digesting the moment. "Now what?" she finally blurts.

"Now what ... what?" I repeat.

"Do you have any idea who Paul's fiancée is?" Roxie asks in a serious tone.

"Ah..." I stutter. "Not any more than any of us. She remains ... a mystery," adding air quotes.

"What do you think we should do?"

"I don't have the faintest—"

"Please fasten your seatbelts. We're getting ready to land. Oh, and congratulations on your upcoming wedding," the flight attendant says, extending me her hand as if nothing happened over the last two hours. "Wedding? Did I miss—"

"Thank you," cutting Roxie off. I shake the stewardess's hand vigorously.

"So—" Roxie begins as soon as the flight attendant walks away.

"Shh... I'll explain later."

* * *

This little Rocky Mountain airport is a healing balm compared to the mayhem of LAX. As I step off the twin-engine jet, I breathe in the scent of the fresh mountain air, crisp, refreshing, and with a hint of wood-burning fireplaces. I halt, glancing at the thermometer after passing through the sliding doors into the terminal, knowing full well that this town is known to have snow as late as Memorial Day weekend. The number takes a moment to register; it says forty-one degrees.

"How are we getting over to Paul's engagement party tonight? It was a cute idea to have the engagement party out at Trail Creek Cabin, but given the fact that it's the only place in this little valley you can't drive to, we're going to get frostbite or, better yet, freeze to death on those horse-drawn wagons."

"Chastity, thanks again for the pills," Sam announces, sidling up to me. "Can't convince you to have tea with me later?" His smile flickers up at the corners.

"Well, I could squeeze—"

"She'll have to take a raincheck." Out of nowhere, Grant grabs my arm, spinning me around. "Does trouble follow you everywhere?" he asks, helping me lift my bags off the conveyor belt and eyeing Sam warily. Sam signs "call me" as he walks out of the terminal. "Who was that anyway?"

"No one in particular. Hey, you," changing the subject, "you're alive!"

"Yeah, we took the earlier flight." Grant makes it sound like that's about as complete an answer that I'm going to get. I glare at him.

"Right. And thanks for ignoring all of my messages," I add sarcastically. "I don't know if I should punch you or hug you, but I guess the latter will suffice." I hug him, lowering my voice to a whisper. "By the way, I had a little chat with Charlie." His eyes widen.

"Chase—"

I put my hand up. "Don't start. I did, and I found peace. The big question in the room—where have you been since Nana's party?" I eye him slowly from top to bottom; he reminds me of a zombie. He has huge bags under his eyes and looks like he hasn't slept in weeks. I reach into my purse, pulling out a little box. I press it into the palm of his hand. "Sorry, it took so long to give it back," I whisper into his ear.

"You don't have to," he squeezes my hand. "Keep it."

I shake my head, lowering my voice again. "No, I need to let the past go, and that starts with letting go of your ring." Brody approaches from around a pillar with Maddy in her car seat carrier.

"Don't think I didn't hear you, Chase. I think it sounds romantic to have a party in a woodsy log cabin. Just think, we can snuggle, sing 'dashing through the snow,' I mean dirt, 'in a one-horse open sleigh,' I mean wagon, and be merry," Brody chuckles, transferring Maddy to Grant. "You seem on edge, Chase. Are you sure you're okay?"

"She's fine, boys," Roxie interjects, pulling me toward the car rentals. "Do not tell anyone you're unsure of this marriage and that you may be in love with Paul," she instructively whispers in my ear once we're out of earshot, "and keep it to yourself, or else you'll be in deep doo-doo!"

3 5

A few hours later and in near darkness, Roxie and I arrive outside the Sun Valley Inn. We park in the little lot and jog over to the sea of unfamiliar faces huddled around three old-fashioned, horse-drawn wooden wagons parked at the end of the soccer field. I spot Paul and grab Roxie's arm, weaving the two of us through the crowd before finally reaching him as he's about to step into one of the wagons.

"Happy engagement," I yell unabashedly as Roxie, and I follow closely behind him. *Happy engagement? Where did that come from? I'm not happy he's engaged.* The driver hands us a couple of blankets, and we scurry over to one end of the wooden bench next to Paul.

"It's good to see you." I wrap the blanket around my shoulders and then engulf Paul in a giant hug, his bushy beard scratching against my cheek. "Someone's looking a little too wilderness with the long mountain-man hair," I nervously joke like I always do when I feel at a loss for words. "Maybe a haircut before the big day?"

"Come on, you. You know I'm still as handsome as ever," Paul refutes, puffing out his chest.

I look over at Maddy, who's buckled in her carrier, which is on Brody's lap. She waves to me with the help of her daddy.

"Hi, Maddy," I wave back. Grant is next to them near the other end of the bench, a beer bottle in hand; the two of them return a smile, looking over at me.

"Isn't it good to see us too?" Brody chimes in. I let out a chuckle since all three of them have so many clothes on that they look like abominable snow people.

"Yes," I laugh aloud, waving again, "always!"

"So, where's your mysterious fiancée, Elizabeth Fairfax-Worthington?" Roxie abruptly interrupts, throwing an arm around Paul. "Sounds like she's an heir to some obscure mogul," Roxie's words, dripping with sarcasm. I catch Grant rolling his eyes. He lets out a pronounced burp.

"What's that all about?" I raise to Grant, ignoring his gross sound effects. I'm again shocked at my boldness.

"Nothing." Grant leans over to whisper in Brody's ear.

"Okay. What's that supposed to mean?" Roxie adds. "Are we missing something?" She cocks her eyebrow at me first and then at Grant and Paul. "Grant looks like he's on his third beer, ready for a bachelor party."

Paul shrugs his shoulders. "Don't look at me. I'm clueless," raising his hands in surrender. "I promise you, it's an engagement party, and you'll meet Elizabeth very soon. She's at the cabin setting up."

I turn and give Roxie a knowing glance. Roxie pinches her nose, her signal to let me know that something fishy is going on. I give her a slight nod.

"We should get going, sir," Gus, our driver, announces.

"Sure," Paul responds. "Hopefully, Landon will get here soon."

"Landon? Who's Landon?" Roxie inquires.

"My cousin," Paul spouts, sounding annoyed. "Shit!" he mutters under his breath. "Where the hell is he?" *Landon?*

Daphne flashes before my eyes as I recall her mentioning the guys that I'd meet whose names begin with L. *First Lynn-*

Ashbury Paul. Now Landon. Chills crawl up and down my spine as I anticipate this mystery man.

We sit in companionable silence for the next several minutes. The rhythmic sound of the horses' trotting and their periodic snorts, along with the light jingling of the bells on their harnesses, adds a sense of warmth and comfort against the brisk night air.

I hear a 'ping.' Paul pulls out his phone and gives it a couple of swipes. "Gus, can you hold out a few minutes? I just got a text message from my cousin. He should be here at the next rest stop," Paul yells to Gus, who nods agreeably. Another ten minutes pass before we hear shouting. Gus slows down.

"Wait up! Wait for me!"

I noticeably flinch when someone slams against the back of the wagon. Paul unlatches the back.

"Folks, this is my very tardy cousin, Landon." We all give weak waves. I watch as he stumbles up the steps and into the wagon.

"Hello, eeeveryone. Welcome ... welcome ah board. Please forgive my tardiNAHSSS," belching the last syllable. "I'll be your new wagon driver this evening," Landon says with a deep, Texan drawl, attempting to pose as an "el Capitan." He reminds me of the Marlboro Man: tall—about 6'3", I'd guess, clean cut with dark brown hair combed back in place, and golden-brown eyes that exude the confidence only a cowboy from yesteryear could possess. Except for his drunken state, I'm weirdly drawn to him. And then Daphne's message hits me again, sending shivers down my spine for a second time.

"Are y'all ready because I sure am?" he announces as he totters down the steps and over to the driver's box. Paul is at his heels.

"Landon," Paul whispers, reaching for him. Even though he keeps his voice low, I can make out every word. "Sit down, man. You're in rough shape. I know you grew up on a ranch, but tonight is not the night to test out your driving skills." Landon pushes Paul aside and heads for the steps.

There's no doubt in my mind that Paul is nervous. Heavy beads of sweat follow his hairline. "Landon, come on, dude."

Gus, hesitant to leave, securely latches the back.

"Let's get this party started," Landon yells and grabbing the reins, he waves them with reckless abandon. "Giddy up, boys." The wagon lurches with such force that it catapults us all backward. Paul and Gus slam against the hatch. Roxie, who looks over at Brody to see him use the side of the wagon as an anchor, bracing Maddy's carrier against him. I'm surprised when she grabs me. Grant suddenly flashes in front of us. We watch in horror as he bounces over the side and onto the dirt.

"Stop! Man overboard!" I yell. Panicked and without thinking, I recklessly lean over the wagon. I can't see anything in the sparsely lit path. "Stop!" I scream. I turn back, but no one's listening because they are all looking at Marlboro Man, who has decided that it's more fun to jump on the back of a chestnut horse than to use reins.

WHAT THE FUCK is happening?

"Landon, what the hell are you doing? You're going to kill us all!" Paul yells.

Marlboro Man's legs straddle the horse's back. He's holding onto the large harness with one hand while waving his other hand like a bull rider.

"Everyone, look at me! I'm going to do my eight seconds. Start counting. One. Two. Three." His voice sounds strangled.

I see legs swing over to the driver's box. It only takes me a moment to realize that it has to be Gus because the wagon slows down.

"Four... Hey, get the hell out of there! I'm in the middle of doing a trick, you asshole!" Landon yells back at Gus. "Five," he screams, smacking the horses' rear ends. The horses bucking throws Landon off. He grabs the harness, but only barely as he begins to slide, and slipping down the side of the horse, the tips of his feet drag along in the dirt. The wagon jerks to the left and then the right, back and forth, tilting to each side along the way and nearly throwing Gus off the box. I am terrified, but I'm more worried about little Maddy, who is screaming hysterically. Gus pulls on the reins hard, which sends a message to the horses to slow down. With everything returning to normal, I can hear sighs of relief all around me as the wagon comes to a halt.

"I'm fine, everyone," Landon brushes himself off like nothing happened, jogging to catch up. He climbs on board and lands on the bench with a thud.

"Dude, stay there and shut up," Paul scolds his cousin. Landon nonchalantly shrugs his shoulders, then instantly falls asleep.

Oh, Lordy!

Lost in the tumult, Grant slipped my mind until I hear the eerie cry of a wolf from the hills. "What are we going to do about Grant?" I exclaim, my voice visibly trembling. The sound of the wolf's continued howling sends more chills up and down my spine.

I look over at Brody. He looks as if he's about to break, having had to deal with an uncontrollable child, let alone losing his partner. "Grant! Where's my husband?" Brody's wail triggers another outburst from Maddy.

What a mess!!

"Don't worry, sir. I'll drop you all off at the cabin, and return promptly to pick him up," Gus volunteers. His plan helps to calm me a bit. Brody and Maddy? Well, I'm not so sure about.

"My husband, he's not in the soberest state. Are you sure you'll get to him fast enough?" Brody asks.

The sound of trotting hooves gets the attention of Gus, who slowly moves to one side and clears the path for the oncoming wagon. A gaggle of giggles erupts from the darkness as it passes us.

"The cabin's just around the next bend, I'll go find him as fast as I can," Gus responds as he pushes the wagon forward along the dirt path.

Moments later, as expected, we pull up alongside the rustic, historic Trail Creek cabin nestled among a copse of pine trees. A flood of memories flashes through my mind as we head toward the front entrance. "Wow! Give me five minutes, Rox." I wave to her to follow our traumatized group off the wagon and into the cabin, except for Landon, who seems unfazed, now curled up like a baby on the floor of the wagon.

"Okay. Whatever," Roxie says flatly, stepping over Landon.

The cabin has changed very little since the last time I was here. It was Charlie's idea for a family holiday dinner, which became the first of many trips to this wonderful spot. The eye-catching front entrance never ceases to amaze me with its floor-to-ceiling windows that peer into a quaint and cozy living room. It always reminds me of something straight out of a Thomas Kinkade painting. I notice somebody sitting on one of the couches in front of the immense natural-stone fireplace.

I'm abruptly met with the pleasant aroma of the woodsy surroundings. I take in a deep breath and release it slowly; my eyes closed. I force my thoughts to linger to the past, hoping to ignore Landon's prodigious snores, but to no avail. It doesn't help that the idiot is such a hottie.

Holy Mackerel! Daphne couldn't have meant this wild wagon driver would be part of my future? God, I hope not! He's crazy as all get out. I shake my head to rid the thoughts. My eyes glide over to another window off to the left side of the cabin, where people are bustling around the oversized dining room. I see Paul standing with some guys, tilting back his head, letting out a giant laugh. Paul. Dear God! I'm about to meet his future wife, so it can't be him either. I drop my head in my hands. Now what, Chase?

"Earth to Chase, you've had your five. Everyone's gone inside. Your turn," Roxie peers up at me, holding drinks for us.

"Thanks, Rox." I exit the wagon with Roxie tagging along, still holding on to our drinks. As we head toward the cabin through the heavy wooden double doors, I stumble straight into the back of a man leaning against a post. His drink ejects like a rocket and flies through the air, splattering a foot away from an oblivious crowd. I clutch his arm in a death grip, holding myself upright, hoping to regain my bearings.

"Are you alright? You look like you've been chased by a bear," a baritone voice says with a familiar Texas accent as he sets me right. I blink at him in surprise as my stomach goes all topsy-turvy. *What is it about his piercing golden eyes stare at me that turns my tongue to mush?* I feel the heat rising on my face, most likely turning a deep shade of crimson. I look at him, speechless, half-hoping he'll quote Dad's favorite actor, John Wayne. "A man's got to do what a man's got to do" is the only thing I can imagine coming out of this gorgeous man because as I stare at him, he really embodies the iconic Old West image of a rugged man. If he were a structure, he would be the San Francisco Golden Gate Bridge, powerful and immense with sleek lines.

I'm smitten with this mysterious man, my Mystery Man. I can't help but stare. He looks oddly like the crazy drunk wagon driver, though.

"Chaaasssse, come hug papa bear." Recognizing the voice, I find a disheveled version of Grant stumbling up to me, Jaydon, at his side.

"Oh, my heavens! Where did Gus find him?"

"Actually, I found him," Jaydon announces.

"And, apparently, the fall didn't affect him at all; he's even drunker?" Roxie adds, staring hard at Grant.

"How is that possible?" I ask, raising my voice to compensate for the background crowd noise. "God, Grant, how many beers have you guzzled down between the time Jaydon found you, and the time when you arrived here?" Grant holds a pointer finger in the air, waving his hand weakly. He opens his mouth to speak.

"Chaaase, don't worry," Jaydon interrupts and belches lightly, totally ignoring Roxie's sarcastic questions and Grant's lame hand wave. "I already called the ambulance. Brooody's waiting outside for them to arrive."

"Can you all excuse us?" Brody interrupts, rushing back inside with Maddy, who looks snug in her carrier. She lightly sniffles as she drinks from a bottle. "The ambulance is here... Oh, my GOD, honey. Look at you!" he says in one breath, sidling up to Grant.

"Is Maddy doing better," I yell as Jaydon leads a bedraggled Grant toward the door.

"She's just fine. It's amazing how warm milk can calm hysterics in a matter of a few minutes," Brody answers, hurriedly trailing behind Jaydon and Grant outside. I watch as a paramedic helps them into the truck.

"Logan!" A woman's voice calls out, averting my attention. I turn to see Mystery Man talking to a woman who appeared at his side, dressed to the nines in a short black and white sequined dress and shiny black stiletto heels. Her giant ring catches the light, shimmering like a disco ball. "Logan, I will let the chef know that you're going to bring the cake out."

"LIZZIE?" I gasp in shock. "What. Are. You. Doing. Here?" I spit out.

"*URSULA?*" Roxie screams, her voice booming. "I didn't recognize you without the white hair and vomit."

"WHAT. DID. YOU. CALL. ME?"

"Holy shit, you couldn't be … could you … she's Paul's fiancée, Elizabeth Fairfax-Worthington," Roxie deliberately emphasizes, now that her identity is revealed.

"How… Why… Your… Name… What?" I stutter, recognizing the unmistakable facial features of one of my Prissy Posse arch-nemesis. "You… look…"

"Ravishing," Ursula finishes, one hand snarkily placed on a hip. "I had hair extensions—in case you're wondering." She flips her hair over her shoulder for a dramatic effect. "They have a way of reshaping a person's life incredibly."

Both Roxie and I stand immovable, our jaws dropped. *She looks amazing. I'll give her that.*

"Oh, and the name change… In case you're wondering, I got it legally changed to the name of one of my great-grandmothers. I thought it would complete my new transformation." Ursula eyes both of us, expecting a response.

"Hey girls, I see you've met my fiancée," Paul says as he approaches our shocked little group. He looks at the two of us and then back at his fiancée before planting a long kiss on her cheek. "What's going on? You guys look like you saw a ghost! Are you okay?" Paul eyes us warily.

"Ghost of Christmas Past is more like it," Roxie whispers to me, draining her drink.

Elizabeth (Lizzie) presses her lips together, smiling that same fake smile that I've seen so many times over the years.

"Nothing, baby," she says, looking over at Paul. He gives me a sidelong glance. "Honey, shame on me, I guess I forgot to mention that Chase, Roxie, and I go way back. We are high school classmates. We were all such good friends." She purses her lips for a moment, then pinches her nostrils one at a time, releasing sizable sniffs.

"Sweetheart, you getting a cold?" Paul looks at Ursula innocently.

"Don't you worry, darling. I'll make sure to up my vitamin C." she replies, her eyes steady on us.

"Sure, she's going to take her vitamin C, the bitch. I know what she's been snorting to keep her stick-thin," Roxie whispers in my ear.

"Geesh! To think all you girls know each other." Paul scratches his head. "Small world, isn't it?"

"Yeah. Small world," Roxie replies, smiling smugly to Ursula.

"Well, back to mingling," Paul says with a wave of his hand. Just as Paul and Ursula turn to leave, a pair of arms immediately grab me from behind.

"Ah!" I screech. I look up and see Jaydon smiling. He spins me around and toward him, pulling me into his arms a second time, but now wrapping me into an all-too-familiar tight bear hug.

"Chaaase, you look so warm and cuuuuddly." He squeezes me even tighter. He reeks of alcohol. Suddenly, it's like a reenactment of Pepé Le Pew and the squirmy Penelope Pussycat. My bug-eyes get the attention of Roxie, who spits out her drink and breaks out in raucous laughter. I stick out my tongue at her as I wriggle my way to freedom. I peek over Jaydon's shoulder in search of my Mystery Man, who I learn has a name: Logan. *Another L!* Daphne passes through my mind as I pan the room. I don't see him anywhere. He seems to have vanished along with Paul and Ursula.

"Okay, enough with the touchy-feely, Jaydon. Chase likes her space. Wait. You never told us how you found Grant? Were you on the wagon that rescued him?" Roxie asks.

"Noooope. Different wagon. I was just about to get ON," he belches again, "when Paul texted me. The nice driver supplied me with a high-density flashlight. I spotted a body near a diiitch. Grant didn't know what hiiit him; heeee was out cold. By the waaay, is that for me?" Jaydon looks at the two drinks Roxie's holding.

"Why not," Roxie interjects, handing him a rum and coke in one hand. "Sorry, I drank more than half. You know, unexpected nerves and all. But I don't like the taste, so you can have it."

"He doesn't need more alcohol, Rox. Look at him. If he keeps this up, he'll turn into a bumbling mess in no time flat."

"Chase, it's a party." She winks, taking Jaydon's arm and ushering him toward an empty seat in the packed dining room. "Follow me." Roxie settles him in. "I'll see you in a bit, okay, sweetie?" she says, giving him a quick peck on the cheek. She turns and grabs my hand, leading me to a table in a quiet corner. "What the hell are we going to do about Ursula? Who's going to tell Paul?" she whispers once we sit down.

"I'm still processing." I begin massaging my forehead.

"He won't marry her, right?" Roxie counters. "He. Cannot. Marry. Her."

"I know that. Rox, don't you remember what the Prissy Posse click did to me in high school? They pretended to be so nice and perfect when the whole time they had connections to help them accomplish their dirty deeds. If they were that with it back then, there's no telling what type of entourage they have now. Look how ASSon turned out!"

Roxie lets out a "hmm," followed by silence.

"What I can't understand," I offer, "is how Paul could buy into her evil schemes hook, line, and sinker. Look at him! It makes me want to throw up. Even with her hair extensions, she's still the same bitch." Across the room, I watch as Ursula rubs against Paul suggestively. Paul, in turn, eats it up by giving her a deep kiss—tongue and all—and a squeeze on her rump.

"We've got to find a way to tell him. Maybe we can set up a sting operation ..."

"And who are we going to recruit? Your Dad?"

"No, silly! Just you and me," Roxie shouts. A few heads turn in our direction.

"Great! Why don't you try that again, only this time use a megaphone?"

"Shut up! You know what I mean, you idiot," Rox whispers. "We just need to think, think, think..."

"Before it's too late, and she becomes..." I can barely say it... "Mrs. Max—"

"Hi, ladies. What are you doing hanging out here way off to the side?"

Roxie and I look at her strangely. We have no idea who she is.

"You don't recognize me with my wig and glasses." She takes off her glasses and removes a sliver of her real hair.

"Malefi—" Roxie begins.

"Joan?" I croak. The look of surprise on our faces couldn't have been more noticeable. *The third member of the Prissy Posse has arrived. Dear Lord! Help us all!* "What are you—"

"Disguise," she says flatly. "I'm probably one of the last people you want to see, let alone talk to," Joan begins, pulling an empty seat and making herself comfortable as she leans in close to us. "I, ah..." she begins, whispering. Roxie and I cup our ears, hoping to catch every word she has to say. "I came to apologize," Joan continues, "for all the years Lizzie and Julie secretly tortured you, Chase. I'm really, truly sorry; I didn't step in and stop them. I don't expect you to forgive me, but you know me; I like to keep it real. I'm trying to turn a new leaf after everything that happened lately, and this time I have to step in and say something."

I rub my eyes a few times, thinking that I'm daydreaming, but flinch when I open my eyes and find Joan (aka Maleficent) standing there, a bit red in the face but waiting patiently.

"Happened lately? I ... I'm..."

"Stunned." Joan finishes my sentence.

"Ee-yes," I reply slowly.

Speechless, we stare at her, waiting for more info as we eye her panning the room.

"Julie eloped. I think she was afraid she would lose her millionaire fiancé if he found out that she purposefully got Grant drunk on his birthday just to get pregnant. Plus, since neither she nor her fiancé was excited about starting a family so soon after getting married, she convinced him that she'd put Maddy into foster care."

"What? On April 14? Last year? Foster care? I thought her rich hubby was the fa—" I raise.

"Nope. Not what you thought," Joan finishes. "I'm sick of her nonsense, treating us all like her pawns. She is no goodie-goodie. She pretends to be blaming others for the things she's doing—like being the town pot dealer."

"Wait. What ... did ... you ... just ... say?" I blurt. "I'm really confused."

"Who? Medus— I mean, Julie? And who knocked her up, anyway? She can rot in hell for all I care," Roxie rants, clearly more confused than me.

"Julie," Joan's response to Roxie's question. "I'm talking about Julie. Sorry for the confusion."

Joan looks at me, a look of shock written on my face.

"Julie and Grant, I mean," Joan clarifies.

"You're not saying what I think you're saying, right?" I quip, uncertain what the hell I'm saying, anyway. "So, the baby is Grant's," Roxie blurts.

"But what about foster care?" I add.

"That was a lie," Joan whispers.

"OH!" I look over at Roxie. It's like a light bulb just went on above her head. "That's why the adoption happened so quickly. But wouldn't he have to take a paternity test—"

"She threatened him," Joan interrupts.

"How?" I add.

A moment of silence passes. We watch Joan nervously pan the room a second time.

"I can't stay long. So," she continues without waiting for a response, "you're probably wondering how Elizabeth nabbed Paul, right?"

This time, she waits for a response, but we remain transfixed.

"Well, let me put it this way: one thing led to the next, and now she's supposedly with a child. So, the rest is history. That's all I can tell you for now."

My heart plummets. "With child?" I mutter under my breath.

"What a bitch," Roxie says through gritted teeth.

"She claims it was 'simply love at first sight.' To be honest, I think Paul's a genuine guy."

"First sight, my foot," finally finding my voice. "Wait till I tell—"

"Oh, I wouldn't bother if I were you. You don't want to go there because things could go very wrong for you, Chase. Elizabeth has it all figured out. You need hardcore proof."

Rox and I glare at her. Chills go up and down my spine for the umpteenth time today. I've lost count. Silence across the table again.

I think back to what Charlie said when he took Joan to our senior prom: *"she's not like her friends. At her core, she's honest and decent."*

"Listen, I think I've said enough for one night. Just watch out for yourself, Chase. Lizzie has eyes planted all over. Here's my number, at least for now," Joan pulls out a sticky note and hands it to me.

"For now?" I question.

"Throw away phones. I don't want to leave a trace. I'm not kidding around. This is no game. Please, believe me. I'm for real. If you want to talk more, call me."

Joan stands up without warning. "By the way," she says, looking at me, "it's nice to see you've ditched your scarf."

I grab the area around my neck, but there's nothing to pull. I smile weakly, watching her walk across the room to the nearest bathroom.

"I don't know what to think," I finally speak up after several minutes.

"Yeah. It's kinda—"

"Happy engagement party" blasts through the loudspeakers. The announcement in that all-too-familiar baritone voice cuts Roxie off. Logan is balancing a cake in one hand while holding the microphone in the other. Singing to the tune of "Happy Birthday," he leads the crowd to join in. On the final note, he twirls around once while raising the cake high above his head before plopping it down in front of Ursula and Paul. "Blow the candles out," he purrs in his Texas drawl. Although my mind is still reeling from the cryptic conversation with Joan, I can't help but stare at him.

"Who is that guy, anyway? He's hot!" I suddenly blurt, my candidness surprising me once again.

"Oh, that's Paul's cousin, Logan."

"How do y—"

"Paul has twin cousins. The Ritter boys," Roxie says matter-of-factly. "Paul's Instagram, sweetheart! When are you going to get on board and join the fun?" Roxie smiles widely. "Identical twins. Equally as hot. By the looks of it, one crazy idiot buckaroo act back there," she points in the direction of the entrance, "and one not so crazy," she points at the singer. "Lots of twins—you and Charlie, my dad and your dad, Landon and Logan."

The room erupts in a fit of applause and hollers of "encore, encore." Logan half bows before he sings the song all over again. *This is bizarre! Twins?!* I watch as Logan swings his arms one final time before he belts out the final note. The drunken crowd continues its hoots and hollers, giving him another round of vehement clapping. Logan points to Paul. "Floor's yours." Paul waves his arms, getting the audience's attention. The whole room grows eerily quiet, waiting for him to speak.

"Thank you all for coming. We're honored," Paul says, hugging Ursula, "that you would share in our celebration. What we neglected to tell you is that we have a second surprise. After seeing my best friend Grant adopt his daughter Maddy—and I'm sorry he, Brody, and Maddy couldn't stay tonight—it made me realize that I also want to be a father. I strove to find a woman who loved me as much as I loved her, and someone who also wanted to create a new life." He laughs as if he's the luckiest person in the world, patting Elizabeth's belly. "What better gift is there than the gift of a child. Let's face it guys, the only reason we're getting married is because we accidentally knock—" Elizabeth playfully shoves him in the side. "Oops, not funny. So, I guess our secret is out of the bag. We're having a baby."

"OH, FUCK, IT'S TRUE!" Roxie hollers. Everyone in the room turns in her direction; she ducks her head for a few seconds then immediately pops up again. Roxie, who has never let a personal embarrassment hold her back, exclaims, "Oh yes, what a joy. Let's raise our glasses and toast to the happy couple," and then promptly sits back down. A collective cheer

404

and clinking of glasses follow, the audience oblivious to Roxie's comments. I catch Paul grimacing, and for a good reason: he and I are probably the only people in the room who know Roxie's grin is as phony as a three-dollar bill.

"Chase, this situation is seriously fucked up," she mumbles under her breath. "The Prissy Posse bitch from high school has no right to end up with the nice guy. And to think Joan was telling the truth."

"Tonight, is getting weirder by the minute, Rox," I whisper back. "I didn't know that having children and building a family were the most important things Paul craved. He didn't reveal that secret to either you or me, Rox." I nervously pick at my nail polish.

"Baby, I need your loving! Let's sing again," Logan belts out before he transitions to another song.

"Hey Chase," Jaydon slides into the chair next to me, "since your datebook is empty, you could always go out with him," pointing to Logan. He gives my waist a little pinch.

I roll my eyes and shake my head in disbelief. "Thanks for the advice," I answer flatly.

I look back and catch Paul kissing his bride-to-be. I observe her face. She's smiling, but her eyes are hard, too controlled. For whatever reason, I continue staring, but something is different this time as I notice that she moves ever so slightly, so Paul doesn't kiss her full on the lips. I notice a familiar face standing just behind him. It's Joan, looking more like herself and in a totally different get-up. She catches me looking at her and winks.

"I need some air," I announce quietly to Roxie. I slip out the side door, thinking about Ursula, who's spent her whole life creating a bogus persona, a sick one to boot. There's no doubt in my mind that the high-school bitch is faking her love toward my friend. *But Why? She could have picked anyone. Dare I ask Joan what's going on? Would she spill the beans on her friend?*

* * *

"See you at the after-party," Paul yells to the audience as he and Ursula exit the cabin, enter a wagon bedecked in wedding décor, and head toward the parking lot. Moments later, three wagons arrive to transport the guests.

"The wagon will take us back," Jaydon says after-the-fact. "I'll go get Roxie," Jaydon straggles up next to me, breaking my thoughts; my head still in a fog about Paul and Ursula.

"You go sit in the front of the wagon," I instruct. "I'll go get her. You're about to pass out."

I grab his arm and escort him outside. The fresh air hits me as the two of us walk in solitude to the wagon.

I settle him in with a blanket. Jaydon reaches out and grabs my arm just as I turn to go back.

"By the way," he whispers, turning to a serious tone, "what did you mean about Ursula, the sea witch, and my brother?"

"Huh?" I give him a dumbfounded look.

"Listen, I have ears. I wasn't born yesterday. I moved over a couple of tables to eavesdrop when I saw Joan sit with you gals. I've got my own opinions about the slut he's planning on marrying. All I have to say is that you and Roxie have a lot of explaining to do, if you are talking about Elizabeth."

I look at him straight in the face. "You really don't want to know."

"Actually, I do. I knew something was off with her. Shall we draw straws on who tells my brother?" I'm shocked at his sudden admission.

"And have him hate us all?" I say, raising my voice a bit. "Let's see how it plays out. Be right back. I'm going to get Roxie. Stay put in the wagon. I don't want to lose someone else tonight."

"Aye, Aye, Captain. When you find her, tell her I'm ready for the after-party!"

"Oh, that's just peachy," I scowl. "I can hardly wait."

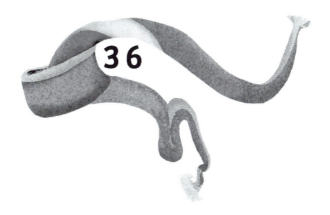

36

It's close to 10 PM by the time we park our rental car on the main drag of this little town, down the street from the El Dorado restaurant. Even from this distance, I can hear electronica pulsating through its walls. "Chaaaaaase, Roooooooxie," Jaydon drawls, extending an arm for each of us to join him.

I'm not too excited about this prospect, but it's the most logical solution after watching him totter soon after exiting the car. I'd rather be in bed than to go to an after-party, considering the disturbing events that took place earlier. The only thing I can think of as we walk side-by-side to the front of the club is our surprise conversation with Joan. *How am I going to tell Paul that he's walking into a trap?* Jaydon stops dead in his tracks, snapping me back to the present as he immediately starts chatting with a group of guys by the door, taking long drags off of their cigarettes.

"I really need to use the ladies' room." Roxie's crossed legs accompany the look of desperation on her face.

"Ooookay, you two go in," Jaydon offers. "I'll be riiiiiight behind you." We look at him incredulously. "Reeeeeeeeeeeally," he says, trying to convince us that he's got his act together as he nearly topples into the bouncer. "I'll be just fiiiiiiine."

"ID's now," the guard says with more sharpness than I expect, standing and holding out his hand like a sentinel.

"By the way, you see the blooooooonde one?" referring to me. "She's seeeee-ven-teeeeeeen," Jaydon says, winking. My thoughts elsewhere, I'm caught off guard. Frozen in place, I give the bouncer a deer-in-the headlights look. The bouncer looks at me and then at Jaydon. By the shocked expression on his face, I realize he actually believes him. *Oh, shit!*

"Sir," suddenly finding my voice, "he was only joking. I assure you I'm well past the legal age—for everything." *What the hell did I just say?* I don a sheepish grin, hoping he doesn't catch my accidental double entendre. *Talk about putting my foot in my mouth and pushing it all the way up to my hips...* Now, he's glaring at me in complete silence, giving me a seductive once-over. I kick Jaydon hard as I pull out my ID and shove it in front of the bouncer's face.

"OUCH! What the he—"

"See the date of birth?" I say, cutting off Jaydon. "I'm telling you the truth. I'm thirty, not seventeen."

He flips my ID over and scrutinizes it.

"This looks real. Where did you get it?" He's mystified.

"I'm telling you, it's real." I shriek as I snatch it back and shove it into my purse.

"I really have to pee. I can go right here if you want?" Roxie begins to pull down her leggings—her knee-length top acting as a cover for her supposedly exposed bottom—when he promptly dismisses us with a wave.

Roxie quickly puts herself together and grabs Jaydon and me to follow her inside. I can feel the palpitations of my heart against the beat-and-grind electronica rhythms. I screw up my face when I see the Mexican restaurant wait staff dressed in Mariachi band attire, pouring bottles of tequila instead of strumming guitars.

"Okee, dokee," I mutter under my breath. "Now, if that isn't surreal, I don't know what else—"

"Miss," a waiter interrupts, "You look like you could use one of these," he holds out a drink, smiling wanly. I wave him away.

The room's bustling with energy as people bounce around; some dancing but most nursing a drink. We find a table and leave Jaydon while Roxie and I push past colliding bodies pinging to the monotonous beat towards the sign for the ladies' room near the back wall. A ridiculous group of scantily clad women, more like a mosh pit than the expected long line, dance in place, awaiting their turn.

"I'll just be a sec," Roxie says, looking at me and then at the group of men to the left, eyeing us like dessert. My eyes widen.

"You can't be serious," I yell over the music.

Roxie quickly pans the room, lightly nodding her head. "Okay. How 'bout you sit with Jaydon instead of waiting for me? I'll be fine."

I watch as Roxie pulls her leggings down again, this time in front of the cattle call of women. Two of them promptly grab her and yelling, "move," partition the line to create a clear path, like the parting of the Red Sea, to the next available stall. I chuckle lightly, knowing that she's got it covered.

"Good idea," I mumble under my breath as I make a beeline back to Jaydon, who's slumped over on the table, asleep. Even though it doesn't have the underground-den-of-iniquity feeling Velo has, I still don't feel comfortable in nightclubs. A tall, buff guy plants himself in front of me, blocking my path. I try to scoot past him to the right, but he bars my way. I keep my eyes on the ground as I try to maneuver to the left; he blocks me again.

"What's your problem?" I ask, finally looking up. In the dim lighting, I'm able to make out that the guy has perfectly styled, cropped dark hair, an olive complexion, broad shoulders like an athlete, and a strong jaw with the glow of stubble.

"Just wanted to say hello," the guy says with a husky Texas accent. His piercing golden brown eyes stare at me. "I know you," he says, reaching forward as if he's going to pull me in for a hug. He smells like petrichor, the fresh earthy scent that comes after a morning rain; it's intoxicating, almost like a drug.

"Ah, excuse me?" I step back.

"Yes, yes, I remember now. I saw you at Paul's party earlier."

My heart is thudding so hard it hurts. He leans closer. He stares at me in astonishment, and there's an awkward silence as his lips, so close to mine, makes me yearn for a glass of water—his aura is drying me out completely. It's stupid to feel this way because I'm sure he's not going to kiss me.

While I hesitate to respond, a warm arm sweeps around my waist, pulling me back against his chest. "Logan, knock it off and stop hitting on her," Paul jokes, punching his cousin in the arm. My mouth drops open. *OH. MY. GOD! That was Logan?* My mind reverts to Daphne's foretelling of meeting more than one guy with the letter L. *Could Daphne be right? This guy is indeed sexy as hell and hopefully more reasonable than his counterpart.*

"You are? Who?" I feign indifference, looking right at him, blushing. "The crazy wagon driver?"

"Ah, no, little lady," he chuckles. "That would be my brother Landon, who's passed out at the hotel. I'm Logan. You bumped into me at Paul's party. A pleasure to make your acquaintance again."

"Come on, Chase, let's go find Roxie," Paul says, tugging on my hand, urging me to follow. "Trust me; my cousin's a bit..." I look between Logan and Paul.

"A bit what?" I spit out.

"Charming, of course." Logan takes my other hand in his. "I'm going to borrow her for a dance if you don't mind, cousin?" he says, smirking at Paul.

"Not a good idea," Paul whispers to me. I stand motionless for a moment before Logan tugs again on my hand. I turn to look at Paul, and he shrugs his shoulders and shoots me an 'I warned you' look. *Sorry*, he mouths. I feel movement within my hand and look to see his fingers intertwined with mine. *Uh oh...* We pass Roxie, who appears to be in deep conversation with a guy. I flick her arm enough to get her attention. Her eyes widen; she looks like she is about to choke in shock.

Logan leads me onto the dance floor for a fast song. Shimmying his hips and shoulders, he attracts a swarm of women clad in clothes made for hourglass Barbie dolls. The women push me out of the way as they close in on all sides, dancing circles around him. I slow to a standstill, paralyzed, half-wondering if this is a bizarre nightmare or a joke that's gone badly wrong. My spirits plunge as I watch Logan dance. He's bouncing his head to the beat, face flushed. His hair glistens from sweat as he murmurs into the ear of a cute brunette. I try and catch his eye; when I do, he only shrugs. *WTF is wrong with him?* My head churns with murderous thoughts.

I fumble, my heel catching on the front of someone's shoes. An arm swoops around my shoulder, squeezing, pulling me upright. I look over, and it's Paul, a duplicate knight in shining armor, saving me from the humiliation of falling and being ditched. He presses his lips to my ear.

"Dance with me." Paul kisses my forehead, pressing his hand against mine reassuringly before leading me to the opposite side of the dance floor. He spins me around a couple of times, and we smile at each other. I'm easing back into a happy mood.

"Grant never told me that you're such a good dancer," Paul says.

"Thank you, but I normally have two left feet," I say shyly.

Paul's bright eyes light up, and his face is suddenly passionate as he clutches me a bit tighter. He moves his hips so gracefully it's like he's a born dancer. I do my best to match his rhythm, swaying my hips when he sways his and spinning around when he indicates for me to do so; he's actually leading me in a salsa. Surprisingly, the strange music fits.

"I've missed hanging out with you," he smiles and holds my gaze for an extra second. My heart is beating so hard it feels like it's going to burst from my chest. *I like Paul.*

"Holy smokes, Chase!" the little Chase Angel, says, roaring in my ear. "It took you long enough to figure out. He's been right in front of you this whole time."

When the song finishes, Paul motions for a waiter to bring water while ushering me towards the booth where I left Jaydon. Paul rolls his eyes and shoves his brother against the wall before he sits next to him. I flop down, sinking into the cushions on the other side. The waiter shows up with water. I take a sip as Roxie appears and sits next to me.

"This one here is way past drunk, you think?" Roxie says loudly, nodding toward Jaydon.

"Like that's nothing new?" Paul laughs. "Listen, you two, I know Jaydon's in good hands. I wish I could stay, but I have to get back to Elizabeth. Thanks for the dance, Chase," Paul says, sliding out of the booth. I watch him disappear into the sea of dancers who are waiting anxiously for a different band to set up.

"Wait a second," Roxie's mouth goes wide, "you and Paul were dancing?" She pauses before continuing. "But I saw you with Mr. Hunk-a-Hunk."

"Whoooooooooooooooo's Mr. Huuuunk-a-Huuuuunk?" Jaydon mumbles, lifting his head slightly.

"Ah, the dead speaks," Roxie answers.

"Giiirrrrrrls," Jaydon's breath reeks of alcohol as he attempts to sit up. "My twin cousins are ... forget it. Whaaaaaat ... are ... we going to do about the seeeeeea witch?" He makes a scary face, sticking his hands up like claws before he slumps back down and begins to snore.

"Our first song goes out to the little lady in the back booth with the long blonde hair who saved me on the plane!" a familiar voice says into the microphone.

My head snaps as I look at the stage, catching sight of the atomic red Mohawk. Mr. Rooster stands front and center, the microphone pointing right at me. "This one's for you, doll." The lead singer points his finger directly at me before diving back into a crazy, energetic song.

"Doll?" Roxie says, her eyes popping out.

"I ... um... That's Sam! What the hell is he doing here?" *Can this day get any crazier?*

"Ah! Your plane fan! And a momentary fiancé!" Roxie exclaims, recalling what I told her about the strange incident on our way here. "So, I guess you're going to have that cup of tea after all?" She grabs my arm and shakes it wildly.

"Cup ... of ... teeeea? With..." Jaydon lets out a loud burp, "Saaaam? Your fi-AN-cé? You're engaged?"

"Oh, boy," Roxie blurts. "It's time to take this skunk back to the hotel. He'll never make it tomorrow morning."

"What's tomorrow morning?" I look at Roxie, confused.

"Filming. Jaydon mumbled earlier about him and Paul having to film early in the morning and needing to be in one piece like that's really going to happen! Anyway, do you want me to leave you the car, or do you want to call it a night and come with us?"

"I would be happy to take her back to the hotel." Warm hands start to massage my shoulders. I turn my head, Logan's standing behind our booth.

"That's a brazen thing to say. I'm not going anywhere, especially with you," I say, folding my arms over my chest. "Paul had to rescue me after you ditched me on the dance floor. How many phone numbers are in your pocket now?"

Logan smirks like a film star. "I had no control over those girls. What can I say? The women like me." Logan is such an arrogant prick. "You were the only one I thought about while dancing with them. I watched you move. You didn't tell me you were a dancer."

I sit back on impulse and stick out my tongue at him.

Roxie lets out a chuckle. "You mind?" she says as she takes my water and throws it in Jaydon's face.

"Hey, whaaat'd you dooooo that for? I'm wiiiiiide awake," Jaydon says as Roxie attempts to drag him out of the booth.

"A little help here!" Roxie yelps.

"Move," Logan instructs Chase as he pulls Jaydon out of the booth. "Pull the car up. We'll meet you at the door."

Moments later, Roxie returns, and Logan buckles Jaydon in the passenger seat. I pull on my coat.

"Have fun, Chase," Roxie yells. "I'll come back and pick you up if you end up needing a ride. See you back at the hotel."

"What? You can't leave me here and with him," I say, shocked, pointing at Logan. "You can't do that."

"It's not every day that you get to have a gorgeous man fight for you," Roxie yells. I notice Logan grinning from ear to ear. "Don't look so worried; I'm one call away. Plus, Paul's still here, if you need immediate help."

"Thanks for keeeeeeping me company," Jaydon adds, smiling stupidly.

"Right." Roxie rolls her eyes. "See you all back at the hotel. Take care of her, Logan. She's extra special cargo."

And with that, Roxie and Jaydon drive away.

"Would you like a drink?" Logan offers once we enter the restaurant.

My mind is in a jumble. First, all this stuff about Grant, Medusa, and Ursula, then Roxie leaves me with Logan! My eyes begin to scan across the room in search of Paul. I sure did miss the moment not dating him, didn't I?

"What did you say?" I ask Logan flatly.

"What's your poison?"

"My poison? Oh, Coke, I guess," I say robotically.

"Whiskey and coke or rum and coke?" He starts walking towards the bar.

"Uh... Just plain coke." My mind's rattled. *I can't believe Paul is having a baby with that witch.* I look over my shoulder again and see her snuggled up under his arm. Our brief moment on the dance floor was just that, a moment. Nothing more. "On second thought," I yell over the music, but the ambient noise drowns out my voice. I madly wave my arms to get his attention.

"What's up, my love?" he says in my face, his breath reeking of alcohol.

"Don't call me that. Listen, forget the drinks. I've changed my mind. I'm ready to go. Please give me the keys, Logan. You're not in any shape to drive." I'm surprised when he willingly surrenders them.

* * *

I stop alongside the hotel in the near-deserted parking lot, putting the car in park.

"Is this okay?" I ask, turning the ignition off. Without warning, Logan leans over the center console. I stiffen, half-expecting that he's leaning in for a kiss. He pops open the side door compartment, reaches in, and slips out a quarter.

"I'm going to flip a coin. Heads or tails?" he says, as he flips the coin between his fingers.

"Okay, wasn't expecting that." I unbuckle my seatbelt. "As I said earlier, I'm going to call it a night."

"Oh, come on." He caresses my thigh as I give him a look that says I think he's gone mad. "Humor me, heads or tails?" He asks again.

"Fine. If it will make you happy, heads." Logan flips it, catches it, and puts it smack down on the back of his hand.

"Tails," he says.

He clutches my shoulders. "I win. We get to make out before we go inside."

"We get to what? Make out?" I look up at him. "Did you really just say that?"

"Well … yes. Remember, making out in high school? It was such a rush." He brushes his hair out of his eyes.

I'm not exactly following. "I'm sure we had two very different high school experiences," I laugh.

He turns toward me, his strong arms lifting me off the seat until I'm straddling him. He brushes the hair out of my eyes, cradling my face in his hands. He traces his index finger along my bottom lip, which sends a shiver up my spine.

"Your lips are so beautiful and soft." He leans in and presses his lips against mine as if he's moving in slow motion.

I pull back, looking at his parted lips. Logic and any ideas of his presumptuous personality and man-whore behavior notwithstanding vanish as I admire his handsome cheekbones and his pillowy lips. He looks like a Grecian god with his chiseled face and body. *It's just a kiss, nothing more, nothing less.* Logan cups the back of my head, bringing me forward. His lips meet mine again, and he kisses me harder this time, sucking on my lower lip. I'm breathing hard, and my body heat warms a few degrees. I'm positive about that.

With every kiss, he releases a soft moan of pleasure. He kisses a trail along my neck, down to my collarbone. He softly, seductively kisses my shoulder. *This feels nice!*

"OUCH!" I flinch backward as much as I can in the compact space. My back hits the dashboard. "YOU BIT ME!" I yell, twisting to look at my shoulder at the damage. *Am I bleeding?* "I can feel your teeth marks imprinted in my skin. What the fuck is wrong with you?" I screech, rubbing my shoulder, trying to dull the pain. "Do you have some kind of vampire fetish?"

"You don't like to be bitten?" Logan leans towards my shoulder again, attempting to bite me again. I push my hands against his chest.

"I think most women don't want to be bitten," I fume, shocked and breathing hard. He looks at me, bewildered, as I scoot off his lap and back into the driver's seat.

Logan's phone rings. He takes it out of his pocket, looks at it, but doesn't answer. It proceeds to blast with a symphony of incoming texts. I lean over and catch the first of many.

Claire: WHERE ARE YOU? You told me you'd call me, and you didn't.

"Who's Claire?" I ask coolly, catching his gaze. "Because she seems as perturbed as I am. I didn't know you had this effect on so many women."

"My girlfriend," he says nonchalantly.

"Your what?" I lean forward, grasping the steering wheel like it's my lifeline.

"You heard me. Girlfriend." The mask is off. If his nightclub stint wasn't enough, this proves Logan's another brazen player and just as bad as his twin brother, Landon.

This is the icing on the cake. "You've got to be kidding me. Why the hell are you making out with me if you have a girlfriend? Don't you think that maybe you should've mentioned that before now?" I say, my voice raised a couple of more decibels.

"If I would have told you, then you wouldn't have made out with me. Plus, I really wanted to kiss you." He smiles, smugly. It takes everything I have to keep from slamming him in the face.

"Correction. You wanted to bite me." What a farce of an evening! "This night just keeps getting better," I say with heavy sarcasm. I hope I have some vampire and angry face Amoremojis to add to my spreadsheet under "Meet a bunch of hot guys."

"Don't be such a prude. We had fun. What's the big deal?" Logan retorts, like a jock.

I look straight at him. "Listen, buster. Read my lips: I DID NOT HAVE FUN. You cannot go around biting women without their permission!" I scream at the top of my lungs, shoving him hard before exiting his car.

"You were the best kisser ever—NOT! You suck!" Logan spits out as I slam the door shut. I drop my head, walking towards the entrance to the hotel. *How did this go south so fast? How could I have reverted so quickly to being a teenager, fantasizing about making out with a hot guy? Or is it that I'm really that scared of growing up?* "I'll go for the latter," I say aloud as I ride the elevator alone up to the 4th floor. "And so, what if his name starts with an L," I continue on my tirade. "I can't go around thinking every guy whose name starts with the letter L is significant. I do know one thing: I have to ask my dates if they've bitten anyone before. As fetishes go, this isn't one I can stand behind.

Bottom line: "fuck the male species!"

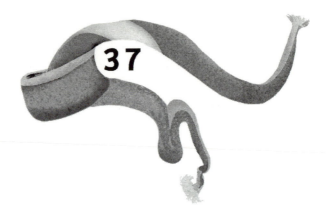

37

June gloom is in full force. It has been pouring nonstop since I woke up, and now low-lying ominous clouds block out any view of the mountains as I stare out the floor-to-ceiling windows. I've spent the last forty-five minutes on a yoga mat on Dr. Brennan's floor, doing a list of breathing and meditation exercises to mitigate my levator-ani pain before switching to a discussion of my love life, or lack thereof.

"This spreadsheet you've been working on," Dr. Brennan, finally getting a word in edgewise, "did you add more Amoremoji stickers? Is that helping you cope with your emotions?" He sits with a pad on his lap, occasionally scribbling notes.

"Yes, I guess," I respond, answering the last of his rash of questions. I roll up the mat and take a seat on the La-Z-Boy chair, flipping the lever to a more reclined setting and stretching out my legs on the footstool. "I'll never pick a guy solely on looks after the crazy twins from Paul's engagement party. Both of them turned out to be egotistical jerks." I look up and see he's busily scribbling again, so I continue. "Love isn't about the way a person looks; it's about how someone makes you feel inside and how you feel for them. It's about wanting to make their life better; it's about this undefinable chemistry."

"Uh ... huh ... yes ... exactly. Also, it helps to pay attention to what a man's saying, to better understand him." Dr. Brennan clears his throat, "and if you take the time to look beyond the surface—"

"Look beyond the surface?" I rudely interrupt, untying my ponytail. "Then explain how I never guessed Paul would get engaged without telling any of us?" I blurt, collecting my hair and knotting it in a little bun on top of my head.

"Does that make you feel hurt that he didn't share that with you before the invitation arrived?"

"In all due respect, Dr. Brennan, you make it sound like what Paul did was perfectly normal. How was I supposed to react? Okay, forget that for the moment. The only thing I'm thinking about now is that Paul needs an intervention. Pronto. He can't pick Ursula." Dr. Brennan gives me another one of his startled looks, promptly putting his pen down. "Sorry," I cower lightly, "I mean Lizzie. Elizabeth." He has no clue that I knew her from high school and how she tortured me. But my hour's almost up, and I don't want to get into it now. "They dated for a few weeks, she gets pregnant, and now they're getting married? There's something desperately wrong with this picture."

"Hmmm..." He scribbles some more. "Do you think an intervention may be a little extreme? Here's a guy, that from what you've shared with me, has shown interest in you for years. He's not driven by sex in the least. Instead, he has shown you genuineness. You just have had a hard time recognizing it surrounded by men who purely want a sexual encounter with you. Now, he's given up and, instead, is engaged to someone else. Maybe what you are feeling is jealousy because you truly are in love with him, like when Grant married Brody—"

Dr. Brennan's phone shrills out. "Sorry about that," he says, turning red in the face. He glances at the screen, clearly hitting the decline button.

"Enough. I'm tired of talking about Grant. I finally made peace with Charlie's death, and I just want to concentrate on me and not worry about Grant. I now understand why I chose him in the first place: to fill the void Charlie left behind. He never was the one for me. Part of me knew that all along. I ignored the signs because I was in too much pain and wanted a band-aid."

"Do you feel you have closure with Grant too? And how he betrayed you?"

"I guess. I don't know. My little friend Daphne came by the house this morning. She told me that Logan, aka The Biter, was never the guy she was talking about, nor was his brother Landon. She trotted down the stairs and said, 'It's not my place, but Paul's right; your friend's in trouble.' What bothered me was watching her smile fade when she looked at me for a long moment before continuing down the stairs. Do you think I should be worried about Grant?"

"I thought you didn't want to talk about him?" he rubs his temples. I can tell that I'm irritating him. "If anyone needs an intervention, may I be so bold as to say, he—"

My phone dings with an incoming email, cutting him off.

From: jacquesp@mera.fr
To: ChaseMorg@mylife.com
Subject: Los Angeles

Bonjour, Chase. I arrive at the hotel on Saturday. I leave LA Sunday, if you have time for Saturday dinner or Sunday lunch.
I will be very happy, and if you choose two appointments, you receive a 50% discount. For three, there's an additional 50% discount.
J'ai essaye de faire de l'humor
Je t'embrasse

"Holy shit! Was it a full moon last night? Nope. Did I wish on a shooting star? Not that I can remember. It's inconceivable to think he'd get on an airplane and fly 5,659 miles to see me!"

I spit out, rereading his email aloud to verify that my eyes aren't playing tricks on me before typing in my response.

From: ChaseMorg@mylife.com
To: jacquesp@mera.fr
Subject: Re: Los Angeles

I'm spending the whole time with you. Saturday dinner, Sunday lunch. I guess this means I get a 100% discount? You are very funny. We'll have lots of fun together. I'm really looking forward to seeing you again.

The moment I hit send, my email immediately chirps back.

From: jacquesp@mera.fr
To: ChaseMorg@mylife.com
Subject: Re: Los Angeles

Ma cherie, I am the happiest man in the world! À bientôt

I respond immediately.

From: ChaseMorg@mylife.com
To: jacquesp@mera.fr
Subject: Re: Re: Los Angeles

À bientôt

"Now what? An almost total stranger is making a grand gesture. He's flying from Europe to have dinner with me AND spending the weekend. Unbelievable! I'm not ready for this." I

421

look to Dr. Brennan for help. When he gives me the deer-in-the-headlights look, it hits me that I just performed *une grand faux pas*. "Oops," I sheepishly utter. "I'm soooooooooo so—"

"Let me get this straight," he interrupts. "Jacques-Pierre's supposed to arrive this weekend, correct? From Europe? And you've never had one date? Let's be realistic; it's a long way to fly for dinner."

I'm genuinely shocked at his response like this was all a part of our discussion.

"Ee-yes, I mean, I hope so," I say. "Is there something I missed? Something you read between the lines?"

When I feel confident that he won't go berserk on me, I walk over to him, handing him my phone so he can view the emails.

"The thing is," I add, "his name doesn't start with the letter L, so he can't be the one."

"First of all ... You can return to your seat, Chastity," he nods toward the La-Z-Boy. "You do realize that you totally ignored my no-cell-phone policy." I look at him incredulously.

"And it's okay for your phone to go off?" I blurt, surprised at my bluntness.

Silence.

"Point well taken." Dr. Brennan reddens for a second time. "To continue," he clears his throat again, "you've been fantasizing about having a man make this kind of grand gesture to you for a long time. I will admit, I had my doubts until I just read the emails for myself. He, like Paul, seems to be genuinely interested in you, and that makes you happy. You know, Chastity, you have tunnel vision again. You first focused all your attention on Grant, making him the one, and now you're focusing on two different men, neither of whom begin with this magical initial L, to be the one. Have you ever thought to take the road less traveled and try something new? Just say 'yes' without fast-forwarding to a result and what initial their name begins with."

"But," I raise, finding my voice again. "I'm freaking out. My mind is going to be reeling with crazy sex scenarios. So, do I, or don't I go? I have to consider the result. Don't you see?" I ramble. I take in a few deep breaths to quiet myself. "There's another thing."

"And that would be," Dr. Brennan's pen is at the ready. "Paul's baptismal name also includes an L."

"Oh, I see."

But I can tell that he really *doesn't* see as he scribbles on his notepad.

"Okay. I admit that this all sounds ... weird."

"I'm glad that you said that. I would agree with that statement." Dr. Brennan glances at his inconspicuous timer.

"But I can't dismiss the fact that everything Daphne has mentioned so far has been spot on," I say evenly. "Hmm..." Dr. Brennan mutters quietly. I can tell that he's still not convinced. "I respect what you're saying."

More silence.

"Listen, I didn't know Paul was going to get married and have a baby. I didn't know Grant would be a father so quickly. I didn't know my dead brother would come to visit me. I don't know how to navigate the murky waters that make up my life."

I flinch when the buzzer dings.

"Time's up. This has been enlightening, Chastity. I have written out four questions for you to consider seriously: Are you planning on having sexual relations with this stranger? If yes, isn't that a far cry different from your desire to wait until your wedding night? Why are you turning this into sex when Jacques-Pierre hasn't even led you down that path at all? Lastly, do we need to talk about you trying to sabotage your relationships by pigeonholing men into just wanting one thing from you?"

Silence. I swallow hard a couple of times.

"I ... I don't know," I begin sheepishly.

"Well, that's a good sign that you need to contemplate my questions, which we can discuss more in-depth during your next visit." He hands me the sheet with the questions. Putting his glasses down on his desk, he eyes me cautiously. "I think we're beginning to make progress. Dealing with your past is a huge step in the right direction. You'll notice by letting go of the past, your stress will decrease, and so will your levator-ani pain episodes. So, until next time..."

"Thanks, Doc. Well ... wish me luck. I will need it with graduation and then Jacques- Pierre's arrival."

"Ah, yes, your degree. That's another wonderful accomplishment. I'm proud that you stuck to your degree against all the odds that you faced. You're a strong woman, Chastity Morgan. Life has dealt you an unexpected hand, and you momentarily lost yourself, but look at how you turned everything around. Chastity, your life is what you make of it. And Luck?" he adds, "Well, it is just that: luck. You don't need me ever to wish you luck. Remember that."

"You're a genius, Doc. You're right. Life is what I make of it. Forget luck," I reply, shaking his hand a little too vigorously. I drop my hand as soon as my phone beeps with an incoming text. I thank him before rushing into the waiting room to check my phone.

Jacques-Pierre: I have never crossed an ocean and a continent for a woman before. À bientôt.

"Hold on a second ... he's never flown this far for a woman?" I shriek. The receptionist glares at me. "Oh ... ah... Sorry!"

I quickly set up another appointment, then race out to my car. All the while, my heart is beating so hard that it feels like I have an entire percussion section inside of me. *His name might not start with the letter L, but in a few days, my life is going to change; Prince Charming's galloping in on his white horse, or in this case, the Airbus 380.*

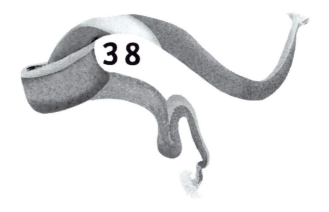

38

The end of the road at last. It's graduation day, and I'm decked out in a flame-red doctoral gown that screams, "Hi! I'm Elmo!" I look around the crowd, half-expecting to see Sesame Street characters seated tightly together in their section. After twelve years, marching in step toward my bachelors, master's, and now doctorate degree, I'm rewarded with ridiculously colored, heavy regalia on a 105-degree day. It would be just my luck to graduate amid a heatwave on the hottest day of summer. Regardless, as any sweet and slightly obsessive-compulsive person would, I've taken every precaution necessary. Like an undercover agent, I concealed the following gear beneath my graduation uniform:

- Cell phone (aka my lifeline) with the sound turned off—check.

- Evian water to prevent dehydration—check.

- Nut bar to stave off hunger—check.

- Cough drops to suppress a tickle in my throat—check.

- Anti-anxiety meds to quash any stage fright—check.

All I have to do is walk to the center of the stage; bow down so that my academic advisor can place the doctoral hood over my robe; shake hands with the dean, and then get the hell off the stage without tripping or fainting. *Easy enough, right?* The only way to get on and off the stage in one piece is to wear comfortable shoes. I opted for ballet flats. *I can't trip and fall in flats, can I?*

Being the center of attention isn't my go-to, even though that's been a consistent theme since high school, so I mutter a blessing for serenity before my name is called.

My cell vibrates as I stand in line, awaiting my turn. It's a text from Roxie. She's sitting on the far-right side of the designated grassy area alongside the college football stadium with my dad, my mom, Henry, Nana, Gramps, Uncle Mason, Aunt Kate, Uncle Herb, Brody, Maddy, Brent, and Daphne, who gives me an encouraging little wave. *Hmm ... Grant must be in the bathroom. Where is he?*

> Roxie: Almost your turn. Before you get up, look at your eleven o'clock. Gorgeous professors do exist in engineering.
> **Me: Where? I don't see anyone but an old bald guy.**
> Roxie: Your 1 o'clock.
> **Me: Ah, target spotted! Nope. He's an anomaly; handsome, yes. That's Dr. Milton from France. He's on loan from Paris, teaching this quarter. Most engineers are like asexual plants—they wouldn't know a woman from a slide rule!**
> Roxie: LOLOLOL! Good one!

That's my motto, and I'm sticking to it. Certainly, this last year has confirmed that. I didn't garner one date from a fellow engineer. My name is called. "Dr. Chastity Ann Morgan." the dean of engineering announces. Hearing this new title is both empowering and surreal. My emotions are all over the place;

I'm hot, and I'm cold (even in this hottest of days). I hear the dean clear his throat to reread my name.

I look over at my family and see Uncle Mason and Roxie mouthing "don't fall." My dad looks ecstatic, as a proud father would be. My mom wipes away fresh tears of joy, and my brother Henry fans himself with the program. *Figures!* I turn to see Brent approaching the middle aisle, ready to snap a perfect picture. My feet start moving, and without even realizing it, I've managed to keep my composure and make it to the center of the stage. The dean hoods me and then shakes my hand. Flashbulbs go off, momentarily blinding me. I blink a few times, ASSon is front and center snapping photos for the department. I look at her, and she smirks, flashing the camera a few more times. *I bet she's trying to sabotage my big day by blinding me and trying to make me fall.* I look at her warily.

"Chase, you cannot let her get the best of you. Chin up! You won!" the little Chase Angel says, cheering in my ear as I prance off the stage to frenzied applause from the far-right quadrant.

I subtly turn and give her a thumbs up. *I'm done. Done! I didn't even trip and fall over anything.* I let out a sigh of relief.

Okay. So now that I've completed a twelve-year collegiate chapter of my life, I have no clue about what to do next.

"Hey, you did it," Brent walks over with my family, holding a giant bouquet of pink roses. "Now, you just have to get married and have sex, and you will have completed all of your fairytale plans on your Excel spreadsheet," he says, whispering in my ear. "Are you sure you don't want me to help you out with those last two things, minus the marriage part, of course? I still think we should all be dolphins. But then again, it's you, and for you, heck, I'll marry you if you ask nicely enough." He gives me a little wink. He's wearing a cream-colored, three-piece suit, minus his signature fedora that makes him look quite dapper.

"How do you know about my Excel spreadsheet?" I whisper back sternly, elbowing him in the side.

Daphne runs up and hugs me. "I told you that you would do well in school." She gives me a big smile and hands me a card. "You guys believe nothing I tell you."

"Actually, that's not true. I *do* believe you," I respond, giving her a second hug. I look up and see Brody and Maddy approach. "Brody, Maddy, so sweet of you to come." I embrace them in a group hug. I look beyond them, expecting to see Grant trailing behind them ... "You're alone? Where's Grant?"

His eyes fall to the ground as the corners of his mouth turn down.

"Brody, what happened? Where is he?"

"I don't want to ruin your day, Chase. It's okay. He's been having food poisoning issues, off and on. We'll talk about it another time," he reassures me.

But I am not reassured. Something's not right. How does a person have food poisoning issues? Maybe he missed the news report about the recall on lettuce. A second later, Daphne's concern instantly flashes before me.

"Open it, Chase," Daphne says, smiling.

I rip open the envelope and pull out the card.

"AHHHH!!" I screech, dropping the card, as a wind-up-butterfly flutters above our heads. I put my hand against my chest, breathing slowly, "You scared the heck out of me!"

Brent's playing with the newfound toy, winding the rubber band between the wings, re-releasing it, and making Maddy laugh. Daphne's in stitches as she hands the card back for me to read:

It's about the journey.
All you have to do is believe. Happy Graduation!

"Huh? Journey?" I eye the little girl. "Please, don't tell me I'm going on another trip? I'm better with flying, but I don't want to go on some wild journey."

"Chase, love, let's take a family photo," Nana interrupts. It's the first time I've ever seen her without a martini in hand. Instead, she's armed with her iPhone, trying to organize our group. "You, Mr. Handsome, who stole away Chase's fiancé, and that little cutie, come, stand here," She points in the direction of where she wants Brody and Maddy to stand. "Chase, love, you stand in front, between your mom and dad.

Mitchell, stand next to Kate and Herb. And Roxie, love," she spots Roxie off to the side. "I'm not used to seeing you in a nice dress." She shakes her head in disbelief. "Where's the young beau who has finally transformed you?"

"I'm not ready to introduce him to all of you," Roxie laughs. "I don't want him to run for the hills."

"Oh, love, that's just nonsense. Everyone loves us. Henry, love, stand next to Roxie." Nana grabs the hand of a girl passing by. "Would you be so kind as to take a photo? I would like to remember this day: my granddaughter, Dr. Chastity Ann Morgan, finally graduating. I want to see you get married too, little love, but I've given up on that ever happening," she adds before handing over her iPhone.

I roll my eyes. What in the fuck is she saying? Way to ruin my moment, Nana!

"Mom, let's enjoy today," my father puts his arm around Nana, squishing in for the picture.

"Smile for the camera, everyone," the girl hollers, "and say cheese."

"Cheese before sex is always best!" Brent laughs out.

Uncle Mason lights up like Christmas. "Hey, that's my line."

"It baffles me that he's not your dad's real son. He acts just like him with his ridiculous antics," I whisper to Roxie.

"It's the environment," she laughs. "He's picked up things. Are you ready for tomorrow?"

"Never been more ready," I smile as we fan out from our huddled position.

"Ready for what, Chase?" Brent looks from Roxie to me.

"Girl talk," Roxie pats his arm.

"*C'est manifique!* He's really handsome," Daphne beams.

"She's in on your little secret, and I'm not? I feel hurt!" Brent's mouth turns down into a fake pout.

"Ahhh ... poor little baby, I think you'll recover just fine." I laugh, patting his arm.

"Are you all ready? One, two, three. Smile everyone," the girl says again. She snaps a series of photos. The irony hits me like a ton of bricks while manufacturing my best smile. This should be a happy occasion, except now I'm worried about Grant. And then there's Paul. Joan's words keep playing back in my head:

"*Oh, I wouldn't bother if I were you. You don't want to go there because things could go very wrong for you. Elizabeth has it all figured out.*"

So, am I truly ready for Jacques-Pierre, for life? With so much baggage on my plate, I'd say the old adage of "the spirit is willing, but the flesh is weak" is pretty apt.

39

The wooden floorboards creak under my feet as I stomp around my room, fidgeting, biting my nails like an unrepentant drug addict. I graduated; I have my PhD. I have achieved a third of my fairytale ending, and all I need now is the man and a job. My mind's reeling—sometimes you have to accept the truth, and sometimes you must accept defeat, failure. But what about accepting the consequences? Right now, that's what I'm forced to accept: consequences of a handsome, near-stranger who is coming to visit me for the weekend! I know it isn't a splendid idea; it isn't even an okay idea; it's a bit ... cuckoo, to be precise. And I know that I call everything out of the ordinary cuckoo, but I've been brainstorming, thinking of the possible misfortune ahead. As a result, I've come up with a hundred reasons why he shouldn't come, three of which stick out:

- He may be a womanizer.
- He's too old.

- He's geographically undesirable. (Duh! That's a no-brainer!)

This whole email courtship is madness. I may be 100% cuckoo, but shouldn't I at least be deliriously happy that he's flying 5,659 miles to see me, instead of pacing around my room like a nervous wreck? Confession: I've been basking in the idea of him. But now that he's just minutes away from touching down in Los Angeles, and his name doesn't start with L, I have this gnawing intuitive feeling that something's not quite kosher. It's like that funny feeling you get when you get scared, and your hair on your arms stands on end. What he has to say in his recent text doesn't help either:

> Jacques-Pierre: I can't wait to see you, ma cherie. Sorry, I thought I'd be able to pass through customs like an adulterer out the back window, but they stuck me in a customs line with what looks like a bunch of Italian mafias. Flagging a tax now.

Adulterer? Does that mean that he's married? Or is he simply being flip? *Shit!* Maybe I should run for the hills while I still have the chance. My phone pings again:

Jacques-Pierre: I'm suffering through LA traffic. If you believe in this miscreant driving me, I should be with you in fifteen minutes.

Fifteen minutes? I scramble for my purse and keys. I jump in my car, buckle my seatbelt, and gun the accelerator up the tree-lined street to the hotel. When he said he was coming, I couldn't exactly suggest he stay with me since I still live with my parents.

Four minutes later, I step out of my car at the exact moment a guy over six feet with coffee brown, perfectly combed hair steps out of a black sedan. My eyes widen, and I do a double-take. He's wearing aviator sunglasses, a black ski jacket with a rabbit fur collar over a heather grey tracksuit. It's the first time I'm giving him a good look over. *Wow! He's got to be much older than I. Maybe the internet was correct. 50s? Whatever! He looks damn good for his age.*

He waves a hand in greeting, marching towards me with such confidence my knees turn to water. Leaning down, he cradles my face in his hands, kissing me lightly on each cheek while flashing me his film-star dimples.

"Bonjour, ma cherie."

My heart skitters as he pulls me flush against his body. His scent fills the air: cinnamon and cloves, like the first time I saw him. He softly brushes his thumb across my cheek, sending a shiver up my spine. *God, I'm so inexperienced. Why do I have to resort to lust immediately? Help me, someone!*

"Bon ... jour, Jacques-Pierre," I whisper, my breath catching. *And someone, please pinch me while you're at it too! This is too surreal for words.* I can't believe that he's standing here directly opposite me, openly staring at me, eye-to-eye, instead of hiding behind a screen of words.

Why did I fret about him coming to visit?

"Why? Well, Chase," the little Chase Angel scolds, sitting on my shoulder with her arms akimbo, "because it's rather unnatural that you've never had a proper date, yet here he is, having traveled thousands of miles to see you. Maybe that's why. So, here's your chance: go get him, tigress!"

"I have a gift for you in my suitcase," Jacques-Pierre whispers, breaking my rattled mind. Taking my hand, he leads me through a swarm of people in the lobby towards the front desk to retrieve his room keys. We follow a bellman as he unlocks the door to Jacques-Pierre's assigned room, holds it open for us, wheels in his suitcase, asks if the temperature's perfect, and tells us he'd be happy to get anything for us. Jacques-Pierre hands him a bill, assuring him that everything is perfect. The bellman lightly bows, then exits, closing the door behind him.

"*Ma cherie*, sit down." Jacques-Pierre guides me to the sofa. He unzips his bag, pulling out an orange box tied with a piece of delicate orange and brown ribbon. "Here, I thought you'd like this." He hands me the box embossed with the words Hermes. *OH. MY. GOD!*

My eyebrows rise. "For me?" He nods. "Should I open it now?" He nods again, eyeing me like a hawk as I untie the ribbon, slowly lifting the lid and discarding it on the floor. I riffle through the crinkly white layers of tissue paper until my fingertips graze over the baby-soft fabric. "I love it," I say, as I carefully unfold the dainty, pale blue-and-pink chiffon scarf. I wrap it around my neck and caress it like I would a newborn. "But you shouldn't have. You barely know—"

"I noticed your scarf on the plane," he interrupts, looking up at me as my eyes start to water. "If you don't like it for any reason, you can take it back and get something else." He casts a downward glance.

"No. No. It's not that. Really, I love it! It's just that..." I quickly lean over, kissing him on both cheeks.

"Jacques-Pierre, it's beautiful!" Just because Charlie gave me a scarf for our 28th birthday, does that signify that Jacques-Pierre may be the ONE?

His arm snakes around my waist. Before I know it, I'm pulled onto his lap. He strokes my leg, gradually moving his hand further and further up my thigh. Although I'm liking this, I can't dismiss the fact that I'm uncomfortable. I lightly push his hand away.

"This is almost like the movie *Pretty Woman*," he says, ignoring my hesitation. "If I were staying at the Beverly Wilshire Hotel, it would be," Jacques-Pierre coos, brushing a lock of hair out of my eyes.

"Er ... huh? Excuse me?" my voice high-pitched with shock. I press my lips together, taking a second to process what his words mean. *Did he just compare me to the pretty hooker in a smash Hollywood hit? Since when did I turn into a prostitute? ME! Virgin me? With girl-next-door looks? Someone who doesn't wear anything too short or too low cut? How could he think I'm a prostitute? I need to call Roxie. Pronto.* I feel around for the phone in my dress pocket, but all I feel is emptiness. *I put it ... I put it ... SHIT! It's in my purse.* I'm the most paranoid person ever; I never leave home without my phone, pepper spray, and whistle. Now, I'm in a possible code red situation in a hotel room with a guy I thought I liked who thinks I'm a prostitute.

"Oh, *ma cherie*," he says, pressing his body against mine, kissing me, darting his tongue between my lips. I put my hands against his chest and push him away. "Whoa! Slow down, cowboy," I gasp for air as our lips part. His mouth stays open in total euphoric bliss. He's breathing raggedly, his cheeks are flushed, and he's panting like a rabid dog.

In one swift motion, I tumble out of his grip and onto the floor. I get my bearings, and in one fell swoop, I scoop my phone from my purse and stick it in my pocket. He sinks into the sofa, head tilted back, tapping his fingers on the armrest. The atmosphere becomes hushed and intense.

"Jacques-Pierre," I smile and continue, "how about we head to dinner?" I return to the chair across from him. I take his hand and hold his fingers, giving him a sign that I'm slowing things down.

"You want to head ... to dinner? Now? But why?" Jacques-Pierre's eyes shoot sparks.

"Yes," I shrug. I'm praying this will momentarily kill any ideas of sex. Dr. Brennan was right. I need to face the reality of what's in front of me. And what's in front of me is a HORNDOG.

"I don't get it. Why can't you be my dinner and dessert?" Jacques-Pierre eagerly leaps to his feet and stands in front of me. He kneels, and reaches for my zipper and pulls it halfway down my body. Again, I'm shocked when I feel a light breeze against my now bareback.

"Wait a second," I jump out of the chair and tug at my zipper to get my dress back into place.

"Don't you want to make babies with me?" He says this as if it's the most ridiculous notion he's ever heard.

"Make babies? With you? What?" I shriek, perplexed, touching a hand to my belly, my chest caving in. "You ... You want to have a baby with me?"

"Oh no, *ma cherie*. I only want to have sex with you. It's an expression," he laughs, his eyes dancing with glee up and down my form. "I'm just joking."

"Oh…" I hesitate. "Well, at the rate you're going, that's not going to happen either."

"*That was a bold move,*" I hear the little Chase Angel on my shoulder say.

But what happened to the guy who wrote the sweet romantic emails? I think, reflecting on my little angel's comment.

"God. I must be bipolar," I blurt.

His bright eyes turn oddly cold, his features tightening. "Are you all right, *ma cherie*? You … you don't find me attractive? You don't want me to seduce you?" Jacques-Pierre says with a frosty smile, heavy with condescension. He stands up, pacing the room.

"Yes and no," I respond, my voice raised. "Sex is a big deal, not something you just jump into before dinner. And definitely not dessert." Dr. Brennan's voice comes through me. *I can't believe I had the gumption just to say that. This is not at all how I pictured my fairytale date. The instinctive words from this Frenchman—excuse me, Swiss—are anything BUT romantic.*

"Sex is a form of communication," Jacques-Pierre says. "That's all. I don't understand why you're making such a big deal out of it." He sounds frustrated. He walks over to the minibar, grabs a water bottle, and takes a long swig.

"Okay, I'll buy the communication part, but it's got to be meaningful, not just something that gets used over and over again from one person to the next. For me, it's—" I mumble now, avoiding his eyes. I can hardly bear to say it out loud because, frankly, it's none of his business. Frustration boils inside of me.

"For God's sake, I wasn't lying when I confessed to you on the airplane that I'm still a virgin!" My voice becomes high-pitched again.

"A virgin. *Vraiment?*" He peers down at me, smiling. "I thought you were joking with me. Really? All this time you've remained a virgin? You've never slept with anyone?" Jacques-Pierre sounds so incredulous. I shrug sheepishly. "Wow, I've never slept with a virgin before." For a moment, he looks lost in thought, almost like he's replaying a distant memory. "Are you a lesbian?" he suddenly locks his gaze on mine.

"No, I'm not a lesbian. I'm a virgin." I stare at him hard. I'm not ashamed anymore to be a thirty-year-old virgin. It actually feels good to be different. I feel proud of myself that I've not succumbed to horny men like him that want to bed me.

"Well, then, I'm confused. Why don't you want to have sex?"

"Because I want to be in love when I have sex for the first time. I'm not a one-night-stand girl. Call me weird, crazy, unrealistic, but I can't help who I am. I can't exactly press a button and reprogram myself. Although a few months ago, I thought I could break that for a brief, unrealistic moment. But it's not who I am. I'm the girl who wants my one true love."

"*OH, MERDE.*"

"Did you just say 'Oh, Shit'?" I nearly choke with astonishment. What happened to the romantic guy that I thought was the ONE who wished me beautiful dreams? Not the one saying, "OH, SHIT" because I won't jump into bed with him. I feel my world swiftly crumbling. It's like that moment when you're playing Jenga, and you just realize that you've pulled out the wrong block, and the whole structure falls apart.

"*Ma cherie,*" he kneels next to me, pressing his lips to my forehead. "Are you sure you don't want to—" he gestures towards the bed, patting it lightly.

"Uh-uh, YEP! Why don't you shower, shave, and clean up for dinner, and I'll see you in a few minutes in the lobby," I say, standing up. I grab my purse off the desk.

"I've never had dinner first with a new ... romantic pursuit ... before ... We usually just—" He looks over at his bed again.

"You just what?" I pause for a weighted second. "Have sex?"

"Well, yes."

"You're unbelievable." I rub my forehead, trying to calm down. I'm beside myself. He clearly hasn't been listening to a word I've said.

He reaches for my hand. "Just give me a second." He looks down at his pants. "Without attention, it will need to calm down before I do anything."

My eyes flash to his zipper, to the current area bulging in his pants. "Oh, good God," I mutter under my breath, my hand shading my eyes. "I feel like I'm with a horny teenager. How old are you exactly?" I say, rather loudly.

"Fifty-three. Why?"

"More like fifteen," I mutter. "At your age, you're supposed to be mature and know how to control yourself, not acting like ... like ... this," pointing to his pants. *The dude just doesn't get it, does he?* I shake my head lightly. "You ... should ... be ashamed of yourself," I stutter, again surprised at my boldness. "I'm a far cry from the girl in *Pretty Woman*. Think about that while you get ready for dinner." Leaving the scarf behind, I grab my purse and head toward the door. I turn before I leave. "Listen, the man I met on the plane, the man who sent me all those romantic emails, he's the one I thought I was going to spend time with tonight. How about we start over?" I give him a light pat on the shoulder. "See you in the lobby," my last words before closing the door.

Retreating to my default sanctuary inside the closest hotel powder room, which is conveniently off the lobby, to calm down and fix my makeup, I put my purse on the vanity and stare at my reflection. I always used to think it strange in movies when actresses did the same thing, especially when they were alone and speaking out loud.

"Would a normal red-blooded woman have jumped at the chance to have sex with him right then and there? Am I not normal?" I say quietly. "You know what? I'm not. I'm not having sex without love. I don't care how many men run from me, hate me, I'm not giving into their wants." I look at myself in the mirror, my chin raised a little higher as I spout out my words. "Dr. Brennan was right. I have to take control over my life from here on out. And that means taking control over my wants and not hiding in the past with these ridiculous antics that men pull. Sure, it's a distraction, but now that I've come to terms with Charlie's death, I don't need bad distractions anymore. I need *real* love."

I pull out my cell and begin dialing Roxie.

"Hello there," says a man with a thick New Jersey accent.

I hang up the phone and hit the call button again.

"Roxie's phone, how can I help you," says the same man.

"Hhh ... hi," I squeak. "This is Chasity Morgan. Is Roxie—"

"It's for you, love. Oops!" The mystery man drops the phone. I hear fumbling.

"Oh, knock it off. You're not getting any lovin' later if you act like this," Roxie teasingly says. "So, did he dip into your chip?" she asks when she takes the phone.

"What the hell type of thing is that to say to your frien—," the mystery man says in the background.

"Dip into your chip?" I cut in. "Excuse me?" I'm totally baffled.

"Chase, I'm dying here. Come on! Is he so sizzling hot that you want to ravish every inch of him?"

"Hey, that's not nice. Aren't I the only one who's sizzling hot?" repeats the male voice.

"Shush," Roxie says to him. "No more fake pouting."

"Is that your boyfriend? I can't quite place his voice, but I know I've heard it before."

"Yes, he is. So, Jacques-Pierre—" Roxie quickly changes the subject, "you can't keep me in the dark, Chase."

I clear my throat. "Well, he's definitely handsome, but it's like I'm stuck in a bad movie. I have a horndog on my hands. He was all over me five minutes after he arrived, ramming his tongue down my throat like a jackhammer. What would you do if someone inferred you were a prostitute?" I move the phone away from my ear; Roxie cackles loudly.

"You've ... got to be ... joking! No ... guy would ... look at you ... and think you're a ... prostitute," Roxie says, laughing hysterically. I patiently wait for her to calm down. A woman enters the bathroom and goes into the nearest stall.

"He certainly did," lowering my voice but to no effect. My voice reverberating off the tiled walls. "Think *Pretty Woman*."

"Oh, I LOVE, LOVE, LOVE that movie," Roxie screams. I muffle my phone with my hand. "Richard Gere and Julia Roberts. It doesn't get any better than that."

"He said our getting together was like that." I say louder with the toilet flushing, masking my words. "He said our situation is exactly like the one in the movie *Pretty Woman*," I repeat, buying ambient-noise time. "He even showered me with a lavish gift."

"What?" Roxie says flatly. "That's not funny. I'm completely at a loss for words."

"Exactly." I pluck a tissue off the counter to wipe away my smudged mascara. The woman washes and dries her hands and quickly exits. "He even had the nerve to say, 'I never make it to dinner because we have sex first?' Who the hell says that?" My phone vibrates with an incoming message. I pull it away from my ear to look at it. "Hold on, he just texted me. Let me put you on speakerphone."

"What did he say?" Roxie's voice echoes throughout the bathroom. I turn the sound down.

"Okay. Here goes..."

Jacques-Pierre: What would you like to drink? I'm in the bar. And where are you anyway? You said you'd be waiting for me in the lobby.

"Hmm..." Roxie says thoughtfully. "Well, I'd say ditch him. Who cares if he flew all the way from Europe? That was his choice. And don't let him use that to make you feel guilty. Listen. If he turns out to be scary, pretend to have food poisoning after dinner and call it a night. Considering that he still wants to talk to you after you turned him down, it's possible that he's just a little sex-crazed like you said. Remember: you don't have to have sex with him to be a nice friend for the weekend, even if he does think you're a lady of the night."

"Trust me, he ain't getting no lovin'. I need love, Rox," I say snarkily. "No matter how hard I've tried to throw caution to the wind and have sex, it's just not me. God! What was I thinking? No man flies halfway around the world for conversation. The reality is, a big part of me thought he would get down on one knee and profess his love for me." I run my hands through my hair. "I was such a naïve idiot to think that!"

"Your biggest problem is that you always see the good in people, even when they show you otherwise. Promise me you won't get mad at me?"

"Oh, God, what did you do now?"

"I didn't give you that list for you to actually do it and make it into an Excel spreadsheet. I gave it to you as a distraction, so you could see that the hookups weren't you. You are a romantic, true, and true. I just thought that if you lived the other way for a date or two, then what Grant did to you wouldn't matter anymore, and you would go back to being you faster. Reverse psychology, as Dr. Brennan would say," she laughs.

I take a moment to ponder Roxie's ploy. Anger immediately rises as I replay uncomfortable scenes over the past months, but then it quickly dissipates when I recognize how much I don't want those types of relationships, anyway. I simply want to be loved and accepted as me. I smile widely, acknowledging Roxie's pure genius.

"I love you, cuz."

"I know," Roxie replies matter-of-factly. "Call me if you really need an SOS. Go to dinner. See what happens. Bye."

I stare at the phone for several seconds, wishing she didn't hang up so quickly, but at the same time, I'm wrapping my head around Roxie's insightful comments. Rushing to freshen up my lip gloss, I try to shake off my stupidity as I walk down a long hallway with framed photos of Hollywood's glamorous celebrities from yesteryear, pre-1960, all black and white.

"*Bonjour.* Want a sip of my Mojito?"

I jump like a jackrabbit. Jacques-Pierre pushes his minty drink towards my lips as his arms wrap around me from behind. He takes me by the shoulders, turning me around. "*Je suis desole.* Let's start over. I'm sorry for my childish antics. *Bonjour*, Chase, I'm here." He kisses me on each cheek with a beaming, wistful look in his eyes.

"This is not how I pictured our first date." I shake my head as a little laugh escapes my lips. "Let's get in my car and head to the restaurant."

He sweeps an arm around my waist and guides me towards the valet. "Is it better?" He hands the attendant his drink.

"Different," I say, stepping into my car, fastening my seatbelt. I pull out of the driveway, heading towards the restaurant, just catching the tail end of the yellow light.

"*Ma cherie*, I'm going to—" Jacques-Pierre begins, facing me in his seat. He massages my thighs slowly. Leaning down, he kisses me along my leg.

"No! What the hell, Jacques-Pierre?" I stifle an uncomfortable laugh as he hikes my dress until my panties are visible to him. I slap his hand hard. At the same time, I inadvertently floor the accelerator.

My hands grip the steering wheel a bit tighter. At the next red light, an elderly woman pushing a walker moves closer to my window to take a peek inside. Her eyes widen when she sees Jacques-Pierre trying to wedge his head between the steering wheel and my legs as if he expects it to morph to the size of a golf ball. Her mouth opens.

"Stop this instant. What happened to putting away your antics?" I yell to Jacques-Pierre, slapping him on the head. "You're not behaving. Sit back in your seat, and for God's sake, put your seatbelt on!"

I floor the accelerator the moment the light turns green. In a matter of seconds, a wail of sirens fills the air. I look in my rearview mirror; lights are flashing so brightly they could light up a street. Jacques-Pierre immediately fingers his hair in place and sits up straight. I hit my blinker and pull over to the side of the street. I'm sweating bullets. *This can't be happening.* "Shit!" I scowl. "Don't. Say. A. Word," I say through clenched teeth. Jacques-Pierre obediently folds his hands. I roll down my window to await my fate. I watch through my side-view mirror as a police officer in his late sixties approaches.

"License and registration, please." The officer bends over to examine Jacques-Pierre.

I gulp, fumbling as I reach in the backseat for my purse to retrieve my license. "I ... I ... I'm so sorry, Officer," I ramble. "I didn't know I was doing anything wrong. I'm not one to break the law. It was at a yellow light after all—"

He holds up his hand to silence me.

"Is everything okay, ma'am? You were going 65 mph in a 50-mph zone."

"Um ... Sir?"

"Also, are you aware that your passenger is not wearing a seatbelt?"

"I'm so sorry, Officer. He's Swiss, and they don't wear seatbelts in their country." I spout off a bunch of hullabaloos about how I've been trying to show him all the touristy spots in LA. I can tell my long-windedness falls on deaf ears as he scribbles on his pad.

"The Swiss have seatbelts, Miss..." he looks down at my driver's license again, "Morgan." The officer brandishes a piece of paper in front of my face. My shoulders slump and my mouth turned down. "Here's your ticket, Miss Morgan. I'm waving the seatbelt stipulation this time. And Sir," he bends over to talk to Jacques-Pierre, "when you're in America, you need to follow basic rules. Is that understood?" Jacques-Pierre nods.

As soon as the officer's out of sight, I pound the steering wheel in frustration. "This is just great! I've never gotten a ticket before. I guess I should be thankful it's only for a speed violation, and not for indecent exposure. You behave until we get out of this car. Are we clear?" I order, half serious, half shocked, pulling out onto the road. Without incident, we arrive at the restaurant ten minutes later.

"Oh, *ma cherie*," Jacques-Pierre begins as soon as I park, "I very much like this domineering side of you." He leans over to kiss my cheek. "I'm sorry, I couldn't help myself. I promise to be a gentleman." "Fine! Misbehave one more time and I'm taking you back to the airport." My patience is wearing thin. "I'm very hangry."

"You mean hungry?"

"No. It's my term for when I'm hungry and angry. It's hangry."

"Oh, I wish I could help satisfy your appetite." A smile flickers in his eyes as my mouth opens to speak. He throws up his hands, "I meant snacks from the plane. I don't have any," he laughs nervously.

"Doesn't matter, we're here." I hand my car keys to a valet while Jacques-Pierre and I exit. I rush ahead of him to the entrance of a local, authentic Caribbean restaurant. The walls are painted a calming sky blue. I look up at the ceiling where there is an ethereal scene of cherubim floating among puffy white clouds, some with bows and arrows. It's a perfectly romantic setting, but I have my doubts that our time together will be less than that, judging on his recent conduct. We take a seat at one of the heavy wooden tables with wicker chairs. I happily lose myself in the succulent dishes, more comfort food than I imagine: a king's banquet of fried pork, Conch salad,

Anguilla rice, peas, fresh fish with plantains aplenty, and the most delightful crab dumplings.

"So, *ma cherie*, how have you been?" He leans forward, listening intently, resting his elbows on the table between us.

"I've—" I look at him wearily. In the midst of the craziness, here I am again beguiled by his suaveness.

"*Idiot! What's wrong with you?*" I hear the little Chase Angel on my shoulder yell. Regardless, I drink him in. He looks at me, cocking one eyebrow up, the beaming smile from this provocateur goads me. *This guy must have charisma descended from Helen of Troy.* My thoughts begin to run wild. "*Charisma of a trickster, you, dumbass!*" Chase Angel says, kicking my ear lightly.

"Ouch!" I rub my earlobe and shake my head to rid my conscience. Jacques-Pierre curiously arches an eyebrow.

"I've—" My thoughts are jumbled. I have trouble meeting his eyes without blushing. The lunatic manages to keep me under his spell. *At least he's finally acting his age—for the moment.* My thoughts float back to the recent past. *I've been good. I just graduated from school. Got my doctorate.*

And for the first time this evening, we actually engage in genuine conversation, which surprisingly flows easily. I have to constantly keep my guard up so that I don't allow him to bewitch me.

In due time, the waitress clears our plates, and we order coffee while perusing the dessert menu.

"Would you like to share a banana soufflé or something sweeter?" the waitress asks. As I glance up, his lips curl up at the sides.

"The soufflé sounds delicious." Jacques-Pierre smiles like the Cheshire cat. He ever so lightly strokes my leg underneath the table before he pulls his hand away. "Sorry, *ma cherie*." He patiently waits for the waitress to leave before he starts up again. "*Ma cherie*, you're a different kind of woman,"

"What you mean is that I'm an old-fashioned, odd bird with very strict morals. I hear that a lot."

"It's more than that. I've had ... many women."

"To be sure." I purse my lips, looking firmly at him.

"Well, I have to say that you are the first woman to—how do I say it—put me in my place. Most women ... melt before me. Tonight, you slapped reality into my life." He stares at me. The seconds feel like minutes. "I have to say that I am ashamed of myself. You are a strong person." He extends his hand, intertwining his fingertips with mine. "I've never met someone like you. It's to be admired, your strength in character. If I had daughters, I would have wanted them to conduct themselves like you..."

He continues on for another ten minutes, telling me about his sons. The rest of the dinner goes without incident.

"Fini?" he asks after I take my last mouthful of soufflé.

"Yes, I'm finished.

I collect my purse. He wraps one arm around my waist as he leads me back to the car, opening the driver's side once I unlock it.

"Merci, and on the way back to the hotel, no crazy antics, okay?" I give a small laugh. "I don't need another ticket."

"Yes, of course, *Ma cherie!* Whatever you say." Jacques-Pierre dutifully buckles his seatbelt.

When we return to the hotel; he retreats out of the car. I briefly look up to see him standing next to me, his mouth spread into a giant grin as he opens my car door.

"How about this: we'll start over in the morning. Tomorrow's a new day," I say, shutting my door and rolling down the window. "Hopefully, a less sex-crazed one," I mumble under my breath.

"You're leaving already? I was hoping we could take a dip in the pool."

I lean over, kissing his cheek. "Goodnight. This has been a lovely dinner. I'll be by around ten tomorrow morning. I'll bring my swimsuit, just in case," I say, before driving away. *One night down, half a day to go!* Roxie may be right: I think I can do this.

4 0

The headboard of my bed pounds against the wall. The window panes are rattling like a freight train whipping through a storm.

"EARTHQUAKE!" I scream, running towards my door frame like a good student. Dad pounded it in our heads, day in and day out: *Doorframe kids, doorframe!*

"Charlie!" I pound on his door, but he's not waking up. "Charlie!" I say again, pushing through his door in a flat-out run. He's sitting at his desk, sketching a picture. The desk is wobbling, his chair is wobbling, but he's still drawing.

"Get up, you moron!" I grab his arm, yanking it hard. "Didn't you hear me? Earthquake!" He doesn't move; just continues drawing. My eyes spot something out the window under our big hundred-year-old oak tree in the backyard; it's a boy sitting under it that looks like him and a little towheaded baby boy, not more than three years old, sitting next to him.

"It's not about the destination, Chase," I hear Charlie say. "It's the journey that gives us meaning and makes us feel fulfilled." The floorboards beneath me start to break. "Read it..." he looks at me again, smiling.

"Huh?" I gasp for air, sitting up in my bed, my hair clinging to my sweat-drenched head. "Huh," I breathe in again. The sun is just beginning to rise, its glow, lightly shining through my curtains.

Read what, Charlie? I pull at my hair. My dream felt so real. I grab my phone and dial Roxie.

"Hey, are you sitting down?" I whisper as I mosey down the steps and into the kitchen to find something to eat.

"Sitting down? Look at the time? It's seven freaking o'clock in the morning here. What do you think? I'm still tucked ... IN BED," Roxie yawns, the last word indistinguishable. "You know I'm not one for early mornings."

"I'm sorry to call so early. Wait, you're in New York? Ah, never mind. I'm just... I had the weirdest dream about the journey... And then there's Jacques-Pierre, who is more than likely passed out like a baby right now, and—" I ramble, not certain why I'm feeling insecure.

"I said to be nice; I didn't tell you to drug him." Roxie laughs. "And what journey?"

"That's not funny, and I didn't drug him. Charlie kept mentioning something about a journey in my dream. Do you suppose he was talking about all my weird dating experiences?"

"Don't know. Possibly. And why are you talking to me when you have a gorgeous guy at your fingertips?"

"I'm not at the hotel. I came back home," I willingly admit.

"You WHAT?" Roxie shouts. I move the phone away from my ears.

"I'm telling you, he's a horn dog! He acts more like a fifteen-year-old than a mature fifty-three-year-old man," I explain.

"Roxie, is everything all right with Chase?" I hear a man's sleepy voice in the background. "Tell her to give the poor guy a little lovin; that way, he won't go home frustrated."

"LYNX!" She screams. "Go back to sleep. Hold on a second, Chase. I'm going to go into another room."

"Lynx? Why does that name sound familiar? And tell him, not a chance," I shriek.

"He's only kidding," Roxie says, laughing too easily.

"How did I get myself into this situation?" I mumble through a spoonful of yogurt.

"For starters, like I said yesterday, you wanted a man who would make a grand romantic gesture. Well, he did. He just arrived with different expectations that went against your fairytale-romance guidelines. So, how'd it go at dinner?"

"Thankfully, much better. He was back to being normal again. Although I did get a speeding ticket."

"Seriously? You?" Roxie laughs so hard she's coughing. "By the way," once her fit is over, "have you talked to Paul?" Her tone turns serious. *She never ceases to amaze me; how she can flip emotions in a moment's notice.*

"Uh, yeah. He texted me a few days ago to say he was on his way to film another segment. Why? What's going on? Spit it out."

"I was checking Facebook, and he's with Ursula up in Alaska. She posted something strange, saying that she's his producer and is running his company."

"His producer? Are you sure Lizzie wrote 'producer'? He would never let an outsider run his company."

"Yes. Producer. The sea bitch is his producer, Chase. She clearly has her claws in his company, trying to take it right out from under him," Roxie bellows, sounding frustrated. "We need to sit him down and talk to him right away. He cannot marry her."

"When are you coming home?" I ask nervously.

"Roxie, come back to bed," Lynx yells in the background.

"Just a moment, Lynx! I will be home tomorrow. Chase, don't worry. We'll talk later about Paul. Good luck today. You can do this; it's only a few more hours. Gotta go!" And with that, Roxie hangs up.

Lizzie, a producer? Charlie and the journey, which is exactly what Daphne said in my graduation card. Ugh ... I can't handle this. I need a shower ASAP!

* * *

I arrive at Jacques-Pierre's room, exactly at ten o'clock. I knock gently on his door.

"Good morning, *ma cherie*. You're just in time for a morning walk. Come with me." Jacques-Pierre looks like he just crawled out of bed, shirtless with a pair of jogging pants. He slips on a navy-blue T-shirt. When he's not looking, I steal glances at his fine torso, complete with a six-pack. It takes all I have and then some to keep from staring, mouth agape

"*You can't deny that he's gorgeous,*" the little Chase Angel says, laughing.

"Did you sleep well?" he yells loud enough for me to hear, pushing the door of the lobby open.

"Yes, how about you?" I yell back, trying to keep up. We exit the hotel to jog the tree-lined streets. The air outside is sweet with the scent of eucalyptus and perennials.

"Mm-hmm ... I had a wonderful night dreaming of you." Jacques-Pierre rubs his hands together, as we jog side-by-side down the sidewalk that runs along the side of the hill. "What shall we do today? My flight's a little earlier than I thought. I need to leave the hotel at noon," he says.

"Oh?" I'm surprised. *Did he change his flight since he didn't get what he came for?* "We can have a light breakfast after our walk, coffee, and then we can relax by the pool before your flight. I can drive you to the airport if you want." No waffling around for us this morning. I'll keep him on such a tight schedule that he won't have time to think about sex. I pump my arms harder, catching up to him.

"Sure." Jacques-Pierre looks like I just popped his bubble. I imagine he had his own X-rated plan for the day, and I say too bad to that. "Did you bring your bathing costume?" he asks, stepping in front of me and jogging backward.

"Bathing costume?" I furrow my brows. "Do you mean my swimsuit? It's under my tracksuit."

"Ahhh... Well then, I agree with your detailed plan," he says, raising an eyebrow playfully. *Oh God, I know that look.* I can't help but chuckle.

"May I ask you something?" he says, briskly pumping his arms beside me. I love a fast jog, heartbeat rising. "Do you plan to have children?"

My chest caves in. I feel like I just got punched in the gut. I jam my hands in my pockets, unnerved, slowing my pace.

I don't get it. Why do men keep asking me this? Is it a trick question? If I tell them the truth, what Dr. Patel told me, will they run away?

"Why do you ask?" I say with a muffled voice, dodging the question. I pick up the pace while trying to get a good look at his expression.

"Well, you're kind of old to have them, aren't you?" He gives me a sideways glance before stepping off the sidewalk and crossing the street.

I stop dead in my tracks at the curb. "I'm kind of what? Old?" I yell. "I'm not old!" I point my finger at him. "You're the one who's twenty-three years my senior."

Jacques-Pierre scurries back and takes me by the arm, coaxing me forward across the street. "No. That's not what I meant. What I meant is ... that with me, you get a man and you get a child, because I'm incredibly talented at acting like a baby." He rubs my arm, his tender smile letting me know he's kidding around.

"Okay. That's an awkward joke, wouldn't you say?" *He has no idea why I just said that.* I trail off, thinking, feeling my heartache, saddened that we even have to speak about this. I turn us around, and we silently head back up the hill towards the hotel.

"Chase?" I jump like a jackrabbit, hearing my name being called along with Frank Sinatra's soothing voice. I turn to see Brent on his bike, cruising up the other side of the sidewalk along with Daphne on her scooter.

He grabs her hand, dragging her across the street.

"Brent, I want to go home," Daphne whines, pulling her scooter behind her.

"Funny running into you here. What a coincidence!" Brent smiles awkwardly.

"Coincidence?" Daphne yells, her arms akimbo and acting more like his mother than the neighborhood kid. "*You* were the one who asked me where you could find Chase, and then you forced me out of the house." Daphne looks at him like he's gone mad. "She's a grown woman, for heaven's sake..."

"Kids," Brent chuckles nervously, lifting his fedora, scratching his head, "they say the damnedest things. I'm Brent, by the way," extending his hand toward Jacques-Pierre. "And you are?"

"Jacques-Pierre," he replies, shaking Brent's hand weakly.

A lightbulb seems to go off in Brent's head; he lets out an audible gasp.

"You dragged me to French class for him?" Brent shouts to me. "Please, tell me you're kidding?" Jacques-Pierre stands rigidly, folding his arms and eyeing Brent and Daphne curiously.

"Oh Lordy, lord," Daphne mutters, slapping her forehead. "This is so embarrassing."

"Um..." I look at the three of them.

"You need an intervention. Pronto," Brent blurts out.

"I said, Grant. Grant is the one who needs the intervention," Daphne yells, grabbing Brent's arm. "You never let me finish—"

"No, you didn't. You told me Chase—"

I throw up my hands. "That's enough, you two!" I scream. "You're making no sense! Paul is the one that needs the intervention, Brent."

I glance at Jacques-Pierre, who is smirking at the strange display.

"On that note, I need some coffee." And without warning, I turn and make a mad dash back up the hill to the hotel to clear my thoughts.

Jacques-Pierre dashes after me. "Race you to the pool," Jacques-Pierre shouts.

"Chase, wait up!" Brent yells. I can hear him peddling after us.

"Let it go. She needs to figure this out for herself," are the last words I hear Daphne yell to Brent as I turn the corner. Jacques-Pierre and I come to a screeching halt at the pool, closely followed by Brent.

"Tie!" he exclaims, ignoring the fact that Brent is trailing us as we make our way to a pair of chaise lounge chairs by an umbrella table near the far edge of the pool. A waiter greets us with menus as we settle in our chairs.

"We have plenty to choose from on the menu. Also, the breakfast bar is open, if you want to go that route. Can I start you with some coffee?" the waiter says in one breath.

I raise my hand like I'm in school.

"We'll have two coffees," Jacques-Pierre orders.

"And you, sir?" the waiter says to a slightly bedraggled Brent.

"I'll..." He's gasping for air, bent over, hands on his knees. "Have—"

"He's not staying," Daphne interrupts, scooting to Brent's side, yanking on his arm.

"I agree with Daphne. Nice to "bump" into you," I air quote to Brent. "But it's time for you to go."

"She'll be fine. Trust me. She won't say yes." Daphne grabs hold of Brent's hand and nudges him to turn around. "Bye, Chase. Bye, Jacques-Pierre. Sorry to bother you."

"Oh, not at all," Jacques waves to Daphne. "It was all very ... amusing."

Brent mouths "talk to you later" before heading back to their bikes.

"Interesting friends you have, *ma cherie*. Who is that strange man with the funny hat, anyway?"

"Who? Brent? He's ... a friend," I smile sheepishly, realizing that I didn't know quite how to explain his relationship to Roxie or me for that matter.

"He seems to ... how do I say ... like you," Jacques-Pierre smirks.

My eyes widen. "How can you tell?

"A man understands the vibes of other men, especially when they're after the same woman." Jacques- Pierre gently rubs my arm.

"Oh." I shade my forehead with my hand, hoping to hide the redness in my face. Jacques-Pierre's chair begins to buzz oddly. He rummages in his back pocket to pull out his phone.

"One second." Jacques-Pierre holds up a finger. *"Bonjour, ma cherie,"* he says over the phone followed by a trail of French words spoken rapidly. I try to translate, but it all sounds like mush to me. The second he hangs up his phone, it rings again. *"Bonjour, ma cherie,"* he says a second time with a lilt to his voice. It's obvious to me that he's talking to a different woman. *And he's calling her "my darling" too? Is that a common French thing to do, or is it what I think it is?*

By the third time his phone rings, he excuses himself. *"Sorry,"* he mouths before going to the other end of the pool to answer it. I hear another *"ma cherie"* in the distance. My thoughts immediately drift to Daphne's statement about needing to figure it out for myself. *Figure out what Daphne? That he's a womanizer? That he's a sham?* I can feel anger rising up within me. *And what did Charlie mean about the journey and reading it? Why does everyone in my life speak in double entendre?*

"Excuse me, miss, but it looks like you could use a Bloody Mary, heavy on the vodka," says the waiter who appears out of nowhere.

"Oh! Sorry. I'm ... fine. It's a little too early for that. The coffee is wonderful, by the way. Could I get a refill?"

"Certainly!"

The waiter scurries off to retrieve a carafe and pours steaming hot coffee into my cup.

"Thank you!" my eyes fixed on Jacques-Pierre as I cup my hands around the alluring drink.

The waiter bows, and then quickly disappears into the hotel.

I can see Jacques-Pierre in the distance, placing his phone back in his pocket before making his way back to me.

"All good?" I ask in a noncommittal tone.

"Ahh ... *Oui!* Yes! So, *ma cherie, je suis faim.* Let's order something to eat." Jacques-Pierre leans back in his chaise, sipping his coffee.

For a few seconds, I sit there, gazing at him, expecting him to say something more about his phone conversations, and why he called three different women *"ma cherie."* I also wish Brent and Daphne didn't show up. I can't get Daphne's words out of my head. I look up and notice Jacques-Pierre giving me a curious look.

"Everything okay?" Jacques-Pierre asks with real concern, or at least I hope he's sincere. "I've really enjoyed this time with you, *ma cherie*." He takes hold of my hand, pressing his lips gently against my wrist.

I flinch when I hear him call me that name. I can tell that he's in sappy-romantic mode again; it's in his eyes.

"Did you know that swans mate for life?" he announces out of the blue.

"Yes, I knew that."

He leans closer to me so that he's face-to-face with me, staring into his eyes.

"And your point?" I respond, tired of his mushy lines.

"Well, something happened yesterday that got me thinking," he starts messaging my hand. "I've never met a woman like you. I feel you pushed me to the edge. I didn't like it, but at the same time, I did. Have you ever seen the movie *As Good as It Gets?*"

"With Jack Nicholson and Helen Hunt?"

"Yes. That's the one," Jacques-Pierre smiles broadly.

"What about it?"

"Well, that's you and me."

I turn away, so he doesn't see me roll my eyes.

"You make me want to be a better man," Jacques-Pierre says, this time grabbing my other hand.

I have no choice but to look straight at him. My hands involuntarily begin to tremble.

"Oh, *ma cherie,* you are freezing. Let's take a dip in the Jacuzzi. You'll warm-up."

I nod and dutifully pull off my tracksuit. He eyes me carefully as I remove each piece of clothing. He frowns a little when he sees me donned in a one-piece, Olympic-style bathing suit. I walk over to the Jacuzzi and dip my toes in to test the temperature. He watches me as I walk down the steps and slip into the bubbling water.

"It's great! Come on in," I urge.

"I'll be right back. I need to change into my bathing costume," he says abruptly, jogging into the hotel.

"Ouch," I gasp. Something poked me in the back. I see a sleek-looking paper airplane sitting right behind me. I look around for the culprit, but no one else is around except me. I open the neatly folded paper to find words scribbled across the middle:

Look under the floorboards ... and remember, a zebra never loses his stripes!

"What the heck?" I look around a second time. I crumple it and toss it near the Jacuzzi steps, my mind reeling from the cryptic message.

Jacques-Pierre returns wearing pink floral swim trunks with a matching pink polo shirt and black flip-flops.

I give him the once-over. "No pink flip-flops?"

"These are the only things the gift shop sold," Jacques-Pierre says, hopelessly looking down at his feet.

He slips off his shirt, which reveals his solid, smooth, and lightly ribbed chest again, glistening with the faint glow of an old tan. For fifty-three, his body looks amazing—toned and fit but not pumped up like a twenty-something gym rat who's taken too many steroids. He glides over to where I am, wrapping an arm around my waist. My stomach does a topsy-turvy thing, making my heart skip a beat. His cryptic phone calls suddenly don't seem that important.

"Chase," the annoying little Chase Angel says, making another appearance. "What are you doing? You're letting your emotions control you, instead of you controlling your emotions!" I shake my head.

"What's wrong, *ma cherie?* A bug get in your hair?"

"No. No. Nothing like that. Can I ask you a question?"

"Ask away, my sweet," Jacques-Pierre hugs me closer.

"If I make you want to be a better man, then who were the other *ma cheries* you referred to on your phone calls?"

"Oh! Oh!" he stalls. "Oh, I call all the women in my life '*ma cherie.'* That's all," he chuckles.

"Ah-huh," I answer flatly.

"Well, if I'm special, how about calling me something like 'sweetie.'"

"SWEE-TIE," Jacques-Pierre emphasizes carefully.

"Yep. Sweetie."

"Okay. SWEE-TIE it is," he chuckles again but nervously.

"I think I'm warm now," I announce, releasing myself from his grip and moving toward the steps. I clamber up, scoop up the crumpled paper, and grab two oversized hotel towels from a rack. I wrap one tightly around my body while the other I place on top of me once I snuggle into my lounge chair again. I feel unsettled; my mind still rattled over the way he answered my question. *Something just doesn't add up. I think he's hiding something.*

Before I know what's happening, Jacques-Pierre grabs a towel, and wrapping it firmly around his waist, sidles up to me on my chair. He smells of cinnamon and cloves again; it's intoxicating. He strokes my hair, kissing me around my face until his lips reach mine, kissing me slowly and softly before he dives in full-passion. He subtly crawls until he's on top of me, his heart pounding against my chest. I feel like butter melting atop a warm slice of bread. He breaks his kiss while gazing longingly into my eyes.

"*Ma cherie,* I need to leave. I have to write a few emails before my flight. Walk me back to my room?"

"Okay, on one condition." I pause. "No more '*ma cherie.*' It's sweetie. Remember?"

"I love it when you're feisty."

Jacques-Pierre peels himself off, offering his hand to assist me. I stand up and gather our clothes and we head to his room.

Once inside his hotel room, Jacques-Pierre turns on relaxing classical music, adjusting the volume above a whisper. He leans down and kisses my forehead, trailing down to my eyebrow, nose, and finally my lips.

"Sit on the couch and watch some television for a minute, Chase. I mean, Sweet-tee." He gently grazes my cheek with his thumb before walking out to the patio. With his reading glasses on, he begins typing away on his laptop.

A talk show is on. I have no idea what they're talking about because I'm lost in my thoughts. What am I going to do about him? On one hand, all Jacques-Pierre thinks about is sex. And I want to kick that guy in the nuts, slow him down. But on the other hand, he's back to the guy who wrote me the romantic emails, being so attentive, gentle, and kind. That guy makes me want to cuddle in his lap. Why did he come out to visit me? That's still unanswered. Wouldn't it have been easier for him to stay in his country and find someone else to have sex with? Unless it's the chase (my name says it all) that thrills him, and the game's afoot.

I walk over and reposition his laptop and sit down on his legs, gently running my hands through his hair. "Whatcha doing, little boy." Jacques-Pierre tugs at the zipper on my jacket.

"Come here," Jacques-Pierre says, pulling me in close.

He leans his mouth down next to my ear, "I've had a wonderful time with you, Chase," he whispers. "I didn't realize that it could be this much fun to be with a woman without having sex. This is a rare moment in my life, one where I feel truly happy." My heart melts in disbelief. The naughty schoolboy has managed to charm me. He tilts my chin up to look at him, his eyes, sweet and vulnerable.

* * *

He cups my cheeks, pressing his lips against mine one last time in the middle of the terminal, where long lines of people wait to check their bags. My knees weaken as he pulls me in closer.

"*Ma cherie.* I'm sorry. Habit. Chase, swee-tie, thank you for the ride, but now it is time for me to say goodbye and go through security." He pulls away. I'm breathless. He grabs his suitcase with one hand and looks at me longingly. I will actually miss him. *Go figure?* I would never have guessed this outcome, considering the way this trip started. Jacques-Pierre clasps my hands before wrapping me in his arms so that I'm flush against his body.

"*Au revoir*, Chase. I will miss you." He kisses each cheek with formality, and then plants a soft, intimate kiss on my lips—the moment will definitely linger in my memory for hours afterward.

I watch as he turns and steps through security. As he collects his bags, Jacques-Pierre turns one last time to wave goodbye. My spirits plunge. I do my best to hold back tears.

My shoulders sag, and a tear trickles down my cheek as I stand in the middle of the airport. And I fail, wailing. The vibration of my phone brings me back to reality. I look down and see the call is from Roxie. "Hi," I say through sniffles, wiping my eyes with my sleeve.

"Chase, what's wrong?"

A loud alert blasts in my ear. I pull my phone away to look at the incoming text. It's from Jacques-Pierre. "Roxie, let me call you right back."

"I really need to talk to you..." I hear her saying as I click off. I swipe my phone and see that Jacques- Pierre has sent me a text:

> Jacques-Pierre: Drink?
> **Me: Sounds yummy! I could use one right now. Have a wonderful flight!**
> Jacques-Pierre: No! Drink with me now?

Drink with him now? That makes no sense.

> Jacques-Pierre: Simply turn around, Chase.

Huh? I scratch my head. Jacques-Pierre's scent fills the air a second before I feel the sudden touch of his warm arms wrap around my waist, squeezing me into a tight hug. He turns me around to face him. My mouth splits into the widest of grins. I can't fathom this moment because Jacques-Pierre's standing right in front of me.

"What? What are you—"

"They delayed my flight. It's a sign. I am supposed to be here with you, and look," he says, holding up the expensive scarf.

"Chastity? Is that you?" I glance up from Jacques-Pierre. My mouth drops open.

"Vincent?" I'm shocked. A strange tingly sensation overwhelms my body. I shiver slightly as he walks toward me, wearing his spiffy flight attendant's uniform, but slows down when he sees me in Jacques- Pierre's arms. I break free and walk over to him.

"What are you ... doing over here?" I stutter.

"Can you believe it? I'm here at LAX. Never expected to see you again, and in an airport of all places. I was just working on our flight from D.C." He looks at me again. "Chastity Morgan. I was starting to wonder if I'd ever see you again."

Jacques-Pierre walks back up to me.

"Oh. Sorry. Vincent, Jacques-Pierre." The two men shake hands, both eyeing each other suspiciously.

"I take it this is another one of your ... friends," Jacques-Pierre asks flatly.

"Yes. A long-distance one, as a matter of fact." I glance at Vincent again. I'm shocked to see him here. Jacques-Pierre glances at Vincent and then back at me. With his cocky smile forming the deepest dimples of the weekend, Jacques-Pierre totally disregards Vincent's presence and leans over, gently pressing his lips to mine. He pulls away, tucking a lock of hair behind my ear before kissing my forehead and wrapping the scarf he bought me around my neck. "I want to marry—"

My phone chimes loudly, interrupting Jacques-Pierre's stunning announcement. I glance over at Vincent, a look of shock and remorse written all over his face. I turn to my phone, and my eyes widen when I see the caller is from my grandmother. "Nana barely calls," I mutter to myself. "I'm sorry," I announce to both men. "I have to take this."

"Nana? What's up?" I ask nervously. "This is not a good time—"

"Honey, I was walking Lacy by the park," she says quickly. I can hear her breathing fast. "And Grant was being loaded into the back of an ambulance."

"A what?" I yell in shock.

"Yes, honey. I heard the paramedics say he was unresponsive."

My eyes go wide; my phone crashes to the ground. I suddenly feel lightheaded, and then everything goes dark.

ACKNOWLEDGMENTS

First and foremost, I would like to thank my editor, Anita Lock. Without her hard work, dedication and patience this book would not be possible. Stephen King said, "to write is human, to edit is divine." This couldn't be more fitting when it comes to you, Anita. You are an angel, and I feel so lucky to call you my friend. Thank you for making me a better writer. It's been one heck of an incredible ride, and I look forward to doing it all again.

I would like to thank Julie Gustafson and Shari Ryan from Mad Hat Books www.madhatbooks.com for putting my book together and making it look so beautiful. You are incredibly talented ladies that provide exceptional independent publishing services for writers. Thank you for helping me get out in the publishing market. I couldn't have done it without you.

I would like to thank my Beta Readers, and especially Alexa and Sheila. Your insight and jargon were exceptionally helpful.

I would like to thank my family. I love you all, and I'm so grateful for your love and support.

For the man I call Mr. Smarties that showed me the meaning of true love, passion, and undeniable chemistry. A huge thank you for inspiring me. ;-) I'll always love you.

I would like to thank my clairvoyant friend, Daniel, for his constant encouragement. You were right...on everything. Wow!

I would like to thank Kevin K. and his 17th-floor team. You have all been such incredible mentors. Thank you for taking the time to teach me about finance. I so appreciate your loyalty and kindness.

I would like to thank Eric Barnard. You are an exceptional artist and incredible friend. Thank you for making my photos look so beautiful.

Lastly, if it weren't for Grammie and Grampe, I may never have followed my dreams. Thank you for making this possible.

ABOUT HOLLY

Holly Brandon breaks free from her analytical side to produce Life in the Chastity Zone. Holding a Ph.D., M.S., and B.S. in Civil Engineering, Holly is best known for her published works in the Journal of Earthquakes, Earthquake Engineering, and Engineering Vibrations and Earthquake Science. Unbelievable as it may appear, many of the scenes in Life in the Chastity Zone are based on true-life experiences. Holly invites readers to follow Chastity on her crazy and hilarious adventures in her search for love and happiness. With more to come, Life in the Chastity Zone is the first in an unforgettable, brand-new Chastity Zone series.

Website: www.authorhollybrandon.com
Facebook: https://facebook.com/holly.brandon.315
Instagram: https://instagram.com/authorhollybrandon

@ authorhollybrandon

@ lovebooktours

Printed in Great Britain
by Amazon